Death of a Diva

Death of a Diva

FROM BERLIN TO BROADWAY

Brigitte Goldstein

ISBN: 0692246665
ISBN 13: 9780692246665
Library of Congress Control Number: 2014911842
Pierredor Books, New Brunswick, NJ

For Nicole,
my pillar and light,
with gratitude and love

PART I

NEW YORK NOIR

ONE

New York City, July 1941

Suddenly, the summer doldrums had come to an end. A murder on Broadway may have been enough to break the lethargic spell a seemingly endless heat wave had cast over a weary public; the violent death of an international movie star aroused a wave of general indignation equivalent to a rallying cry for retribution stoked by a frenzied battle of the daily headlines.

"DESDEMONA STRANGLED!" screamed the tabloids in outsize, bold letters.

"STAR OF STAGE AND SCREEN BRUTALLY MURDERED!" headlined one mass-circulation daily.

"RENOWNED SHAKESPEAREAN ACTRESS STELLA BERGER FOUND DEAD!" intoned the newspaper of record.

"PROMINENT ANTI-NAZI VOICE SILENCED!" bemoaned the German-Jewish émigré paper *Aufbau.* "Wherever she appeared," the editorial explained, "the applause subsiding, she issued without fail a passionate clarion call to join her in prayer that her homeland and the world might soon be delivered of the Nazi scourge."

All news outlets reported the killer still at large.

On that morning I was getting out of the subway on my way to class at Hunter College. As was my habit, I stopped at the news vendor's kiosk on the corner of 57th and Lex to glance over the day's headlines when I felt a leaden hand weigh down my shoulder. A droning voice drummed into my ear: "Misia Safran?"

I nodded, all flustered. Still stunned by the headline my mind refused to comprehend, I was utterly confused. My brain felt pulverized, as if it had been struck by a meteorite.

"You'd better come with us to the station," the voice said.

I slowly turned around and came face-to-face with two uniformed police officers. They had boxed me in on both sides as if they feared I might attempt a dash into the crowd. I was far too paralyzed for any such move and followed them like a sheep to slaughter. At the same time, I told myself this could only be a mistake. My meek inquiry into the reason for my arrest was met with shrugs. When I insisted, I received a cryptic, "You'll find out soon enough."

Realizing the futility of pressing further, I got into the backseat of the squad car, pulled up my legs, and leaned my face against my knees. A sinking feeling weighed my stomach down. What was going on? What possible reason could there be for the police to take me into custody? All this came in the midst of that terrible, terrible news. Tears streamed down my cheeks as I muttered to myself over and over, "Stella Berger dead?"

I could not believe it. Stella Berger, my idol and mentor, had been killed in a savage attack in her dressing room. My thoughts wandered to the front page news of the last few weeks: the daily press drumbeat about the German army's advance on Moscow and an almost quixotic British attempt to win over the German public with a propaganda campaign. While the ongoing war in Europe had been casting its shadow across the Atlantic for many months, for most Americans it was a battle fought in a far-off place. The war raged on another continent with an ocean in between and barely affected the daily lives of ordinary citizens. Isolationist rabble-rousers and a few attention-seeking politicians decrying the presence of "multitudes of foreign elements allowed to freely roam the city streets of this country" were fringe elements, attracting small crowds on street corners and in city parks.

The violent death of a celluloid icon at the height of her triumphant run on Broadway, however, was a stab in the city's heart and its famed theater world. It was also fodder for the isolationist grindstone. Even those who had never heard of Stella Berger or her critically acclaimed Ophelia to Olivier's Hamlet were likely to seize on the tragic event for their own agendas. Berger's Ophelia had electrified London audiences back in 1934, spreading her fame beyond the German-speaking world where she had reigned supreme on stage and in film for more than a decade before the Nazi regime had forced her into exile abroad.

TWO

The police inspector heaved his considerable bulk onto the table at which I was crouching and slid to a halt just short of crashing into my much frailer physique. He lowered his glowing moon face close to mine, and his rancid breath stung my nostrils. His eyes glowered menacingly. His every move was obviously calculated to intimidate and browbeat me into confessing complicity in a horrendous crime that had left me shattered in body and soul.

"Let's see now if we can get somewhere," he grunted and leaned sideways over a stack of papers he had pulled from a folder and flung down between us. I recognized the statement I had filled out at the front desk on entering the precinct, where the two officers who had arrested me in front of the news kiosk had unceremoniously escorted me. My interrogator was sweating profusely, breathing heavily, and frequently interrupted his questioning to dab his brow with a lily-white handkerchief. I too felt intense discomfort from the stifling heat in the cell-like room, lit dimly by a single bulb dangling from the ceiling. Three sides of the windowless walls oozed sweat through the flaking, glossy paint of washed-out green. The inner wall of the room sported a full-size, yellowing mirror dotted with brownish blotches.

"So I understand you were personally acquainted with the victim," he continued after skimming my statement in front of him. I simply nodded. My mouth was half open, and my throat was parched and constricted. My voice failed to produce a sound. The little fan in the corner huffed and puffed mightily but with little success in providing relief. I held on tight to the sides of my rickety, wooden chair and used every ounce of will I could muster to keep from fainting.

"In fact she was your benefactress. Wasn't she?" he droned on. He slid off the table and rid himself of his jacket, exposing large patches of wetness on the underarms of his white shirt. Again he pulled out his handkerchief and dabbed his forehead. Keeping his eyes fixed on the papers, he pulled up another chair and sat down directly across from me at the table.

A long pause ensued. His labored breathing was similar to the whistling of a steam engine, and his occasional grunts and lip smacking were the only sounds in the overall silence. I watched him from below hooded eyes as he continued to read with the undivided attention one might give a suspenseful mystery novel. To fight a sense of helplessness, I told myself that this was a war of nerves. He might think I was too young and a woman to see through his game. Little did he know or guess that despite my youth I had seen something of the world. I had encountered police tactics before in my native Berlin. In fact I had witnessed the Gestapo brutalizing my father and even roughing up my mother. *You might think you are very clever and fierce, officer of the NYPD*, I thought to myself, *but I can tell you are no match for the ruffians operating in their underground torture chambers in the German Reich. Even if you play tough and try to strike fear into the hearts of those in your power, you are still American. You don't have it in you. You don't have the guts to rough up a person the way they do over there. They know how to destroy not only the bodies but also the souls of those who fall into their hands.* I reassured myself that this was America—the world's greatest democracy. It was very unlike the brutal dictatorship that I had fled with my parents a few years before.

Then his next blow struck me like a hammer coming down on an anvil.

"She was kind enough to help you get a job, and what did you do in return? You murdered her!" The last sentence exploded from his wide-open mouth like the roar of a lion as he lunged across the table with the full force of his heft. I ducked down in the chair. His glowering face came at me like a hurtling projectile, and I wasn't quite fast or low enough to avoid his spittle spraying my face.

"Murder!" he roared again before falling back into his chair. Gasping and with streams of sweat trickling down his padded cheeks, he was the image of a warrior spent from the heat of battle.

"No, no!" I protested.

"So you insist on denial. You deny the eyewitness reports that claim you opened the door for a man described as a vagrant—the same man these eyewitnesses saw running from the victim's dressing room. You could do yourself a lot of good if you came straight out and confessed. Help us find the killer who might be out there looking for his next victim, which could be you."

"How could I have anything to do with her death? You said it yourself. She was my benefactress. I was forever grateful to her. I adored her. She was like a goddess to me."

Maybe that was a bit too much melodrama, but it summed up my feelings. He, however, seemed quite unmoved by my lachrymose protestations. He reiterated his threat. "I am advising you that failure to cooperate with the police in this investigation will make your situation worse. We are looking here at possible deportation."

"But I am cooperating," I whimpered. I was close to panic now. "What else can I tell you? You have all I know right in front of you in writing. I made out a full statement and answered all questions put to me truthfully and to the best of my knowledge."

I had been cooperating from the moment the two police officers confronted me at the kiosk and handcuffed me without explanation. He had the evidence of my innocence right in front of him. The sun, I thought, will bring the truth to light. Now his accusations and threats made me doubt the wisdom of having put my faith in a system where the individual was supposed to be innocent until proven guilty. My adversary seemed to have no compunctions about pronouncing me guilty without a trial. This police officer accusing me outright of murder seemed to give this cherished doctrine the lie.

At this moment of my greatest distress, the moment when I was losing all hope of ever making him believe I was speaking the truth, the door swung open. With agile step in walked a suave, slender man in a perfectly tailored, gray, striped double-breasted suit. His smile exposed a perfect row of white teeth below a thin, carefully trimmed mustache. His shiny black hair was slicked back with pomade. He was elegant as if plucked from a movie set. For a moment I thought I was seeing George Brent in the flesh.

"That's enough, Mulligan!" he hissed with a flippant wave of the hand.

So Mulligan was the name of the still-panting inquisitor. It sounded something like Molotov when he first mumbled it. Mulligan hurriedly picked up his crumbled jacket from the chair, and, without another look at me, he headed for the door. The papers with my statement were left on the table.

I knew someone had been watching the proceedings from behind the mirror. Why else have a mirror in such a room than for others to observe, intervene at a necessary or opportune moment, or release some of the pressure on both questioner and questioned? Still I gratefully accepted a glass of water from a woman who slipped as noiselessly as a phantom in and out of the room as the new cop boned up on my statement.

"Don't mind my colleague. His Irish blood tends to heat up in this weather," he said politely. He flashed his brilliant whites though without offering an apology.

And your German blood remains cool and collected. Above the fray. The thought popped into my head before I had even heard his name.

"I am Lieutenant Frank Dettelbach," he introduced himself, extending his hand. My instinct had been right, though he pronounced his name the American way with the ending sound like "back."

"Murder, as you no doubt know, is a serious matter," he continued with grave mien, as if I needed reminding of the gravity of the situation. He then unexpectedly began to talk about his upbringing in the Midwest. His ancestors had also been immigrants from Germany, fleeing political persecution. They had come several generations further back though, in 1848. My fear he might subject me to a long discourse on the history of German immigration to America turned out not to be justified. Instead he bemoaned the loss of German culture and identity among the descendants of these immigrants over the generations. He, however, knew enough German to get by and would gladly conduct our conversation in that language if it made me more comfortable. Somewhere in my head an alarm went off. I assured him I was perfectly comfortable speaking English. I told him it was almost my mother tongue now since I had received much of my education right here in New York. He nodded. I thought I noticed a slight irritation as if his advances had been rejected. He turned his attention back to those irksome papers, which seemed to serve as stage props. He rustled through them with exaggerated attention while continually smacking his gum.

He seemed impervious to the stifling air in the room. The lingering, rancid odors from Mulligan's bodily excretions mingled with a pungent smell wafting from Dettelbach's direction —Old Spice aftershave or underarm deodorant or both. Mixed in were the not-altogether-pleasant smells from my own perspiring body. When he turned his attention back to me, he spoke in carefully composed moderate cadences. His voice was almost unctuously soothing. But rather than putting me at ease and lulling me into a sense of security, it alerted in me the instinct of the hunted confronted with the hunter's cunning. Something about his bearing put me on my guard. My eyes and ears were on the lookout for traps and snares. He was slender and suave with impeccable manners, impeccable civility, and sympathetic expressions. I knew his type was much more treacherous than the ranting Irishman.

Not that I took this man to be a Nazi and the NYPD the equivalent of the Gestapo. The psychological props employed in the cellars of Gestapo headquarters went far beyond mere paper rustling, pregnant pauses, and even the occasional rant. I could not claim I was being tortured. No blinding beams of light were wearying my eyes for hours. There were no hot irons, whips, drugs, or needles. Nobody laid a hand on me. The psychology applied here was intended to cause the subject enough discomfort to elicit the desired confession. This would satisfy the public's desire for results and law enforcement's desire to close the case, pass it on to the district attorney, and move on to the next case. Even this kind of pressure, I had heard, was often enough for the police to obtain false confessions.

My new inquisitor tried a different tactic when his rather clumsy attempt to establish a bond between us through our presumably common fatherland failed. Maybe they called this "alternate tactic one" in the police handbook. He leaned back in his chair, crossed his legs, pulled out a silver cigarette case from the inner breast pocket of his shiny pin striped suit, snapped it open, and tendered me a cigarette. I refused. He took one out for himself and tapped it down on the case before putting it between his lips and lighting it with a silver lighter. The initials FHD were engraved on both lighter and case. He placed the case next to him on the table and kept snapping the lighter open and shut while inhaling and exhaling deep drafts with a satisfied mien. The air in the room was now a toxic brew of sweat, perfume, and smoke. This not only made it hard to breathe but caused my head to throb with such intensity I feared it would explode any minute.

Don't crumble, I kept telling myself. *Don't let him think his tactic is working.*

"If it bothers you, I can put it out," he said with a benevolent smile and stubbed the butt into an ashtray. The entire ritual was repeated over and over, and at the end of the two hours, the ashtray overflowed to the brim. He patted down his already-flattened hair with both hands, wriggled his tie loose, and said in a hoarse whisper, "Well, let's see now what we can do here." Ever alert to being pounced on again, I held the piercing gaze of his gray eyes. Wordlessly I waited for his next move.

"From what I see here," he began, pointing at my written statement, "you do admit to opening the theater door to a man from the street and letting him in about halfway through the afternoon performance. Right?"

I nodded.

"What you don't tell us is the identity of this man and why you would act so irresponsibly. Why would you break the trust of people who put you in a responsible position?"

"I felt sorry for him," I managed to say. "It was a mistake."

"You felt sorry for him," he repeated, and his eyebrows raised. "Well, we'll get back to your motive later. Right now I need to know who this man is. Who is this man who was so deserving of your pity? Is he a friend? A relative? An accomplice? A spy? A lover, perhaps?" His voice leaped upward, getting louder with each enumeration until it reached a fever pitch with the last possibility proffered.

"Who is he?" His fist landed on the table with a big thump. All that fake friendliness was gone. His eyes bored into mine like a snake's zeroing in on its prey.

"I don't know," I whimpered. Tears flooded my eyes against my will. "I'm telling you the truth. I don't know who he is. Some penniless vagrant violin player. He asked if he could just see a little of the performance."

"His name! I want his name!" He tapped his fingers on the table and ignored my assurances the man was a total stranger to me. I knew nothing about him except he had been playing the violin on the sidewalk outside the theater entrance every day since opening night.

"And you let him in out of the goodness of your heart?" he said with a derisive grin. "He then went on to murder the star of the show, and you want me to believe you had nothing to do with it."

I gave up. There seemed no way of convincing these police officers of my innocence. The cards were obviously stacked against me. Doubts began to creep into my mind. Was I really completely innocent?

Had I made myself the inadvertent accomplice in a murder? Did I not have myself partly to blame for being in this situation? I had allowed a street musician's wistful gaze at the marquee where the name "Stella Berger" shone in bright letters to touch me. Seeing him day after day from inside my perch in the ticket vendor's booth, I let the lilting melodies of European schmaltz beguile me. Soaring from his violin in a standoff with the blare of midtown traffic, his melodies touched something in my heart akin to nostalgia for a bygone era.

None of this could I disclose to Lieutenant Dettelbach. He was from the Midwest. His ancestors had arrived on these shores almost a century ago. What did he know about the old country and its culture? That home had spit us Jews out like so much refuse. They called us unworthy of living and vermin deserving to be crushed under their boots. I feared I would just make myself the butt of Dettelbach's derision were I to mention any of this.

"From opening night on he appeared every day before the performance began. He sat on a crate directly opposite the theater entrance and played the violin," I tried to explain.

"OK," he said in a calmer, encouraging tone. "Go on. What happened next?"

"I didn't pay too much attention. There's no shortage, as you know, of panhandlers on Broadway. I thought nothing of him picking that particular spot. It was a good spot. From what I could see, passersby and theatergoers generously rewarded him for his efforts. People seemed to like his playing."

"So you would say he had some money? Didn't you say you pitied him because he didn't have money for a ticket?"

"Well, yes. I believe that's what he said. He spoke poor English. It was hard to understand."

"He spoke poor English. Here's something to go by. What kind of accent did he have?"

"I would say Austrian or Hungarian."

"Excellent! Bravo! That narrows it down to a few thousand fiddle-playing immigrants in this city." He clapped his hands as if he had hit the jackpot. "Now if you will be so kind to give me his name and address, you can be on your way, and we can do our job."

I shook my head. He still didn't believe me.

"Where were you at the time of the murder?" he continued. "Waiting for him in the back alley? In a getaway car perhaps?"

"I wasn't there. I left right after I let him in. Besides I don't have a car, and I don't drive. You can check it out."

"Where did you go then?"

"I had a class, and I left early before the end of the performance."

"A class in the summer? What kind of class? Where?"

"A lab class. At Hunter College. A summer course."

"You are a college student? Interesting. Amazing."

What was so interesting and amazing about it, I could not fathom. He could see I was of college age.

"What's the program you're in? I presume you have witnesses who saw you there at the time of the murder."

"Pre-med, and yes, my lab partner can testify to my being there the entire time as well as other students and the professor."

"OK." He waved this information aside like some irksome fly.

I noticed yet another change in his demeanor. The raised eyebrows with which he looked me over bordered on something resembling respect.

"Pre-med? What do you know?" he mused. "Only in America. The land of opportunity. Give us your huddled masses and…here you are! You wouldn't sacrifice such a splendid opportunity for a brilliant career and secure future in our wonderful country by getting yourself involved in some vile act like murder, would you?"

"Of course not!" I replied somewhat haughtily. What seemed a momentary faltering in his determination to connect me to the crime emboldened me. I seized the opportunity to press my case. "That's why you have to believe me. I made a grave mistake. It was rash and thoughtless. I realize that now, but I had nothing to do with the crime. And I have no clue about this man's identity other than he plays the violin."

He gestured toward the mirror. This was apparently a signal to whoever was behind it. A middle aged woman carried in a pitcher of water and paper cups. I couldn't figure out whether she was friend, foe, or just some neutral flunky. She picked up the overflowing ashtray from the table with a look of disgust and poured its contents into a trash can. With arms akimbo, she gave the lieutenant, who was just lighting up another one, a disapproving stare.

"If you would like to get up…maybe you would like to avail yourself of the…" He waved toward the door. I gladly took up his offer to stretch my legs and escape from the confinement of what felt like a torture chamber. Also I urgently had to go. The woman silently escorted me to the ladies' room. An inscrutable nod met my thank-you and smile. There was still no way of telling whether she was an ally. I caught a better glimpse of her through the mirror in the washroom. She looked haggard but well-groomed.

Unlike my matted hair with its long strands knotted from sweat, hers was tidy, neatly combed, and tied back. The face that stared back at me from the mirror was more than just haggard. It was outright appalling. My face was smudged, my eyes were hollow and underlined with dark rings, and my cheeks were caved in. The cornflower-blue, sleeveless summer dress I had ironed in the morning was all crumpled and stained. I repeatedly doused my face with the cool water I collected from the faucet in my cupped hands. I let it run over my hands and arms and up to my elbows. It was a soothing ritual I didn't want to stop. All too soon, however, my escort tapped me on my shoulder and jerked her head to indicate it was time to go back into the lion's den where my inquisitors were awaiting my return.

Dettelbach looked refreshed, and so did Mulligan, who was now rejoining us. There was a spread of coffee with Dixie cups and dough-nuts on the table. Mulligan, who was already feasting, invited me gal-lantly to partake. From somewhere he had commandeered a floor fan that whirled up the stuffy air and blew it out the open door. It was a big relief, but I had no illusions. This sudden atmospheric change in the room did not dupe me. I knew it was all part of the game: trick, trap, and go in for the kill.

"Well, back to business it is," said Dettelbach, his mouth still half full. Though I seemed to have detected a slight trace of cordiality in his tone, I soon sensed him slipping back into his Jekyll and Hyde character.

He bade me retake my seat with a gallant gesture, and the pair took their seats opposite me. Two faces stared me down, though they were two very different faces. They were like a Laurel and Hardy act. This comedy team was known in Germany as *Dick und Doff*, which translated to something like Fatman and Dullard. I immediately tried to chase this silly thought from my mind. Dettelbach was thin but no dullard, and Mulligan, though of some girth, was nobody's fool either. My motto was to never underestimate an opponent.

THREE

In the course of the interrogation, I had an opportunity to size up my adversaries more closely. Dettelbach, I already knew, was as trustworthy as a wolf or maybe a fox. Mulligan, however, appeared in a very different light from my first encounter with him. A twinkle in his eyes gave him away as a decent, kind man. He was obviously devoted to his work and sometimes had to play rough in the line of duty. I could also sense in him genuine distress over the terrible crime that had occurred on his watch. *Here is a straightforward character*, I told myself. *He might even become an ally at some point.*

"Let's start at the beginning," said Dettelbach. Though the younger of the two, he outranked Mulligan and took charge of the interrogation with the authority of a presiding judge.

"State your name please," he began.

"My name is Misia Safran."

He gave me a puzzled look. "That's not what you wrote down here." He pointed at those paper props again.

"I'm sorry. My given name is Artemisia, but everybody calls me Misia." I still cursed my mother for sticking me with such a fanciful name to suit her artistic follies.

"Fancy, fancy," he mumbled as if reading my mind. He shook his head derisively. Mulligan flashed me a broad, sheepish grin. "Artemisia Safran. That's not very German, but let's leave that aside for now. What is the place and date of your birth?" Dettelbach continued.

"I was born on August 19, 1921, in Berlin, Germany."

"Name of parents?"

"My father is Paul Safran, and my mother is Tillie Werther."

"Hold it right here!" He jumped up. If he had had a whistle he would no doubt have blown it full blast. "What kind of game do you think you are playing here?" He had the annoying habit of ending his sentences with the word here. "Explanation!"

"My father's name is Naphtali Safran, but he is better known as Paul Safran." Was I overly sensitive, or did I see a disdainful smirk cross his face at the mention of my father's obviously Jewish name? I put it out of my mind and explained, taking care this time to be very precise. "My father was a well-known musician and composer in Berlin in the 1920s. My mother's legal name is Ottilie Safran, née Wertheim. She's a singer and actress. Tillie Werther is her stage name." Mulligan nodded.

"Until they threw you all out," I heard Dettelbach mumble under his breath.

"Actually we ran for our lives." I corrected him.

"Where are these parents of yours now?" Dettelbach's tone was getting increasingly cantankerous.

"They went to California a few months ago."

"And they left a young girl alone here in the big city. Why didn't you go with them to California?"

"I didn't want to interrupt my studies. Besides I'm a grown woman. I can take care of myself."

"As we have seen." I sensed a rising hostility that had not been there during our earlier one-on-one session. Something had irked him. I ratcheted up my vigilance and was determined not to be drawn into a battle of wits I couldn't win.

"Where in California can they be found? We'll have to speak with them."

"They are staying for the time being in Hollywood."

"Doing what? Enjoying the scenery?"

"Visiting friends and also looking for work."

"They're communists?" he asked.

17

I was totally nonplussed. "What do you mean?" If he meant to bewilder me, he surely was succeeding.

"Not everybody in Hollywood is a communist, Frank," Mulligan remarked. He was obviously unable to hide his irritation at the turn Dettelbach's questioning was taking.

"There are plenty of them, Tom. Plenty. You better believe it."

I cut in on their exchange. "I still don't know what you mean."

"I mean are they members of the Communist Party? Do they believe in world revolution? Do they like Uncle Joe? Why didn't they go to Moscow? Did they come here to overthrow the government? That sort of thing."

I was speechless. What could I say? Of course they weren't members of the Communist Party. Of that I was certain. I didn't even know whether there was such a thing in the United States of America, the center of capitalism. A freely elected, two-party system governed this democracy. As far as I knew, my parents weren't very political at all. They had their music on their minds all the time. We never talked about politics at the dinner table or elsewhere, except when the Nazis emerged and the political situation became a personal threat.

I remembered many of their friends back in the Weimar Republic days. They used to get all heated up while bandying about words such as proletariat, capitalist exploiters, and free artistic and sexual expression. I was little then and living mostly with my very bourgeois, buttoned-up grandmother who made no secret of her disapproval of her daughter's (my mother's) bohemian lifestyle. I presumed my parents leaned to the left like most intellectuals back then, but I doubted they had any sympathy for the Soviets or Stalin. I might have even heard them express abhorrence for some of the things that went on there, such as the famine caused by Stalin's bureaucrats or the show trials of intellectuals who ended up either dead or in Siberia. I don't think they paid close attention, though. Since the early 30's we had been moving from place to place, from Berlin to Prague to Paris to Spain. We landed in New York in the fall of 1937 before America closed its doors to refugees from the Nazi tyranny.

The story of how Paul and Tillie met and fell in love became part of our family lore that filled my childhood. No family gathering was complete without someone, usually one of my mother's five sisters, dramatizing Tillie's romance with a bohemian wandering minstrel, or klezmer, as Cousin Manya from Krakow would say. My grandmother, Fanny Wertheim, née Liebermann, was the matriarch of a side branch of the prominent Berlin department store Wertheims. She frequently referred to her daughter's marriage to an Eastern European Jew as the union of a commoner from the land where the black pepper grows and a princess from the urbane confines of Charlottenburg. It was a union she could never quite bring herself to accept in her heart of hearts, but in the end she said she gave her blessing since she did not want to stand in the way of her daughter's happiness. In reality she had no choice. Her daughter was as headstrong as she, if not more so, and she would have run away and cut her family ties.

Ideology and politics had little to do with Paul and Tillie running into each other or better yet being pushed into each other's arms inside the revolving door to the Romanesque Café on November 9, 1918. That was the day when the Kaiser abdicated his throne and Germany was declared a republic. Tillie and a flock of her girlfriends were filled with youthful euphoria about witnessing history in the making. They were marching down Kurfürstendamm in solidarity with the masses of factory workers streaming into the center of Berlin from the outlying working-class suburbs, clamoring for bread and an end to the war. Their hoisted red flags and banners fused together into a seamless crimson baldachin that virtually blotted out the sky, so it was reported.

At the corner of Tauentzienstrasse, Tillie was awestruck to find herself in front of that famous haunt where all the great minds, artists, and poets rubbed elbows, sipped their coffees, and exchanged ideas and lovers. The Romanesque Café was the place of her dreams. Whenever the subject came up later, she told me it was her holy grail. Eager to see inside and perhaps espy a famous person such as her idol, the poet Else Lasker-Schüler, she rushed into the revolving door unawares that the chamber was already occupied. The door closed, started to move, and with a croak came to a standstill. No amount of banging on the glass wall made it budge. She looked around for the fellow detainee and came face-to-face with an angry man in a Prussian army uniform with a bandaged head behind an enormous suitcase.

"Couldn't you wait your turn?" he yelled at her and pointed at a sign outside. "Can't you read? It says right there. Just one person at a time. See what you did? You probably caused a short, and now we're stuck in here."

For the next half hour, they were stuck in close proximity to each other inside the door. He rolled his eyes and tapped out some rhythm on top of his suitcase. She was all red-faced about her faux pas and torn with guilt and remorse as if she had committed a mortal sin. An impatient flick of his hand waved off her profuse apologies. She wanted to crawl deep into a hole. It was the most embarrassing moment of her life. When they were finally released from captivity, she tried to sneak away, but to her surprise he held her back. Very politely and with a gentlemanly bow, he invited her to a cup of coffee. The romance developed from there. Even though the sisters' embellishments about the hand of fate in this encounter became the official version, my mother insisted it was not love at first sight. It was more like on second or third sight. At any rate, in the following months and years, Tillie and Paul were among the regulars at the legendary café, and she did meet and rub elbows with many of the intellectual lights hanging out there. Among them was the divine Lasker-Schüler.

Could it be said my parents were communists back in Weimar days? I didn't know, and if they were, what difference did it make? Like most intellectuals and artists, they harbored left-wing ideals. Some were so lofty they didn't fit into the official agendas of either the Socialist or Communist Party. But what possible relevance could this have for the situation I found myself in here in New York? What did it have to do with the murder of a beloved movie star? Would it prove my guilt if they were card-carrying party members? I certainly had no connection to any ideology or party. I was trying too hard to build a life for myself in America. Dettelbach's erratic questioning was truly befuddling. Where was he going with this? A suspicion arose in my mind. Could it be he was trying to make the murder of an internationally renowned actress out to be part of a communist plot?

"You haven't answered the question." Dettelbach's menacing tone brought me back to the present. "We are waiting for your answer, Miss Safran. Maybe I should repeat the question. Are you, your parents, or all three of you communists? Are you perhaps spies for the Comintern?"

I was still racking my brain for how to respond to this ridiculous accusation clearly meant to entrap me any possible way. I heard Mulligan's voice. "Does this really do any good, Frank? I don't see how this helps us solve this case."

Dettelbach turned with blustering fury toward his colleague. "I am trying to establish motive here, Sergeant Mulligan.

Turning toward me, he once again his volatile demeanor changed: "So here you are, a young refugee, all alone in a big city." His patronizing tone dripped like oil from his lips. "You must at least have a boyfriend."

"Not really," I mumbled.

"You mean to say a nice looking girl like you doesn't have something romantic going on? No fiancé? Are you playing us for fools?"

"I don't have a real boyfriend or fiancé or anything like that, but..."

"But?"

"I've been dating someone on and off. Nothing romantic, as you would put it."

"What is his name?"

"I don't see what he has to do with all this."

"Name please," he thundered.

"His name is Curtis Wolff. I believe it's spelled with two f's."

"And where does this Curtis live? What does he do?"

"He's a law student at NYU. He lives somewhere down in the Village."

"So you haven't been to his place?"

His snarky tone made me want to punch him in the filthy snout.

"I think we have enough testimony for now," Mulligan once again intervened.

Somehow our earlier confrontation seemed wiped out. He had turned from adversary to ally.

"I'll say when we have enough." Dettelbach rose. His hands on his belt buckle.

In the end they let me go. I was told to go home and not leave the city. Everything was suddenly a big rush to get me out of there. Maybe they were eager to get home for supper. Maybe they had families, wives, and children waiting for them.

I walked out into the street. My head was spinning, and I felt anything but relief. I breathed the stale air in and out deeply to stave off an anxiety attack. It was early evening, still light out, and with no lessening of the record temperatures. I looked around for a subway station. Lower Manhattan was unknown to me. My lodging, a rooming house for young women, was uptown on the West Side. Eschewing the underground that was surely as airless and stifling as the little room from which I had just escaped, I started walking due north. I was fully aware of the two shadows I was dragging along behind me. I decided to ignore them.

FOUR

Germans call it "Schadenfreude"—a mischievous delight in someone else's misfortune. My tails would have to take a long walk with me. Although these hapless fellows were not the ones who had grilled me for hours in that stifling, little room. I pictured my two inquisitors spending a cozy, quiet evening in the bosom of their families—although I could be wrong, especially about the chain-smoking Dettelbach. He might very well be boarding at a rooming house like I did or a mid-town flophouse. He might be spending the night coughing, smoking, and chasing his beer with shots of schnapps or the other way around. I had no idea if that was what people did. Movies had mostly formed my ideas about American life. In my mind Mulligan, the Irish-American, was more likely to be a family man whose wife welcomed him home with a tasty Irish stew while his five children hopped around on his knees. I tried to chase these silly imaginings from my mind together with any thoughts of my day at the police station.

As the sun began its flaming descent into the Hudson River, I picked up the pace and began to walk more briskly. Zigzagging through the side streets, I hoped to give my pursuers a run for their money. Then again I felt sorry for them. I thought of walking up to them and inviting them to take the hike together, but I refrained. They probably didn't want me to spoil what might well be for them a cat-and-mouse, cloak-and-dagger kind of fun.

When I reached Times Square, it finally hit home. The force of a powerful punch to the stomach overwhelmed me. I gasped for air. My entire body trembled. My eyes glazed over. I leaned against the side of a building to keep from collapsing onto the sidewalk. I was no longer able to keep myself from facing the reason I had been arrested and interrogated. Stella Berger was dead. Murdered. A shining light in a darkening world had been snuffed out. Stella Berger, the tiny woman with a larger-than-life personality, had captivated her audiences, and in recent years she had inspired so much hope among fellow exiles. Stella Berger was no more.

Stella Berger is dead! How could it be? The thought went round and round in my head, gyrating like a spinning top and creating circles of changing colors before my eyes. Somehow I managed to pull myself together and walk on. I paused in front of the theater on Forty-Fifth Street where she had enchanted her audiences night after night. The theater was now draped in darkness, and yellow police lines marked "crime scene" cordoned off the area. Again I breathed in and out deeply to stave off an anxiety attack. Then I realized I was standing in the exact spot where the violin player, the man who was now hunted as the prime suspect in the crime, had played his soulful Kreisler and Sarasate tunes. His wistful gaze had been fixed on the marquee from which beamed her name in bright lights. Those lights were now extinguished.

The anticipation in the Jewish refugee community had been electrifying. Stella Berger was coming to New York. The announcement, several months in advance, had made the headlines. The coming of the Messiah couldn't have generated greater excitement.

"FAMED SCREEN DIVA ON BROADWAY," screamed the tabloids.

"ANTI-NAZI STAR DEBUTS ON NEW YORK STAGE!" read the headlines of the mass-circulation press.

"LEGENDARY THESPIAN TO PLAY SHAKESPEARE!" stated the paper of record.

"STELLA BERGER, ICON OF GERMAN CINEMA AND STAGE, COMES TO NEW YORK!" enthused the German émigré paper *Aufbau*. (I had a small part-time job editing and proofreading at the paper then and am proud for having contributed the word "icon.")

Madam Berger was to star at the Shubert Theater playing Desdemona to Robeson's Othello. Many among the exiles remembered her in this role at the Deutsche Theater in Berlin in Max Reinhardt's production. It had a long run and then went on tour in other German and Austrian cities. In those days she was hailed as the foremost Shakespearean on the continent. Her reprise of the role in New York was a moment, if not of hope, of pride for the émigrés. One of their own had become a persistent thorn in the side of Joseph Goebbels, and a growing host of admirers outside the German-speaking world were celebrating her. Unlike many in her profession who faltered at the language barrier, her Austrian-inflected English charmed her English audiences as much as her Austrian-inflected German had enchanted millions of German theater and moviegoers.

About the time Stella Berger signed the contract for her Broadway engagement—the actual appearance was still months off—my parents decided to seek their good fortune in California. Since our arrival in New York in October 1937, they had had gigs here and there at downtown dives and nightclubs, appearing as the "Safran Duo," "Paul and Tillie," or "Tillie and Paul." They just about made ends meet, but the local entertainment world was still smarting under the lingering effects of the Depression and provided meager bread. Besides, with anti-German sentiment on the rise, German pop songs were not much in demand even if Jewish artists wrote and performed them. Among their fellow refugees who might appreciate the Berlin wit and charm of Paul's compositions and Tillie's sultry renditions, few were inclined toward a nostalgic walk down Unter den Linden, and most didn't have enough means to spare for a night out on the town.

They turned, therefore, to a repertoire of mostly American jazz and some French chansons in the manner of Edith Piaf. In other words their act was derivative and imitative, as my father would say abjectly. Although Tillie's performances found much praise, presenting secondary material wasn't much to the liking of either of them. Several attempts to break into a Broadway musical production ended in failure. Finally they declared themselves to have had it with New York. In Hollywood they hoped my father might ride the coattails of famed film composers such as Friedrich Hollaender and Franz Waxman. Both had been part of the same crowd in Berlin's artistic circles. In fact the better known members of this crowd were now populating the Hollywood Hills, and they inspired hope that the atmosphere would be more congenial and opportunities for recognition of their talents would be more plentiful than in New York.

Although professional recognition never materialized on the scale my parents felt their talents merited, they very quickly felt at home in balmy Southern California. The clime bore little resemblance to the windswept north German plains. As they had expected, the atmosphere in émigré circles of German citizens of the Mosaic persuasion (counting even those who had very little knowledge of or connection to that persuasion) was indeed congenial. It abounded with opportunities for renewing old friendships if not the gigs they longed and hoped for.

The Hollywood Hills had become the home of a dazzling galaxy of exile celebrities, musicians, writers, poets, and playwrights with whom they were on familiar "Du" terms. Their relationships went way back to their more impecunious days when many of them lived in dingy, rented, cold-water walk-ups and nursed single cups of coffee for hours at the Romanesque Café, where they debated obscure philosophical points and recited their latest poetic outputs far into the night.

At one of those endless parties thrown by the famed uprooted, one such felicitous encounter was with Stella Berger. They had known each other in the days after the Great War when she was a struggling actress and late-night regular at the cabaret dubbed *Der Taubenschlag* (the Dovecote), Paul and Tillie had set up in an abandoned warehouse in the rear of a factory yard off Friedrichstrasse to showcase his tunes and her voice. To Stella's credit she never let her later success and stardom get in the way of acknowledging those early friendships.

At my mother's urging, I called on her during rehearsals at the Shubert Theater in New York. I was graciously received, and through her good word with the theater management, I was hired as an usher. Then I filled in at the box office when she opened as Desdemona.

A woman with a sourpuss face had answered my knock at Stella's dressing room door. I knew immediately this could not be Stella Berger because of her unusual height. Stella, the waiflike creature, emerged from behind the woman's back. She waved me in with a smile. The woman rolled her eyes seemingly disapproving of me and disappeared. I had heard that attendants to stars were often very possessive and felt called upon to guard their precious charges against an intrusive public. Later I saw the same person with the same sour mien several times in Stella's company as she was getting in and out of her limousine, and I felt confirmed in my original assessment of the nature of her role. At the time the magical atmosphere emanating from the star wiped the unpleasantness of this brief encounter from my mind.

I sat in the lavishly appointed dressing room at the edge of a rose-colored velvet chair opposite this petite woman. She was robed in a crimson silk sarong embroidered with gold cranes. Her reddish brown curls were fashionably bobbed. (On stage she was to wear the waist-long, blond wig I saw propped on a dummy in the corner.) Her stunningly huge, dark eyes fixed on me with a gentle smile, and she sat in a semi-reclining pose on a likewise rose, velvet Recamier chaise-longue. I was simply star struck. I had never been in the presence of such glamour. As if reading my mind and sensing my discomfort and awe, Stella gave off a gurgling laugh and made a sweeping gesture at the surroundings—the lighted, gold-framed mirrors and makeup tables, the matching rose of the wall and upholstery coverings, the plush carpeting, and the elaborate costumes on the rack.

"Don't mind this. It's all American taste."

Hearing her famed, growling voice in Viennese-inflected German addressing me, fairly made me swoon.

"We had none of this in Berlin," Stella continued. "Even at the Deutsches, we got dressed and made up in a crowded dump. No stars. We were all equals. And to think here in America, the land of equality, they make such distinctions. You should see the fuss they make over the sta-a-ars in Hollywood! Like royalty!" She stretched out the word "star" with ironic disdain, raising her eyebrows as if all this was just part of the show and had to be put up with.

"But let's talk about you."

Without asking how I took it, she poured me a cup of tea with sugar and milk and pushed a plate of chocolate-covered biscuits across the table with a gently prodding nod.

"Misia!" she mused, letting the word roll sensually from her lips. "What an unusual name."

"It's short for Artemisia," I explained. As always I was a little embarrassed about the subject of my name. "My grandfather often took my mother on business trips to Italy, especially Florence, even when she was very young. He thought she had artistic talent and should be exposed to the finest art. That's where she discovered the Renaissance artist Artemisia and fell in love with her at fourteen."

"Yes. I remember your grandfather very well. Max Wertheim. A prominent art dealer in Berlin. I attended several openings at his gallery on Friedrichstrasse—the fashionable side near Unter den Linden. Very bright, spacious exhibition halls. He had exquisite taste. Good family," she added.

I just nodded and suppressed the tears welling in my eyes at the memory of my grandfather who had passed away in 1935. It had probably been of a broken heart as it was not long after the Nazis trashed his gallery and hauled off his beloved collection of artwork.

She gave me another thorough appraisal and then burst out, "My heavens! How you have grown since I last saw you."

I had no idea when that might have been. I certainly had no recollection of ever meeting her in person before.

As if to answer my doubt, she continued, "We won't count the years, but the last time was when you were just starting to walk. From the time you could crawl, you were always underfoot at the Taubenschlag. In hindsight I wonder what your parents were thinking letting you be up at all hours in that dingy cabaret café of theirs with that billowing smoke and ear-shattering music. It was like Bill's Ballroom in Bilbao. With your papa accompanying your mama on the piano, we could have listened for hours, and we did. To us it was paradise. Every Friday and Saturday night from midnight into the graying dawn, we sat around frail, little tables. We smoked and drank wine or Berliner Weisse beer, and our faces glowed in the candlelight. These were wonderful, memorable, yet terrible times. The music, theater, and literature created in

28

those days offset all hardships. It's all gone now. Nothing will ever bring back those glorious days."

With that allusion to a popular Brecht and Weill song, her eyes glazed over. She seemed to drift off into a world that for me was but a vague childhood memory of ghostly figures and blurred shadows behind a veil of smoke. From the time I had reached the age of cognizance, my mother's voice was more of an irritant and cause for embarrassment than pleasure and pride. A child doesn't like to see her mother in a slinky lamé dress lolling sensually about a piano with a cigarette holder stuck in the corner of her mouth and emitting husky, suggestive sounds to the delight of a smitten audience at her feet.

"After a while you were no longer there. You must forgive me, but I never found out where they put you. We were so absorbed with our own lives and so lost in our dreams. We put all energy into making it. We all wanted to make it big. We wanted recognition and earthly rewards for what we were sure were our God-given talents, even though in the open we expressed our absolute disdain for material possessions."

Here again her eyes radiated a forlorn glow as her mind seemed to take flight to that far-off, almost mythic, sunken place they called "Weimar." Though, it wasn't the actual Weimar. That was the city of Goethe and Schiller. Theirs was Berlin—city of Brecht and Weill, Tucholsky, Lasker-Schüler, and others who brought glory to this metropolis for a brief span of time.

"My grandmother intervened," I replied abruptly to the question she didn't ask. "I was about three when she literally stormed the Taubenschlag. Brandishing a huge umbrella like a sword, she was ready to do battle. She lifted me off the floor where I was entertaining myself in the sawdust by stacking beermats for dominoes. She too thought that a smoke-filled, noisy joint, as she put it, wasn't a proper place for raising a child. She took me out to the family residence in Charlottenburg where I received a proper education in all things proper. I rarely saw my parents, and my return visits to the Taubenschlag were even rarer. I saw them mostly at family gatherings until I was thirteen, and then the Nazis came to power. They soon left Berlin after several raids on the

Taubenschlag by the Nazi thugs. Like so many, my parents started to wander from place to place. I came in tow."

"Yeah. We all became wandering Jews then, and we still are in a way," Stella mused. "Well, not everybody realized what was happening right away. Many thought the "spook," as they called it, would go away sooner or later. Your parents were more prescient than most."

I felt a hardening come over her. She sat up straight. Her muscles tensed, and the glow in her eyes dimmed. Her pupils contracted into a harsh, piercing glare. I began to writhe in my seat. What had I said or done? Then I realized this sudden transformation had nothing to do with me. "Never put your trust in men, Artemisia. I always put my trust in friendship, and to a certain extent I still do, but I have learned to be more selective."

I was deeply touched hearing my full name. Nobody ever called me that. Was she signaling her trust in me?

"We were all friends and colleagues—George, Kraus, Gründgens, and Jannings. Or so I thought," she added between her teeth. "We appeared in films and on stage together, and we experienced the joys and sorrows of our characters as if they were our own. We celebrated our triumphs together and comforted each other when the occasional flop brought us down. They all sold their souls to the devil!"

She proclaimed the last sentence with the pathos she put into her roles.

"I have often pondered the question of what I would have done. How would I have reacted had I not been born of Jewish parents?" she continued in a quieter, more reflective tone. "Would I have abandoned my Jewish colleagues and friends? Would I too have made a pact with the devil? Who knows? Marlene didn't. Maybe I too would have looked out for my career. Still I cannot forgive those erstwhile friends of mine. I wasn't much of a Jew, you know," she said with a cynical laugh. "It was Goebbels who reminded me where I came from and what I was—a Jewess. I was born in Galicia in Poland. Did you know that? I, the quintessential Viennese girl! And yet he offered to make me an honorary Aryan. He never forgave me for turning him down. Such an honor, and I spat in his face!"

I didn't know whether I should be taken aback or flattered to be witness to this outburst that laid bare a totally different side of her. Just as suddenly as she had launched into this rant, she straightened herself up, and the light went back on in her eyes. With a dazzling smile, she accused herself of being silly. *The consummate actress,* I thought.

We chatted for a while longer about this and that. She eventually turned the conversation to more practical considerations concerning me and my plans for the future. She wholeheartedly applauded my decision not to go with my parents to California and seek an elusive fortune in show business. It was much better to study to become a doctor and eschew the entertainment world.

Rehearsal was called. She tendered her hand to say good-bye but then thought the better of it. She pulled me toward her delicate frame, which was about half a head shorter than mine, in a surprisingly firm embrace. She told me I could stay for the rehearsal if I wanted. She would be alone on stage practicing Desdemona's monologue. I gladly accepted, but I was sorry I hadn't brushed up on my Shakespeare in advance of the interview.

I heard her speak this soliloquy on opening night and many times thereafter, but never did it touch me as deeply as on that afternoon when I sat alone in the dark, empty theater still under the spell of the encounter with this most extraordinary woman. Some described her as a boy/woman because of her ageless, hermaphroditic physique. Even at forty, however, in her comportment, manner, and style, she projected the image of the quintessential woman. She was comfortable in her skin and even had a touch of femme fatale—the real kind. I had never seen her as Wedekind's Lulu, her signature role before she established her reputation as a Shakespearean, but I could well imagine.

As I left the theater, the director stopped me. If I wanted to, he said, I should see him in his office. "When convenient," he added brusquely and making no attempt to hide his annoyance at not being able to turn down a request from his star. At least that was the way I, always probing behind the outward facade of human behavior, interpreted the blasé, disinterested manner he projected when I saw him a few days later.

As usher on opening night, my senses were dazzled by the galaxy of celebrities, stars, and politicians I guided to their seats. Laurence Olivier and Vivien Leigh, Marlene Dietrich and Jean Gabin, Max Reinhardt and Helene Thimig, and Kurt Weill and Lotte Lenya were among the celebrated couples who entered via the red carpet. Hedy Lamarr glided in alone and took everybody's breath away, including mine. The mayor of New York was there and members of the city council. Representatives of cultural organizations showered Stella with flowers and praise when the curtain fell.

The one who remained distinctly in my memory was one Herman Krueger, president of the German-American *Kulturbund*. A short, stocky man, the suspenders holding up his trousers barely reined in his beer belly. He waddled on stage and huffed under the weight of an outsize bouquet of red roses. She listened graciously to the sickeningly sweet effusion he heaped on her in American-accented German. He spoke in long, winding clichés about the extraordinary honor it gave him to be able to greet the incomparable Stella Berger—a truly worthy ambassador of German culture to the world. She raised her eyebrows, and baring her bright, shining teeth, she accepted the accolade. It might have looked like an amiable smile to some watching, but I knew what was in her heart.

At the end of the performance, she stepped in front of the footlights. She raised her hands begging for silence. When the applause subsided, she spoke directly to the audience. She urged all those present to pray with her for the timely defeat and obliteration of the Nazi scourge. A standing ovation and shouts of "Victory!" followed the minute of silence. I looked around for the man from the German-American Kulturbund. If he was still there, the standing crowd obscured his corpulent figure. Stella Berger's appeal to her audience at the end of each performance became her signature.

I often saw her from afar, but we never had another opportunity to speak. I saw her on stage where she became the vulnerable Desdemona whose skin she assumed totally. On occasion I saw her getting in and out of limousines. A troop of men in dark suits always surrounded her.

If they were bodyguards, hangers-on, or an entourage of ardent admirers every celebrity seemed to keep, I could not tell. Neither did I know which one might be her husband and manager, the famous director Alexander Levary. I shut myself off from rumors of scandal, of their breakup and divorce. For me she was an immaculate saint.

I remembered my mother telling me about Stella. In those early days after the war, even before she gained fame and was just an ordinary regular at my parents' cabaret, there were always three or four "lovelorn" young men around her and one tall woman—her mother hen. They all spoke Viennese German except for the tall woman whose diction was more Bavarian. My mother said this with raised eyebrows and the Berliner's supercilious yet indulgent smile when the subject of German dialects came up.

Once Stella made it into film, my mother added with puckered lips, she was apparently too busy to come to her old haunt at the Taubenschlag. She also never saw any of the young men again except for one sad sack, as my mother referred to him. He was a poet who came by occasionally to recite his poems to an appreciative audience.

"Beautiful poetry. Very expressionistic," she mused nevertheless and sent up that nostalgic gaze into an indistinct distance.

All the displaced "Weimaraner," as I dubbed them, assumed that look when they spoke about those halcyon days in that far-off place now lost in the miasma of time. That poet had also disappeared from the cabaret scene by the late twenties. She always felt sorry for him, she said. He seemed so forlorn and out of sorts. She didn't know his name, or she didn't remember it. What she did remember was that Stella called him *Xaverl*—a Viennese term that was part endearing and part mocking. He was probably Hungarian, she added with pride for her ability to place people's origin from the way they spoke.

Seeing Stella and her entourage, this conversation with my mother came back to me. I wondered whether one of those men with Stella might be Xaverl, the Hungarian poet.

FIVE

My parents' venturing three thousand miles away from New York had affected their lives only slightly; they were still wanderers in search of their holy grail. My decision to stay in New York turned my life, the course of which I had so carefully planned, upside down. *None of this would have happened,* I told myself, *had I gone to California with my parents.* I would never have met Stella Berger in person. To me she would have been a movie star and just a glimmer on the silver screen. Her murder would have been a great shock. My mother would have broken out in hysterics and locked herself up for a few days under the pretense of one of her migraines, but it would have been something far away. It would not have affected our daily lives. I didn't go to California, though, and I was there at the crime scene. Not only was my life profoundly affected, but I had put it in grave danger in a thoughtless moment of misguided charitableness. This is how I came to view the situation while turning the sequence of events over and over in my head. I continued to walk up Broadway, away from the theater district, and toward my rooming house on Ninety-Fourth Street on the Upper West Side.

I had had good reasons for wanting to stay in New York, not the least of which was a desire to unhitch my life from that of my parents. Maybe it was my upbringing in my grandparents' thoroughly bourgeois, upper middle-class home in an affluent part of Berlin that made me regard my parents' bohemian lifestyle with some disdain. Of course my mother had been raised in the same home with her five sisters, and all of them had married into what my grandmother called "proper society." Two of my aunts had married out of the faith, but their husbands were a judge and a defense lawyer respectively. One could, therefore, shut one's eyes to their one shortcoming of being goyim. For reasons my grandmother found hard to discern, my mother had always been the rebel. She was also the most gifted. Even as a young girl, she had scorned bourgeois values. She called it Philistinism but not directly to her parents. She was too well brought up and respectful for that, but she chastised their social class on a broad, abstract level. She always cited my grandfather's compromise (his caving in, she said) to bourgeois values by sacrificing his great artistic gift on the altar of the capitalist god, Mammon. He became a successful art dealer and accumulated great wealth. He built a beautiful mansion in Charlottenburg and a lakeside villa in Grunewald with a dock and sailboat, gave his daughters the finest Swiss boarding school education, and took them all on extended vacations to European artistic capitals where they stayed at the grandest hotels. "At what cost?" Tillie moaned on numerous occasions. She, however, benefitted from her father's extended business trips to Italy, as he arranged for art and singing lessons with outstanding instructors only the wealthy could afford. Yet, she insisted, a penniless, starving artist shivering in some garret and disowned by his wealthy family while fulfilling his destiny would have conformed much better to her romantic ideal of a father.

Being a musician in and of itself was no detriment in my grandmother's eyes (my grandfather maintained neutrality). She had the greatest admiration for a Rubinstein and a Heifetz. But her prospective son-in-law was a klezmer—an itinerant *Musikant*! The matter was finally settled and her mind put at ease when this klezmer musician of indistinct lineage performed for her Chopin's "Revolutionary Etude" with such panache that she proclaimed Horowitz couldn't have done it with more feeling. It was a slight exaggeration to be sure, but Naphtali Safranovsky, alias Pavel Safranov, alias Paul Safran, had conquered enough of her heart to be admitted into the bosom of the clan. The wedding took place in a beautiful, traditional ceremony at the great synagogue on Oranienburger Strasse on Sunday June 30, 1919. It was the day after representatives of the new republican government signed the Allies' peace terms at Versailles.

My father spoke very little about his family and his growing up in Poland. All I knew was he came from the Polish town of Grodno. Whether he was born there, moved there later, or went to school there was never clear. He was fluent in Yiddish, Russian, and Polish. His German was quite idiomatic but overlaid with a heavy, rolling Slavic accent. He also seemed to have at least a smattering of knowledge of the Torah and Talmud and the basics of Jewish observance, but it was no more than a vestige from what I presumed was a former life. I picked up a few hints that his father's family was in the lumber business. At other times they seemed to be dealers in fabrics and sartorial supplies. Maybe they were both or neither. Where my father was concerned, one could never tell fact from fiction or reality from fantasy.

Somewhere along the way, there must have been a falling out. Once when I asked about the origin of our family name, he said his ancestors had been in the spice trade. He said their caravans had carried precious goods from the Middle and Far East to medieval Europe. Thinking back now, I am sure that was another of his romantic fantasies. As a child I adored my father. I loved to be drawn into his tall tales and didn't ask questions whether anything was true or not. During his wandering years, he traveled with a band of itinerant minstrels all over Eastern Europe. From Riga to Odessa, there wasn't a town or village in the entire Pale where they didn't perform at weddings and market fairs. At some point along the way, probably as they moved west into Poland, he changed his name to Pavel Safranov, and as they got even further west, he became Paul Safran and went solo. At the outbreak of the war in August 1914, he found himself in Prussian territory. Hating Czar Nicholas more than Kaiser Wilhelm, he enlisted in the Prussian army and spent the war years entertaining the troops on the Eastern Front. After the Treaty of Brest-Litovsk took Russia (by then the Soviets) out of the war, he drifted toward Berlin, landed a gig as a piano player at the Romanesque Café, and fell in love.

That was about as much as I knew about my father. He was witty, easygoing, and always up to fun and pranks. He was *ein Spaßvogel*. Only his music he took very seriously. My mother tended toward mood swings from exultant to the high heavens to sinking into the pit of melancholy without warning or visible reason. She was also quarrelsome and let my father have it for the slightest infraction, but he couldn't have found a better interpreter of his compositions. She had some operatic training as a soprano, but her natural voice was more comfortable in the lower registers, and she found her calling as a cabaret singer in the suggestive style of a French chansonette.

They set up the Taubenschlag shortly after their marriage with some financial support from my grandparents, even though they had suffered severe financial losses due to the war and the inflation. Paul and Tillie soon gained some local fame and appreciation. Not long after my mother showed signs of pregnancy, but this didn't hinder her from performing almost up to the last minute before giving birth. If Paul hadn't called his mother-in-law to let her know Tillie had gone into labor, I would likely have had the stigma of being born on a table or the floor of a smoke-filled nightclub dressing room. My grandmother arrived in a limousine at the eleventh hour to haul her daughter off to the Charité Hospital. In short order I came to see the light of the world.

My parents were incorrigible bohemians and completely lacking in any sense of the practical. Money, if they made any, ran through their fingers. The only reasonable thing they ever did was get out of Europe in time to make it to America. Once here they continued in their old way. They moved from gig to gig for meager pay and always held to the fantasy that somehow the land of opportunity would bring them their due recognition. Didn't Marlene Dietrich, Stella Berger, Max Reinhart, and even that little guy from Hungary, Peter Lorre, gain fame and fortune? How often did I have to listen to this claim?

How removed from reality they were struck me like a revelation during our life in New York. Maybe I was just growing into adulthood. When we arrived I was seventeen and still in high school. In the three years since, I had matured and come to see the world for what it was—not some dream world my parents hankered after. This was a major reason I resisted the move to California with them. I was old enough to stand on my own feet and follow a path divergent from theirs.

Then there was Curtis Wolff, the NYU law student I had been dating on and off for a few months. I really liked him and wanted to see where it would go. I also liked the company of his friends down on Washington Square. They were easygoing and fun. They were what I considered normal, young people. They were unencumbered by the Weltschmerz afflicting most people around me and causing them to blow up over the most insignificant matters.

For some totally inexplicable reason, my mother objected. She said I was too young to tie myself to an older man. Curtis was twenty-five.

"It's only a date!" I protested. "You got married when you were nineteen to a man twelve years your senior."

"Things were different then. Times and circumstances were different."

That was the excuse and explanation for everything. I didn't want to get into a debate about how things were different. I already knew about the times and circumstances. Of course this was America, and thank goodness things were different here.

"You speak like an American!" she snapped.

Maybe she thought it was a mother's duty to object to a daughter's choices as her mother had done. "Is that what's bothering you?" I asked. "That he's an American?"

I was completely perplexed. Curtis was about to become a lawyer and was from an apparently prosperous Jewish family, although that didn't matter to me. His forebears had come from Germany and settled in Chicago several generations back. His mother's great-grandfather came in the nineteenth-century wave of German migration to America.

"We're just dating. Having a good time every once in a while," I reiterated. "I'm not getting married. My studies come first."

"You can study in California," she insisted.

There was something much more profound and perhaps irrational that tied me to New York. It made me lie awake at night for hours with my heart pounding and my throat parched with anxiety. It was the specter that turned my dreams into nightmares and haunted me with intimations of impending doom. Could I (should I) confide in her and tell her the real reason I wanted to stay in New York? California would remove me another three thousand miles from the events in Europe. Maybe it was just an excuse, but I felt leaving New York would sever the last thin thread that tied me to my grandmother. Somehow I felt I could still reach across the waters to her. My mother of all people should understand, but I wasn't sure she would.

"I worry about Omi," I said.

"Sweetie, we all worry about her," she said in a softened tone. "We must take comfort that she's not alone. Aunt Trudi is with her, and Aunt Malli is still trying to get them both out."

My mother's sisters had all managed to leave Germany with their families after the November pogrom the Nazis called *Kristallnacht*. Amalia, called Malli, went to England. Grete went to Palestine, and Eva and Anna found refuge in South America. My grandmother felt she was too frail to leave and start life over in a foreign land, and feisty as she was, she wouldn't give those thugs the satisfaction of letting them drive her out of the country where she had been born and lived for eighty years. Not to speak of her ancestors going back centuries. Gertrud was unmarried and stayed with her. I saw no reason to share my mother's optimism. For me the signs were clearly on the wall. The noose around the Jews still in Germany was tightening every day and every minute. My grandmother had already been forced out of the family villa in Charlottenburg and had had to sign over the house with all other possessions and assets to the state. She and Aunt Trudi now shared one room in an apartment in Berlin-Schöneberg in a *Judenhaus*. They were cramped in with other dispossessed and displaced Jews facing an uncertain future.

"Aunt Trudi is working in some factory in Lichtenberg from dawn to dusk. Omi is alone all day with strangers. What can Trudi do when she gets home, worn out and exhausted? You know all this. Why can't you face up to what is happening?"

"Of course I know. Of course I do. I read her letters. You needn't remind me." My mother winced and wrung her hands. "But what can we do? If we could make enough money, maybe we could do something. Help them to somehow ease their lives or even get them out."

I wanted to scream at her to stop deluding herself. She could never make enough money in time, and even if she made a million dollars tomorrow, money wouldn't do anything. It was too late. I didn't scream, though. I tried to let her down gently on the harsh ground of reality.

"We must be prepared for the worst," I said softly.

"You are such a Cassandra," she said and wiped her tears. "I need to lie down."

This was her way of handling a difficult situation. For the next three days, she was lying flat on her back in bed in her darkened room with a migraine. I applied hot and cold compresses to her forehead but thought better of bringing up the subject again. Two weeks later Paul and Tillie Safran boarded the overland train for the promised land of California.

"I hope you can find a way to support yourself," my mother said as we said good-bye. "You know we barely have enough for ourselves right now."

I told her not to worry. I would find enough work, and I still had the job at the newspaper. I remained standing on the platform until the train had disappeared into the crimson, western sky. I would miss them, but I was also relieved to see them go so I could start my own life.

About a month after their departure, my mother called long distance. For a moment I thought they had struck gold. She was so excited about what she had to tell me the cost of the call seemed no object. They were settled in among a crowd of old friends. It was like Berlin in the olden days, my mother said, a veritable dream. They also had a few prospects—possibilities in the film industry. *Whatever that means,* I thought. She was about to hang up when she seemed to remember something. Maybe it was the reason for the call in the first place.

"Before I forget, I think it could do you a lot of good if you called on Stella Berger. You know? The famous actress. We knew her from way back. She is going to be in New York this summer, on Broadway no less. I believe she's doing Shakespeare again."

I knew very well who Stella Berger was. Who didn't?

SIX

I saw him right away. He was sitting on a stoop opposite my rooming house on West Ninety-Fourth Street. Due to the strictly enforced rooming-house rules barring male visitors at any time, I always went down to the Village to meet Curtis. It, therefore, came as a big surprise to see him sitting there. His presence was quickly explained, though. He had heard of the murder and my arrest and wanted to offer emotional and legal support.

"That's very sweet of you," I said somewhat embarrassed. I really would have preferred him not getting involved. "So far I haven't been charged with anything. They let me go. Maybe they think I will lead them to the killer."

"That's probably their calculation. I see you have two guardian angels." He pointed to the two gentlemen at the corner guzzling bottles of Coke. "Looks as if you gave them a good workout."

"I think you should leave," I said. "Consorting with a potential accomplice of a murderer could get you into deep trouble."

He gave a throaty laugh. "You? A murderess? Don't make me laugh."

"I don't think the detectives are laughing. They think I really had something to do with it."

"Then we'll have to prove them wrong."

Did he see himself as my savior or a knight on a white horse? *Typical American*, I thought. I reminded myself, however, he was a law student and soon to be a member of the bar. I probably could use some legal

41

advice, especially since I didn't have a penny to my name for a defense or whatever else I might need down the road, which was still shrouded in uncertainty.

Hold it, I told myself. *He's a boyfriend.* It would hardly be ethical or proper to exploit the relationship.

"If you think there's something wrong with me representing you, think again," he said, guessing my qualms. "Let's go someplace where we can talk. Let's go to my place."

"That's a hundred blocks away!" I protested. "I just walked that distance and couldn't do it again. I'm dead tired. My feet are hurting."

"There's the subway," he replied. "Or even better, we can take a cab."

Rich kid. Just as I thought. I didn't want him to think I was going out with him because he had money to burn, but he insisted. After what I had gone through that day, I needed to pour my heart out to someone.

"What are we going to do with those guardian angels?" I asked as we stepped into the cab.

"They're on their own," he replied. "We're not even supposed to know they are there. Then again, whom are they kidding?"

I leaned back in the cushions. Suddenly it was "we." It was no longer just me alone in the world. I closed my eyes and quietly savored the closeness of a strong, male body. I was grateful for the mindfulness he showed of my need for silent contemplation after the day's unsettling events.

He asked the driver to stop at the corner of Bleecker and MacDougal, which was half a block from where he lived.

"The posse has already arrived," he said and extended his hand to help me out of the car.

I didn't know what a posse was, but I too spotted a different set of police officers right away. These two wore colorful Hawaiian shirts and were licking ice cream.

"I have to hand it to the NYPD," he said. "They wasted no time tracking us down. Their stakeouts might be a bit obvious, but their researchers are surely on the ball."

I was learning a lot of Americanisms from my date. This, however, wasn't a real date, and I still had reservations about drawing him into my troubles.

Instead of going straight to where he lived, he grabbed me by the elbow and steered me in the opposite direction. "You must be starved. I hope you like Italian. I know a nice, quiet Italian restaurant with a mean chicken cacciatore."

As if to voice its agreement, my stomach responded with a gentle growl that I hoped he didn't hear. A single candle flickering in a red-tinted glass globe lit our corner table. The chicken cacciatore and a nice Chianti to go with it were indeed delicious. Even after I had nibbled profusely on the crusty Italian bread dipped in olive oil, I was still hungry enough to fall over my food with utter disregard for the punctilious table manners of my upbringing at my grandmother's house. No matter how hungry you are, she would say, always approach the food with reticence. Cut small portions, and chew with slow deliberation.

These were indeed different times and circumstances I found myself in. I was in a world far removed from the polite society of Charlottenburg, and I pleaded mitigating circumstances for myself when I thought back on it later. Red-faced, I apologized to my companion for my uncouth behavior.

He laughed it off, and with typical American insouciance, he shrugged. "Think nothing of it."

He ordered coffee for both of us and then a second cup that eventually got cold. We talked, or rather I talked. He reached for my hands, and we kept them firmly entwined as if holding on for dear life. Our eyes locked without flinching, and I told him everything sotto voce. My mouth broke open like the box of Pandora, spilling thoughts and feelings I had never before put into words. I told him about the woman I had idolized. I spoke of her kindness, generosity, and great art.

"She was a beacon of hope for the world in these dark times," I proclaimed. "And now a murderer's hand has brutally extinguished that light." He squeezed my hand when he saw tears welling up in my eyes. "Am I being too sentimental?" I asked.

"Not at all. It's good to let go," he said. "Let's make this a festive occasion and have some more wine." He waved to the waiter with a nod at our empty glasses.

Thus encouraged I went on. I told him about the violin player, a panhandler like so many in the streets of New York, the police were now seeking as the prime suspect. I told him what I would never have told the police officers who had interrogated me. "I broke the rules and let him into the theater." I paused, fumbling for the right words. "But I also let him seduce me."

"How do you mean?" A puzzled look appeared on his face.

"No. It's not that." I laughed nervously. I was ever fearful of being misunderstood and that the right words wouldn't come to me. "In the weeks since opening night, he played those schmaltzy Gypsy tunes while sitting on a crate near the curb opposite the theater box office. Day after day I sort of let the music melt my heart. Whenever I heard him play, I got this knot in my stomach. It was a longing for my old world. The loss came over me. The music was part of a culture I had grown up with. It seems all gone now. Destroyed by the barbarians."

I worried if he would understand what I was trying to say.

"Don't misunderstand me," I added quickly. "I love America and wouldn't want to go back over there." I had been speaking to the plant behind him and avoiding eye contact. I turned my face toward him now. I was apprehensive about having aroused his anger or scorn, but he just nodded with that gentle, understanding smile of his.

I went on and tried to sound very American. "You know, the Old World isn't all that it's cracked up to be. Is that how you would say it?"

I told him of my near-birth on the sawdust-strewn floor of a dingy Berlin cabaret. I told him how the grand entrance of my umbrella-brandishing grandmother rescued me from that fate and ensured I was properly birthed in a proper hospital.

"Slight exaggeration," I said, and we both laughed. "But it's not too far from the truth. Maybe it wouldn't have exactly been on the floor, but the kitchen table or some backroom pallet would have done fine for my mother. Several eyewitnesses have confirmed one thing. My mother was still singing while in labor. And still I didn't inherit her voice...or her winning personality." I remembered the way my mother could captivate any company with wit and charm. My grandmother called it her "prima donna allure." Even among the circle of Berlin artists, she stood out, and that circle was not lacking in alluring prima donnas.

He protested against my "unjustified modesty." I protested back and assured him I was perfectly fine. "I never aspired to be like my mother. I realized early in life how different we were, and I was grateful for her total disinterest in making me a little inkblot of herself. Of course, we also lived apart for a good part of my formative years."

"Fascinating," he said with a sympathetic nod.

Was he psychoanalyzing me and my relationship with my mother? He was a law student, but nearly everybody I knew had read Dr. Freud and played amateur psychoanalyst at the drop of a dime. It was like a parlor game but a very annoying fad. I was, therefore, surprised and even not a bit gratified when he professed his complete ignorance of the famous Viennese soul explorer's theories.

"If you like cabaret," he said, unabashed about this gap in his education, "maybe you would enjoy this one singer. I think she was European. German or French. My friends and I used to love her. We even followed her around for a while from a place in the village called Jacqueline's to the nightclub at Hotel Albert. A few times she was at the Village Vanguard. What do you say? Let me find out where she is now."

"You won't find her. She's in California."

"You mean..."

"If her name is Tillie Werther, yes."

"Well I'll be darned! I've been dating the daughter of Tillie Werther without knowing it."

"Would it have made a difference?" I asked.

"Of course not!" he said quickly. "It's just a funny coincidence. Even after all you told me, I didn't put two and two together."

He ordered more wine, and we polished off the entire bottle. The conversation returned to the murder case. I expressed doubts that the violin player had actually done it.

"Why would you say that?" he asked.

"Just a hunch that there's more to the whole thing than just a vagrant intruder. What would be his motive? Nothing was stolen."

"Well, I guess we should let the police figure this one out and not play amateur sleuth." I noted a slight irritation about him, but I filed it away under insignificant miscellany.

I was more interested at that moment in finding out something about his life, family, and upbringing, but he evaded my direct questions. He only repeated what he had already told me. He came from a Jewish family of lawyers and real estate developers in Chicago. They were of German origin dating back several generations. He wouldn't go into more detail.

Looking back, searching for clues among the sequence of events I unreeled over and over in my mind, I pinpointed this romantic moment in the glow of the candlelight in the Italian restaurant as the moment I fell in love with him. Why? Because I wanted to. I had never been in love before. Influenced by the movies, it seemed the thing to do. His good looks helped. With his chiseled features, strong chin, prominent nose, warm honey eyes, and dark-blond, wavy hair, he could have competed with any movie star. There was something more than just being pleasing to the eye, though. I felt an irrepressible desire to kiss his soft, full lips. His seemingly permanent smile revealed an almost too perfect row of sparkling whites that made me besotted. Maybe I lost all good judgment because I was starved for the warmth and security I hadn't felt since I had left my grandmother's house. I knew I was starved for love. My body was ready for physical closeness. I yearned to be held, to be made love to, and to make love. I was twenty-one and had never experienced the love of a man.

Unlike American teenage girls, I had not been into boys. There were not even any boys around during my teenage years I could have fancied. I spent puberty as an appendix to my parents' adult world. I was an extra in a drama that unfolded on a constantly changing stage. Had I had a sister, it might have been different. I might have had someone to share my thoughts, feelings, and fears with. As it was, feelings were something I kept unexpressed and buried deep inside. My parents were in the business of survival. I realized that. Their life together was a daily struggle. I would only have sown seeds of discord had I demanded their attention. Something did rub off on me from my parents, though. I had inherited their craving for success. I had set my sights on what I regarded as a more realistic, practical goal that I knew I could achieve. Even after we had settled in New York, and I was in high school, boys were just not part of my equation to reach the goal I had set for myself.

I had met Curtis Wolff at the *Aufbau* office. I was editing an article he submitted about the Joint Distribution Committee when he complimented me on my English language skills. With a touch of arrogance, he had added, "For a refugee." The article contained nothing original. It was just a summary of the origin of the organization and the services it provided for the homeless and uprooted. The information could have been gathered in any library. I wondered why we were publishing it at all. The editor explained it might be useful for the readership to have the information at their fingertips. We had a few editorial meetings in which we went over his work, and I thought his pieces were nothing to write home about. I made a few suggestions for changes in style and content, and I pointed out a few factual errors. When the article had been put to bed, he asked me out to celebrate what he called his first publishing success. We saw each other off and on for a movie or a beer with his friends in the Village. I came to enjoy the company of these freewheeling people.

Once or twice I invited him to a Friday night young people's gathering at Congregation Habonim. Despite his German-Jewish ancestry, he didn't seem to fit in with all those German refugees. I noticed him twitching uncomfortably and regarding the crowd with a detached, even scornful eye. He seemed reluctant to get into a conversation with anybody, and he certainly was unfamiliar with the Hebrew prayers. After the third time, I gave up. I never asked him to accompany me again, and he never asked to go back there. Maybe it was the language. All that chatter in a foreign tongue might have made him feel like an outsider.

He was the first man I ever dated, though nothing romantic had come of it then. Even in the darkness of a movie theater, he never tried to kiss me. The romantic comedies and dramas unfolding before us on the silver screen kept us spellbound but failed to light a fire in either of us. Back then I was perfectly fine without such complications. My mother had gotten all nettled over nothing. If I had told her what really went on (or didn't go on) during our dates, she would have declared him not normal in the head or elsewhere. To her a platonic relationship between a man and a woman was something to scoff at.

Now there was this sudden even though welcome shift in our established protocol. Without ado or declaration, he was acting like a boyfriend. It was as if we had always been a twosome. The change made we wonder for a moment, but the day's events had put me in need of companionship. Besides, why shouldn't I stir his romantic interest? Though no drop-dead beauty, I wasn't ugly. I was slender and kept myself well groomed. While never a fashion bug, I was a graduate of the finest Swiss finishing school in Davos, and I knew how to comport myself in a pleasing manner. We were young, intelligent, educated, unattached, and Jewish. I was a damsel in veritable distress. He was a gentleman extending a helping hand. Maybe he had just been shy before. Now we had gotten to know each other better, perhaps he was less reticent to make his feelings known. It also, no doubt, did his manly pride good to play the role of my protector from the police, and I was more than ready to strike out into uncharted territory. I was game for almost anything heretofore untried, especially on this day that had already turned my life upside down.

What a day it had been. First there had been the crushing news about the murder of a woman I worshipped, followed by my arrest under suspicion of complicity in the crime, and then a grueling police interrogation. Next there had been this totally unforeseen godsend. It was not exactly *Deus ex machina* since I was not off the hook with the police yet, but it suggested the possibility of love, intimacy, companionship, and who knew what else.

We left the restaurant on MacDougal. My stride on wings, my head dizzy from too much food and wine, I felt his arms around my shoulder and the warmth of his body pressed against mine. We laughed. I felt the hair rising on the nape of my neck and a strange rushing sensation up and down my spine. Only the fear of being seen by the police made me hold in a scream of happiness. I looked around carefully. The Hawaiian shirts were nowhere to be seen. Maybe more inconspicuous colleagues had replaced them and were lurking in the shadows. Curtis shrugged off my concern.

"They must have packed it in for the night." He giggled. "Even police officers need a rest."

We giddily staggered along like two inebriated children down Bleecker Street toward what I presumed was his place. He fiddled with the keys, as his hands were a bit unsteady from the wine. I stood back, leaned against the side of the building, and caught my breath. I was happy but still on the lookout for any spies. There were no police in sight as far as my blurry eyes could see. It was way past midnight, and the street was empty. Only one skulking figure, a man in a long, buttoned trench coat, moved in the shadow of the building across the street. Something vaguely familiar about him attracted my attention. Then my gaze met those wistful eyes. He was looking straight at me with an imploring, pleading stare. My heart contracted. My companion's back was to the street, and he was still struggling to get the key into the lock. He was unaware of the panic that came over me. I turned away and faced the building. Finally the door opened. I entered quickly and passed into the foyer without a word. Those wistful eyes were like needles in my back.

I didn't know why I didn't tell Curtis about the man who had obviously been following us. Or maybe I did know. I didn't want anything to burst my bubble. I didn't think of it consciously then, but I wasn't going to let anything or anyone spoil this enchanted moment. Though I was inexperienced in the art of lovemaking, I hurtled myself into his embrace. I faked more than felt the wild, passionate abandon just to forget those wistful eyes outside.

At some point I must have fallen into a fitful sleep. A clattering noise nearby woke me and made me sit up with a start. I found myself in a strange bed in a strange room redolent with the aroma of strong coffee.

"Good morning, my darling." Curtis walked in with a tray of breakfast dishes and flashed his brightest smile. "Did you sleep well?"

Darling? I thought. *Now I'm his darling?* Then I remembered. I jumped out of bed, pulled the top sheet around me, and bunny-hopped toward the window.

"They can't look in here," he grumbled at what surely must have appeared like rude behavior. "The apartment over there is unoccupied."

That wasn't what worried me, though. The street bustled with people. Some had grocery baskets, and others were carrying briefcases. It was a regular early morning street scene. No wistful eyes were anywhere, but he would hardly show his face in the daylight.

"If you're looking for the snoops, they haven't taken up their post yet." He poured the coffee and offered it to me with a piece of buttered toast. When I failed to reach for the offering, he slapped it on the table. "You shouldn't worry. They're probably busy following other leads by now. I'll go down and get the paper. Enjoy your breakfast."

The cheer in his voice was gone. His tone was cold and formal. This was hardly surprising to me. After a night of passion, I should have made at least some show of affection. We were lovers now, and I knew I should explain myself. I should let him know about the man who had been lurking in the shadow—the suspect the police were looking for all over town. It seemed too late to tell him now. He would surely wonder why I had held back. We could have alerted the police and had him arrested. Maybe the case would have been closed for me. That would have been the right thing to have done, but something had kept me from doing what reason dictated. By not turning him in, I had made myself what the police accused me of being: an accomplice. Would this law student understand my motive of not wanting anything to spoil our romantic moment? Was this reason enough to neglect my civic duty? Was it the true reason?

I took a small bite of toast and chewed thoughtfully, but I was unable to swallow much and put it back on the plate. I sipped the coffee and savored its soothing aroma. I looked around the apartment. It was a sparsely furnished one-room studio. The bed, a mattress on the floor, still showed evidence of having been slept in. Next to it was a dresser that could have come from Goodwill. The one bookcase contained a few worn paperbacks but was mostly empty. What passed for the kitchen was a corner with a small icebox and an open cupboard with a few dishes, a pot, and a pan. A hot plate with two gas burners and a toaster were on the counter. Both were in need of cleaning. At least there was a bathroom with a shower.

All in all a modest abode for a rich kid, I thought. There were no wall decorations, pictures, photographs, posters, knickknacks, or memorabilia of any kind. The room was completely bare of any distinct personality or imprint of a personal touch. *Anybody could be staying here*, I thought with a pinch of disappointment in my stomach. There was something incongruent between this lodging and the person who had made love to me the night before. Was he really that bland?

I walked over to the dresser in a desperate search for something personal. Hesitating at first I overcame my fear of being caught snooping and opened the creaking top drawer. There had to be a trace of this apartment's occupant somewhere. Using two fingers I lifted the neatly folded underwear. No mother's hand had sewn in name tags as was customary where I came from for a son or daughter going away to school. I was about to put the disturbed garments neatly back in place when I felt something hard tucked between them. Against my better judgment, it had aroused my curiosity enough to take a closer look. I fumbled for it. Recognizing the metal object with a black and silver striped ribbon attached, my blood curdled. I let it drop from my hand back into the drawer. No longer concerned about leaving any evidence of my indiscretion, I slammed it shut.

My breathing was staggered, and my knees were shaking. I collapsed on the only chair in the room. It was near the table on which the breakfast he had prepared for me was still untouched. What had I gotten myself into? What kind of a person had I permitted myself to fall in love with? Persuading myself he deserved the benefit of the doubt, I tried to rationalize away what I had found. What was the big deal anyway? All that had come down on me in the last twenty-four hours had obviously been more than I could handle. It had set my nerves on edge to such a degree that every minor thing blew up into a monstrous crisis. Maybe he didn't even know it was there. Maybe this wasn't his apartment, and he was just subletting. The lack of anything personal associated with him was evidence of such a possibility. Then I reminded myself he was a Jew. This thing was no doubt a collector's item—the kind of war memento many people fancy.

At last I was breathing more steadily. Yes. That was what it most likely was. How could I think this Iron Cross to have any other meaning? These items were so commonplace. I was no expert, but they were probably traded all over the world. My Aunt Sophie's husband, the judge and war veteran, had his Iron Cross Second Class proudly enshrined in a special display case in his home. Then a gang of SA thugs trashed his home to express their displeasure over some of the verdicts he had passed down against their fellows and made off with it.

Nevertheless I felt an irresistible urge to be cleansed. I wanted to wash off all contamination not only from this object I had held but from the one who had touched me and invaded my well-guarded private sphere. An irrepressible yearning to return to my pristine state propelled me from my stupor toward the shower. The running water took its time to heat up. *One more frustration in my way!* Finally the temperature was just right. I stepped in and was ready to surrender my body to the soothing balm when I heard the door open. A cheerfully mocking voice called out. "Honey, I'm back."

I had no choice but to reply. "I'm in here."

My lover wasted no time stripping his clothes off and hopping into the narrow stall with me. The smoothness of his body pressed against mine, and the flood of his tender kisses overwhelmed me once again. We whiled away the rest of the morning making love and exploring every nook and corner of his Spartan little flat for possibilities of enhanced rapture. Tossing all reservations to the wind as overheated fantasy, I sank into a sea of oblivion where nothing existed beyond the boundary of my body. I had no memory of the police, Iron Crosses, murder, war, the evil (or good) people do, or throbbing violins. My perception of the world was confined to the narrow circle of my lover's touch. The warmth of his body fused with mine we trailed off into a state of otherworldly bliss.

SEVEN

The world would not be sidelined forever. Mundane thoughts wormed their way back into my consciousness. They came as fragments at first. Bits and pieces of memory intruded ever more insistently on my mind while I still clung desperately to the blissful state of oblivion induced by the new sensation of carnal knowledge. Gradually the splintered thoughts started coming together and formed complete scenes from the day before. Flashbacks drawn from the recesses of the distant past were interspersed.

My head was resting on my lover's chest. The steady beat of his heart soothed my soul like the hum of a cat's purr. I looked up at him. He flashed his pearly whites at me. All was well with the world. I hadn't felt so at peace since the days in my grandmother's house. Then suddenly, with the brute force of a giant Behemoth unleashed, the real world beyond the window of our garret on Bleecker Street tore into the idyll we had spun from the flimsy threads of illusion. The world of human depravity, evil, cruelty, and murder returned.

"You know what," I said, sitting up. "I think Dettelbach has a grudge against Jews."

"What makes you think so?" Curtis mumbled.

"From the things he said, his reaction to my family name, and references such as 'you people.' Maybe we are sometimes a little too sensitive, but after what is going on in Germany, can you blame us?" I grabbed him by the shoulders and shook him playfully at first and then more insistently to get a reaction.

"He prides himself on his mid-western German heritage," I continued. "He even offered to conduct the investigation in German. Can you imagine? What arrogance! I could practically feel the condescension. It reminded me of a lot of people I came across back in the fatherland. I insisted on English of course. At first he was what we call *scheinheilig*, hypocritical. He presented himself as the good cop, but it didn't take him long to show his true colors."

Curtis kept his back turned. I shook him some more.

"Come on. You are from Chicago. You must have come across that kind of attitude, even if your family has been there for several generations. To the anti-Semite, a Jew is a Jew no matter how assimilated."

"Why are you picking on the Midwest?" Curtis burst out. "There are prejudiced people everywhere. Even here in New York. Especially here in New York. Couldn't we change the subject?"

Somewhere in the back of my mind, a little bell rang, but I ignored it. "I just thought this was a common denominator between us—the burden and heritage all Jews share. It's a history of two thousand years of persecution, oppression, expulsions, and violence."

He raised his voice impatiently. "Come off it now. Aren't you laying it on a bit thick? Sure. It's rough for Jews in Germany right now, but it couldn't be as bad as you paint it. And Hitler isn't the first to hate the Jews."

"Exactly my point," I yelled back. "Yes. There was Jew hatred in Germany and elsewhere before. Plenty of it. I experienced it myself when I was only eight years old, and that was before the Nazis came in."

Now that I had introduced a personal aspect, he seemed more sympathetic. He came up to me from behind and buried his face in my freshly washed hair.

"Why don't you tell me?" he murmured. His warm breath was in my ear and once again I succumbed to his embrace.

Despite lingering misgivings about what I thought was his attempt to downplay the Nazi threat to the Jews, I felt my heart and knees soften. I let myself sink into his embrace and took him on a journey into the most secret oubliette of my memory. I was about to release the spec-ter I had kept chained up in there all those years. Holding nothing back, I revealed to him something I had never spoken of before. Not even my grandmother knew about this painful episode of my life. I wanted to make him understand what it was like to be Jewish in old Europe.

"My first encounter with anti-Semitism goes back to the time when I was eight years old going on nine," I told him.

"My grandmother had decided to send me off to a boarding school at a Catholic convent in Bavaria. She thought I could benefit from instruc-tion in the art of needlework. Knitting, embroidering, and crocheting, this was the holy trinity of a girl's education. Like finishing school. You might wonder why she picked this particular school. My grandmother had some special relationship with the mother superior that went back to their childhood. Several of my aunts had attended this school with very satisfactory results. Except for my mother, of course. She much preferred fingering the piano, violin, and later the guitar. That was all before I was born. By the time I was enrolled in this school, my grand-mother's old friend had regrettably passed away, but my grandmother was sure the instruction I would receive would still be beneficial toward my becoming a well-rounded lady. This was the year 1929, and the atmosphere in the country had changed dramatically from the idyl-lic time before the Great War. So began my year of great agony. I was reminded every hour of the day I was a Jewess. I was not only excused from all religious activities such as attending daily Mass and religious instruction, but I was also excluded from all inner circles. The cliques of girls formed around their interests, which tended toward all things Bavarian.

"Also my Berlin German was so different from their southern cadences. It elicited snide remarks about Prussians and racial slurs as well. Not only was I made to feel like some foreigner, I also utterly failed needlework. The only subjects in which I excelled were geography and languages such as French and English. The more my language teach-ers held me up as an example, however, the more I was decried as the outsider. I also showed an early talent for writing, but the topics I chose were too dramatic for the nuns' tastes. I told, for example, the story of the fatal accident of a boy on a bicycle I had once observed in dramatic detail. I received failing grades every time.

"Lonely and outcast, I began to wet my bed several nights a week. This was where the new mother superior, who did not know my grandmother, charged into action. I was publicly shamed and pilloried at assemblies. It was then I first saw the face of Jew hatred. The face contorted with unconcealed loathing was indelibly imprinted in my mind. This woman mocked a helpless, young girl and set her up to ridicule, and she jeered at the Jewish people who would produce such a misbegotten child.

"My ordeal did not end there. I was blamed for every accidental calamity and was constantly accused of wrongdoing without knowing what it was exactly I was meant to have done. The punishment imposed on me by the mother superior was hours of confinement in dark closets, and sometimes I was banished to the dank cellar with the rats."

My voice rose by several decibels. "Fingers were pointed at me for any little mishap that occurred within those cloister walls from which there was no escape!"

"It's all in the past." Curtis tried to hush me and calm me down.

"In the past?" I shrieked. "Don't you understand? That was only the beginning of what is going on now."

"I do understand," he assured me. "But now you are here in America."

I blew my nose with his proffered handkerchief. "I don't know what came over me. I don't even know why I'm telling you all this."

I disengaged myself from his embrace and sat up straight. "But I did escape," I said. When I saw his questioning look, I added, "I hitched a ride with a workman and made it all the way to Munich to my Aunt Eloise's house. My grandmother had given me the address just in case I needed something. Well, I needed something all right. I needed to get out of that hell. I fell violently ill, and my grandmother took me back home. I never told her the details. Just that I hated needlework. The following year I was sent off to a finishing school in Switzerland to perfect the language and etiquette skills deemed fitting for a daughter of higher social circles. I never wetted my bed again," I concluded with a laugh.

He covered my face and neck with kisses, but I disentangled myself. There was still an unsolved murder, I was still under suspicion from the police for being an accomplice to that murder, and the wistful eyes I had seen in the shadows the night before were still somewhere out there.

"I need to go home to my place," I said and looked around the room for my clothes and shoes.

"What on earth for?"

"At the very least I need a change of clothes and underwear," I said trying to make light. In reality I felt a great need to be alone. I had to think through all that had happened in the last thirty-six hours. There were so many questions and mixed emotions. For instance, why had the police dropped the surveillance? Or had they?

"I need time alone to think," I said.

"OK. I'll get a cab."

"Please don't. I'd rather take the subway."

"That's not advisable," he said in a suddenly commanding tone. "The killer is still out there, and he probably knows you spoke to the police. It wouldn't be safe. If you insist on taking the subway, I'll have to go with you."

"There's one thing I don't get. If the police think I can lead them to the suspect, why drop the tails? Maybe they just learned to be less conspicuous. Maybe they exchanged their Hawaiian shirts for more subtle garb."

"They didn't drop it," he said calmly. "I'm your tail."

I looked at him in disbelief.

"What did you say?" I thought I had misheard. Then he repeated it: "I am your tail."

The scream that rose from my throat must have sent tremors into the foundation of the building and echoed along the entire block. He wrestled me down and covered my mouth with his hand so tightly I almost suffocated.

"I trusted you," I roared when he released the pressure of his hand a bit.

"Let me explain," he pleaded.

"What is there to explain?"

"Listen to me. You gave the police my name, and they came after me."

"I wouldn't have mentioned anything about you if Dettelbach hadn't insisted I had to have a boyfriend. To get him off the subject, I said I had been seeing someone occasionally. He, of course, wanted to know the name and address. I didn't even have your address. Just that you were a law student."

"Well, that was enough for them to track me down. They hauled me in and worked me over as if I was the criminal. In the end they let me go, but I had to work for them. Keep an eye on you and report anything suspicious. Once they thought I was doing their bidding, they withdrew their men."

"Meaning the Hawaiian shirts peaked in the window, saw you were making love to me, and were satisfied you were on the case. So that's why you suddenly changed your behavior. I should've known. We went out for months, and you never came on to me. Not even a kiss. Then you suddenly turn into this romantic, lovey-dovey Romeo. Gullible, stupid me fell for the whole spiel."

He protested it wasn't exactly the way I put it, but I just wanted to get out of this apartment, roll up in the corner of my room at the boarding house, and shut out the world.

"I gotta get the hell out of here!" I slipped into my clothes and shoes and collected whatever belongings I had on me when I permitted myself to be lured into this mousetrap. "If you need to follow me, do it from a distance like your friends the Hawaiian shirts. I don't want to see you. I can already see the smirk on Dettelbach's face when he reads your detailed report."

Without looking back to see whether he was following, I flew down the four flights of stairs and out into the sweltering, relentlessly hellish heat. My white blouse was already clinging to my skin. With staggered breath I looked up and down the street for the nearest subway entrance. I picked up my pace, wove through the crowd of people, and hoped to lose my presumed pursuer. I was about to cross Sixth Avenue for the Uptown train when a figure in a dark suit and overcoat abruptly obstructed my path. When I looked up, I met a pair of gray-green eyes. They were now a shade more imploring than wistful.

"Oh shit!" I exclaimed.

What had I done to deserve all this? I was unable to decide what to do or where to go. I knew I couldn't turn around. My erstwhile lover was in hot pursuit of me. I could feel his breath in my neck.

PART II

A WISTFUL VIOLIN

ONE

He said his name was Viktor Erdos. Later it came out that this was his nom de plume. He was born Chaim Erdreich in a small Hungarian town in the Carpathian Mountains at the time of Kaiser Franz Josef's benign rule over the Austro-Hungarian Empire. He was the youngest of five sons of a prosperous violinmaker. Erdreich string instruments, particularly violins, were renowned throughout the Hapsburg realm and beyond for their excellence in artistry and sound quality. He carried a specimen from his father's workshop under the trench coat he was wearing in July. This made him conspicuous on two counts: the bulge it produced and the fact the police were looking for a violin player. It was no wonder he was anxious to be rid of the instrument but couldn't bring himself to simply abandon it in the trash somewhere. Then again he was not likely aware what the police knew and were looking for. At any rate, he stated the violin was a burden and asked if Curtis or I could safeguard it for him for a while.

All this came out in a long drawn-out exchange that bordered on the bizarre. The language barrier put me into the position of interpreter of his heavily accented English interspersed with his very pronounced Austrian German to which my Berlin ear was not quite attuned. In the end the story emerged piecemeal, and I was able to put together the pieces of the puzzle of who he was and his relationship to the murdered Stella Berger.

I found myself at the corner of Bleecker Street and Sixth Avenue. I was sandwiched between this scruffy, disheveled stranger in a bulging, rumpled raincoat with pleading eyes and the man to whom a few hours before I had been making passionate love and from whom I was now running away.

"Let's hear what he has to say," Curtis whispered in my ear.

"Not here," I said.

"My place then," he said with a firm voice.

His place! I had just gotten away from there! Did I really want to go back to a place full of memories from the last twenty-four hours, during which I had experienced a scale of extreme emotions from total bliss to abject humiliation?

We obviously formed a rather conspicuous trio, even in New York where weird characters were commonplace. The first order of business demanded we get off the street and out of the public eye. The apartment (the Wolff's lair I realized) was the logical solution. Once again I felt trapped, and the desire to change into fresh clothes was almost over-whelming. Then I looked at the man with the pleading eyes. He was in need of help and maybe even something to eat. From somewhere deep inside me, a voice wanted to know who he was. What whim of fate had conspired to bring us together in the streets of New York? I resolved to find out.

I motioned him to follow, and we made our way back down Bleecker Street in a row. I led. The man was behind me, and Curtis brought up the rear. Fortunately it was beginning to get dark, as we hoped to attract as little attention as possible. We especially wanted to avoid any police who might be patrolling the neighborhood on the lookout for a bedrag-gled hobo with a violin.

Mounting the four flights of stairs proved arduous for our guest. He stopped repeatedly, held onto the rail with tremulous hands, and bent over huffing and puffing to catch his breath. I looked back and was worried he might not make it to the top. Notwithstanding his slight stature, it would hardly be possible for either Curtis or me to carry him. He finally did make it, though, and spared us creating a spectacle that might have brought out any neighboring tenants.

I offered him a chair and a glass of water with a familiarity of the place as if it was my own. He sat down and took a sip. Again I noticed the tremor in his hands. *Maybe it's nervousness. Understandable under the circumstances,* I thought.

We sized each other up. Curtis stood to the side with his hands in his pockets and what seemed to me a smirk on his face. *What does he expect? A bout, maybe?* I thought.

"Can I get you something to eat?" I asked the man.

He nodded, but then he said, "A cigarette please."

The man's pulmonary distress apparently derived from a smoking habit. This became a cause of considerable distress for me as the evening passed into night. Besides his disturbing wheezing and coughing, he ran through the supply of smokes Curtis had on hand in a very short time. Curtis offered to run down to replenish the stock, but rather than running the risk of having him alert the police, I insisted on doing the errand myself. There was no telephone in the apartment, and I was sure he had no other means of communicating with his buddies at the precinct before I had a chance to hear out the man's story and the explanation for his behavior at the theater. When I returned with a carton of Lucky Strikes and a fresh bottle of wine under my arm, the cost of which very nearly cleaned me out, Viktor was feasting on scrambled eggs, buttered toast, and a glass of wine—leftovers from the feast of love that had taken place in this very room the night before. He even greeted me with a twinkle in his eyes as he and Curtis started lighting up again. *Promising to be a cozy evening,* I thought. *All I have to do is survive the assault on my lungs.*

As it turned out, this wasn't all I had to do. Having satiated his need for food and cigarettes for the time being, Viktor Erdos remained for quite some time in the bathroom.

Ignoring the man lounging on the bed, I walked wordlessly to the window and opened it wide in the hope of letting in some fresh air. A balmy, evening breeze fanned my face and caressed my troubled soul. I surveyed the street below. It was a typical Saturday night in the Village. Faceless crowds sought to be entertained at the myriad nightclubs this part of town was famous for. My parents had appeared at numerous gigs here in various joints to some acclaim from the local press. They even accumulated a small band of loyal followers, as Curtis had affirmed, but the smaller arena wasn't big enough for their egos. They had to go to Hollywood. Southern California was the place where everybody who had been somebody in the Old World was now congregating.

As much as Paul and Tillie Safran were liked and their talents recognized by their peers, they would end up ground down in the Hollywood machine. They would always be hangers-on, part of the entourage, and beggars at the table in the mansion of some international star such as Marlene, Stella, or Hedy Lamarr with whom they had rubbed elbows way back in a now sunken world. When would they realize Hollywood could never stand in for Weimar Berlin?

I wondered how Viktor Erdos fit into this world of the past. He had identified himself as a poet rather than a musician as I would have expected from his expressive playing. He explained he was a trained violinist and had even played professionally back in Vienna before the war, but poetry was his true calling. He stated this stiffly in formal Austrian German when I voiced my amateur but positive assessment of his musical talent. I took his reference to the war to be the one many still called the Great War—the dividing line by which many lives and events were still measured.

Turning from the window, I shooed away these irksome and utterly useless thoughts. Instead I eyed the reality of this ramshackle garret I had attempted to flee and where I was now sequestered with two virtual strangers—a deceitful lover and a possible killer. Curtis was stretched out on the bed, chewing gum, and waiting patiently, he said, for the next shoe to fall. Maybe it was more correct to say he was waiting for the curtain to rise on the drama he expected to unfold. The sound of running water indicated our guest was taking a shower and would not reappear quickly. I decided to take the opportunity to have it out with this perfidious lover of mine. (Several Shakespeare courses were behind me, and I thus delighted in calling to mind the dramatic vocabulary fitting my situation.)

"You could at least have gotten a decent couch in this hovel so we wouldn't have to break our backs on these rickety chairs," I began in rather un-Shakespearean pentameter. My rant sounded more like a spiteful fishwife attempting to fling a hook into her opponent's heart.

"It's not my hovel," he said.

"What do you mean it's not your hovel? What else do you call this? One would think a rich kid from Chicago could afford better for entertaining lady friends!" His betrayal was still enraged me to such a degree I couldn't think clearly. "What kind of place is this then if it isn't yours? A crash pad for a cheap date?"

"If you will let me I'll explain." He jumped up and grabbed me by the shoulders. "I'm not particularly proud, but I had no choice. I had to go along."

"Go along with what?" A dark premonition gripped my heart that his involvement in this police gambit was even deeper than I had first assumed.

"Dettelbach suggested I gain your confidence. He figured the suspect would come out of hiding and contact you if he was sure there was no police surveillance. He also thought it best if I could take you to a private place. I couldn't take you to my place on MacDougal because of my roommate. This here is some kind of safe house the police keep for stakeouts and sting operations. You would think the NYPD could afford something a bit classier." He gave a nervous chuckle, but to me it seemed it was all a big joke to him.

"So it was all some jolly good ploy. And as you can see it worked." I pointed to the bathroom door. "You got your prey in more than one sense. You got two birds with one stone. Brilliant execution."

"Please let's stay on the subject of us."

"Us? There is no us," I screamed. "You did your duty for your country. Above and beyond I'd say. Why be a lawyer? With your talent for deception and choirboy looks, you could have a brilliant career in acting."

He walked over with big strides and grabbed my shoulders with two hands, forcing me to sit. "Now you listen to me!" he yelled. By now I was totally spent, and I slumped in the chair. "Let me repeat this so you get it through your head. I followed what the police told me to do."

"What Dettelbach told you to do," I corrected him.

"OK. I did what Dettelbach told me to do. He uttered all kinds of threats if I didn't. But he didn't tell me to make love to you."

"Worming yourself into my heart is pretty close. And what about this apartment? What was that for then?"

"Hear me out. Dettelbach figured the suspect would be more easily trapped in a nonpublic place. Anyway, back to us. It happened. We had a good time. We understood each other. We seemed to have a meeting of minds and hearts."

"Don't tell me you fell in love," I said in the most scornful tone I could muster.

"Something like that. In fact, yes. I did fall in love with you." He looked me straight in the eyes. His countenance was serious and sincere. I was tempted to fall for his assurance, but then held back.

No. I'm not going to be taken in again. I won't be anybody's fool anymore, I told myself.

"I think you've seen too many movies. Real life doesn't work that way." Something stirred inside me when I realized he had just made a declaration of love to me. I should have swooned or flown into his arms. Following this script should have been a romantic moment, but it wasn't. In real life a brutal murder had been committed, and somehow our lives were entangled in it.

"You had plenty of opportunities to fall in love with me before all this happened. We went out for months. How about those chaste dates we'd been on? You didn't even try to kiss me!"

The bathroom door opened at this moment, and our suspect stood hesitantly in the doorway. Still unshaven he otherwise displayed a more civilized appearance. Without that shabby overcoat, I noticed how small in stature he was. He was at most an inch or two taller than I and considerably shorter than Curtis.

"Pardon me. I don't wish to intrude," he said in German. "May I have a cigarette?" he added when neither of us responded.

"Of course. Here. Please help yourself." I threw him a half-empty cigarette pack and was glad to have something to bridge the awkward silence.

"Küss d'Hand, gnädiges Fräulein!"

Unaccustomed as I was to Viennese verbal conventions, I counted myself lucky he didn't make a motion to seize my hand and place a kiss on it. Instead he fingered the cigarette pack with a tremulous hand and quickly extracted one of those treasured sticks. He stuck it between his quavering lips and lit it with a match from the matchbook I had handed him. He eagerly drew on it with his face raised and eyes closed before blowing out the smoke in a cloud of nicotine. He repeated this ritual several times, coughing lightly and exuding a gratified sigh like an addict finally getting a fix. Unless he was feigning it for some reason, I judged his English to be rather rudimentary. This assessment was confirmed in the exchange that followed, and I hoped he hadn't heard or understood much of the heated quarrel to which his reemergence from the bathroom had put a temporary end.

Curtis walked over to the guest (or suspect) and placed a patronizing hand on his shoulder. "I'm sorry, old man, for the inadequate seating in this place, but please make yourself at home." Curtis gestured toward the bed as the most comfortable accommodation but was politely rebuffed with a bow in my direction. Apparently Viktor did not deem it proper to accept such an invitation with a lady present.

A perfect Viennese gentleman, I thought. Only he was, as we were to learn, neither Viennese nor Austrian, discounting that he was born in the Austro-Hungarian Empire and spent most of his adult life in the imperial city. Rather he was a Hungarian Jew.

Hungarian, Jewish, Viennese, whatever, I told myself and was impressed that the legendary breeding and refinement of the now defunct Danube monarchy was still alive among refugee panhandlers in New York City.

"What do we do now?" I asked Curtis with a slight roll of my eyes toward our guest. With a deliberate mumble, I added, "Don't you have to hand him over to your friend Inspector D?"

"If you're trying to needle me, you're succeeding splendidly. Inspector D is not my friend. Your blurting out my name got me into this unpleasant business in the first place."

"Unpleasant business? So that's what it is for you?" My voice leaped into the upper registers and almost reached shrieking level. I was about to fire off another diatribe when the pained expression on Viktor Erdos's face made me stop.

"Sorry. Go on. You were saying..." I waved Curtis on in a more subdued tone.

You really shouldn't let him turn you into a shrew, I told myself. *This isn't you.* Thinking it over, doubts seeped into my mind. I wondered if I was to blame for my shrewish outbursts more than Curtis. Yes. I felt hurt and betrayed, but was it really all his fault? The memory of our love, passion, and tender moments of embrace came back to me. I remembered the immense happiness I had felt in every fiber of my body and that I had seen in his warm, content gaze he showered on me. It had seemed genuine then—a union of mind and body as I had never thought possible. Could it all have been nothing more than a lie and pretense?

"I'm curious to hear first what the man has to say for himself." Curtis assumed a straightforward tone reminiscent of a good cop. "And since we're up against a language barrier, I'll need your help. Can we bury the axe for now?"

A hollow feeling of regret twisted my stomach—a sense I had done him an injustice. I nodded my agreement to a truce only too willingly.

TWO

Before another word was spoken, Viktor Erdos took his violin case off the floor and placed it on the table. He waved for us to gather around.

How interesting, I thought. *The suspect is taking charge of the proceedings.* He obviously didn't feel he had anything to fear from two quarrelsome lovers. What ensued was an exchange in two languages, though to me it was at least three. I was frequently stumped to find the right English translation for his Austrian idioms. As I fielded questions and answers from both sides, however, it occurred to me more than once that Curtis understood more than he let on. His explanation that his high school German was coming back to him was not very convincing as he had previously claimed total ignorance of the language in the company of other German speakers.

I shall relate the exchange in English as I remember it and omit the frequent breaks for back-and-forth translation. The search for *le mot juste* also took time. Since the police apparently didn't find it necessary to stock their hideout with various foreign language dictionaries, the translating became at times rather cumbersome.

"I need a caretaker for my violin," Viktor Erdos said in German with a pleading look in my direction.

Up to that point, he had spoken very little except for monosyllabic answers to questions about his need for a smoke and drink. He surprised me, therefore, with how forcefully he stated his request. As he opened the case and laid bare to our amazed eyes a beautiful, shiny violin, a lit cigarette dangled from the corner of his mouth. The fumes made my eyes sting, but I realized this was how it would be, and I had to put up with it if I wanted to find out anything about him and his connection to Stella Berger.

"As you can see, this is a magnificent musical instrument of great value." He lifted the violin gently from the case. He took care not to drop any ashes on it and began to stroke its outline with the fondness of a lover caressing a woman's smooth skin.

Your mind seems on a one-track course, I scolded myself. I again noticed the tremor in his hands and the delicateness of his fingers that fluttered like gentle, little birds as he drummed out some rhythm on the violin's body. Those hands had certainly never done any rough work.

"I really couldn't." I raised my hands. "Why don't you..."

"Sell or pawn it? Impossible. Simply out of the question," he stated brusquely. "You must understand what this instrument means to me." He turned his eyes toward the window and assumed that wistful gaze as if summoning a memory from another time and place.

Was he putting on an act, or was this all real? I looked at Curtis. He shrugged indicating he'd rather stay out of this. His head was tilted, his eyebrows were raised, and the corners of his mouth sagged as if biting on a lemon. *Like a movie gangster,* I thought. Realizing I couldn't expect any support, I tried to assess the situation. The primary suspect in a murder was demanding I understand something about a violin. Was Viktor even aware of the jam he was in? Then curiosity got the better of me. I wanted to know the significance of this violin whose sounds had gotten me into trouble.

"Why don't you enlighten me," I said.

He kept stroking the instrument and lowered his wistful or perhaps loving gaze on it. "They don't make these anymore." He turned it over and pointed to almost imperceptible letters etched into the wood. I leaned forward and tried to make them out.

"It says 'Lazar Erdreich, Maître Luthier,'" Viktor read for me. "My father made this violin for my thirteenth birthday when I became bar mitzvah. Here. Feel the smooth spruce top and the beautiful pattern of the maple bottom. Luthiers from all over the world get their wood from the Carpathian Mountains. Even the famed Stradivari imported his wood for his instruments from there."

Viktor had suddenly become very talkative. I could see the passion radiating from his eyes for this instrument he was cradling. Pride in his father's work swelled the speech that came bubbling out of him like a mountain creek in springtime. He had me so completely enthralled with his heartwarming tale that I forgot about Curtis.

"Hello there," Curtis burst out. "What's going on?"

"I thought you wanted to stay out of this," I said mockingly.

"I thought we agreed to set the personal invective aside," he retorted with a mixture of irritation and hurt.

"Sorry. That was uncalled for." I put a mollifying hand on his arm. From then on I resumed my role as translator and related what I heard as best I could.

Before he had it officially changed to Viktor Erdos, his name was Chaim Erdreich. He was born in 1890 in a remote village in the Hungarian part of the Carpathian Mountains—an outpost of the Austro-Hungarian Empire. As he put it, it was in the "k. k." realm. He was the youngest of five sons of the violin maker Lazar Erdreich and his wife, Marta née Szekely. Viktor was not only the youngest but also a late-comer. He lagged seven years behind the brother before him. His brothers were in the lumber business. They were all as tall and burly as the trees in the ancient forests they felled and transported down the river. To Lazar Erdreich's chagrin, none of them had the patience or artistic disposition to follow in his trade. They did, however, provide plenty of raw material for their father's workshop.

"My father always said the luthier's work was both art and craft," Viktor stated. "Manual dexterity, which can be perfected through diligence, only goes so far. It has to be complemented with an artist's vision, a musician's ear, and a poet's imagination. The finest violins are handcrafted from scratch," he continued. "So are violas and cellos for which my father's workshop was justly famed as well."

Lazar Erdreich's prayers for a son who would carry on his trade finally seemed to be heard when his wife gave birth to another son.

Viktor's birth followed several miscarriages and a stillbirth that had dashed all hopes. His wife had hoped for a girl who would spare her the worry about the perils posed by the rough world of the woodsmen. She had married a sensitive artist—a pious man with the soul of a poet. Her only disappointment was that the mountainous forest environment seemed to have formed their offspring.

"They are good, upright men who abide the laws of the Sabbath and kashrut," Erdos said. "It was I who became the renegade." He paused to stare at the wall with a forlorn look into a world where nobody could follow. "But that came much later," he added. "I am getting ahead of myself."

His mother was compensated for her disappointment with a boy who was the opposite of his brothers. Even fully grown he still was dwarfed next to them. The baby was delicately built, and during his first year, he was prone to fevers and wheezing coughs. The mother passed many a night at his crib, unable to close an eye for fear of losing him. Afraid he might choke on his food or ingest some foreign substance, she kept breast-feeding him into his third year. His third birthday brought the most traumatic experience for both mother and son—a custom called *upsherin*.

"I don't remember who cried the loudest, my mother or I," he said and shook his head. "I saw the scissors approaching my head like the mouth of a giant monster ready to swallow me. I screamed uncontrollably as the scissors were passed around among the men present. Clip after clip my golden locks tumbled to the floor. *Upsherin* means shearing, and I indeed felt like a sheep being shorn. In the end all I was left with were two dangling locks on the side of my head. Then they placed a yarmulke on my head and dressed me in a little *tallis* with *tzitzes*. I don't even know if my father or one of my brothers did this. I heard laughing and cheers of mazel tov. I was now ready for study and no longer a baby. The worst of it was I was taken from my mother's care."

He closed his eyes and dropped his head between his curved shoulders. I was afraid he might start crying. Fortunately he pulled himself together and continued. "I heard my mother sobbing, but I didn't dare look up for her. When the Rebbe said something about humans being

74

like trees and that the study of the Torah might make me grow as big and strong as the magnificent trees in the forests, a shriek reverberated from where my mother was gathering my precious locks into a basket. She sounded as if her baby had been struck by lightning." Again he paused.

"Why," I probed softly. "Why was this custom so upsetting to your mother? I can understand a young child at such a tender age being horrified. I remember my first haircut at nine. It was as if a part of my body had been severed. But your mother must have witnessed this traditional custom many times with her other sons. It's not like circumcision."

"Ah, there you are wrong!" He gave me a scornful look as if to chastise me for making assumptions. "You don't understand."

"No. I don't understand. How could I," I said. The vehemence of his reprove took me aback, and at the same time, this melodramatic display about something as trivial as a haircut bemused me. "Hair can grow again."

"Not according to whoever made that law. It had to be kept short except for those ridiculous sidelocks."

I had had enough of this subject and wanted to go on. I was more interested to hear about how he learned to play the violin, but he apparently wasn't done reminiscing about this hurt inflicted on him at such a tender age.

"My mother loved my hair," he began again, and I saw Curtis rolling his eyes in resignation. "You can't see it anymore, but I had the most beautiful golden curls. They were admired by all," he said.

"At two they grazed my shoulders, and by the time I was three, they draped my upper body like a cape. My mother had brushed my hair with slow, long strokes twice a day—in the morning and at night before putting me to bed. I felt as if I was a princess in the fairy tales she read to me. Those were the happiest moments of my life, and they had come to an end. She still read me stories of magical, mythical creatures—dragons, unicorns, dwarfs, enchanted princesses, kings, queens, and good and bad witches—but the bond woven between us through the daily hair brushing ritual had been severed.

"She read most of these stories to me in German, which was her first language. She loved German literature. Not only fairy tales but Goethe and the like. The classics and romantics. She passed this love on to me. Although I grew up speaking Hungarian and Yiddish, German was always my preferred language. It was my mother's tongue.

"I inherited my blond hair from my mother," Erdos went on. "Her family name was Szekely. She came from a pious, Jewish family in Transylvania. Her father was a *sofer*, a Torah scribe, as well as a scholar. He came into conflict with the community and was almost put under *cherem*, a ban, for keeping a library of secular books many people considered heretics. My mother didn't have to go to *cheder*, the school where only boys studied, so she devoured all the secular works in her father's library."

Two of her brothers were apprenticed to kosher butchers, and the youngest had a beautiful voice. He became a cantor. She met my father when he came to her town to deliver an order of violins for a local klezmer band. He stopped at the butcher shop where she was helping behind the counter, and their fate was sealed. There was some opposition, but that was an obligatory ritual in those circles—an initial back and forth about conditions and dowries. My father just wanted to take his bride home. One brother objected because he didn't have the right *yiches*, family tree, meaning he wasn't a Szekler. A rather ludicrous reason. Who knows how they got the name?" Erdos shook his head. "Family legend had it they were descended from the Szeklers, a Magyar tribe of warriors famed for defending the Kingdom of Hungary against the Turks in the sixteenth century. An absurd contrivance to my mind."

"Who were these Szeklers?" I was eager to hear more about these people and their history.

"As I said they were a warrior clan or tribe. Most likely Magyars. Most of them lived in the mountains of Transylvania. At some point a few centuries back, some of them became Sabbatarians and Judaizers. They began to live by the laws of the Old Testament for which they were frequently persecuted and massacred.

"Persecution and laws to suppress their practice didn't deter some from following their beliefs and passing them on through several generations. In the last century, they got permission to join the Jewish community. There were quite a few intermarriages. So it's possible, though doubtful, that my mother's family or part of it had Szekler blood. My uncles wore their Hasidic garb and liked to brag about being warrior descendants. It's more likely the blond hair came from some forebear marrying one of the Saxons, the German settlers in that region."

Three was also the age when Viktor was enrolled in *cheder*, the one-room school where boys began their studies. He first learned the aleph-bet so he could read the Hebrew texts. Bright as he was, he caught on very quickly and soon was in a class studying the Torah. The class began with the book of Vayikra, the third book in the Jewish Bible.

"Why start there and not at the beginning with creation?" I asked.

"That's a very good question," he replied. "The rationale is something to the effect that children are pure, and they should first become acquainted with the laws of purity and holiness rather than the confusing stories of the patriarchs. Of course most of what is called studying is really learning by rote. They drill little kids to rattle off passages without the slightest understanding of what it means. Like parrots."

Viktor was a smart, curious little boy. Twirling his blond sidelocks, he pored over the text, and rather than memorizing the words, he got to thinking. He asked lots of questions. The laws of family purity especially apparently caught his attention.

"The place where I grew up was a primitive, backwoods area. Uncultured, coarse, superstitious, Slavic peasants surrounded us. There were Ruthenes, Ukrainians, Poles, and Slovaks. The Hungarians weren't actually much better." His squinting eyes flashed utter disdain and contempt for these people. He took a long drag on the cigarette between his thumb and forefinger with his little finger splayed out. With a slight cough, he slowly exhaled a thin stream of smoke through puckered lips.

Where does this guy get off? I thought. His mannerisms had started to irritate me. He was the most wanted man in New York City, and here he behaved like Richard Tauber playing an effete count or some other dandy in a Viennese operetta. Maybe it was a big mistake to sit and listen to his story, and maybe it was all made up to garner sympathy. Something about this man made me uneasy. In fact he gave me the creeps. I was in a mood to cut him off and hand him over to the police.

I was therefore grateful to Curtis when he broke into the man's harangue against various Eastern European ethnic groups.

"They probably didn't have much love for Jews either." Curtis's sarcasm was unmistakable, but not to clueless Viktor. He just carried on.

"You can be certain of that." he replied. "But that wasn't the point I was trying to make. I only brought that up to give you an idea of the kind of place I grew up in." Viktor said he saw people doing things for which, according to the biblical laws of purity and holiness, they should have been stoned to death or expelled from the community. When he asked his teacher why these people—men and women, men and men, and even a shepherd and his sheep—were not stoned to death as the law required, he was reprimanded with five hours of detention in a dark cellar. He was six, and in the darkness of that cellar, he began his journey toward doubting the validity of the laws of the Torah and the very existence of God.

The next day the rabbi, whom the teacher had informed of a precocious child in their midst, took him into his study and pressed him for the names of those he had observed in these ungodly acts. The seeds of his rebellious spirit had been planted, though. No amount of threats from this holy man would make him give up names. In the end he said he only saw goyim.

"That wasn't quite true, but the rabbi let it go at that, and I was off the hook," he concluded.

Chaim said he continued attending *cheder* and broadened his learning, as was expected of all boys. The more he learned, though, the more his doubts deepened and his conviction grew that a superior being had not given those laws. Instead he suspected men who sought to control the masses by portraying human nature as sinful created them. He no longer asked his teachers questions. It only got him into trouble. His father had his mind on his work. The only person with whom he could share his thoughts was his mother. She did not always agree with him, but Viktor said he thought that was probably for fear of being found out and shunned. She did, however, encourage him to think independently and admonished him never to take anything at face value.

About the age of five or six, Chaim began to take a keen interest in his father's business. He would hang out for hours in the workshop and avidly observed the basic steps of instrument making. He eagerly watched the designing, molding, shaping, and gluing as his father turned out carefully handcrafted violas, cellos, and even some guitars. His father's particular passion was building violins. He was, therefore, only too pleased to see his youngest son's eagerness to learn the craft, and he soon let him try his hand on a learning model. The boy proved his mettle with chiseling, planing, purfling, molding, and gluing, and he applied himself with the full concentration and patience the work required.

Those same qualities came to the fore when Viktor expressed his wish not only to build but to play the violin. Lazar Erdreich, a good fiddler himself, instructed his son in the rudiments, but by the time Chaim was ten, he had sailed beyond what his father was able to teach him. His mother and father agreed only a professional teacher would be able to meet the challenge. The closest town where a suitable teacher might be found was Munkács, a three-hour horse-and-cart journey.

The family was fully behind furthering their wunderkind, and even his brothers shared gladly in the task of shuttling little Chaim to Munkács once a week for a two-hour lesson. His mother was the driving force and personally traveled to the city to find what she called "a classically trained" teacher. It was also at this time Chaim befriended a group of Gypsy musicians and spent much time harmonizing with them.

"My mother was not very pleased with this turn toward what she called 'devil's music,'" said Viktor. "But my father rather liked this music with its frequently dazzling violin trills. From my mother came a constant refrain of Bach, Beethoven, Mozart. Or what about Brahms and Liszt. To which my father would reply that they too use Gypsy elements in their compositions." It was to no avail, though. She was determined to get her son away from that vulgar influence. So Chaim went off to Munkács to perfect his classical training. The instruction he received there was competent, but all too quickly it became inadequate to his vaulting talent. His Saxon teacher told his parents that lessons once a week were not enough. More intensive training was necessary for the pupil to reach his full potential. The teacher gave him a letter of introduction to one of the finest violin teachers in Debrecen. Since this meant he would have to lodge there, the Saxon also recommended he enroll in the local German gymnasium.

Erdos's narration became vague and even evasive at this point. There were obviously things he was not willing to share. As much as I could gather from some of the dropped hints, Debrecen was the turning point in his early life. He was fourteen and past bar mitzvah age, and he had already shed the outward signs that would mark him as a Jew. Those blond sidelocks, though not as blond anymore, were the first to fall. The conflict Chaim had nurtured about Jewish law turned into outright rejection of all that was Jewish. Curiously enough his friends at the boarding school were other Jewish students. There were only a handful of them, and they too wanted to fit in with the wider society and sought to distance themselves from their Jewish upbringings. We used to call them self-hating Jews in Berlin.

Their admiration for German *Kultur* was boundless. They memorized and recited German poetry, and they kept up with the latest trends in literature, art, and music coming out of Vienna and Berlin. Their readings also spanned a wide variety of philosophy and history, German and otherwise. They read everything from Descartes and Rousseau to Kant, Hegel, and Nietzsche. In their insatiable hunger for knowledge, they also devoured the great works of Roman and Greek history from Gibbons, Montesquieu, and Mommsen.

"Most of all we yearned for fin-de-siècle Vienna," he mused wistfully. "Vienna was the navel of the earth, our promised land, and the Valhalla of our dreams."

Many exchanged their Jewish names for less blatant monikers that made them seem more Magyar or German. From this ferment of self-reinvention arose Viktor Erdos—a new, European man. Like many of his contemporaries, he liked to style himself as a *Weltbürger*. He became a citizen of the world, a man without country, religion, or ties. He was a man at home everywhere and nowhere. The fact he had seen very little of the world beyond the confines of the Eastern Austro-Hungarian Empire made his aspirations all the more lofty.

These aspirations received a boost from the discovery of Karl Marx. The *Communist Manifesto* and especially the tract "The Eighteenth Brumaire of Louis Bonaparte" turned him and his friends into instant true believers in Marxian doctrine. These writings informed their views of history, economics, and politics. In all-night debates they bandied about concepts such as class struggle, historical materialism, means of production, and monopoly capitalism—none of which anyone really understood. Alienation was a favorite topic and a concept they readily applied to their own situation and place in the world.

"Karl Marx was our prophet; *Das Kapital* our Bible!" Viktor Erdos declared. "We marched under the banner of revolutionary intellectuals. The old religion—the opiate of the masses—was dead for us." He extended his chest and defied us to refute his stated truth.

Neither of us took the bait. I didn't know about Curtis's experience, but all I knew about Marxism came from overhearing adults around me either approving or refuting it. I was not versed enough to engage in a debate with a zealot. I changed the subject to a more practical consideration.

"With all that reading, debating, and marching, how did you find time to practice the violin?" I asked.

He rummaged through the cigarette pack, extracted the last one, and lit it. He slowly went through the motions as if carefully considering his answer. "That is a somewhat touchy matter," he finally said and puffed nervously in and out. "My father was fully expecting to soon hear about my first public performance. He was crafting an instrument especially for that anticipated event. Violins are made not only with superb artistry but with love," he started to preach again. "He applied all his skill with great love and care. The result was this violin here before you."

Something wasn't quite right. Earlier he had said his father made the violin for his bar mitzvah. Instead of pointing out this discrepancy,

I said, "So you disappointed your father and mother. You let them down in your pursuit of some ideology."

"You could say that," he replied. "But I had to make a choice. Did I want to pursue a self-indulgent career for personal fame and glory, or did I want to devote myself to helping create a better world for the benefit of all mankind? I still practiced every day as part of my studies, but I knew even then I would never be a concert violinist. The fire Beethoven, Brahms, and even the Gypsy songs had once ignited in me had gone out. It was all part of the bourgeois oppression of the masses. It was a youthful whimsy, but in those days a calling of a different kind fired me up. I exchanged the bow for the pen, and I vowed to serve the cause of the working class with my poetry."

He said it was about the time of his graduation from the gymnasium that news of his mother's death reached him. He returned home devastated and afraid the loss of his beloved mother might have had something to do with his switch from musician to poet. Again his narrative was getting vague and evasive. It was clearly difficult for him to speak about the mourning period. All I was able to surmise from his incoherent hints was that he strayed off directly after the burial into the mountains and trudged alone through the forests for an indistinct period of time. Asked how he sustained himself, he had no answer. This period was a complete blank. I pictured him kicking up the fallen leaves underfoot while contemplating his past and future, picking berries, and maybe trapping a hare to roast over a fire.

Some kind of epiphany must have eventually befallen him, but he did not want to reveal it. All he admitted was he decided then to seek fame, glory, and maybe even fortune by bringing class struggle to the *Kaiserstadt*, the glamorous city of Vienna. When he reemerged at his father's house in the village of his birth, he was unkempt and wild-eyed like a mad backwoodsman. He bade his father and brothers farewell. He would sever all ties to his birthplace where his mother's spirit still filled the air with sweet and bitter memories. With the violin case housing his father's parting gift wedged under his arm, he descended from the mountains into the plain below.

"Very touching," Curtis growled when Viktor paused to light another cigarette. "How does all that relate to the current situation? Where does Stella Berger fit in?"

"Patience, my friend! Patience! I am coming to that. Just bear with me." I could see that Viktor's patronizing did nothing to rein in Curtis's growing impatience.

"So you admit that you knew her?" said Curtis.

"Of course, I knew her!" Viktor replied indignantly. "I knew her before anyone had heard of her. I made her what she became."

"Then why did you have to sneak into the theater?"

"We had a falling out several years before. I wanted to tell her how sorry I was. You will understand once you hear the whole story. She was still a child when we met in Vienna."

THREE

Vienna, Austro-Hungarian Empire, 1908

At the height of its splendor, the benevolent Kaiser Franz Josef had ruled the Danube monarchy for some sixty years when Viktor Erdos alighted on the banks of its capital city. The empire had known its setbacks and tragedies—an attempt on the Kaiser's life, the suicide of Crown Prince Rudolf, the anarchists' assassination of Empress Elisabeth, and intermittent wars with defeats and triumphs. Though Austria had lost its predominance within the German realm through two lost wars with Prussia, Hapsburg rule over its Slavic subjects held firm despite sporadic unrest and rebellions. The empire had waltzed on into the new century unruffled and confident of an eternally brilliant future.

Viktor Erdos was in his nineteenth year. His violin and a small, tattered, cardboard suitcase containing his meager belongings (toiletries, one change of clothing and underwear, and a few books and pamphlets) were his only possessions. He checked both cases in a locker at the railroad station and set out to explore the city of his dreams. For three days he wandered about town in a trancelike state. He breathed in the atmosphere, sampled a variety of tortes with whipped cream, and curled up on a park bench to sleep under the stars as balmy July breezes fanned his brow.

What he saw in the city enthralled him. It was as if he had emerged into daylight for the first time. He eagerly took in the grandeur of the boulevards, the Ring, the majesty of Saint Stephen's Cathedral, and the magnificent splendor of the imperial residence at Schönbrunn. He waited in a crowd below the balcony for the Kaiser to appear and greet his subjects and was disappointed to learn His Majesty and entourage were at one of the imperial summer residences in the province. The palace guards stood at attention and were stiff like the lead soldiers he had played with as a child. Their sparkling, golden helmets; drooping tassels of eagle feathers shading their eyes; and debonair, sky-blue uniforms embellished with shiny, gold decorations and medals left him openmouthed. A patriotic fever seized his heart and made it beat faster. He tapped his foot to the beat of the Radetzky March that was blaring in perfect harmony from the shiny instruments of a military marching band parading around the plaza in equally perfect formation.

Then he remembered he was supposed to hate the Hapsburgs. Inevitably he would stray away from the splendiferous side of the city and enter its more squalid parts. Instead of being dazzled, he was appalled. Instead of ambling along bright boulevards, his path led him into narrow, murky streets. Instead of opulence, he met privation. Tattered rags replaced shiny uniforms and pompous attire. Pushcarts and wheelbarrows took the place of elegant carriages and automobiles. Ramshackle huts and gray, cramped tenements displaced palaces and urbane residences. Instead of elegant boutiques displaying exclusive merchandise in bright windows, he came upon dingy little shops littered with inferior wares. Instead of hushed, polite conversation and soothing music, a cacophony of languages, street vendors shouting, hordes of noisy children playing and fighting, and women bickering filled the streets. *Lumpenproletariat*, Karl Marx had dubbed such people.

His sense of indignation and disgust for such a discrepancy between the classes was aroused. His conviction of the need for class struggle was confirmed. He retrieved his violin and suitcase and rented a room in the working-class district of Ottakring. The landlady, a widow, provided him with a sparsely furnished, dimly lit room and a peasant breakfast in exchange for a few shillings and music lessons for her sixteen-year-old daughter.

"What do you know?" I sneered. "A scenario straight out of Schnitzler."

"I am glad to hear the lady is familiar with the work of my good friend Arthur Schnitzler," Erdos snapped back with an irritated sneer of his own. The sneer was either for the disruption of his narration, my insinuation he was lying, or both. "Whatever you might think, there was nothing Schnitzleresque going on," he forcefully protested.

Maybe a bit too much, I thought.

"And if you must know," Viktor continued, "we dropped the lessons shortly after since the girl had not the slightest interest or talent."

I apologized, and he took up the thread again.

The mother, he said, played a passable zither, and she also had friends in musical circles. So it came about that she introduced the almost penniless violinist to a band of Schrammel musicians. For the remaining summer months and into autumn, he and his newfound colleagues traveled the environs of the city on weekends and some weekday evenings. They bounced from beer gardens to dance halls to *Heurige* wine taverns—places of amusement where the common folk waltzed and swayed to popular tunes, ate their fill of sausage and cheese, and quaffed the local beer and freshly pressed wine.

Viktor Erdos was in his element. He had found a home. By way of the music of Strauss and Lehar, he felt connected with ordinary, working people. For the same reason, he also relished the repertoire of Alpine peasant folk songs that the Schrammel brothers, who gave their name to this kind of music, had popularized throughout lower Austria. In the technique and fervor he brought to his playing, he clearly outperformed his comrades, as he called them. They were carefree musicians—simple country boys who had a good time making music together. They freely acknowledged his superior musical skills and that those skills helped them gain some acclaim in local dance halls. However, what didn't go over so well was his habit of lecturing them on topics such as the origins of folk music, his sounding off on the regional differences and commonalities of harmonic and melodic structures, and the origin and development of the counterpoint.

If this wasn't enough to make him out to be some kind of oddball in the eyes of his fellow musicians, he also lectured on class struggle and imperialist oppression. Bandying about words such as "alienation" and "consciousness" finally caused the beer mugs to overflow. He took it upon himself, without official party credentials, to introduce the Marxist gospel to several workers' club meetings in his neighborhood. Imbued with his mission, he spoke out of order, offered unsolicited opinions on issues under discussion, and was soon pegged as a pesky agent provocateur.

It wasn't long before someone in the audience called him a Jew. Others chimed in. Even without proof a chorus arose calling for him to get packing. He refused to leave and tried to stand his ground above the growing din of "Jews aren't wanted here!" The police dispersed the crowd, which was on the verge of becoming a lynch mob, and saved him from bodily harm. He fled the scene under police escort.

As Viktor related it, his landlady greeted him at the doorstep, his belongings in her hands. "I have nothing against you or your people," she said. She conceded he was a good lodger, but had she known, she couldn't have rented to him in good conscience. For some reason, she seemed compelled to add: "One can't be careful enough nowadays."

"She had a habit of emphasizing her good conscience," Erdos said with a disdain that apparently hadn't diminish in all the years since. "How they presumed to know I was a Jew I still don't know," he added. "I had none of the appearance and habits of those in the district where I found lodging next after a long search throughout the city."

The next lesson Viktor Erdos was compelled to learn was that no matter how he tried to blend into the gentile world, something Jewish tenaciously clung to him. It didn't matter that he changed his name, attire, allures, or speech patterns. It didn't matter how ostensibly he sank his teeth into roast pork. He had to come to grips with some hard facts about fin-de-siècle Vienna. There were certain districts of the city where Jews were unwelcome, and he had a better chance of finding a suitable place to live in the second district known as Leopoldstadt.

"I resented being pushed into a ghetto overrun with eastern Jews with whom I no longer had anything in common," he mused. "I should have been free to live anywhere I wished and could afford."

He was, however, an impecunious musician and certainly couldn't afford to live in the precincts of the Jewish upper bourgeoisie in the first district. He should have been happy living among the proletariat, but this was a proletariat of poor Jews. His Marxist, world-embracing outlook stopped short of any narrow parochial or tribal concerns.

The sights and sounds of this shtetl transplanted onto an island between the Danube and the Danube Canal fairly made him cringe. The smell of garlic and cabbage wafted about men bedecked in broad-rimmed, black felt hats and black overcoats trailing at their ankles as they clustered on almost every street corner. They punctuated their excited chatter with vigorous hand movements, offending his sensibilities. Even the women, whose prematurely aged faces bore the marks carved by lives of drudgery, aroused little sympathy in him.

"These babushkas walked about hollow-eyed with heavy gaits and packs of children in tow." He crimped his nose at the memory all those years later.

Only the scents of Friday afternoon appeased his contrary spirit. He would then meander through the streets and eagerly breathe in the aroma of freshly baked bread, roasting chicken, and bubbling soup. The memories of his mother then filled his heart, and he didn't know whether to rejoice or weep. He did both, he admitted, with a wistful gaze.

Pulling himself back from the brink of this brief, sentimental interlude, he added defiantly and somewhat incongruently, "Wealthy Jews like my friend Stefan Zweig didn't have to put up with ghetto life. They resided in a palais on the Ring."

"Yeah, yeah. Life is so unfair." His whining got my ire up. "Even Zweig had to make a run for his life recently. To the goyim we are all the same." I deliberately used a Yiddish word that was generally banned from polite discourse.

"Let me finish." He raised his hands as if to fend off an attack. "In the end the move to Leopoldstadt turned out to be the greatest blessing of my life. On an icy November day in the gray rear yard of an overcrowded tenement complex between Novaragasse and Taborstrasse, I first met Stella."

FOUR

The months trailed off into that nebulous purgatory of time between late November and December when the temperatures speak of winter, but the calendar still holds onto autumn. Vienna experienced an early snowfall that year, and Viktor Erdos's existence reached a low point. Shivering in his cold-water, unheated flat, he convinced himself the whole world had conspired with the elements to make his life miserable. The only warm meal he got all week was the Friday evening handout at the Jewish alms house where the well-off from the first district volunteered to ladle out soup and cholent for their indigent co-religionist brethren.

He was several weeks behind in his rent, yet his landlord chose not to throw him out into the cold. He had considered playing the violin at a street corner, but his fingers were too stiff and his mood too glum. His meager efforts toward finding indoor work at a coffeehouse or a dance hall were without success in a city teeming with aspiring, hungry musicians. He neglected to answer the letters his father sent every week. They always expressed the hope of hearing soon about his son's debut on the concert stage. How could he explain he had given up on a musical career? How could he explain he had never even auditioned for admission to a conservatory? Viktor could not present himself to a panel of judges when he did not know what it was inside of him that paralyzed his every move. Rather than disappointing his father, he draped himself in silence.

"I know now it was cowardly and probably caused him more pain than if I had told him the truth," he said. "He was a forgiving man and would probably have understood what my problem was even better than I did back then. Years later I discussed the matter with my friend Dr. Sigmund Freud. He made me see it was fear of failure and not being able to live up to my father's or blessed mother's expectations. I have often thought about his theory that the loss of my mother had a stunting effect on my ambitions. That part of the consultation I had with him was all right. But he also suggested something about my relationship with my father and mother that I still think is total nonsense. I adored my father. He was the kindest man. My regret is not having had a chance to speak with him before he died."

Meanwhile Viktor Erdos turned from playing the violin to writing poetry. Although he adhered to no school or particular trend and did not have any contact with the leading literary lights of the time, he intuitively leaned toward iconoclastic meter and expressionist imagery. His early poems painted a series of bleak, desolate landscapes. He explained these were reflective of the state of his soul then. They gave free rein to the anger, disappointment, and self-loathing stored inside him during those months alone in the city of his dreams. His later poems were less personal. He took up more universal themes—mostly rants riddled with Marxist clichés and exhortations to the masses to rebel against injustice and exploitation. In this vein he advocated the overthrow of the bourgeois regimes and capitalism and the establishment of world communism. He did so in language so obscure and convoluted, however, the average worker was not likely to comprehend. Since he didn't have a desk, his writings remained by and large at the bottom of his underwear drawer. This was not the case for all of them, though.

"My good friend Karl Kraus published several of my works in his prestigious literary magazine *Die Fackel*."

He obviously wanted to impress us with all the famous people whom he described as friends. The names he kept dropping were familiar to most in the German-speaking world, especially if one had grown up among writers and artists, though I doubted Curtis had any inkling of who these people were.

"Why don't you cut the crap and get to the point about this Stella?" Curtis broke in gruffly.

He had been in the background quietly smoking and drinking whiskey while leaving it to me to periodically push our visitor through his self-absorption, self-pity, and self-justification and prod him to go on with his story. Now Curtis's belligerent tone and slurred speech made me turn toward him with alarm. I stayed the hand that held the half-empty whiskey bottle ready to pour another shot.

All I needed at that moment was a drunk spoiling for a fight. Not wanting to get embroiled, I withdrew. We had a long night ahead, and I had no idea what the morning would bring.

I turned with a smile to Viktor Erdos who was downing a shot as well. "Please go on."

Nice company I'm keeping, I thought. *Wonder how long I can go on before my lungs and head explode?*

"Yes. Stella. Of course you want to hear about Stella." His eyes glazed over with that familiar wistful gaze as if calling forth a ghost inhabiting a long-forgotten saga.

Since he didn't believe in God, he didn't believe in the saying that God closes one door and opens a window. Still, just when he had reached the nadir of despair, something happened that almost made him a believer, except he exchanged God with fate.

He was crossing the inner yard of the tenement complex where he had been living for two months. Without a proper overcoat, he had to make do with the thin, unlined jacket he had brought from home. He was shivering and eager to get out of the cold, when the sight of a young girl in a flimsy red dress on a stone bench halted his step. She was hugging her knees. Drawing closer he noticed she was softly sobbing.

"I told her she shouldn't be out in the cold staircase without an overcoat."

"She lifted her head with an astonished look. Her big, brown eyes were red from crying, but they captivated me from the first moment."

"You don't have a coat either," she said.

"Then we have something in common," I replied.

91

"You are funny," she said and wiped her eyes. We both burst out laughing.

"Why are you crying out here in the cold?" I asked.

She pointed to a window from which a stream of angry shouts could be heard. He had become so used to the shouting, quarreling, and arguing throughout the tenement almost day and night. He had trained himself to pay no heed until he couldn't hear the noise anymore.

"I guessed she was talking about her parents. I now remembered passing this girl a few times before in the staircase. She must have been from the family directly above me where there always seemed to be a quarrel going on when the man was home.

She told me that they were always fighting, as soon as he got home from work."

"My brother and sister don't seem to mind. They just shut their ears. I am different!" she added with a self-confidence that made me take note.

I asked her what they are fighting about to which she replied, "Money. What else? She shrugged. "She says he doesn't bring enough home. He says she squanders his hard-earned wages on trivial things."

Viktor didn't know what else to say, but he couldn't tear himself away. She already had a hold over him. "Still, you shouldn't be out here without a coat," I repeated after an awkward pause. "If you don't want to go home, why not stay at my place until things calm down upstairs?" I suggested.

"My mother told me never to go anywhere with strange men," she replied.

"She's right. You should never do that," I agreed. "You have nothing to fear from me, though. Of course that's what any fiend would say. If you'd rather, we can sit outside the door on the stairs and pass the time chatting."

Viktor went on to describe how they raced each other up three flights of stairs and collapsed laughing and huffing on top of the drafty staircase in front of the door to his flat.

He offered her a blanket, he said, but she shook her head so resolutely her curls flipped back and forth. She pulled her legs up again and hugged her knees with a soulful look. "You are a good person." She used the German familiar as he had done, since she was still a child.

"In what way are you different?" he asked after he had settled down at a considerable distance from her so she would not feel threatened. But he also got a good look at her. She was a waiflike child of about eight or nine. The most remarkable feature were here big dark eyes that sparkled a self-confidence unusual for her age.

"In every way," she replied. "I want to get out of here, and I will once I get a good education in all things that interest me."

"And what interests you?"

"First I will learn to speak proper German. Then I'll study the literature of the great playwrights and the great roles of women on stage, and I'll become a famous actress."

At first he was tempted to make light of this. Surely many little girls have such dreams. But seeing her big, dark eyes shining on him, he thought better of it. This little girl indeed seemed different. Not that he had much experience with girls of any age, but he had a gut feeling. She also seemed very self-aware about her shortcomings and how to fix them. He had noticed her speech right away—the distinct rolling diction of the Jews from Galicia colored her Austrian German.

"You would have to work on your speech," he confirmed.

"You could teach me."

"To speak German? I'm Hungarian. I hardly qualify."

"I have an ear for it. Your German is very pure. Better than that of most Austrians."

"If you think so," he replied. "Maybe it is because it was my mother's tongue, my *mameloshen*. She was from Transylvania and grew up among the Saxons there. I must have gotten it from her."

"Will you teach me then?"

"We'll have to see. Right now I need work. I'm all out of money and have rent to pay. And most of all I need an overcoat."

"What do you do?"

"I play the violin. I earned some money playing with a Schrammel band last summer, but they didn't want me anymore when they found out I was a Jew."

She nodded her understanding and seemed neither surprised nor bothered by this.

"You should speak to my father," she said. "He's a waiter at a coffee-house in the first district. He might know somebody who can give you work. In return you can give me lessons. He would like that. He always says the education in the schools around here is lacking."

She said she had just started third grade, but her father felt his children weren't studying enough secular German culture.

"Then you are eight years old?"

"Papa was an actor. He traveled all over Galicia with a Yiddish the-ater company. His most popular roles were Hamlet and King Lear in Yiddish. The name Bruno Etzel was very famous, but he wanted more. He wanted to reach a wider audience. His dream was to appear on stage at the Burgtheater. We left Drohobycz and came to Vienna five years ago. He studied hard to learn classical stage German, but it never seemed good enough. The only role he got was Shylock in some small theater. Now he waits tables."

He listened in silence. *Another failed existence*, he thought. *Like so many who come to Vienna with high hopes.*

"Mama was studying modern dance and ballet in Lemberg when she met Papa. When they got married, they moved in with his parents in Drohobycz. He still traveled a lot with his theater group, and she was stuck with the children who came in quick succession. We never hear the end of how bearing children ruined her chances for a dancing career and also her figure.

"She still moans about her missed life. How often do we have to hear her moan, 'I could have been a Grete Wiesenthal? If only...'? Papa wasn't to blame. It was the world she came from. That was another reason we came to Vienna. He wanted his children to grow up in a world free from a religion with so many restrictions. As you can see though, the only difference between here and there is the tenement we live in."

She sighed and then jumped up. "Nothing will keep me here!" she declared with unexpected pathos. "That's why you have to help me."

Her sparkling eyes turned upward and exuded such fervor and resolve. Her outburst erased any doubt he might have had that she would indeed do it.

Suddenly all was quiet upstairs. Deeply engaged in conversation, they had stopped paying attention to the squabble. Now the silence was almost deafening. They held their breath and waited for the scuffle to resume. They could have heard a pin drop.

"They are making up," the girl whispered. He looked at her perplexed. "You know," she insisted. "I just hope she doesn't get pregnant again."

"Oh." He finally caught on. "If you are the youngest..."

"You aren't very smart in certain things, are you?" She chuckled. "It doesn't mean she didn't get in the family way over the last eight years." She jumped to her feet. "I guess I'd better go now. Remember what I said. Go talk to Papa. He's very nice. Look him up at the Café Central in the evening."

He called her back once more.

"What is your name?"

"Sorele Ettelberg, but the name that will shine over the Burgtheater one day is Stella Berger."

"Stella Berger! I like it," I told her. "I like the sound of it."

"What's yours?" she asked.

"It was Chaim Erdreich, but I changed it. Now it's Viktor Erdos."

"I like that too. It has a distinguished ring to it," she said smacking her lips. "Good-bye for now, Viktor." With that she flew upstairs, taking two steps at a time.

"So you fell in love with an eight-year-old girl?" I concluded when he broke off. Viktor's long look of rebuke came my way like a flaming dagger I will never forget.

All right, I thought. *My faux pas.*

To me it seemed a sincere apology could smooth it over. To him, however, it was more than a casual remark spoken without thinking. I had put my foot in my mouth, but I had also overstepped a line. I had violated a sacred boundary. I had trod on forbidden ground "If you mean what I think you mean, you are totally off the mark," he finally said. Disdain dripped from his mouth like pus from an infected wound. "I wouldn't expect you to understand. How could you with your bourgeois morals?"

95

"I don't think you know anything about my morals," I replied. I was now on the warpath myself. "Maybe you should enlighten me about yours. They are very fuzzy indeed."

He stuck another cigarette in his mouth and squinted as he lit it. This seemed to have a calming effect on his jittery nerves and thin-skinned ego.

"When we were first sitting together in that drafty staircase, she appeared like an angel—an ethereal being from another dimension." His wistful gaze was pinned on some water spot on the wall.

"When spring began to burst into bloom in the Augarten and the Prater, we took long walks or sat on a bench and studied the classics of German drama. She learned in no time all the important roles—Gretchen, Minna von Barnhelm, the Maiden of Orleans, and many more. She recited Goethe, Schiller, and Kleist with such conviction, depth of feeling, and passion. A revelation overcame me. She was more than an angel. She was a being of a higher order. She was a goddess."

Who can argue with that? I thought and tried to keep a straight face in the presence of so much schmaltz. Having experienced the great acting art of Stella Berger on screen and stage, however, I could not argue his point. Her performances enraptured me too. At the age of eight, though? A goddess? At the height of her fame, her pathos roused audiences on two continents to their feet, and a few critics actually did call her a goddess—the divine Berger. Viktor Erdos, however, didn't seem to mean it in a metaphoric sense. His gushing wasn't mere hyperbole. He really believed in her divine nature as a gift from the gods to the world.

"You might find this melodramatic," he said as if he had read my mind. "Nein, ich habe mich nicht in sie verliebt." He protested vehemently he had not fallen in love with her. "My feelings for Stella Berger were never that vulgar and commonplace. If you must know, I venerated her. I worshipped at her feet. I was a priest officiating at her altar. I never desired to possess her body. We would embrace and kiss each other on the cheeks, but it was never...it never ever had anything to do with erotic desire."

What could I say? He smoked, and Curtis was fast asleep on the bed.

FIVE

Viktor's situation improved in December when he received a surprise package from home. Lazar Erdreich had bundled up some warm clothing, boots, and a thick overcoat his son had left behind. The simple mountain apparel was not in the prevailing style of the capital, but Viktor was very grateful. An even greater surprise awaited him when he put his hands in the coat pocket and pulled out a sizable wad of money. It was enough to last him until spring. He could pay the rent and, if spent judiciously, afford three warm meals a week at a restaurant.

He wrote a long letter of thanks to his father telling him about the coffeehouses he was now frequenting regularly and all the famous people with whom he took his coffee and discussed art and politics. Would his father be impressed? Not likely. Names such as Schnitzler and Hofmannsthal meant nothing to him. He might, however, take some pride in the praise his son's first poetry reading reportedly earned among these prominences. Even the legendary critic and publicist Karl Kraus had taken an interest in young Viktor's writings and promised to publish a selection in his literary magazine *Die Fackel,* which was the holy writ of the art world. Kraus could make or break careers and did so many times, Viktor wrote. There was no greater honor than a man as formidable as Karl Kraus hailing one to be a new Loris—a reference to Hofmannsthal who had taken the literary world by storm at sixteen.

Viktor continued on for several more pages, dropping names right and left. Among them was a young man named Stefan Zweig, the scion of a wealthy, upper-class Jewish family as Viktor emphasized. Lazar Erdreich had never been to Vienna and certainly would have no idea about the layout of the city and its districts. Such a consideration, however, didn't hinder his son from lavishly describing the opulent Zweig home located in the first district where he had recently attended a soirée. (Viktor wondered if his father had any idea what that was.) Viktor had gone at the invitation of the family's youngest offspring. His new friend was also an aspiring poet and devoted coffeehouse habitué.

Viktor neglected to reply to the little note he had found attached to the wad of money. It asked about his progress on the violin and expressed the hope, as so often before, that he would be admitted to the conservatory. Only this time a slight doubt seemed to have crept in. There was no reference to a debut concert. Maybe Lazar Erdreich had come to realize that his son would never fulfill his potential for becoming a concert violinist.

Viktor knew his father would rather swallow his disappointment than disparage his son. He let the matter slide and did not touch on it at all in his reply. Instead he played up his literary friendships. He was gaining recognition and acclaim from important people, as he called them. It was just for a talent and passion other than music.

Viktor Erdos had indeed made his entry into the coveted world of the first district across the canal. He had become a regular of the literary coffeehouse circuit in the inner city. He had found a place where he was at home and connected with kindred spirits. His friends were people like him who shirked manual labor and whose hands were made to fill reams of notebooks with the outpourings of their minds. They were people who appreciated the finer things in life, even if they couldn't afford them, but for whom a good cup of coffee would do. The latter was an acquired taste but one Viktor took to with the enthusiasm of the true Viennese. As tribute to his changed circumstances, he adopted some of the habits and appurtenances of those with whom he wished to blend. He grew a mustache, lovingly nurtured along from sparse working material, laid out the cost for a walking cane with a copper nob, and acquired the habit of smoking cigarettes, which became the biggest item in his budget. He had eyed in the window of a hat maker a broad-rimmed fedora for winter and an Italian straw hat for summer, but those had to await the better times Viktor was sure would come. Any sartorial changes would have to wait as well. For the time being, the suit from home would do if subjected to regular brushing and pressing.

Viktor lingered over coffee for hours and smoked cigarettes, which he soon began to consume in increasing quantities. He smoked the cheaper Turkish brands such as Murad or Balkan Sobranie in those early days, as the more expensive Egyptians Emir or Conqueror Extra by Kyriazi Frères of Cairo were still out of reach of his budget. Viktor also became an avid reader of newspapers. Any self-respecting coffee-house made available an assortment of local, national, and foreign language newspapers, and Viktor welcomed this opportunity to broaden his horizons. Perusing and delving into *Neue Wiener Zeitung*, *Berliner Tageblatt*, *Frankfurter Zeitung*, and *Budapest Review* became part of his daily routine. He too became one of those faceless figures at the Café Central holding a spread out newspaper from behind which exuded billows of smoke.

This new Viktor Erdos—Viktor the sophisticate, the man about town, the aspiring literary luminary, the coffee aficionado and habitual smoker—was the creation of Bruno Etzel. As master of mimicry and keen observer of the human cabaret, he was the erstwhile paragon of the Yiddish theater and now maître d' at the Café Central. He was a man of small stature with graceful, catlike movements. His public persona always presented an affable demeanor that was neither fawning nor pompous. His alert, dark, round eyes held a constant though discreet watch over the entire establishment. He never lost sight of anything that might need tending to in the regulars' corner. He was tuned in and attentive to the quirks and habits of each regular. He knew what kind of coffee and newspaper each preferred. His signature Shakespeare mustache was neatly trimmed above and below the lips, and his pomaded, shiny, black, shoulder-length hair was brushed back in the manner of actors and magicians. His black suit with thin, gray stripes was of an outmoded cut and lent him the aura of being from a past world and time.

When he spoke people listened. His voice had the inflection of a trained actor. It was modulated and strong for a man of slight build. In the hinterland of the empire, on the Yiddish stage, his instrument had risen from the softest whisper to a lion's roar. His voice had climbed and descended along a full register of emotions, making his audiences weep, laugh, and anything in between. In Vienna it was ironically the sound of his voice that was the shoal on which his dreams shattered. This master of mimicry could never shed the lilting, musical intonation that betrayed his Galician origin to the satisfaction of those he auditioned for at the Burgtheater and most other stages in the city.

"I won't let this happen to my little girl," he told Viktor. "If you can help her erase any trace of that damnable speech pattern and educate her in the German classics, I'll be forever in your debt. She already has what it takes. She has personality, passion, and purpose. You can see it in her eyes. She has the itch, the fire, and the burning desire I too felt as a child. But she has to start early and not rely on public schools."

So they struck a bargain. Viktor was to spend the afternoons turning Sorele Ettelberg into Stella Berger. Bruno Etzel would gain him entry into the circles of habitués at the Café Central and groom him in the art of becoming the exemplary Viennese coffeehouse *flâneur*.

Viktor Erdos still held fast to his Marxist beliefs and spouted them when the occasion presented itself. He counted the second happiest day of his life when Peter Altenberg, poet and Viennese coffeehouse institution (one of the elect residing on Mount Olympus of the literati), turned to him during a debate on the merits and demerits of a certain metaphor and asked, "What do you think, Mr. Erdos?"

The happiest times of his life were the hours spent with little Stella sitting on the stairwell of their tenement or wandering about in the Augarten and Prater in the blooming spring, the long, hot summer, and the autumn splendor. On cold, winter days, they kept warm by the fire of a local community hall with their heads bent over volume upon volume of reading material. The years went by, and he saw her grow mentally and physically. Though, she always remained petite. He was in awe of the dramatic flair she displayed during presentations to family and friends and in school productions. Wherever she appeared she was the queen. By the time she was twelve, he reluctantly admitted, like his violin teacher in Munkács had told him when he was that age, he had nothing more to teach her, and she should get professional training if she wanted to advance.

"Of course I want to advance," she said and tousled his hair. "Need you even ask, you dumb man?"

"It means we might not see each other anymore or at least not as often."

"Don't make such a sad face." She spoke to him as if she was the adult and he a schoolboy. "We still live in the same building. We could hardly avoid running into each other. Besides, you'll come and visit. We'll play cards and games as we always have. Nothing will change. You know how much Papa likes you."

Much changed, though, after she was enrolled in classes at an actor's studio attached to the Hofburgtheater in the eighth district, the Josefstadt. Somebody had to accompany the precocious but still twelve-year-old to and from lessons to the other side of town. Since Viktor had long since become part of the family and had no other obligations, he gladly took on the role of designated chaperone. He enjoyed the time they spent together on the tramway. This was the curious girl's first time outside the confines of the ghetto of Leopoldstadt. As he had done when he first arrived in the capital, she found no end to marveling at the magnificence of the marble-columned edifices, mansions, and palais lining the elegant boulevards.

"You never told me anything about this," she pouted playfully. "But I forgive you," she added quickly and placed her hand over his mouth to muffle his protest. "You've done so much to prepare me for this brave new world," she quoted. Miranda was a role she had memorized at her father's suggestion and which she and Viktor had read together multiple times.

"Miranda later became one of her signature roles—one among many from Shakespeare. She played that role on the Berlin and Munich stage," Erdos explained. "At twelve she could already recite in German several Shakespearean roles with perfect recall and diction. She could also quote Goethe, Kleist, and more. She had a phenomenal memory," he added.

I would have liked to ask him a few questions. Could she really have been so completely without flaw? Then I remembered him describing her as a goddess. Anybody using such a superlative for a mortal could not be relied upon to be objective. I too had fallen under her spell, but the way I saw her, she was an extraordinary woman and actress but still human.

We sat in silence for a while. I thought over parts of the curious tale he had told while attempting not to inhale too much of the fumes hanging over the room like a stagnant cloud.

"Then Sender came back into my life."

It was a concise, matter-of-fact statement. Out of the blue. I waited for the second part of the sentence or the modifier, but none came. The fragment hung between us like the smoke rings he blew into the air.

SIX

Since no explanation was forthcoming, I went into the kitchen in search of more coffee. When I came back into the room with a steaming pot, he stood next to the open window. He was careful not to show his face to anybody who might be staking out the building. His forehead creased, he cast a probing glance at the dimly lit street below. It was way past midnight. The steps of a few stragglers echoed on the cobblestones of the otherwise empty street.

The strain from listening and lack of sleep was beginning to take its toll on my body. My head felt swelled like a balloon, and my itching eyelids refused to stay open. All I wanted was to lie down next to Curtis and surrender to a dreamless sleep. But I was sequestered in a small space with a potential murderer who seemed compelled to unload his life story. As long as he kept talking and I kept listening, I figured he wouldn't do anything desperate that might include a threat to my life. He was like some sort of reverse Scheherazade.

"When did things between you and Stella begin to change?" I was reclining on the bed against Curtis's back, and Erdos returned to the chair by the table. He propped up his head with his hands and fixed his gaze on some spot on the wall. He avoided eye contact as he continued his tale, which I presumed was at least part fiction.

"It started with Sender," he began. Then, as if he wasn't quite sure of the actual sequence of events, he added, "No. That was much later. It was around the time she started acting lessons that he came back into my life, though."

He hadn't mentioned that name before, so I asked who he was.

"Alexander Levary," he replied.

"Stella Berger's husband?" I was trying to help him over a stumbling block he seemed to have run up against and was unsure he should surmount.

"Yes. Yes." He fumbled around with the almost-empty pack to extract another cigarette. "She married him, but that was many years later in Berlin. By then she was already famous and had a reputation to protect."

As much as I knew, Alexander Levary was a film director and producer who had directed Stella in several of her most successful film roles. At some point they got married. The marriage was always regarded with some skepticism. If I remembered correctly from hearsay, it took place under a cloud of scandal. I was a child at the time and had other things on my mind than adult gossip, but now in this New York garret, I pondered what Viktor meant by Sender came back into his life. There was something about the way he said it that made me hold back any questions. Something told me it was better to leave it up to him to explain in due course.

Viktor's life had taken a dramatic change for which he was not prepared, as he told us. In the evenings he still made the rounds of the coffeehouses. He checked them out to see who was out and about, and he usually settled down for the night either at the Café Central or Café Griensteidl. The major difference in his life had to do with Stella. Although they were still in regular contact, he no longer had her all to himself. He was no longer the one to guide her in her studies and nurture her insatiable desire to learn. He was not her sole audience for whom she performed the roles she had studied. He had to share her with her teachers and fellow students at the actors' studio.

The only time they were alone was on the tramway to and from school. At first she was bubbling over with excitement to tell him about her lessons and the praise and critique she received. She was the youngest student but had already gained the attention of her instructors.

Within a few weeks, however, he noticed a change. She became reluctant to share what was going on and wrapped herself in silence. She kept looking out the window for the length of the ride home. His attempts to start a conversation were rebuffed with a shrug. Her mind seemed elsewhere now—a place she barred him from entering.

This sudden change of attitude toward him, the moodiness, the grumpy responses, and the stubborn silences in the cheerful chatterbox he had known and adored left him totally nonplussed. He took it as a personal rejection for no fathomable reason. That it might have nothing at all to do with him never crossed his mind. He never considered it was about a change in her and her body and that she was going through a phase of development when such behavior was common and expected.

"A penny for your thoughts," he said with a nervous giggle during one of those sullen rides home from her lessons.

She slowly turned away from the window and toward him. He noticed for the first time that her features had filled in. She had an almost womanly look. Her big, dark eyes had a new glow. The sneer launched at him from those eyes went through him like a knife. "You are such a child, Viktor," she said. "You really should grow up."

A tongue-lashing from Stella was something completely unexpected. He did not know how to respond. He simply felt as if his heart had been ripped out of his chest, he said.

"You really should do something with your life," she added in a softer, motherly tone. "I don't need you to take me to the studio. I'm grateful for all you have done for me, but now you are simply wasting your time and talents. How can I respect you when I'm growing, learning, and perfecting my craft, and you're treading water?"

They still talked but not as often. They would still sit down together on the stairs when they met in the hallway. Sometimes her parents would ask him to eat with them, and inevitably a discussion would ensue around the table. Stella always dominated. She had a theory she liked to propose that contrasted the stage and the actor's art with what passed for the real world and people in it. Viktor recognized Shakespeare's influence but said nothing.

"You might think acting is make-believe or a way to escape the real world," she mused. Her face was aglow, and her eyes sparkled with the passion of a truth seeker. "I think it's just the opposite. Through his art the actor holds up a mirror of the real world and reveals aspects of life that remain hidden to most people who can't see the forest for the trees." After giving it some thought, she added, "Actually it should be the other way around. Most people can't see the trees for the forest. Don't you think so, Viktor?"

He was flattered she still sought his opinion and readily nodded his agreement. Before another rebuke came his way, he quickly added, "If you mean people can't appreciate the beauty of small, individual things because they are unable to penetrate the dense foliage that overshadows them, you have a point."

"You, my dear friend, might have the makings of an actor in you!" She laughed and gave him a patronizing pat on the back. "Speaking of a make-believe world," she chattered on. "I might never have been to a coffeehouse in the first district, but I know all about it, and I can tell which world is the fake one."

"How would you know?" Viktor said. His voice crackled with irritation over her attempt to deride a world that was dear to him—the one small realm he had carved out for himself. He wondered where she was going with this other than an attempt to get his ire up. *She's just a child playing childish games,* he told himself. *You shouldn't take her so seriously, as if she was a reasonable adult.*

"Papa tells me plenty of what goes on there," she replied. "And by my own intuition, I can well imagine what those folks are trying to conceal behind a camouflage of outlandish costumes and eccentric blustering."

With the self-righteous certitude of the precocious, she declared the coffeehouse scene to be the actual world of make-believe where people went to escape from real life. The theater, on the other hand, was the place where people went to find their inner selves and discover the deeper, true meaning of life.

One day, out of the blue, Stella declared, "I think every man should have a woman. Don't you think so too, Papa?"

Papa rolled his eyes and told her off with a wagging finger.

"This is hardly a subject for a young girl," he reprimanded her.

"Don't you think Viktor should have a girlfriend or a woman?" she insisted.

"I'm too busy making something of my life to get involved in dalliances," Viktor replied. His face was red to the roots of his hair.

"I know you're in love with me, but I'm too young for you. Besides I don't have any time for dalliances myself as long as I'm working to make something of my life." She bored her big, dark eyes into his with a challenging jerk of her head. "What is it exactly you do?"

All this banter led Viktor Erdos to go deep into himself. He was lying awake at night and staring at the ceiling. That little vixen was right. He was fixated on her but not in the way she seemed to think. He loved her, but he was not in love with her. While thus embarked on an examination of his inner self, he sought out the famed Viennese soul specialist Doctor Sigmund Freud again albeit with not altogether satisfactory results.

The doctor's numerous disciples spread the gospel of psychoanalytic theories around the city and postulated the therapeutic benefits of finding the inner self deep within the unconscious by digging up and scrutinizing childhood experiences. Viktor really had no use for concepts such as the Oedipus complex that were so much in vogue among the youth. He loved his mother and cherished her memory. He also loved and respected his father. To honor both his mother and father was deeply engrained in his consciousness. It was ludicrous to think he had any desire to sleep with one and kill the other. He remembered the unpleasantness of the one therapy session with the great doctor some time ago. Viktor remembered him stroking his goatee as he sized him up with a pitying look when he refused to take the doctor's bait.

"Methinks the gentleman protests too much," the doctor intoned unctuously. "Repression of one's feeling is a dangerous path to take. It can lead to all kinds of neuroses and impair one's functioning in everyday life. It might also be a sign of arrested psychosexual development in the phallic stage. All this can have serious consequences such as homoeroticism."

"Denial will get you nowhere!" he heard the good doctor call after him as he stormed out of the consulting room and slammed the door behind him.

Viktor's relationship with Stella had reached a nadir at that time. What she had said about him refusing to grow up had planted a worm in his brain. In particular the part about respect went swirling around in his head. He had to admit she had more wisdom at twelve than he at twenty-two. Ever since they had become friends, she had had a clear vision of the course she wanted her life to take, and she pursued that goal with an iron will and steadfast determination. All this time he had been content to drift and be a hanger-on. He had clung to her and the famous people at the coffeehouses. His only aspiration had been to be a dilettante poet and a flâneur in the manner of Baudelaire. He came to admit to himself that Stella was right and that his desire to make it in the literati coffeehouse society was a sham and an escape from the real world.

In the course of his soul-searching, Viktor eventually rediscovered the spark of his gymnasium days. He recalled the desire to do his part to make the world a better place. He delved once again into the writings of Karl Marx and decided to become an activist for social justice. As a first step, he matriculated at the university and read philosophy and political economy for which he eventually presented himself for the doctoral exams. In the midst of this new direction, however, another seismic event shook his entire being. Alexander Levary, the man he called Sender, came back into his life.

SEVEN

Back in the days at the gymnasium in Debrecen, Sender Herz Loewy liked to go by the name Alexander Löwenherz. He was a lionhearted swaggerer whose entrances and exits even within the confines of the school walls were calculated to project an aura of dramatic flair. When they met again years later in Vienna, he was trying to make a name for himself as Sasha Levary.

"It seems so many nowadays are anxious to shed their provincial origins by changing their names," declared Sasha Levary. The Budapest native had a gurgling laugh that made the upturned, pointed ends of his thin mustache quiver. "From Chaim Erdreich to Viktor Erdos, world-renowned violinist! I like it. You will go far, my dear friend. Very far."

"You haven't done so badly yourself, Sasha Levary. Still the lionhearted, I presume." Viktor's attempt at an equally cheerful reply aborted into a sour twitch of his mouth as if he had taken a bite out of a lemon.

"It's derived from Hebrew. 'Lev' means heart, and 'ari' means lion," Sender explained.

"I am familiar with the language and its meaning." Sender's condescending tone irritated Viktor.

Was he happy to see his old schoolmate and closest friend from his gymnasium days? He should have been overjoyed and received him with open arms. Instead Sender's appearance out of the blue roused something long dormant in the far recesses of his inner self. A dark sense of foreboding lodged in the pit of his stomach like an undigested meal. What was he afraid of? Was it fear that the friend's presence might jolt him from the path of study he had set for himself? Was it something deeper and more unsettling? Could Freud's theory about the subconscious guiding human behavior contain some truth after all? Could his fear be due to a reawakening of something buried in his subconscious—something he thought was in the past and ostensibly shed with his name? Was it fear of a return of the magnetic power the boy Sender had held over him when they were both adolescents?

They were both adults now. Surely Sender had moved beyond what was a pubescent infatuation. Viktor had. To hell with Freud and his theories!

Sender broke into the stream of his thoughts. "I should have thought I'd get a warmer reception. Aren't you happy to see an old friend?"

"Of course I'm happy." Viktor tried to justify what must have appeared to his friend like a rather bizarre reaction. "I guess it's just so unexpected."

"Don't worry. You're forgiven." Sender gave him a bear hug and came dangerously close to crushing the violin and bow Viktor held in his hand.

The encounter took place at a wine and dance garden where Viktor played in a Strauss orchestra on Saturday nights to support his university studies. Though seated on the podium among the other musicians at a distance from the entrance, he had recognized him right away. Sender's entrance was unmistakable and calculated to draw attention. As he strutted through the door, he flung his broad-rimmed felt hat off his head in a sweeping gesture and let his dark-brown velvet cape slide from his shoulders with nary a look back to make sure the two ushers who followed behind him caught the items. His monocle in hand, he surveyed the hall. Nodding his satisfaction, he clamped the glass into one eye and swaggered through the merry crowd. That crowd, however, was too absorbed in drinking, singing, and dancing to take note of this strange appearance. The waiting staff apparently took him to be of a higher station, though, and expecting a generous tip, they cleared a table for him directly in front of the podium.

"How did you find this place?" Viktor asked during the musicians' recess.

"Easy," Sender replied. "I heard you were in Vienna. Don't ask me how or from whom. Word gets around. I found your address. Should have guessed you would live in that Leopoldstadt ghetto."

"It's affordable," Viktor grunted.

"Never mind," Sender waved his arms about. "It was just a joke. Don't get touchy. Anyway, you weren't home of course. I left a note under your door and was about to leave when a most charming young girl asked if she could be of help. I told her my business, and she told me where to find you. She seemed surprised you had any friends."

"That would be Stella," Viktor said. His cheeks were glowing like two light bulbs.

To Viktor's annoyance Sender leaned back, crossed his legs, and scrutinized him with a probing, amused gaze. "A girlfriend? A fiancée perhaps?" he inquired after a long, pregnant pause. Sender was twirling the ends of his mustache.

"No such thing. Just a neighbor," Viktor replied, and he nervously rummaged in his pockets for a cigarette.

"You smoke?" he asked his companion.

"No. That's one vice I never acquired." Sender gave him a blasé look. "She would be too young anyway," Sender mused.

"But seriously," he then continued, "do you have a girlfriend? A mistress perhaps? Married women taking young lovers seems much in vogue, especially in Viennese high society. So I hear."

"Let's talk about something else." Viktor showed his irritation with a cutting gesture.

Their eyes locked. Despite the discomfort it caused him, Viktor returned his friend's probing gaze. He remembered the boys at school teasing Sender about his dark eyes with their daredevil spark. Gypsy eyes they called them. To Chaim Erdreich they were like magic, and so they were now to Viktor Erdos. He hadn't thought much these last few years about the swashbuckling Alexander Löwenherz, his boarding school roommate, sometime crusader and slayer of Mameluke Turks, and the boy to whom he had played loyal retainer and stirrup holder.

As is natural for adolescent boys, especially since they were confined to an all-male environment and had very little or no contact with the opposite sex, the school was a hothouse of sprouting hormones.

A stream of conflicting sensations rushed through Viktor's body like a mountain stream melting in springtime. Sender had matured. His boyish good looks had developed into handsome features. Viktor considered whether his friend's jet black hair, which was now almost shoulder length in the preferred manner of stage actors of the day, and wondered if it had always been as wavy. Somehow he suspected the locks were getting some help from a curling iron, and the shine was achieved with ample applications of pomade.

"That mustache is really ridiculous," Viktor finally said to break the stalemate their staring at each other had reached.

"You don't like it?" Sender asked. "All right then." He tugged at the handlebars, and the offending facial ornament came off. He emitted a slight wince of pain that ended in a burst of laughter.

"What about your hair? Is that a wig?" Viktor asked. Joining in the merriment, he threateningly extended his hand toward his friend's crown. "Is anything about you genuine?"

"Oh no!" Sender protested and leaned back in his chair. "Don't touch! My hair is all mine. You have no idea what work and care it takes to get it to look that way."

"You haven't told me what you are doing in Vienna," Viktor remarked when they finally caught their breaths and stopped laughing.

"I am on my way to Berlin. You know I was always interested in the theater. Now the great Reinhardt is considering me for a position of assistant director."

Just then the musicians were taking their positions on the podium.

"We'll talk more after you close," Sender replied.

For the next two hours, Sender hurled himself into the festivities. He waltzed about and shed his affectionate attention on the maidens of the people. He talked to everyone from *Schnitzlerian* sweethearts to matronly bakers' wives. Between rounds he quenched his thirst with enough wine to deplete an entire cask to its bottom.

After the incident with the fake mustache, a sigh of relief came over Viktor. He felt the ice had been broken. Maybe his initial unease and even alarm about Sender's sudden appearance after so many years had been unfounded. They had been intimate friends as schoolboys and could be friends again as adults. Sender was still the braggart and fantast he had always been. Maybe this was a prerequisite personality trait for a career in the theater. If what he said was true, he was on his way to Berlin under contract for an apprenticeship with Max Reinhardt at the Deutsches Theater—a promising start for an ambitious go-getter.

Viktor felt a sense of gratification that Sender had sought him out. He had gone to the trouble of finding his address, calling on him, and even coming to the dance hall.

"So you're an aspiring actor?" Viktor asked him over a late-night coffee at the Café Central.

To show he was not completely unfamiliar with the theater world, Viktor took a certain pride in introducing the man who served the coffee as a good friend and a one-time player on the Yiddish theater circuit who was famed for his portrayals of Shakespearean characters from Hamlet to King Lear. Though Sender rose from his seat and politely shook the man's hand with a bow in Austro-Hungarian fashion, Viktor knew very well the meaning of the raised eyebrows and condescending smile. Bruno Etzel was not up to snuff in Sender's universe of Budapest and Berlin. He was, therefore, gratified to see Bruno returning the favor with doubly raised eyebrows. Sender either didn't notice the rebuke, or he shrugged it off as a provincial's impudence.

"Me? An actor?" Sender laughed loudly enough so Bruno, who had turned to serve other guests, could hear it. "Originally that was my idea. I studied acting for a while in Budapest. Did you know I once almost touched skin with Mari Jászai backstage at the National Theater? She was very gracious about it and said a few kind words about..."

"No. I didn't know, and how should I have?" Viktor stopped him short.

"Well, do you know who she is?" Sender huffed indignantly at Viktor's lack of appreciation for his personal contact with the foremost tragedian of the Budapest stage—a woman whose death scenes vied with the most famed demises of Sarah Bernhard.

"Of course I know who she is. I also know you are a name-dropper and show-off."

"Very well then," Sender sulked. "What do you want to know?"

"Nothing in particular."

"This might surprise you, I discovered I would rather pull strings from behind the scenes. I'd rather be involved in producing than appearing on stage. It's so much more creative. My rencontre with Max Reinhardt was a turning point. Sorry, I had to drop another name. But this meeting could almost be described as a rendezvous with destiny. I had produced a short play as a school project, and as luck would have it, Reinhardt happened to be in the audience and my father invited him to dinner. We spoke, and he invited me to Berlin. Get this. I told him I didn't have the means to work without pay and needed a contract to convince my parents, with whom I was living then, to permit me to go. He suggested I check out the theater scene in Vienna on my way and give him a written account. He doesn't want what others write about it but what I see. My own perspective. He made that very clear. And so here I am." Sender opened his arms wide with a bright smile. "What about you? I should have thought you were a famous violinist by now, conquering concert stages all the way to Carnegie Hall."

Viktor sadly lowered his head. He felt shamed by this man who seemed to have his destiny so clearly mapped out. "I just didn't think I had it in me to put up or put in what is necessary. What the world demands."

"That is sad and a waste of a great talent. But you have to suit your-self." Sender made a clicking sound with his tongue. "A real pity. No career, no girl, no mistress, and no lover. What have you been doing? Living like a monk? Or is it that fetching girl in your building you are lusting after?"

"Leave the girl out of this. She's untouchable. Do you hear? Don't even speak her name." Viktor jumped up wild-eyed as if ready to fall on his friend's throat.

Sender spread his hands in mock defense. "Hold it. I don't even know her name. Why does mention of her make you lose control? Did she reject you, or is there something deeper at play here? As young as she is, I bet I could get between her legs in no time." Sender bared his gleaming fangs. "Don't worry. I'm just teasing you to get your ire up. She's not my type. Lovely no doubt and spunky, but not my type if you know what I mean."

"I thought you liked boys," Viktor replied.

"And so do you. Don't you?" Sender's dark, Gypsy eyes bored into Viktor's sky-blues. Both held the gaze, and neither flinched.

The midnight hour had long passed when the black-lacquered fiacre transported the two gentlemen at top speed to an uncertain destination. The two oil sconces attached to the sides lit the driver's way as the carriage careened through the dark, twisting alleyways like a hearse late for a funeral. Viktor's fingers nervously tapped out the beat of the chorus of clattering hooves and screeching wheels hurtling over the cobblestones. Thuds of raindrops dancing on the carriage roof counterpointed the rhythm. He tried to avoid looking at the friend seated opposite him in sequestered proximity. From time to time, he lifted the curtain a hand's breadth to catch a glance of the fleeting scene outside. Sender leaned forward and clutched the silver knob of his cane with both hands while keeping unusually silent. Viktor didn't know whether he should be amused or annoyed to see he was sporting another mustache. This one was pencil thin with neatly trimmed ends. He turned again toward the window. The scenery outside was changing. They seemed to be heading into a nocturnal world populated with female figures of varying ages and maturity standing guard at the corners under streetlamps. A red gleam bathed their scantily clad bodies. Further into the shadows of the squat buildings, elegantly dressed men were engaged in some sort of haggling and dealing.

"Where the devil are we going?" Viktor finally cried out. "What kind of hell is this?"

"Oh, Viktor! After all this time in the big city, you are still little Chaim from the provincial backwater."

"I knew I shouldn't have come." Viktor's face was aglow with shame and loathing.

"Just calm yourself, will you?" Sender placed his hand on Viktor's thigh as he spoke in soothing tones. "We are only passing through this ninth circle of hell to get to where we are going, our ultimate goal. Everything good now?"

Viktor nodded. The warmth from Sender's hand spread through every part of his body and engulfed him with a sensation of being slowly consumed by a wildfire. Bereft of all resistance, he willing gave himself over to its flames.

"So where is it we are going?" he finally asked in a guttural voice.

Sender lifted the curtain and glanced briefly outside. It was still raining. The graying dawn attempted to break through the clouds.

"Just a little longer. Soon, my dear Chaim, we shall arrive at the gates to paradise. The portal to the garden of immense earthly delights!"

EIGHT

Viktor turned his gaze from the water spot on the wall to which he had been speaking and faced me directly. Perhaps he wanted to gauge my reaction to his confession. Would I condemn him? I tried not to avert my eyes. His candor touched me deeply, but I didn't know how to react. I had heard of such things but only in whispered tones and vague allusions. This was the kind of thing even my bohemian parents wouldn't speak of in my presence. As for my grandmother, I was sure such a world was unimaginable in her universe. She would certainly deny any knowledge of its existence.

I held his gaze and showed neither approval nor disapproval. This was his story, and he revealed it to me with unreserved frankness. Once again the wistful expression in his eyes struck me. The passage of time had not been kind to him. Deep furrows had ravaged his forehead. I never was a good judge of age, but to me he looked much older than his actual years. Had a life of debauchery aged him prematurely? I tried to shake off the thought even though it encroached on my mind.

He did not ask me if I was shocked. It probably didn't matter to him what I thought. Then out of the blue, Viktor suddenly said with a nod toward the sleeping Curtis, "I wouldn't trust him."

It wasn't clear whether he meant I shouldn't trust him or he didn't trust him. Two cigarettes later he suddenly burst with speech. "You must believe me. I am not a murderer. I might have done terrible things in my life—things I am ashamed of—but I am not a murderer. All I wanted was

117

to see Stella one more time. I wanted an opportunity to explain and tell her how sorry I was for what happened in Berlin. I wasn't looking to get back into her good graces. I just wanted to explain my side. She surely would have forgiven me. I knew her better than anybody. But Sender made himself the puppeteer and turned her against her true friends. Why did she marry him of all people?"

I said nothing. I had nothing to say. Something had happened in Berlin that had had a profound effect on two lives that converged again in New York.

"I was familiar with her habits," Viktor continued. "I knew she required time after each performance during which she shed her character self and transformed herself completely. She had to be left alone in her dressing room. Nobody was allowed in. No maid, manager, or colleague. Absolutely nobody was allowed to be present while she underwent her metamorphosis back to Stella Berger. So I knew I would find her alone. I also knew from the papers that Sender was in Hollywood. If I could circumvent that woman, Stella would hear me out. I was sure of it."

He rose and walked to the window and back. He looked me straight in the eye. "She was dead," he said with a hollow, matter-of-fact tone. "Her throat had been cut. I turned and ran. On approaching her dressing room, I had been vaguely aware of the figure of a man passing me. I was too preoccupied with rehearsing what I would say to her, but in retrospect I know there was a man leaving her dressing room just as I was getting there. I am not afraid to die. Now she's gone, my life is over. What I want is for the murderer to be found and punished."

"You think it could have been Alexander Levary?" I asked.

"No. Never. Not Sender. What would be his motive? She was his pathway to fame and his bread and butter. Without Stella he is nothing. Besides he was in Hollywood at the time."

"The police will check his alibi," Curtis said.

We both turned toward the bed. Curtis had lifted himself up on his elbows. How much had he heard or understood? I hoped not much. Even if he wasn't asleep the entire time, I thought his German was too limited to catch all that was said.

As it turned out, his German wasn't quite as limited as he had made us believe. When Viktor Erdos had gone to the bathroom, he whispered in my ear, "A faggot in love with a movie queen? The jury will eat it up."

I slapped him in the face and called him a bastard. Instead of starting a row, he took it all with a big grin.

"I don't know about you," he said as if nothing had happened, "but I'm starved. I'm sure our guest is too. Why don't you make more coffee, and I'll go down and get fresh rolls and stuff."

"He will no doubt alert the police," Viktor said when he was gone.

"Why do you say that?"

"Before the third cry of the rooster, he will betray us."

"A Christian reference," I said. "What do you mean by 'us'? He's a Jew too."

"No, he is not." Viktor shook his head emphatically. "He may be of Jewish parentage, but this man does not have a *Yiddishe neshume*."

I almost doubled over as from a punch in the stomach. "I didn't take you for one to put much stock into notions such as a Jewish soul," I managed to say when I recovered my senses.

"Forgive me for seeming blunt. Far be it from me to hurt your feelings. You are in love, and love makes people blind. It's a cliché but true. That's why you have overlooked that his eyes are…there is an expression my mother used to use. His eyes are devoid of a certain kind of tear."

He didn't explain further.

I wasn't in the mood to dwell on my uneasy presentiments about my lover or to explore my misgivings about this whole affair. Before either of us could say anything more, the door burst open, and in strutted Chief Inspector Frank Dettelbach, dapper as ever, and Inspector Mulligan heaving his bulk up the creaking, narrow stairs behind him.

"Couldn't you have found a place on the ground floor?" Mulligan panted volumes of hot breath and mopped his brow with a big, immaculately white handkerchief.

"Come on, Mulligan. You can use the exercise." Dettelbach placed a hand under his colleague's elbow and feigned help. "There you are. See? You made it."

A contingent of six uniformed police officers followed the two. Their guns were drawn, and they were fully alert for the arrest of a violent, armed criminal. Curtis Wolff sheepishly brought up the rear.

"I presume this is the man we are looking for?" Dettelbach pointed at Erdos.

He addressed the question to me, but I thought it safer to play dumb and made no reply.

"Papers!" Dettelbach pushed his hat back and extended his hand toward Erdos.

Viktor pulled a worn, leather billfold from the inside breast pocket of his jacket and carefully extracted a wad of documents. He selected a few with great care with seemingly complete disregard for the inspector's repeated popping of his chewing gum.

"State your name," Dettelbach demanded. His face was menacingly close to Erdos's.

"My name is Viktor Erdos." He moved two steps backward.

"You are a citizen of what country?"

"I am Austrian, but was recently declared stateless." He spoke in halting, accented, but clear English.

"Country and place of birth."

"When I was born, the village was in the Austro-Hungarian Empire, which was also known as the Danube monarchy. Now I am not so sure where it is anymore, maybe Romania. Borders tend to change in the region, and I have lost track."

"Don't get smart with me," Dettelbach snorted.

The underling behind him busily entered the information in a pocket notebook.

"Date of birth," Dettelbach snapped.

"The twelfth of Sivan 5650, which would be the thirty-first of May 1890, according to the Gregorian calendar."

"Typical *Judenschnauze*!" Dettelbach knocked the cigarette from Viktor Erdos's mouth. "Don't think because you are in America you can get away with this kind of impertinence. We have laws here, and insulting an officer of the law carries severe punishment."

Dettelbach was losing his cool. To my own satisfaction, I noticed a faint trace of glee, almost Schadenfreude, flashing over the other officers' faces.

"Cuff him!" Dettelbach bellowed at the officer nearest him. "If he tries to escape, shoot him."

Viktor Erdos did not resist. He calmly held out his hands and followed his police escort to the door. At the top of the stairs, he turned around toward me. "Die Geige! Verwahren Sie die Geige!"

"You can take his blasted violin!" Dettelbach answered my uncertain look.

"Am I free to go?" I asked. "I would like to go home if I am not needed."

"Oh, you are needed all right," he replied. "For now you can go wherever you want, but don't leave town. Tomorrow morning you are expected to report to the precinct. We might need an interpreter. His English isn't that good."

"I thought the chief inspector was fluent in the mother tongue."

"You Jews are all alike. Impertinent bunch. Just wait. You'll get yours soon enough. You are lucky I don't arrest you on the spot for complicity to murder."

I had no doubt he would do just that if he had any evidence against me. I waited for them to be gone. With a sigh of relief, I realized I was alone. I went to the bathroom to wash up. Coming back into the room, I looked around for the violin. I tried not to dwell on what had happened in this shabby dwelling in the last forty-eight hours. If those waterlogged walls could speak, what a story they could tell. The stale odor from cigarette smoke and empty whiskey glasses mingled with the aroma of fresh coffee still simmering on the stove. I tried to avoid looking at the crumpled sheets on the pallet that served as a bed where I once thought I was experiencing love. The violin was leaning against the wall in the corner. I grabbed it quickly and turned to flee, but I found the man I hated more than anybody blocking my path.

"What a rough night. You must be exhausted going so long without sleep. Come on. I'll take you home." Curtis took control as if we were still a couple.

"No you won't," I said. "I'll take the subway."

"What do you mean?" He seemed completely oblivious to how much his betrayal had hurt me and how my feelings toward him had changed.

Did he really think the night with Viktor Erdos had only been an interlude and now we would pick up where we left off? I looked into his gray, carefree eyes. I searched for the tear, but there was none there.

PART III

A DREAM CALLED WEIMAR

ONE

Inspector Dettelbach lost no time compiling evidence and presenting what he called an open-and-shut case to the district attorney, who in turn speedily got the trial underway. A high-profile case such as the brutal murder of an international movie star was a heaven-sent gift for the careers of both men. Such an opportunity could not be wasted, even if the actual evidence was rather flimsy—a few eyewitnesses who saw the shadow of a fleeing man and implicit confession from the suspect.

I was present during most of the long, hot hours of interrogation at the police station. Dettelbach went to work applying a bit of his brutality. Mulligan was next to him and had settled into his natural role of the good cop. He tried to mitigate his colleague's verbal and physical excesses.

"You people think you can come here, break the laws of this country, and get away with murder!" Dettelbach yelled with ear-shattering volume directly into Viktor Erdos's face.

Viktor sat stoically erect and expressionless on that rickety chair I had gotten to know so well. Dettelbach's rants were always against "you people," and he directed his wrath not just against this one suspect but against the entirety of huddled masses who had found refuge from persecution and tyranny on these shores. Primarily that meant European Jews. I was sure if he had his druthers he would put us all on trial and convict us of for whatever crime he could pin on us.

In the case against Viktor Erdos, it was clear from his method of interrogation (mostly browbeating just short of physical assault) he was bent on extracting a confession. Dettelbach wanted to display that confession triumphantly before a press corps impatiently waiting for blood to flow. Judging from the sword of complicity he kept dangling over my head, he expected me to aid him in this scheme. He was sorely mistaken, though.

I am not an employee of the New York City Police Department, I told myself. *I am here only under duress.*

In a way I was glad to be part of the investigation, though. It gave me the opportunity to watch out for any deliberate distortions of Viktor Erdos's testimony the chief inspector might try to slip into the record. Not too far into the interrogation, I realized his knowledge of German was not as thorough as he had boasted. In fact it seemed a mere smattering of stock phrases he most likely picked up from his grandmother. His pronunciation was an admixture of American heartland twang and what sounded to me vaguely like traces of a Franconian dialect. It was atrocious to my Berlin ear.

Dettelbach frequently asked me to clarify Viktor Erdos's monotonous protestations of his innocence that were delivered in his own admixture of heavily accented, severely flawed English and Austrian German embroidered with the soft intonations of Eastern Hungarian Yiddish. Mulligan's Irish brogue was of little help in untangling this babel of idioms except for the salutary effect his periodic interventions had on tempering Dettelbach's hammering accusations. Caught in the middle of all this mayhem, I felt like a police officer directing traffic flow in a busy intersection while dodging bullets whizzing past me from all sides.

The purported confession of the accused, placed in evidence at the trial as proof positive of guilt, was obtained in a manner that made to my mind a mockery of the American justice system. "For what purpose did you set yourself up as a violin-playing panhandler outside the theater?" Dettelbach began his interrogation.

"I was probably wrong to expect this, but I was hoping the music would reach Stella's ear and attract her attention," Viktor replied.

"So you admit you did something wrong. It was wrong to seek her attention."

"No. I was wrong to expect she would hear the music with all the noise in the street."

"But you desperately sought her attention. What for?"

"I wanted to speak to her."

"What about?"

"A private matter."

"You don't say. Maybe a private vendetta? What kind of private matter does a low-down hobo have to discuss with an international movie star?"

Erdos wrapped himself in defiant silence. Dettelbach crossed his legs, lit a cigarette, and blew smoke rings into Erdos's face. Erdos turned his head to the side. His lips were firmly squeezed together. However, his hands were trembling from what I knew was nicotine withdrawal. This fact did not escape his tormenter's keen perception.

"If you were a bit more forthcoming, we could sit back and enjoy a nice smoke together," he taunted and waved a pack of Lucky Strikes.

"What would you have me do? Confess to something I didn't do for a cigarette?"

"Come on. We all know you did it. You can make this less painful for yourself and everybody. That includes your friend here, this poor, suffering translator. She doesn't look too happy. Just clear your conscience. Maybe you had a good reason to do what you did. Take my word for it. The DA will take any extenuating circumstances under advisement."

Dettelbach was right. I wasn't too happy. In fact my stomach was ready to give up its contents having to translate his tactics of obvious lies and deceptions. I was about to murmur under my breath, "Glauben Sie es nicht," when Viktor Erdos said in English "All right. I'll tell you what you want to know in exchange for a pack of cigarettes."

"Atta boy!" Dettelbach was jubilant. "Here. Take two packs. Take as many as you want. How about a cup of coffee?"

They made themselves comfortable, puffed away, and even laughed and complimented each other and the quality of American cigarettes.

I caught sight of Mulligan rolling his eyes and shaking his head. Dettelbach was an expert at exploiting his preys' weaknesses. I wondered if Erdos could really be so naïve to fall into the trap. Was he so desperate for a nicotine fix he would admit to anything? It was hard to believe, but then I was no smoker. In fact the air in the room was getting so dense it caused me enough distress breathing I asked to be excused.

"Sorry, my dear. We need you more than ever." Dettelbach was flying high with an exultant expression. Tapping his finger on the table, he added, "Every single word he says must be very clear and taken down. Justice will be done. It's in your interest as well."

Mulligan urged a cup of coffee and the last doughnut on me. "You'd better get some nourishment in you. This might go long into the night."

I nodded and thought about the long night I had just passed listening to Viktor Erdos talk about his friendship with a young, Viennese girl who had great ambition and called herself Stella Berger. Unless he was a straight-faced fibber, he could not possibly be guilty of her murder. Dettelbach did Mulligan one better. He had sandwiches and sodas brought in with a fresh pot of coffee. Like a good host entertaining his guests, he passed the goodies around among those present, which now included a stenographer. He was particularly attentive toward Viktor Erdos and made sure he didn't want for anything. He even urged him to relieve himself in the washroom and freshen up. The pressure had gone out of the room, and an atmosphere of almost calm had settled in. No doubt this was the calm before the storm. With a flick of a switch, Dettelbach had turned off the bully and released the charmer. This Jekyll and Hyde act didn't really deceive anyone, but he held all the cards. The rest of us just had to go along.

My mouth flew open, and my stomach gave me considerable trouble when I heard him say, "Whenever you are ready, Doc. Or should I call you 'Herr Doktor'? Either way, we can get started."

I was in a mood to swipe that saccharine grin right off his face. A glance at Viktor Erdos showed him receiving these accolades with the dignified reserve of a Viennese gentleman.

Dettelbach held the reins in a relaxed hand and left the direction of the confession up to the suspect. Of course this too was a deception and part of his game. The chief inspector never really lost control over the proceedings. He was so sure of himself and his method of interrogation. A few interspersed questions would suffice to elicit what he wanted to hear.

TWO

Viktor mentioned briefly his friendship with Stella Berger going back more than thirty years. Then he picked up where he had left off the night before. It was just on the eve of the war. I thought it would highlight his honor and show him in a favorable light to mention his role in tutoring and educating the young Stella, but Viktor Erdos was not out to present himself in a favorable light. He knew as well as I that the inspector had already convicted him of the crime. Erdos would not kowtow to him.

"Everything changed with the war," he began. "I didn't see Stella for several years. When we met again, she was well on her way to fulfilling her dream."

"What dream was that?" Dettelbach asked.

"To become a famous actress, of course."

"Where were you during the war?" Dettelbach changed the direction of questioning.

"In the army like everybody."

"Which army was that?"

Erdos looked up surprised. "The k. k. army, of course," he said partly in English.

"I don't suppose this has anything to do with the Ku Klux Klan?" Dettelbach laughed and slapped his thigh as if he had made a clever joke.

I wondered about the man's mental state. Of course he hadn't meant what he said. It was just a nuisance question to confound the suspect.

"It stands for *Königlich-Kaiserliche Armee*. That's the royal and imperial army of Austria-Hungary," I explained.

"Thank you, Fräulein Safran, for the lesson, but I knew that already. Just trying to keep things on the light side." His glowering look gave him the lie. Turning back to the subject, he assumed a more imperial tone. "Where did you serve? What unit? Maybe we were shooting at each other in Flanders."

"On the Eastern Front. Medical corps," Erdos replied. "I don't understand the relevance."

"Just curious," Dettelbach replied and contemplated his fastidiously groomed fingernails. His lips were puckered as if biting on a lemon. "One hears things here and there about you people and how you seem to always manage to get out of serving in combat."

I had never seen Viktor Erdos jumping out of his skin before. He shot up with a terrible howl, and only the broad table between them held Viktor back from falling on Dettelbach. Shouting across the barrier in two languages ensued. I didn't feel like transmitting the insults being fired across the line from either side. The secretary's mouth flew wide open, and she dropped her pad and pencil in her lap. She obviously expected an uncertain delay in the demand for her services.

However, the altercation ended as quickly as it had flared up. Mulligan intervened. "With all due respect, Frank, this is a murder investigation," he said. "Let's try to stick it."

Dettelbach smoothed back his oily hair with both hands. "OK. Let's get on with it." He sipped his coffee.

Mulligan took over for a while. "Tell us, Mr. Erdos, about your relationship with the victim after she rose to fame. I understand she was Germany's sweetheart. Kind of like Mary Pickford here in America."

"I'm not sure exactly how you mean," Erdos replied with a trace of disdain in his voice. After some reflection he added, "Critics held her in the highest esteem. Audiences adored her. If that's what you mean."

"I'm just trying to put her in the American context," Mulligan said.

From the corner of my eye, I could see Dettelbach. His fingernails still preoccupied him. His face glowed with a smirk.

"Anyway, let's get back to my original question," said Mulligan, and he produced his bright white handkerchief. "What was your relationship with the victim in Berlin?"

"Nothing much to tell. It was cordial. We were always good friends," Erdos replied coolly and distantly.

"So that's it? Let me help you out here," Mulligan said. This time he raised his voice a notch. He was obviously reaching the end of his patience. "This is what I think happened, and you tell me where I'm wrong. You knew her back in the old days in Vienna. She was just a child. You knew the family as friendly neighbors. All good. Then she grew up and went on to study acting. She wanted to become a star. She no longer had any time to waste with a...whatever you call yourself. Perhaps a poet who spends his time fiddling. Then came the war and you served on the front. When you came back, she was no longer in Vienna. She had gone on to better things. She was on the way to reaching the top of her chosen profession. Next thing you know, her name is in all the papers. Her pictures are on the cover of magazines. She's big in Berlin—a stage idol and the premier German actress. Now it occurs to you that you could turn your past acquaintance to your benefit. Sponge off her fame. As we say in New York, you thought you could become a moocher. Get a bit of the limelight to shine on you. So you go to Berlin. It's easy to find where she is appearing. Posters are all over town. You knock on the door of her dressing room. She doesn't remember you and has you thrown out. You don't give up so easily. You stalk her. You make yourself a nuisance. You are obsessed. She has to remember you. She calls the police. They send you back to Austria. Years later you see another chance here in New York. She still doesn't know who you are. You don't understand, and it's another blow to your bruised ego. You explode. All the rage over being rejected and the feeling of worthlessness seething inside you all those years boil over, and you kill her. Strangle her with your violin string."

Mulligan fell back in his chair. He dabbed his forehead and neck with the white handkerchief that had become crumpled in his hand while delivering his monologue with the precision of reading from a script. The stenographer was still scribbling long after he had ceased speaking. Even Dettelbach gave signs of being astounded by his colleague's summation.

Viktor Erdos was first to speak. He had been listening impassively to my translation with his steepled fingers pressed against his lips. Now he slowly lifted his chin, raised his eyebrows, and started clapping his hands in a slow, measured beat. "Bravo, Inspector! Brilliant! Outstanding! Your story might make an interesting fairy tale for a Hollywood movie. Unfortunately the scenario is far, far from the truth."

"Then enlighten us. What is the truth?" said Mulligan.

THREE

I was eager to hear the rest of the tale that had been prematurely cut off at dawn the day before, but I doubted he would ever tell those police officers the full story. He had already left out in this account most of the details he had related during the night. I was sure there was more to it all. I sensed some dark secret he was never going to reveal. For the time being, though, I was eager to lap up any bits and pieces he was willing to share.

"Well then," he began and drew on his cigarette. A coughing spell immediately interrupted him as his lungs discharged a swirling cloud of smoke. He cleared his throat.

"To begin we need to go back to the time immediately following the end of the war. As you know there were revolutions going on all over Europe in the wake of the war. Empires collapsed and monarchies toppled. These were exciting times. Following my discharge from the k. k. army, which was by then simply the Austrian army, I became a reporter for a provincial newspaper owned by a comrade of mine. We had served together for almost four years. After covering the revolutionary upheavals in Budapest and Vienna, I was given the choicest assignment of all—the new Soviet Republic of Bavaria in Munich."

Viktor Erdos spoke of these historical events from the standpoint of the bystander, the impartial observer. His role was that of a news reporter gathering facts about the events as they occurred. He was careful not to let on anything about the Marxist leanings he had professed to the night before.

The freshly minted journalist arrived in the Bavarian capital in February 1919. He plunged right into reporting the fast-changing events. He covered the revolutionary turmoil of the first Bavarian republic that ended with the assassination of Minister-President Kurt Eisner. A regime of workers' councils based on the Soviet model replaced him in a communist coup with the bloody repression of any opposition. Within a few weeks, there was a right-wing countercoup and more bloody retaliation. In his testimony Viktor Erdos touched only briefly on the historical events he had reported on in great detail for the *Klagenfurt Gazette*.

"One might think," he reflected, "that the turbulent events of those days—the demonstrations, riots in the streets, and political uncertainty—might overshadow and even dampen the cultural side of city life. This, however, was not the case. Music halls and nickelodeons overflowed with an entertainment-seeking public.

"The most renowned theater and concert performers played to sold-out houses. One name, while not yet shining in bright lights over the entrance, appeared ever more frequently on the lips of critics and theatergoers everywhere. An ingénue actress whose portrayal of Wedekind's Lulu was creating a stir. People would surrender their hard-earned money to see and hear the great Alexander Moissi, but they came away speaking of Stella Berger."

Among her admirers was Viktor Erdos. He sat entranced in the gallery night after night. How she had grown in her craft! He was not surprised. The little shoot he had nurtured had germinated and fully blossomed. Every moment the petite nineteen-year-old was on stage, an aura of magic swept the entire house. At the end the audience rose to its feet again and again and applauded with enthusiastic appreciation.

The last time Viktor had seen Stella was on the platform of the train station in Vienna. She had come with her father to see him off to war. She was fourteen and at a stage Germans call "Backfisch" and the English refer to as "half-baked."

She kept her promise to write, and they exchanged mostly postcards. His were written on the standard gray cardboard issued for frontline correspondence. Viktor wrote little about what he saw as a medic charged with retrieving the wounded to safety behind the lines under hails of gunfire. Afraid of frightening her, he mostly answered her admonishments to stay safe with assurances nothing was likely to happen to him.

Hers were picturesque cards from the various towns of upper and lower Austria where she said she had appeared in provincial theaters. This gave him an opportunity to follow her trail toward ever-growing success. She described how she advanced from a walk-on domestic in a white bonnet and white apron brandishing a feather duster to a speaking part as sidekick to the main character and eventually the primary role. Somewhere around the summer of 1917, their correspondence broke off. His cards came back unanswered. No forwarding address was available. He assumed her mind was on her career, and she had no time to write silly postcards to an old friend. War and the daily struggle for survival on the front certainly kept his mind preoccupied.

When his new journalistic career brought him to the Bavarian capital after the war, he was astounded to find her fast becoming the toast of the theater world. He hesitated to contact her, though. He did not want to appear like a ghost out of the past. For the time being, he was content to watch her nightly performances and take satisfaction in seeing his premonition that she was destined for greatness gain reality.

"In other words you were stalking her," Dettelbach broke in.

"No. She eventually came to me." Erdos turned away from the inspector with a disdainful look and addressed his account to the rest of those present.

By day he was dashing around town and keeping track of the ever-shifting events of governments being established and toppled and the personalities involved. He gathered material and was always on the lookout for an exclusive inside scoop for his daily report in the *Klagenfurt Gazette*. What soon gained him a wider reputation was not his reportage on the political scene but his impassioned observations of the Munich cultural scene.

His glowing review of the stage production of Wedekind's "Earth Spirit" with special mention of Stella's performance as Lulu was picked up by other news outlets and reprinted in the cultural pages of larger circulation dailies in Munich, Vienna, and Berlin.

The review came also to the attention of the theater people who passed it around with great delight and pride. Even though the press had generally been very positive, there was something different in Viktor's focus on Lulu to the exclusion of almost anything else.

"You seem to have a secret admirer," Alexander Moissi said to Stella. "You are leaving us lesser mortals in the dust."

Stella recognized the byline and immediately put in a call to the office of the *Klagenfurt Gazette*. Late at night on a Monday, the theater's day off, in early May 1919, Viktor Erdos was working furiously against a deadline on his report about the murder of the poet and inadvertent revolutionary Gustav Landauer at the hands of Freikorps thugs in Stadelheim Prison. A gentle knock on the door of the dingy room he rented at a pension in Schwabing intruded on his train of thought. Inclined at first to ignore the disturbance as noise from a neighboring room, he finally opened when the knocking persisted and a woman's voice called out his name.

She walked straight past him into the room without waiting to be invited. With a glance at his desk strewn with papers, she said, "You're burning the midnight oil. Not to worry. I won't keep you. I just wanted to see for myself that it is really you."

She turned toward him with a probing gaze. "It is really you," she concluded.

Before he could say anything, she reached up and pulled his face toward her with both hands. In an old, familiar gesture, she rubbed her nose against his.

"It really is you!" she repeated and burst into that gurgling laughter he had always loved about her. "And all this time I thought you were dead," she added gravely with a sudden change of demeanor. "I shall leave you to your work now. Let's meet tomorrow afternoon."

She designated a particular spot in the English Garden and was gone as quickly as a fairy in the night. He was dumbfounded and uncertain what to make of the tears that sparkled in her eyes like glycerin drops. Was she the consummate actress, or was she really flat-out happy to see him alive and well?

Any doubts he might have harbored were quickly dispersed the next day. They sat facing each other in a gazebo in a quiet, hidden grove in the English Garden. Fields decked out in shimmering tapestries of spring flowers surrounded them.

"I am so happy to see you," she called out and rushed up to him as he walked toward her. "Why were you hiding from me?" Stella said. "Here we are in the same town, and you don't even have the decency to make your presence known. That was very naughty of you."

"I didn't think you wanted to see me," he admitted sheepishly. "At least I wasn't sure. All that fame comes with different friends." He cast a glance at a woman sitting on a nearby bench who was seemingly engrossed in a book.

He hadn't paid much attention the night before. Stella's sudden appearance had overwhelmed his senses. Now he was sure that same woman had lingered in the semidarkness of the poorly lit hallway outside his door while Stella was in his room.

"Oh, I'm sorry," Stella said. "This is my friend Ulla. How rude of me not to introduce you."

Stella made the introductions, and Viktor and Ulla shook hands. She was almost a head taller than he. He noticed her wry smile and tried to smile back, but she quickly returned to her bench and stuck her nose in her book.

"Why would you think such a thing?" Stella inquired.

"Well, for one thing, you stopped writing. My cards came back without a forwarding address."

"The same happened on my end. My cards were being returned. It said addressee unknown or untraceable. I tried to get more information. My efforts were rebuffed with the usual excuse." With arms akimbo and assuming a bass voice, she mimicked the military manner of speaking. "There's a war going on, and the post cannot always be relied upon." When she pressed the matter further, she was told he was missing and presumed dead.

"Then it was all a misunderstanding. Perhaps the k. k. bureaucrats who ran the war from behind the lines lost track of me when I was transferred to another front. There seemed to have been a greater need for the removal of wounded from the frontlines on the Podolian Plain than in the Vojvodina." Bitter sarcasm filled his voice. For a moment his thoughts trailed back to the battlefields littered with grotesque, twisted shapes of the dead and wounded. The dead at least hadn't rent the air and his heart with agonized screams as did those he transported to the field hospital. He kept the vision to himself.

"But you are alive and unscathed, and all is well!" A triumphant tone rang in her voice as if the glorious k. k. army had come marching home from a victorious war.

All was indeed well. Viktor was happy. Stella was happy. She moved from triumph to triumph on her own battlefield: the stage. However, due to her personal charm and kindness, her path toward glory was not littered with wounded or dead opponents.

He couldn't take his eyes off her. For the past weeks, he had observed her on stage where she appeared in makeup and costume. She was Lulu then. The woman before him now was Stella—the princess grown into a goddess. Stella was undisguised and without makeup in a simple, cornflower blue spring dress. A red silk scarf imprinted with a pattern of Japanese flowers wrapped her head. Stella took off her big, dark sunglasses and sank her big, dark eyes into his.

"Don't you ever dare do that kind of nonsense again. Or else," she scolded him with a roguish smile.

Hearing her warble on in this familiar manner, he seized both her hands. "Küss d'Hand," he mumbled and pressing each hand to his lips.

She flittered quickly to other topics and filled him in on her itinerant stage career during the war years from engagements in provincial towns in Austria to Zurich. Her Lulu in *Earth Spirit* drew the particular attention of several important people. Among them was Max Reinhardt. He offered her a contract at the Deutsches Theater in Berlin to play Puck in a production of *A Midsummer Night's Dream*.

"I turned him down." She laughed. "Can you believe it? I turned down an offer from the great Reinhardt!"

No. He couldn't believe it. Although she was exactly the type, she explained, she didn't want to be typecast as a tomboy. She wanted to play the Fairy Queen, but that role was taken.

She rattled on and on. The upshot was she was going to Berlin as soon as her engagement in the Bavarian capital was over. It wasn't the Deutsches, but she just had to give it time. She was sure she would conquer the hearts of the Prussians as well.

Big words for a little person, Viktor thought. *As always.*

"You must come too," she urged.

"I have a job to do here."

"Can't you do it in Berlin just as well?" She pouted and put on her best kitten imitation.

Viktor had the impression she was completely oblivious to what had been going on outside her theater world. Was she aware of the demonstrations, riots, and bloody confrontations in the streets of Munich? Was she even aware of revolutionary upheavals in Berlin or Vienna? Did she even know the German and Austrian Kaisers were gone?

"Of course, I've heard of all this," she said. "Germany and Austria are now republics. You see I'm not as ignorant as you think." Then she shrugged as if to say it's all the same to me.

Viktor attempted to enlighten her about politics and how dangerous the situation still was especially for her. "You are a famous person now. Your name and picture appear daily in the newspapers and magazines. You could easily become a target of the rioting factions. Have you thought of getting an escort for when you leave the theater at night?"

She looked at him dumbfound. "Ulla is my escort."

"She could hardly fend off armed militants."

"She's pretty tall and well built."

Oh, Stella! She had no idea what she was talking about. "She couldn't protect you from those who mean you harm," he said. "I suggest I pick you up and accompany you home from now."

"You, my Xaverl?" She laughed.

He was taken aback. She had used the name the Viennese gave to a sweet but not very bright boy.

"What would you do if it actually came to such a debacle?" Stella asked.

He patted a bulge in his coat pocket from which something was sticking out.

"What have you got there?"

He partially took out a handgun and shielded it from open view.

She looked at him with wide eyes. "And you know how to use this thing?"

"I was in a war for four years. Remember?" His pride was hurt, but he wrote her reaction off to her naïveté.

"I thought you drove an ambulance and took care of the wounded."

"It was still in a war zone, and we came under fire all the time."

When Viktor was mustered out, he reported his Roth-Steyr M07, a self-loading pistol and the pride of the Austro-Hungarian army, as lost. Armed bands of militants who refused to accept the outcome of the war were roaming the countryside and terrorizing the inhabitants. They were looking for scapegoats—leftists they accused of having undermined the war effort. Among their targets were Jews of any persuasion. In view of this situation, Viktor decided it was best to have a weapon. He had become a good shooter and had actually enjoyed that part of the military training. It gave him a sense of being less vulnerable.

FOUR

Stella moved to Berlin in September 1919 to begin an engagement at a small theater for the fall season. Her entrance into the capital of the newly formed German Republic was by no means as glorious as she had imagined, but she was not one to despair. She got to work with an iron will.

Viktor Erdos became part of Stella Berger's entourage. He persuaded the publisher of the *Klagenfurt Gazette* of the necessity of having a correspondent in the place where history was being made, and he forthwith took up residence in Berlin.

Stella's entourage consisted of two young men who served as her private audience. She bounced her dialogues off them. They were students who were unable to find their way back into the academic world after the war. Their source of income was not clear. Somewhere there seemed to be a father from whom flowed unlimited means.

Then there was Ulla whose icy acquaintance Viktor had already made back in the English Garden in Munich. She was introduced to him as the Swiss woman but she was actually German by birth. Ulla Scholz was her full name, and her official title was private secretary, her amanuensis, as Stella put it. Viktor had to laugh. This was quite pretentious for a nineteen-year-old ingénue, but it was also typical of Stella. Seeing Ulla hover over her employer while taking care of everyday minutiae with an admittedly competent hand, Viktor said he would have dubbed her a factotum.

How and where Viktor Erdos was to fit into this circle of intimates was not clear. He had no particular function, except that Stella wanted him near for conversation and as her "father confessor" to whom she could pour her heart out. This pouring out of the heart never really happened, though. Stella was so focused on her work, it came at the exclusion of anything else. She had no mind for backstage intrigues and personal rankling. If this was going on among the divas and prima donnas of either sex, she kept out of it. She seemed to have no mind for anything outside her work, and that included love. As far as Viktor was aware, she was completely celibate and routinely turned down the advances of her most irresistible matinee idol male colleagues. Acting out great and often tragic loves on stage seemed to demand the full measure of her passion.

"I experience love all the time. I know what it feels like to be in love. It's enough to make you shy away from it," she would say. "Love and loss. Love and loss. It's always the same. It drains my body and soul." She pooh-poohed any hint that real-life love didn't always end in tragedy.

Viktor Erdos was not a suitor, a tutor, or a mentor. He was what he had always been to her—a friend. As her fame broadened, so did the circle of hangers-on and toadies. They gathered around her like flies attracted to light. She was becoming quite the diva.

When she first came to Berlin, she was still eager to explore the famed nightlife of the great city. He would accompany her with Ulla and the students inevitably in tow to late-night cabaret performances. The "Taubenschlag" in an abandoned factory yard near Bahnhof Friedrichstrasse was a favorite Saturday night haunt. It gave her a chance to unwind, soak up the local culture, and enjoy the talent after an exhausting performance on stage. Whenever they could manage the time (he was still a working reporter), they would meet at a coffeehouse during the day. She was always solicitous of his opinions about the theater world and her progress, which he followed by faithfully attending her performances.

Their lives coursed along a relatively unencumbered trajectory. They cut a thin swath through a world of perpetual political turmoil and government crises. They saw a plummeting economy and monetary inflation stretching into the stratosphere, which left masses of people in abject misery. Many were destitute and plagued with hunger and disease. Stella and Viktor were lucky to have work. While the money they earned wasn't worth the paper it was printed on, their professional connections tied them over the worst of it.

Viktor Erdos advanced from Berlin correspondent for a provincial Austrian newspaper to syndicated columnists. He became a respected observer of the political and cultural scene. His political analyses aside, he was not reticent to use his pulpit to make himself the foremost promoter of the career of a rising star on the Berlin stage named Stella Berger.

This was a relatively calm, gratifying period in Viktor's life. Despite almost unabated government crises, which gave him something to write about, the economy of the Republic improved markedly from 1924 onward. The currency reform eliminated the most grotesque inflation wherein a loaf of bread could only be had for a barrow of banknotes.

Viktor had acquired a typewriter by then, and this relieved him of using longhand to produce his reports. One night he was typing out with two agile forefingers the details of the Dawes Plan that was to regulate German reparations payments, when a knock on the door of his room in yet another garret broke his concentration. This one was on Rosenstrasse in Berlin Mitte. It was a knock that was to shatter the life he had built for himself.

Ten years had elapsed since he had last seen Alexander Levary. Without a sign of life and with no way of finding out what had become of him, he had presumed he might not have survived the war. Yet the distinctive impatience of the drumming on his door made him jump up and almost overturn the lamp on his desk. There was an imperious assertion of an intrinsic right to being admitted contained in the knock. This could be none other than his long-lost friend who made it a habit of weaving in and out of his life at inopportune moments. The biblical parable of the snake in paradise shot through his mind.

Viktor Erdos paused. His wistful gaze was lost on some point on the green wall of the police interrogation room behind which a struggle seemed to take place that only he perceived. With the exception of Dettelbach, everyone in the room receded into a mesmerized silence.

"All right now!" Dettelbach thundered impatiently. "We don't need all the pithy details of this sentimental reunion between two old school friends. You are obviously speaking of the victim's husband."

"Why don't we call it a day?" Mulligan suggested. "Our poor stenographer must be suffering from writer's cramps."

She heaved a grateful sigh. She put down her pen and rubbed her sore hands together as if in prayer.

I too had reached the point of exhaustion. Hours of racking my brain for the appropriate American idiom to reflect Erdos's often arcane and turgid Austrian German induced a pulsing headache and an irresistible desire for sleep. I wanted to slip into a deep sleep that lasted until the end of all of this, including the war in Europe. Some of Erdos's expressions were so unfamiliar I could only guess at their meanings. He seemed to think, "Why say something in simple, straightforward terms when you can beat around the bush and couch your meaning in pompous, highfalutin phraseologies?"

What might have been commonplace on the banks of the Danube was often foreign to the lingua franca spoken along the Spree of my youth. Nevertheless I was grateful to be of service. I didn't necessarily care about serving New York's finest, who surely had access to other translators, but I was glad to be there for Viktor Erdos. I had come to see him as something of a fellow wayfarer lost in time and place. The more I got to know about him, the more I saw him as a misfit who had lost his bearings in this world and had never been able to find them again.

FIVE

A dim twilight cast an opaque shroud over the sagging city sky. Unfortunately this didn't bring much cooling relief. The scorching furnace engulfing the subway tunnels seared my skin and brain as I cut a meandering path through the crowd in search of the uptown train. All the while the image of Viktor Erdos haunted me. I saw him handcuffed with his gaze wistfully turned upward as he was callously shoved into a padded wagon for the ride to "the Tombs" downtown.

Pressed into a corner seat on the crowded subway train, my mind went over parts of the testimony he had given that day. I knew he had wisely left out many details about his journalistic activities, especially as far as his sympathies for the revolutionaries in Munich and Berlin were concerned. The slightest hint of communist leanings would be welcome grist for Dettelbach's mill.

Something had happened in Berlin he was reluctant to speak about, something that had caused his estrangement from Stella Berger. No doubt it had something or everything to do with yet another return of Alexander Levary. At the same time, I doubted he would ever reveal the true nature of his relationship with the old school friend to the New York City police.

My thoughts wandered to the present Berlin under Nazi rule where my grandmother was still living under increasingly uncertain and oppressive conditions. Intimations of doom crushed my spirit and soul. My aunt's few letters contained only sparse details and contained no mention of the regime or the war. Because she had to be mindful of the censors, vague codes and family expressions only a member of the inner circle would understand couched any hints about their circumstances. Still distraught and in a daze, I mounted the brownstone steps to my rooming house with a sluggish step. Even before I could stick the key in the lock, the door flung open. I was face-to-face with the housemother, Mrs. Weber surrounded by a flock of chattering, excited, young women.

"What kind of home do you think I am running here?" she barked. Her indignation bubbled over like boiling milk on a stove.

"The telephone has been ringing off the hook all day," she informed me. Press members have been camped out in the street all day."

I took a glance back. If there were reporters out there all day, they had gone home by now. The only people following me were my faithful police tails whom I had learned to ignore. Nobody had accosted me on the way here.

When she moved away from the door so I could enter the vestibule, I asked her politely if there were any messages.

"A Tillie Werther called twice from California" she said. "She sounded very agitated, and was hard to understand."

How typical of my mother to identify herself by her stage name and not as my mother, I thought.

"Then there was a female who said she was your lab partner. She wanted to know if you were dropping the course. How should I know?" Mrs. Weber added indignantly.

My chemistry professor had the same question. Then a Mr. Wolff called several times, and he had even had the audacity to show up at the pension's front door. She asserted endlessly that she was running a reputable boarding house strictly reserved for young, working women with impeccable character. I was in no condition or mood to deal with any of this. I didn't want to think about the tarnished good name of Mrs. Weber's establishment or of Mr. Wolff. All I wanted was take a bath and crawl into bed for a long, long sleep.

"Here's your mail." Mrs. Weber waved a bright blue airmail envelope. "It's from over there," she declared. She jerked her head in some indistinct direction that presumably meant the other side of the Atlantic.

She was also from "over there"–from Germany. But she had come to America twenty years earlier at the end of the Great War. She was an immigrant and not a refugee. As she made clear, her kind of people were the right kind of people and clearly not from my sort of people.

In my room I ripped open the envelope and read my aunt's letter over and over. I tried to read between the lines and search for hidden clues. All I could gather was that the situation was getting worse. The noose was tightening. Arbitrary rules were passed daily to make their lives unbearable. My heart sank. My worst fears were coming true. What would become of my Omi? My mind raced over what we should have done. Why didn't we force her to leave? Then again, how would we have forced her? My parents had been targets of the storm troopers from the onset of the regime. Most other family members had dispersed to the far corner of the Earth. They had landed wherever they could find a foothold. The octogenarian matriarch would not budge. No. She would not give the usurpers the satisfaction of dislodging her. Besides, what could they do to an elderly woman whose days were numbered? she kept saying.

What could they do to an elderly woman? That was what I was asking myself as well. Yes. They could unsettle her daily existence and cause her discomfort. They had evicted her from the villa in Charlottenburg and forced her into cramped, inadequate quarters in a *Judenhaus* in the inner city. They had rationed the food and limited buying hours to one day a week. My Omi would meet all this valiantly and stoically. I was sure of it. What else could they possibly do to her? Crush her spirit? Never. The note I found appended to my aunt's letter made me smile and cry all at once.

"My dearest child, despite what your aunt writes in this letter, never permit your spirit to sag. Be assured I have found much solace of late in reading the old fairy tales. Remember Little Red Riding Hood? The Big Bad Wolf might eat Grandma, but the spirited little girl destroyed him. You are always in my thoughts and prayers. Your loving Omi."

It was funny she should bring up the Big Bad Wolf. Had I myself let a wolf deceive and lead me astray? *What a silly thought.* Dealing with

Curtis Wolff would have to wait for another time. Another session with Viktor Erdos at the police station was scheduled for the morning. It might be the last. Then I would hopefully be free to tend to straightening out my life and going on with my studies. I collapsed on the bed in my room at the end of the hallway. I curled up in a tight fetal position. *I will have to find a different place to live.* It was the last thought I had before I slipped into a dreamless slumber.

Early the next morning, before Mrs. Weber started patrolling the floors, I snuck into the lone common bathroom for a quick full-body cleansing. If she found me out, I was likely to get expelled on the spot. Violation of the rule about only ten minutes of tub time on weekends was a capital offense. *Let her expel me,* I thought. I was not about to face another sweltering session in close quarters with my body still reeking from a concoction of excretions from the day before. My hope the other parties might have the same consideration was soon dashed.

SIX

Dettelbach opened the second day of the interrogation with a sharp, "OK. Let's cut to the chase." He said he would no longer tolerate long-winded beating around the bush with sob stories of war and reunions. (I suspected he had prepared this speech with the help of a diction-ary.) Heartwarming as they might be, Erdos should reserve them for the memoirs he would have ample time in prison to write. Here such details were beside the point.

"Let's get on to Berlin!" he shouted as if coaching a sports team in a championship game or spearheading a political campaign. What hap-pened there, he surmised, was more likely to get to the crux of the mat-ter and establish the all-important motive.

"So you followed her to Berlin," Mulligan interjected.

Dettelbach fortified himself with a fresh doughnut and coffee, which the stenographer had brought in. Erdos puffed with obvious relish on the cigarette Mulligan had offered him from a pack placed like bait in front of him on the table. In fact the murder suspect looked rather refreshed that morning. He shot me a bright, familiar glance.

Must have gotten a good night's rest at the Tombs, I thought.

What we had learned so far was that Stella Berger did not take Berlin by storm. The admiration from critics and audiences she had enjoyed in the Bavarian metropolis did not automatically guarantee equal success in the German capital. After all, the provincial town of Munich could

150

hardly compare to Berlin. The tastes and predilections of Bavarians and Prussians were worlds apart.

So once again Stella had to cut her teeth on a variety of secondary roles on lesser stages around the city. The stages were definitely lesser than the Deutsches Theater—the holy grail of the acting world ruled over by the legendary, formidable Max Reinhardt. Her unshakeable faith in her talent and destiny, however, winged her steps from rung to rung on the ladder leading her to the top. In rare moments of dismay and gloom, she sought succor from Viktor Erdos. Neither Ulla nor the toadies around her could take the place of the man who was her first teacher in elocution—the man who never sought anything for himself and was always self-effacing in his devotion.

Fame, in the person of Max Reinhardt, ineluctably tapped Stella on the shoulder. The great superintendent whose offer back in Zurich she had turned down had been closely following her progress. Now, he decided, her time had come. She had matured enough for the Deutsches. Tendered on the emblematic silver platter was Ophelia, opposite matinee idol Franz Lederer's Hamlet. Her success was instantaneous. Audiences gushed with enthusiasm. Critics spilled cascades of ink in praise of the German Sarah Bernhardt. Her rise to stardom was, in the hyperbolic trade lingo, meteoric. Viktor Erdos found himself in the shadow of her fame overnight. As she moved from success to success on stage and later in film, she refused to hear about any change in their relationship.

"I'm still the same person and friend," she assured him.

But how could their relationship have remained the same?

As I grappled with rendering Erdos's florid speech patterns into more down-to-earth English, I noticed Dettelbach fumbling with his cigarette lighter. He snapped it open and shut with increasing ferocity until at last he smashed his fist on the table and turned to me.

"Fräulein Safran!" he thundered, making me feel somehow at fault. "Tell Herr Erdos or Erdreich or whatever his real name is to cut the crap."

I tried to keep my composure and passed on the message in a somewhat altered form. "Bitte fassen Sie sich kurz."

"Yes. Cut it short. That's putting it politely." Then Dettelbach bellowed in his best German, "Sparen Sie uns den Scheißdreck."

Nothing escaped the keen nose and ears of that bloodhound. I couldn't help but chuckle, however. I was glad for the comic relief he had inadvertently provided. I gleefully whispered the translation of the inspector's remark into Mulligan's ear and instructed the stenographer on how to spell it.

"No need to enter this into the record." Dettelbach waved his hand with a sour expression. "Let's get back to where we left off yesterday."

So back we went to our grim task. Dettelbach was bent on extracting a statement from the suspect that would be incriminating enough to take the case to the district attorney of the borough of Manhattan.

"What was your relationship with the deceased's husband? You said Alexander Levary came to visit you. When exactly did this visit take place? And what was the reason for his visit? Circumstances please without sentimentalities! Let's cut to the chase."

Apparently this was a favorite expression of his. Viktor Erdos turned his wistful gaze toward me, and for a brief moment our eyes remained locked in silent understanding. I nodded imperceptibly. I would not betray him.

"Fräulein Safran, we expect a faithful rendition of the suspect's testimony," Dettelbach proclaimed suddenly. "No editorializing please!"

Had he noticed something? His keen eye was likely to catch even the most imperceptible nod. I assured him I was doing my best. At this point I did not want to risk being taken off the case. I had waded waist-deep into this swamp and had become too emotionally immersed to let go now. On a more mundane consideration, the police department did reimburse me for my time and effort. It was a small sum but a much-needed padding of my sagging finances. So on we went.

Viktor Erdos followed Dettelbach's dictate and made every effort to cut to the chase. What he left us with was a bare-bones story of two friends separated by war. He used none of the high-flying, baroque verbal flourishes he was capable of chiseling with his poet's hand.

Viktor and Sender hadn't seen each other since September 1914. They were both mobilized about the same time and had time only for a brief good-bye. While still in basic training, they wrote to each other a few times. When their respective regiments were sent off to places unknown along the expansive Eastern Front, they lost contact. At war's end, each believed the other dead.

Five years went by. There had been no sign of life from Sender until that midnight knock on the door. Stella's career was taking off just then. Viktor was an established news correspondent. Sender's sudden, unexpected appearance was like a resurrection. He was haggard and thin like a skeleton and limping, but seemed otherwise healthy.

The story of where he had been keeping himself changed frequently. Sometimes it was a stay in an Austrian military hospital. Other times it was an isolated sanatorium in the Alps to tend to slow-healing war injuries or a protracted incarceration in a Siberian prisoner of war camp where he stayed on after his release since he had no means of making his way home. Wherever he was in all this time, he was now restored to health and in Berlin.

His prewar prospect of an assistantship with Max Reinhardt, if indeed it had actually existed, had fallen through. The great director looked hurriedly at him when Sender waylaid him in the theater lobby. He knew nothing about a promise from almost fifteen years before. Sender was incensed.

"That's the way it goes," Sender said. "You drop out of sight to serve the fatherland, and you cease to exist."

Viktor stayed neutral. He could see Sender was not a little bitter and irrational. He was desperate and hungry. He offered him a glass of Scotch and a cigarette. He eagerly consumed both.

Sender told him he hung about the theater for several days trying to construe a scheme to gain a private interview with the overlord of thespians. All he needed was a chance to explain his circumstances and make the director appreciate that the powers-that-be had taken charge of his life. He was sure any patriotic citizen would understand. He wanted to explain that all the horrors of war and the hardships of imprisonment in a merciless climate far from civilization had done nothing to make him doubt his ultimate calling for the theater.

Whatever Sender had actually endured in those years, it didn't make a dent in his sense of self-importance or his tendency to lay it on thick. Viktor, nevertheless, felt sorry to see his old friend in a truly distressed state. For old times' sake and for their long-standing friendship, he promised to do everything for him he could within his limited means.

"There is one thing you can do for me." Sender's voice suddenly changed to the sotto voce of a *souffleur*. By the light of the midnight oil, his dark eyes took on a hypnotic glow.

"Yes. There's something you can do for me," he repeated.

A pregnant pause followed. Viktor looked up, alarmed. The smirk on Sender's face portended what was coming.

"Introduce me to Stella Berger."

Viktor puffed on his cigarette. His eyes followed the smoke rings circling his desk lamp. Here was the rub. There was always a rub where Alexander Levary was concerned. Something had to be in it for him if he paid a midnight visit to an old friend.

"And you think I can do that?" he said.

"I remembered the name when I saw it on life-size posters at the theater," Sender went on. "Her picture shines from every *Litfass* column in this city. She has grown since Vienna. I only saw her briefly then, but I remember a little girl with fiery eyes. You kept her from me then and maybe with good reason. I've got to hand it to you. You were absolutely right about her. You recognized her potential."

"Her talent," Viktor cut in. "I saw her talent."

"Yes. Whatever. Her talent. I'm sure she must have that too. Then I saw your byline in a newspaper column. I put two and two together. You had to be in Berlin. Wasn't so difficult to track you down from there, comrade. So here I am."

"And what exactly is it you expect to get out of such an introduction?" Viktor gave him a cold stare. "A conduit to Reinhardt?"

"Something like that did cross my mind I must admit. But it seems she's a person worth knowing in her own right."

Viktor made the introduction. Alexander Levary became a regular at Stella's villa in Dahlem. He made himself the life of the party. His talent for telling tall tales found an appreciative echo among the pleasure seekers who flocked there. When he wasn't tapping out the latest steps on the dance floor, he banged out popular ragtime and jazz tunes on the piano. He had picked them up somewhere, and it surely was not in the frozen Siberian tundra. The lilting tones of Viktor's violin were no match.

All around him Alexander Levary (Sasha, as he was now called) exuded an eroticism and dissoluteness that inebriated men and women alike. Word got out about licentious revelries at Stella's Dahlem villa—bacchanalia more lavish and lascivious than in old Rome. The tabloids reveled in stories about orgies and debauchery obtained from anonymous insider sources.

Alexander Levary never hit it off with Reinhardt. Sender reminded Viktor on more than one occasion, however, he got something even better. He got Stella Berger. He became her manager, publicist, and all-around spokesperson. When she broke into movies, he directed most of her films at the UFA studios. All this happened over Viktor's head and behind his back. For the first time, Stella was making major life decisions without consulting him beforehand.

Viktor Erdos began staying away. He withdrew into himself. He frequently read his poetry at the Taubenschlag where he found an audience appreciative of any kind of wallowing in human misery. He wrote of rivers of bitter gall engulfing his dejected soul and of the poet hitched to a rickety tumbril carting the wretched and debased to unmarked graves. This was his most productive poetic period.

One night he spotted Stella. She sat alone in a corner watching him intently. He had just finished reading a poem that spoke of fame casting its shadow over love.

"But we are not lovers," Stella said when he sat down next to her.

"No. Not in the traditional sense."

"Did you ever want to sleep with me?"

"No. You were always sacred to me."

She laughed out loud. She seized his head with both hands and shook it. "Xaverl. Xaverl. My dear, wonderful, inimitable Xaverl! Only you could say something like that."

He wriggled free and leaned back.

"Are you sleeping with Sender?" he inquired.

"With whom? Oh, you mean Sasha?"

"Yes. Sasha. Alexander. Whatever he calls himself now."

"I thought you were friends. You don't seem to like him very much."

"It's much more complicated than that."

A long silence ensued between them. Her sparkling, dark eyes rested on his face with a look of probing curiosity. With her hand against her cheek, she tilted her head and nodded almost imperceptibly. He was bewildered. For her nothing seemed to have changed. The intimacy and camaraderie that had existed between them seemed unbroken.

"You didn't answer my question," he whispered softly.

She threw her head back indignantly. "The answer is no. He is useful to me. He's fun to be with and have around. My guests appreciate his wit and charm."

"In contrast to me."

She patted his hand. "You will always be my Xaverl. I wouldn't want to change the slightest thing about you."

In the end he was helpless to withstand her luring call to return to her circle. What role he was to play there was unclear to him, but she assured him there would no role-playing. He should just be himself— her oldest and most trusted friend.

"If all was so honky-dory, why did Stella Berger sever her relationship with you?" Dettelbach interjected.

"The Nazi thugs started to harass her. They attended the theater where she appeared and the movie houses where her films were playing. They disrupted the performances with rowdy behavior and tried to bar people from attending. She needed to put an end to that."

"What does that have to do with anything? Makes no sense," said Dettelbach. "The question at hand is: What was the reason for your falling out with the deceased? Did you have a fight? An argument?"

"Yes. We argued. I would say we had a heated discussion."

"What was the nature of this argument?"

Viktor hesitated. "A private matter," he said. "It had to do with Levary."

"You were jealous and then she showed you the door? She threw you out."

"You could put it that way. We parted on not the best of terms. I was willing to apologize and make it up to her after a cooling-off period. But then she married Levary. I never understood why she would do that."

"What did you do then?"

"I returned to Vienna. I had an offer to work for a newspaper there."

"A Zionist propaganda newspaper I understand."

"I don't know what source you are looking at. It was a legitimate paper that advocated the return of the Jews to Palestine."

"What was the name of the editor?"

"Oskar Rosenfeld."

"A Zionist agitator. You were a travel correspondent, and you visited Palestine several times on Zionist missions. Is that so?"

"Yes. I was to report on conditions in the Holy Land and prospects for emigration and settlement. What does this have to do with anything?"

Dettelbach waved his hand and kept flipping through the papers. "Why didn't you stay in Palestine? Isn't that where all Jews want to return? Instead you came here to America."

"Not all Jews."

"Why didn't you stay?"

Erdos started to speak but broke off. He raised his hands and shook his head.

"I'll tell you why you preferred to come here to America. Stella Berger wasn't in Palestine. You knew that. You came here looking for a chance to waylay her and take your revenge on her."

"Absolutely not!" Viktor Erdos lost his composure. His voice filled the small room with thunderous protest. "I came here as a refugee Austrian citizen after the Anschluss in 1938. Stella Berger was in England at that time. How could I have been following her to New York?"

"You were informed about her whereabouts then? You kept track of her every movement. Didn't you?"

"I read the papers. Her name appeared on occasion as any famous person's would. Her anti-Nazi activities especially made the headlines from time to time in the Western press."

"Let's cut to the chase!" Dettelbach was visibly impatient. "Let me lay out the scenario for you. You made your way to New York, and you waited patiently. With the war in Europe intensifying, you figured England wouldn't hold out forever against the Blitz. You calculated she had to turn up in New York sooner or later. Then your wish came true. You found yourself together with the subject of your obsession in New York. The woman whom you could never forgive for having scorned you and who married your rival was coming to Broadway. You set yourself up outside the theater playing your schmaltzy tunes to attract her attention, but she paid no heed to a wretched street musician. Her engagement was limited and nearing its end. You became desperate. You had to act. You had to do something before she would disappear from your sight again. Maybe she would go to Hollywood and be far out of your reach. Then a gift from heaven fell into your lap. You seized the opportunity our good-hearted ticket vendor here provided. You entered the star's dressing room. You knew her habits and calculated she would be alone after the performance, and you strangled her with a violin string." Dettelbach was screaming this at the top of his lungs.

Viktor Erdos just shook his head. He was close to tears but made no attempt to refute the accusation.

"You had the motive, and you had the opportunity. You are the murderer!" Dettelbach rose and shuffled the papers in front of him into a neat pile. He turned to his partner. "We are done here, Mulligan. Case closed. Book him for the murder of Stella Berger."

SEVEN

"We were all more than a little puzzled over the marriage." My mother recollected the incident when I spoke with her on the phone that evening. "Sasha Levary! He was well known around town for his...well, for being someone from the left side. Not the political left, if you know what I mean."

I knew perfectly well what she meant. Despite her bohemian and somewhat unconventional lifestyle, she had never quite gotten over the prissiness of her bourgeois upbringing when it came to sexual matters. This was reflected in the expression she used—*von der linken Seite*, a German euphemism for homosexual.

"Did you know Alexander Levary? Did you ever meet him?" I already knew about the nature of the relationship between Viktor and Sender, but I was curious to hear the impression of someone who was there but still an outside observer.

"Oh yes. On several occasions. He came to the Taubenschlag once or twice with Stella. She was no longer a regular then, but we were friendly enough for her to invite us to the villa. You should have seen the place. Fabulous."

"Yes. I've heard about it, but..."

"Your father and I were somewhat taken aback about what was going on there and eventually stopped attending. We had our own circle."

"Yes. What kind of things were going on there?"

159

"Well, there was wild dancing. Exotic almost. There was music I had never heard before. Sort of jungle type stuff. Just drumbeats without a real melody. Sasha was always at the center and acting in the most uninhibited, lewd manner. His limp from a war wound didn't hold him back. Then there was the drinking. Not wine or beer but hard liquor—schnapps, Scotch, and vodka mixed with who knows what. The worst was the hashish they passed around. Made people do crazy things. The Taubenschlag was a monastery by comparison."

"What about Stella? Where was she while this was going on?"

"Oh, Stella was there but completely clean. She wasn't even into nicotine. I never saw so much as a cigarette in her mouth. For Stella I would put my hand in the fire. She didn't drink or sniff. Neither did her friend Xaverl. I guarantee it."

"His name is actually Viktor. What were Stella and Viktor doing then? If she disapproved, why did she tolerate this kind of behavior in her house?"

"That's what we couldn't understand. The two of them stayed on the margins while the guests engaged in...well, I needn't go into the details. Suffice it to say the word "orgy" is no exaggeration. What hold Sasha had over her is still a mystery. There was also this tall woman. I've forgotten her name."

"Ulla."

"Yes. Ulla. You are better informed than I. Anyway, this woman never left Stella's side. It was as if they were attached at the hip. She hovered over her like a protecting angel. Maybe she was trying to shield her from the evil raging around her."

"How did this Ulla take Stella's marriage to Levary?"

"That I wouldn't know. We weren't all that close, and we had lost contact by then. The scandal with the Nazis was the last straw. We had to save our own skins. As you know those thugs roughed up your father on several occasions."

"Yes. I've heard it all." Knowing my mother's tendency for going off on tangents with personal stories, I tried to keep the focus on Stella. She did anyway.

"You shouldn't be so dismissive of what we had to go through." I could see her sulking face before me. Then she quickly skipped to the real reason she had called. "I'm sorry we won't be able to come to New York. We would like to be there with you when you have to testify at the trial."

"That trial could be years away," I said. "But what's your news? I can feel you have something you're dying to tell me."

"Well, the Safran Duo has signed with the film industry for a spy movie. No major roles, but I am to play a singer with your father at the piano. We'll be in a scene set in an Austrian wine cellar populated by Nazi types. Just the way Hollywood pictures it. We have already been promised a similar gig in a movie about the French Resistance. In that I will exchange the dirndl for a leather outfit. Once the money starts rolling in, we'll be able to set up a regular allowance for you."

"That's wonderful. I'm very happy for you. This might turn out to be a whole new career for the two of you."

"Indeed. There's an entire industry of war movies. They always need singers and musicians for creating *couleur locale*. The possibilities are endless as long as the war goes on." She broke off suddenly, and I heard her sobbing at the other end of the line. "To think," she said between sniffles. "To think we should be making money off that horrible war while our dear mama, your Omi is still..." We both burst into tears. "Maybe with the money..."

My mother didn't finish the thought. She knew as well as I did it was too late. Emigration for Jews from Germany had been halted. Those still there were trapped. No amount of money could buy them out.

I told her about the latest letter from her sister and her mother's addendum about the Big Bad Wolf. Clara Wertheim was the matriarch of the art house Wertheims, and she was not to be cowed by even adverse circumstances.

"She has no illusions about what the outcome will be," I said. "She wants us to be strong. Even if it is too late for her to be spared the worst, we must pray and fight within our means for the eventual defeat of this scourge. As Stella did. Your appearance in those war movies is probably the best you can do to inform the public."

"What a mature young lady you have become," my mother said in a still-quavering voice.

I believe this was the first time she expressed some pride in me.

"But now we have to hang up. This call is getting much too expensive," I said, intent on not letting this exchange blossom into a cross-country melodrama.

"You are always the practical one," she said. "Always the voice of reason."

"Steeled in the cauldron of life," I said.

I reminded her she wasn't a big movie star yet. We still had to count our nickels and dimes. Then I quickly pressed down on the cradle of the telephone before she could go off on another tangent.

The seismic events that had shaken the ground beneath the path I had set for myself still left me in a state of daze. I tried to regain my bearing and get back into a daily study routine. Even while my eyes peered into the microscope, however, I saw a ceaseless parade of the cast of characters in the melodrama of love and deceit into which I had inadvertently been drawn—Curtis Wolff, my dubious lover; Alexander Levary, the husband and shady agent variously named Sender or Sasha; Viktor Erdos, the suspect, failed violinist and self-described poet, and loyal friend; and Stella Berger, the goddess and victim of an untimely, violent death. They held sway over all my thoughts. They never left me completely, but in time they gave me enough space to finish my course with a good enough grade to look forward to continuing my studies in the fall semester.

August brought some relief from the oppressive heat. Soothing showers and even thunderstorms were a welcome break. By early September, with regular subventions from my parents, I was able to move out of Mrs. Weber's pension for young, unmarried girls of impeccable character and repute and into a small studio downtown. It was small but mine. I was in heaven. My furnishings were sparse. Besides the bare necessities of a bed and a dresser, I acquired a small desk with a chair and a bookshelf from Goodwill.

On top of the shelf I placed the unopened violin case. Lying in bed I often rested my eyes on it and wondered about the journey it had taken from its place of origin in the Carpathian Mountains. Viktor Erdos had beguiled me with the lilting sounds he coaxed out of it in the street, but I had never dared open the case since he had entrusted it to me. I feared it might turn out to be a Pandora's Box. If I opened it, all sorts of trouble might spill out. Then again, it was hard to imagine there could be more trouble than had already been spilled. I took the case down one night and opened it with a fluttering heart. Even to my unschooled eyes, it was clear I held in my hands an instrument of shining exquisiteness. I lifted it with both hands above my head like a sacred object. On the bottom was etched "Lazar Erdreich, Maître Luthier." I wondered what had become of this master violin maker. Was he still alive? What was his fate and that of his other sons? Hungary was not in the war, but it was allied with Germany. The lives of the Jews were certainly affected.

My other haven in this interim period was the medical section of the New York Public Library. I hit the books, buried myself in texts on anatomy, physiology, neurology, the lot.

Then there was the matter of Curtis Wolff. He had persistently turned up or waylaid me in various places. I had consistently brushed him off. Living now in his neighborhood, though, I could no longer avoid him. I agreed to meet a few times at a café around the corner from Waverly Place where I lived. We talked and came to an agreement to cool it for a while. After the trial we would reevaluate our feelings.

"I'm going to offer my services to defend Viktor," Curtis said in parting.

"But you are not a lawyer yet."

"You don't even have to be a lawyer. Anybody can act as defense counsel. Besides I don't think many American defense attorneys will want to put their reputations on the line and rush to take on the task of defending a penniless immigrant."

On this point he was proven wrong. Some of the heaviest legal guns in America threw their hats into the ring. Curtis would have to settle for assistant counsel at best. I pointed out it would in any case be a propitious career start for a novice. In a strange twist, the course of events were to prove me wrong again.

PART IV

NEW YORK *DANSE MACABRE*

ONE

The first time I laid eyes on Alexander Levary, the image I had formed of him splintered into a thousand pieces like a mirror shattered by a hard object. He entered the courtroom with his signature limp, but otherwise he bore little resemblance to the man Viktor Erdos had described during the night in the garret on Bleecker Street two months before. I had seen him as tall, slender, suave, and debonair. This man was of medium height and so portly as to be almost pudgy. His hair was cropped short, thinning, and white-gray. He reminded me more of an aging Peter Lorre than the great rogue of the German cinema Alexander Moissi to whom he had been compared. Testifying for the prosecution, he projected none of the swagger and poise Erdos had endowed him with. If anything he seemed unsure, hesitant, and evasive in his answers to the prosecutor's questions. His English was fluent but heavily accented with a Hungarian growl reminiscent of Bela Lugosi.

Disappointed as I was to see my image of him demolished, I had to remind myself that the man Viktor Erdos spoke of had been thirty years younger. Time had a way of ravaging the human physiognomy, and it had not been any kinder to Alexander Levary than to the rest of humanity. He was no Dorian Gray. Only his eyes seemed unchanged. They were indeed of the darkest black with a daredevil spark. Even from my distance, I could see why his schoolmates back at the gymnasium of Debrecen would have called them Gypsy eyes.

He had an ironclad alibi for the time of the murder. He was in Hollywood negotiating a contract for Stella with Warner Brothers, he said. Although not a suspect, a host of lawyerly types and assorted folk clad in bulging jackets despite the warm weather surrounded him. It occurred to me he was like the mob bosses in movies. In fact as it unfolded, the entire hustling, bustling scene in the halls of justice had the unreal aura of a movie set. Judging from their grandstanding with the press outside the courthouse, the lawyers were all high-powered publicity hounds. They no doubt brought their client up to speed on the ins and outs of the American judicial system. They likely coached him on what to say and not to say and how to say what he did say. They probably choreographed his every move and gesture as if he was starring in a movie. So I thought.

However, to everyone's surprise and not least mine, the accused, Chaim Erdreich alias Viktor Erdos, shunned the services of the big guns and placed his defense into the hands of the freshly minted counselor Curtis Wolff. For the duration of the proceedings, the defendant sat stoically in his seat. His gaze was wistfully directed at the courtroom walls. Never once did he deign to meet the eyes of his erstwhile friend whose testimony the prosecution asserted would establish his guilt in the murder of Stella Berger beyond a reasonable doubt.

The trial started on September 22. The Honorable Harold Stern presided over the trial. Was this date an omen? Did anybody besides me have any qualms that it coincided with the start of the Jewish New Year and would no doubt extend over the Days of Awe that followed? *On Rosh Hashanah it is inscribed. On Yom Kippur it is sealed.* These familiar phrases ran through my head. I looked at Viktor Erdos. *What will be your fate,* I wondered. His sphinxlike demeanor was forever wistful and inscrutable.

The jury selection was a drawn-out affair. The actual trial was not likely to get underway on that day or even the next. The lawyers had to argue first over who among the pool would be called up to perform their civic duty and who wouldn't sit in judgment. Curtis acquitted himself valiantly in hand-to-hand combat with the titans of his profession. My services were not required. The court had plenty of translators on its roster. A sudden urge for air seized me, and I slipped out.

Wandering around aimlessly through the streets of lower Manhattan, I found myself at the steps of a synagogue. The chant of High Holy services sounded from the open windows. I decided to enter. Although I had previously attended services when the occasion warranted, my mind was not of a particularly religious bend. Now I felt a sudden impulse for something that transcended the earthly sphere. This urge for something I could not put a name on came as a surprise to me. I was even more surprised, though, listening to the cantor chanting the prayers. I found myself haunted by the image of the man accused of having killed the thing he venerated most. He had created an idol—a sin for which he was now to be punished. The reading of the sacrifice of Isaac filled me with profound uneasiness. Where was the angel to stay the hand pointing the knife at Viktor Erdos's throat?

Two days later the lawyers were still battling over potential jurors. Curtis's motion to have the case dismissed entirely for lack of evidence was overruled. The police, politicians, press, and not least of all the general public were out for retribution more than justice. When the jury was finally seated, it was just a day before Yom Kippur, the holiest day in the Jewish calendar. Mercifully, the judge called for a day's recess.

The proceedings resumed in the same atmosphere of chaos and turbulence. I observed the circus perched in a corner of the gallery. Interspersed with the ordinary spectators, I spotted several celebrities. Their big sunglasses and pulled down hats gave them away. One of those incognito visitors I could have sworn was Lotte Lenya. She was there every day the entire time of the trial and followed the proceedings avidly. Another was Hedy Lamarr. To think I showed them to their seats on the opening night of Stella Berger's triumphant run on Broadway only a few months before.

It was hard to figure out who the hecklers were and whom they cheered or jeered. Their staged rowdiness was eerily reminiscent of the Brownshirts' *Krawall* in Berlin. I had the distinct sense of a guiding hand behind the disorder. The judge issued periodic, though empty, warnings he would have the courtroom cleared. His officious demeanor gave an indication he rather relished the brouhaha. Reports of these disturbances would get his statements and rulings once again cited in the morning papers.

Once the actual trial got underway, I tried to take notes, but was unable to control a tremor in my hand and the beating of my heart. When I looked them over later, I found them rather spotty and incoherent.

I couldn't see her face, but I had no doubt she was the tall woman with whom I had crossed paths on the threshold to Stella Berger's dressing room. Now I knew her name was Ulla Scholz. Clad in a classic black suit, she sat in the front row of the visitors' gallery. She was erect like a giraffe and thin as a reed. Her back was as straight as if she had swallowed a stick. A ridiculous black pillbox hat from which a black netting fell over her entire face crowned her shoulder-length, straight hair which gave off an orangey sheen of bottle red, inadequate to the task of glossing over her specks of grayish-white. All in all she was an imposing figure. Her height, even while sitting, made her stand out.

The first witnesses were two stagehands who identified Viktor Erdos as the man they saw running from Stella Berger's dressing room. One claimed the case the defendant was swinging almost hit him in the head as he "stampeded like a bull" through the narrow backstage corridor. Curtis questioned the witnesses' ability to make out a face in the poorly lit area. Others employed at the theater saw nothing but heard shouting and screaming of an indeterminate nature. Curtis got them to admit that was nothing unusual in their work environment. When asked if the screams came from the direction of the star's dressing room, none of them could say for certain. As the star ordered, no one went near that area after a performance.

"This was her habit back in Berlin as well?" the prosecutor asked Ulla when she took the stand.

"Always and everywhere. We always respected her wish to have this time to herself." Ulla had removed her hat and revealed a pear-shaped face, small, squinting eyes, and a pointy nose. She dabbed her eyes frequently with a white, lace handkerchief she held in her hand.

She was a woman considerably past her prime—a fact she apparently tried to plaster over with a thick layer of makeup. She might never have been pretty, but she knew how to comport herself with dignity and poise. On the witness stand, she assumed the doleful demeanor of a woman in mourning. She spoke in soft, measured cadences. Though clearly audible, she was almost whispering. This gave her the air of an insider revealing dark secrets in the interest of justice. Her English was accented but fluent.

"Would the defendant have known about this peculiar habit, and would he, therefore, have been able to choose this particular time to enter her dressing room knowing she would be alone?"

Curtis's objection that the prosecution was leading the witness was overruled.

"He certainly would have that knowledge and could use it toward his purpose."

Another objection was overruled.

"How well did you know the defendant?"

Ulla had earlier identified the defendant as the man she knew by the name Viktor Erdos. It had been ten years since she last saw him. She added that he looked a bit scruffy now, and this elicited laughter from the gallery. She said, however, she had no doubt it was him.

"How well does one ever know anybody?" She rolled her eyes and shook her head looking up to the ceiling as if to extract the answer from there.

Even the prosecutor despaired of such melodrama. "Never mind," he said. "We don't have time for philosophical debates. Did you have any close contact with the defendant during the time you were in Berlin?"

"Yes. I saw him frequently. Practically every day. He was always there. Wherever Stella was, he had to be too."

"Would you say he made a nuisance of himself?"

"I'd say." She gave off a disdainful cackle.

"Eventually there was a row and a split. Tell us about that."

"Counsel is leading the witness!"

The judge waved off Curtis's attempt to break up the cozy little chat between prosecutor and witness as if it was a mere nuisance.

"Were you present at the blowup between the defendant and the deceased?"

"I wasn't in the same room, but the words came clearly through the wall and were heard all over the house. So violent was the altercation."

"So you heard every word. Tell us what kind of words you heard."

"Bitter words. Very bitter words. He accused her of betrayal. She told him she never wanted to see him again. Whereupon he left with the warning she would rue the day. We never saw him again until he turned up here in New York."

"What in your estimate caused this rift? They had been friends, maybe even lovers, going back a long time. Hadn't they?"

"Friends, yes. Lovers, never!" Her voice rose ever so slightly in protest.

"What was it then?"

"He brought the Nazis down on her. It was because of him the SA—the Brownshirts—picketed the theaters and staged demonstrations in front of her villa. Her career, all she had worked for, was in jeopardy."

"Looking at the timeline of these events..." The prosecutor turned to his assistant who perused a folder to confirm the accuracy of the statement. "Yes. From this timeline I understand these events occurred before the current German government took office. What objection would these men you call Brownshirts have at that time?"

"Well, they obviously didn't think Germany's darling of stage and screen should be consorting with Jews."

"Wasn't Madame Berger herself of Jewish extraction?"

She curled her lips and wiggled them around. "That is true." She drew out the words and then quickly added, "But it wasn't generally known. That came out only later."

"Thank you. No more questions."

A hushed murmur rose from the audience. The prosecutor's abrupt halt of questioning just as he was getting to what seemed the crux of the matter surprised everyone. It could only be attributed to fear of treading into dangerous territory that would cast the witness in a negative light and be detrimental to his case.

In good lawyerly fashion, Curtis jumped into the breach the prosecutor had left open and picked up on the selfsame point during cross-examination.

"Very interesting," he mused. He buttoned his jacket as he rose from behind his table as he had seen in courtroom dramas. "Am I right to presume you want the jury to believe Madame Berger showed the defendant the door because he was a Jew? Is that your testimony?"

"Not exactly. Only in a certain sense." She raised her eyebrow. Her disdainful look pierced him like daggers.

"What sense is that? Weren't most people around the star of what one might call Jewish extraction? The director of the Deutsches Theater for one." She started to answer, but he moved on when the prosecution objected.

"Shortly after the breakup, Madame Berger married her manager, Alexander Levary. Or was it before? How did you feel about that? Betrayed?"

"Objection! Irrelevant."

"Sustained."

I shook my head in disbelief. How could Curtis squander the opportunity the prosecutor had handed him in such an amateur fashion?

"No more questions," he said to my consternation.

Ulla Scholz's height loomed even larger as she rose and stepped down from the witness stand with slow, deliberate strides. An audible sigh escaped her lips as she passed the jury box. She let her keen, probing eyes wander from juror to juror. She paused for a split second before each one like a queen reviewing an honor guard.

Alexander Levary, the next witness for the prosecution, displayed none of Ulla Scholz's haughtiness. He comported himself in a surprisingly humble manner. He had none of the flamboyance I had been expecting.

Yes, Levary confirmed there had been one angry verbal exchange between the defendant and the victim. He then stated that the defendant subsequently left Berlin, returned to Vienna, and was never heard from again.

"To your knowledge did the defendant ever try to contact Madame Berger either in person or by letter? It's been ten years since the incident, hasn't it?"

"As I said we never heard from him, except through his newspaper articles. He never contacted her in all this time."

"As her husband you would know, wouldn't you?"

"I am sure she would have mentioned it had he attempted to contact her."

"Did he ever try to contact you?"

"No."

"What was your relationship with the defendant prior to the incident?"

He hesitated for a moment. "We were friends going back to our gymnasium days."

"Where was that?"

"In Debrecen, Hungary."

"Aha! So you have known the defendant for a long time. Longer than anybody. You presumably also know him better than anybody. He introduced you to Madame Berger, and then she married you while he was shown the door. In your assessment of his character, do you think it possible he nurtured a deep resentment during all those years?"

"That's quite possible. He was very possessive of her."

"So, when the opportunity presented itself here in this city, do you think he could have seized the moment and taken his revenge including murder?"

Curtis's objection that the witness couldn't possibly read the defendant's mind was once again overruled. A breathless silence filled the courtroom. No one moved or made a sound. All eyes were on the witness.

Alexander Levary looked down. He was visibly uncomfortable and struggling with the answer. When the suspense reached the cracking point, he lifted his dark, sparkling eyes and looked straight at the impassive Viktor Erdos.

"No. I don't think so," he said. "I don't think so at all."

"You don't think what?" bellowed the prosecutor. He was obviously unable to rein in his impatience.

"I just don't think he would be capable of harming her."

The prosecutor's frustration burst wide open. "Then who do you suppose tied a violin string around the victim's throat and strangled her to death in the most heinous way?"

"Objection! Speculation! Counsel is leading the witness!"

"Sustained."

Curtis was having a field day. On cross examination of Levary he repeated the prosecutor's question.

"No, I don't think Viktor Erdos would be capable of doing Stella any harm," the witness confirmed his earlier statement.

My testimony was last on the prosecutor's agenda. All I had to do was restate the course of my action and how I had enabled Viktor Erdos to enter the theater. Since I left right after for class at Hunter College, I had no knowledge of what happened once the accused was inside the theater.

"This is the story you are going with?" asked the prosecutor.

"Yes. No. What I mean is I am telling you the truth."

The judge asked if the defense had any other witnesses, anybody who could vouchsafe for the character of the accused. "No," Curtis replied. He explained that since the defendant has been living alone in the city no character witnesses were available.

Curtis apparently saw no point in subjecting me to cross-examination. The lawyers then did their song and dance before the jurors.

The jury took its time. I deemed this a good sign for the defense despite a sense of ill foreboding.

"Whose side are you on?" Curtis asked me.

We were having coffee across the street from the courthouse. The tension between us was close to breaking.

"That's what I should ask you. You really botched the cross of Ulla. You blew a splendid opportunity as if you were looking for a guilty verdict."

"That's exactly what would be best for Viktor."

"What do you mean? You can't be serious. A guilty verdict would get him the chair."

"It would keep him alive and in this country."

"This makes no sense."

"You see, he's in a real bind. He entered the United States illegally from Canada, as I just found out. If he is found innocent of murder, they will deport him. They'll send him back to Austria or Hungary and certain death. If he is found guilty, they will lock him up in a high-security prison in this country. Even if he gets the maximum, there will be appeals. He'll be on death row for a long time, and new evidence might emerge for a retrial."

"Meanwhile you'll be able to milk this case for all its worth. You've got it all figured out, haven't you?" His logic made no sense to me. "Wait a moment. Why didn't this come up in the trial?"

"Because he told me about it when I spoke with him in prison. That's why he refused counsel from all the big shots."

"But he did have papers. I saw them at the police station."

"False papers. They are not so hard to come by. There's a whole industry. He slipped through once, but immigration is bound to notice on closer look. Then questions will be raised why he didn't stay in Canada. What was the urgency to get into the United States?"

"So you gambled a man's life on the assumption that a guilty verdict would keep him here, and you could keep him alive with appeals."

"I told you. It is a rock and a hard place."

"More like a Machiavellian plot."

"Never underestimate the power of the devil's cunning."

The devil's cunning got its first do without delay. The jury deliberated for forty-eight hours. The verdict and sentence were foregone conclusions. The public, politicians, and maybe even providence demanded it. *Isaac!* I thought. *Alas. No staying hand!*

Viktor Erdos had the motive and opportunity. So everybody was made to believe. Justice was done. The world's attention could move on to other matters. Most of Europe was under the Nazi boot. There was still a war going on in Russia. The Blitz was still terrorizing the citizens of London. Uncertainty over the outcome and what it might mean for America took center stage again. Pundits gazed into their crystal balls for answers and predictions.

Viktor Erdos was sent up the river to while away his time on death row in Sing-Sing Correctional Facility. Curtis Wolff got to work on his first appeal.

TWO

The sparkling brass sign outside the small office in a town house on West Tenth Street read Curtis Wolff, Esq., Attorney at Law. It was the first item on which the now-famous attorney splurged. He might have lost the case, but his name was made. Requests for his services kept pouring in. There were more than he could handle, and most were turned away.

Besides the new sign and office, there was even something in it for me. I got a much-needed part-time job filing papers and taking out the trash a few hours a week. As for that prickly matter of our relationship, I thought it best to keep him at arm's length. I deferred a solution to our personal problems to another time.

A few days after the verdict and sentence were announced, a surprise visitor appeared at the office. It was early evening and almost dusk. The days were getting shorter, and the unbearable heat of summer had given way to a brisk autumn. Curtis was in his study. He was reading up on appeals in past murder convictions. I was on my way back in from a trash run in the miniature backyard. My thoughts were on an upcoming midterm exam, and I almost ran into the dark figure of a woman who materialized seemingly out of nowhere in the dimly lit hallway.

She apologized more profusely than necessary. It was I who should have been watching my step. She needed to speak with Mr. Wolff about a matter that should be of interest to him. The urgency in her accented English and her general aura behind her thickly veiled face set her apart from the potential clients who came to the office every day seeking representation in automobile accident or personal injury cases. I guided her inside even though it was after hours, and I took her wool wrap. As we came face-to-face in the light of the vestibule and she lifted her veil, my jaw dropped. I made a faint screeching noise. There was no doubt. The woman standing in front of me was none other than Lotte Lenya.

"May I sit down?" Her signature throaty voice, even in English, was unmistakable. "I had to vent my anger somewhere to someone. And since I cannot do it in public, I came here. I think you will understand."

I wasn't sure to whom she was speaking—me or Curtis. It was probably to both of us.

"I had to do something about this woman and her lies. Bald-faced lies! Oh, I could wring her neck. That bitch!"

I had an inkling of whom she was speaking but decided to keep silent and hear her out.

"Nothing of what I'm about to tell you can leave this room. It would be a betrayal of Stella's memory. You must swear to it. But I hope you will find the information useful in some way for your appeal, Counselor."

He nodded. I offered to make tea and put the water in a kettle on a tabletop burner.

She leaned back, closed her eyes, as if collecting her thoughts.

I had been right. She had been in the courtroom. She had taken the time out from rehearsals of an English revival of *The Threepenny Opera*, which was scheduled to open on Broadway later in the month.

"This isn't easy for me," she began and then stopped for a moment to take a sip of hot tea. "My acquaintance with Stella Berger goes way back to our days in Zurich during the war. Long before either of us was famous. I also knew Ulla Scholz then quite well." She stopped again. A pensive frown appeared on her face. "It would be easier for me to speak in German, if that is all right with Mr. Wolff."

Curtis apologized for his spotty German. If she wanted, though, his assistant (he shrugged toward me) could translate. She decided that would be too cumbersome and continued in English after all.

178

"As I said, absolutely nothing of what I will tell you can become public. It would be a disaster, and I would deny it. I would swear by my mother's grave it wasn't true."

She leaned back in the uncomfortable chair. The new furniture was on order but hadn't arrived yet. She took out a cigarette whereupon Curtis scrambled to his feet in a Pavlovian response and gallantly flicked his lighter in front of her face. It never ceased to amaze me how gentlemen seemed to have their hands permanently on lighters in their pockets. They seemed ready to pull them out at the spur of the moment. Lotte Lenya drew a few puffs with a nod of thanks and continued.

"Her official biography describes Stella Berger as a young actress who blazed a trail of triumphs through the Austrian provinces during the war, culminating in ultimate triumph on the stage in Zurich in 1917 and so on. I knew her then, and none of this is true, except that she eventually made her breakthrough. Just not immediately. Believe me. I have no problem with a bit of mythmaking. The public wants that. I'm not here to decry her in any way for it. We all have our secret prior lives. I'm only telling you this to shed some light on her relationship with Ulla Scholz. This too would be immaterial were it not for an innocent man sitting on death row."

Once again my jaw dropped. The certainty with which she pronounced Viktor Erdos's innocence allowed for no doubt she was speaking the truth.

She rose abruptly as if stung by a wasp and crushed her cigarette into the teacup on the table before her. Again she took time to apologize.

Come to the point. Come to the point, my mind recited.

"To put it all in context, you must allow me to begin with a little history of myself before getting to Stella. You'll see how it all fits together."

In those glory days just before the Great War, Viennese high society obliviously danced on a volcano, and Lotte's years of dogged toil in the city's working-class districts finally began to pay off. Her career as a serious songstress and actress seemed to be assured. She had risen from singing on street corners and in absinthe pubs to star of her own cabaret show. Even her occasional, minor dramatic performances had received positive notice. In August 1914 the building blocks she had so diligently stacked up teetered along with the entire foundation of the Austro-Hungarian Empire. She carried on doggedly for a while. This was her modus operandi, and she was determined never to be tossed back again into the dregs. Adversity was not going to make her give up. The war without end, however, finally made her if not give up, leave town for more promising pastures. She would seek fame and fortune in a place not engulfed in war. The natural choice was Switzerland. Zurich was known for its lively Germanophone culture and theater world—an important aspect for someone whose métier depended on speech.

Alas Lotte's high hopes did not translate into the immediate success she sought. The city was teeming with aspiring artists from neighboring warring countries seeking fame and fortune. The number of those willing to wait tables and wash dishes was larger than jobs available. The lines for auditions for even the minutest roles wrapped around the corners of the theaters. Cabarets were in plentiful supply, but so were singers and performers eager for spots in the dingy limelight.

Keeping an anxious eye on her dwindling means, Lotte doggedly made the rounds. Under those circumstances she would inevitably get to know some of the people sharing her fate. They were equally frustrated but equally dogged. Among those aspiring actresses was a tall German woman. Her name was Ulla Scholz. While waiting in the audition line together, they got to talking and befriended each other. There was much time for the exchange of experiences and aspirations. Lotte told the woman Zurich was just a way station for her. Berlin was the place to be as soon as the war was over. Ulla was from Ulm in Bavaria. Berlin for her was the place where the Jews ran the entertainment business. Her dream was Munich. Meanwhile the yellow teeth of hunger began to gnaw on their innards. Ulla came up with a plan that would allow them to keep auditioning and make money at the same time. Was Lotte ready to go into business with her?

There was already considerable competition for the line of work she had in mind, but there was also an endless demand for that kind of service. Financing was not all that hard to come by for a business as promising as the one she envisioned. Employees to make the business run were even easier to find. In no time at all, Lotte and Ulla became the proud madams of a prosperous establishment they called House of Easy Virtue. They figured they might as well call a spade a spade. The steady line of customers pouring in night after night soon provided them with luxuries neither one had ever tasted or dreamed of.

Ulla gave up auditioning. She showed quite a talent for managing the business and kept it running shipshape. The merchant's daughter from Ulm kept the books, trained the help, scheduled and assigned the clients, prepared the payroll, and saw to the hundreds of details to keep the operation running smoothly and elegantly. Lotte provided the entertainment at night. In the daytime she still doggedly made the rounds of the theaters where auditions were held for any part. She even auditioned once for the part of Lulu in a Wedekind play. She wasn't the type or size, but she figured she'd give it a try. Nothing but nothing would make her give up her dream of making it in the entertainment world.

One day in the winter of 1917, on leaving the theater after another unsuccessful audition, she noticed a young girl she had seen earlier in the audition line for Lulu. She was huddled on the steps outside. Shivering in her thin coat, she was crying. She was such a waif and a perfect Lulu to Lotte's mind, but she was passed over for another more robust candidate.

On inquiring Lotte learned her name was Stella Berger. Like her, she was from Vienna. She had just arrived in Zurich. She was almost penniless, and she had no place to go or sleep. Lotte took her home— that is, to the House of Easy Virtue. Ulla took her under her wing.

"She's perfect," she said to her business partner. "So sweet and innocent. Just what some of our clients go for most!"

So Stella was initiated into the business. Outwardly she was very docile. She did as she was told. Ulla used her young protégé's innocence for all it was worth, but Lotte saw something else in those dark eyes. Something made her take note. She saw the glowing embers of a fire. It was like the fire she felt in her own belly that no momentary setbacks could extinguish. She also saw a cold shrewdness that made her wonder who was really using whom.

No matter how long the nights stretched out, Stella was up every morning bathed, groomed, and transformed. Even then Stella's ability to completely slip from one role into another astounded Lotte. From teenage seductress at night to serious aspiring actress in the morning, Stella's life seemed all about role playing. She was a perfect chameleon. Together they made the rounds. Their motto was to absolutely never give up. All they had to do was keep banging their heads against the wall in front of them. One day it would inevitably give way. A breach would appear, and they would emerge into the light.

For Stella the hole in the wall opened up when *Earth Spirit*, for which she had been rejected, folded in the spring of 1918. The girl they had chosen to play Lulu turned out to be an unmitigated disaster, and the production was a flop. A new production was planned, and new auditions were held. This time the director expressed his disbelief about how shortsighted he had been the first time around. How could he not have recognized the ideal Lulu when she stood in front of him? His past error would now be set right.

Given a chance, Stella did not disappoint. Her Lulu enchanted and enticed. A local paper claimed Zurich had never seen the likes of this young woman. The word got around. Soon she played to a full house every night. She came to the attention of the visiting Max Reinhardt, whose offer to take her to Berlin she rebuffed. Lotte couldn't believe at first how she could pass up such an opportunity. Only later did she recognize the calculation behind it. No one would ever say Stella Berger had earned her rise to stardom on her back.

As soon as the guns of war fell silent, Lotte packed her bags and headed straight to Berlin. Stella left for Munich when the season ended with Ulla and two so-called students from Vienna in tow.

When they met again in Berlin years later, Lotte had found steady employment at one of the cabarets. She had teamed up with Kurt Weill, who composed songs for her that found a receptive audience. Stella was building on her Lulu success in Munich, but now she branched into a great variety of modern and classic roles. She expanded her repertoire to include every female part in Shakespeare's plays. Lotte and Stella got together on occasion, but they took care never to let out a word about the bad old days in Zurich.

Yet the reminder of those days was always there. Wherever Stella went, Ulla was in tow. Lotte was baffled. Why would Stella keep Ulla as her constant companion? They were known to be lesbian lovers in certain circles. Lotte suspected Stella nurtured this gossip to keep the men who were swarming around here at a distance. Sex was never of interest to her for its own sake. At the brothel in Zurich, it was a matter of survival, and she had played the nymph true to type. On stage and from the screen, she exuded the rawest, unadulterated eroticism. In real life she was rather asexual and androgynous. She was completely single-minded. Her mind was on one thing and one thing only: her art. Everything else was just props, essentials for the production, in the great drama of Stella Berger's life.

Back in Zurich they would talk for hours about the inner workings of the actor's art. Stella's lack of a basic desire for personal fame struck Lotte. She seemed motivated and driven primarily by an irrepressible need to express herself through acting. Now in Berlin the mantle of fame had been thrust upon her, and Lotte knew this still to be true. Fame and fortune were nice to have for the conveniences the money afforded, but they were never a goal to strive for or a value in themselves for Stella.

Even after they lost contact, Lotte couldn't help but be aware of all things Stella. She just had to open a newspaper, and news of Stella hit her right between the eyes. They had become estranged after a falling out over Ulla. In a moment alone, Lotte questioned Stella about the former madam's continued presence. Stella vehemently rejected her suggestion Ulla might be blackmailing her. Lotte apologized. She said she was sorry if she was out of line. Stella accepted her apology but was very cool toward her from then on whenever they happened to meet.

Stella's reaction confirmed her suspicion that somewhere in a safe place in Zurich, probably a bank vault, a Damocles sword was stashed away in the form of pictures and negatives. She knew Ulla was taking pictures of the girls who worked for her at the brothel in the nude and in compromising positions. She had never understood for what purpose. Now she knew. But what could she do? Nothing. She had her own career and reputation to worry about and a past to hide. Stella was doing fine. Maybe her fear that Ulla would use the weapon she no doubt had was misplaced.

Lotte Lenya paused. Her eyes came to rest on Curtis as if she meant to mesmerize him. She pulled out another cigarette. The ever-solicitous Curtis leaned forward with a lighter at the ready.

"You understand that none of this can be made public," she repeated.

I was sure there was much more to this story, especially where her relationship with Ulla was concerned. It was, of course, her right and privilege not to divulge every detail, but why did she come to us with this story in the first place? I couldn't help but wonder what motive might lurk behind it. What was her agenda? Did she want revenge against Ulla for some reason but couldn't do it herself?

Let's face it, I thought. *If Ulla has the goods on Stella, she no doubt has damaging material on her as well.*

"What would you like us do with this information? In what way could it possibly be beneficial to Viktor's case?" Curtis said this very politely and even deferentially.

"To put it bluntly, I have a hunch. No. I am convinced Ulla was in some way involved in Stella's murder, and I would like you to prove it. She is the one who should get the chair."

"You realize this is a tall order." Curtis kept a straight face. He was businesslike even though this conversation was crossing over into the realm of the bizarre.

"With nothing but a hunch to go on..." He steepled his fingers and tilted his head. "We have no evidence."

She rose abruptly. Indignation flared from her eyes like brandished daggers. Jutting her prominent jaw even further out, she snarled, "I see I've been wasting my time and energy here." Directing her daggers at me, she snapped, "Where's my wrap?"

I hurried to fetch her wrap from the rack in the vestibule. When I came back into the study, she was sitting again with her legs crossed. Curtis was pouring cognac into two glasses. They clinked glasses and cheered. Somehow he had been able to mollify her.

Remembering his manners for a moment, Curtis held up his glass to me. "Would you like a sip? I have only two glasses."

I declined.

She obviously had a way with men. I had the feeling she would have liked me to disappear altogether so she could play her tricks on him. There was no way I was going to clear the field. This was too good to miss. Instead I made myself invisible. I withdrew into the background. All ears, I was a fly on the wall.

They smoked, drank, and laughed as if they were at a cocktail gathering of the swells. She batted her coal black, curved eyelashes at him. He groveled at her feet.

After many years of not seeing each other, Lotte Lenya and Stella Berger ran into each other at a bash of illustrious émigrés in the Hollywood Hills. Stella was on the arm of her husband, Alexander Levary, whom Lotte called the "dapper Sasha." On spotting Lotte on the arm of her husband, Kurt Weill, Stella flew toward them. With arms open wide, she hailed them like long-lost friends. The women embraced and touched cheeks with kisses three times *à la française*. After mutual assurances about how fabulous each looked, Lotte commended Stella for her courageous public stand against the Nazi regime.

"Somebody has to do something to show the world Hitler's true face and intentions," Stella said. She took a look around the room.

"Most people here enjoy having escaped to freedom too much to even put their names on petitions to Roosevelt. There's still a strong sentiment in this country against becoming involved. And most émigrés like to lie low while sipping wine and cocktails. We need the United States and its might to defeat the tyrant who has taken over most of Europe," she stated. Her round, dark eyes glowed with fervor. "Britain alone can't do it. If it were up to the isolationists, Hitler might as well take over the rest of the world. As long as he keeps his tentacles off the United States. And why should they stick their necks out for the Jews?"

The sincerity of Stella's jeremiad bowled Lotte over. She eagerly nodded her agreement. She wondered how Ulla took all this. She looked around for her old nemesis. To her surprise her towering frame was nowhere in sight.

"How is Ulla?" she asked politely after a pause.

"Oh, you know. Ulla is Ulla."

Lotte didn't know what she was hinting at.

"She keeps my household running shipshape," Stella explained. "I have nothing to worry about in that arena, as you can image. It's her gift."

"I'm surprised she isn't here." Lotte hoped things between them weren't all honky-dory, in the American vernacular.

"Sasha is involved in delicate negotiations with Warner Brothers and Louis B. Mayer. He's trying to play one against the other. Hollywood is quite a prudish place and averse to even the hint of scandal. It's all hypocrisy, but Sasha thinks it's better to keep Ulla out of sight."

They chatted some more and found they were both to star on Broadway. At the opening night party for Desdemona, Lotte saw Stella for the last time.

"Now I really must go." Lotte Lenya rose and scooped up the wrap I had placed next to her. "Kurt will start worrying. My visit here is completely confidential. Not even he knows about it."

It was close to midnight. Curtis offered to call a cab. She assured him it wasn't necessary. Her driver was waiting outside.

So somebody does know where she is, I thought. *Probably one of her lovers who was also sworn to secrecy.*

She turned around one more time at the door. "I suggest you start by talking to Sasha Levary. My gut feeling tells me he was not completely forthcoming in his testimony at the trial."

THREE

Whoever made up the saying that surprises like accidents always came in threes might have been on to something. Number two arrived at the doorstep of my apartment a few days after the visit of the cloaked lady to Counselor Wolff's office. I was coming home from a night class in the driving rain. Battling against the wind to close my umbrella while fishing around in my bag for my key, my heart suddenly started to race. Close behind me I felt someone's heavy breathing. I fumbled and tried to get the key into the lock.

"Don't panic. It's only me." I recognized the voice and sighed with relief. This particular visitor was cloaked in a big overcoat covered by a slicker with a hood pulled over his eyes and face. If this was a disguise, it did a poor job of hiding his bulky identity.

"Inspector Mulligan I presume," I called out.

"Shh!" He put his finger to his lips and sent a darting glance over his shoulder. "Open the door!"

When the blasted door finally opened, he pushed past me without waiting to be invited and practically fell into the house. When we were both safely inside, he commanded, "Close the door. Quickly!"

This was all a bit too much melodrama from an otherwise down-to-earth police officer.

"I have to make sure I wasn't followed," he heaved.

He shivered and dripped all over my brand-new carpet. Once again I had the feeling I had stumbled into a movie scene replete with the hugger-mugger of a film noir.

I came to suspect that somewhere a hidden hand was intent on throwing the switch to derail the track I had laid out for my life. I had returned to my studies, and Curtis had put out a subpoena for Alexander Levary to get him back from California. Since he was working on the appeal, this wasn't such an out-of-the-ordinary request. I hoped to have some time to catch up on my courses. My mind was on the upcoming midterms. I was already late handing in several projects, and my grades were in danger of slipping.

Then a recently arrived letter from Berlin gave me cause for grave concern. Since September nineteenth all Jews were ordered to wear a yellow star on their clothing when going out in public. Any infraction brought the severest punishment. Food was rationed to the barest minimum. It was not enough for a full meal but just enough to keep from starving. I suspected my aunt spared me the worst details.

Now there was this most unusual nighttime call from the homicide inspector. An ominous feeling churned my stomach. What might his visit forebode?

I offered to take his coat and bade him to have a seat. He refused both. I wished he would at least get out of his rain boots, but I let it slide. He couldn't stay long, he said breathlessly. He sounded as if some evil villain or an entire band of miscreants had chased him down a dark, narrow alley.

"None of this can become known. Not my visit or what I have to say."

Now where have I heard this bit before?

The trial was over, a man was in prison waiting to be zapped by an electric current. These cloak-and-dagger phantoms were coming out of their closets to haunt and taunt with new leads. I wasn't even the police! Why me? Then I remembered the man with the wistful gaze whose violin playing had touched my heart. I was willing to grasp at any straw.

Turning my attention back to the inspector, I noticed he was extremely agitated. He collapsed on the chair I had previously offered and he had refused. It gave a groan, triggering jitters about my limited decorating budget.

"You must promise not to tell anybody any of this, except perhaps your Mr. Wolff."

He wasn't my Mr. Wolff, but I let it go. It wasn't worth the effort.

"I have family. A wife and five children to feed."

Yeah, yeah, I thought. *I've heard it all before. Everybody has something to protect.*

I gritted my teeth but managed to make it look like the flash of an encouraging smile.

"I could be booted from the force if this came out." He pulled out a bright white handkerchief from inside his many-layered clothing and dabbed his forehead.

"If what came out?"

"I overheard Dettelbach on the phone. Something is going down at the Oktoberfest up in Yorkville. He mentioned a place on Eighty-Sixth Street. A beer hall. Tzoomli or something like that."

"Zum lieben Augustin," I filled in.

"Seems about right. Something is planned there for the night of the twenty-fifth. Something to do with the murder."

I didn't have to ask him what murder he was talking about. There was only one as far as I was concerned. "So what about it?"

"I think we might have convicted the wrong man."

You don't say, I thought.

After the police had done their best to feed the man into the grinding wheels of justice, this inspector now raised the possibility of a miscarriage of justice. My clenched hands were itching to pummel him. Then I reminded myself he had been the moderate one who had tried to rein in his superior's bullying theatrics.

"Why are you telling me this?"

"Maybe you could do something. Go there. Find out what's going on."

I burst out laughing. "Me? Play detective? Excuse me, but this is too funny. It's absurd."

"Not at all. You know the language. You might find out something that could help Mr. Wolff's appeal."

I wondered what kind of strings this man was pulling. Then the sincere, sad look in his eyes won me over. He seemed genuinely desirous to right a wrong. I wasn't sure what I could or would do.

"Before he hung up, I heard him clearly say, 'See you then, and make sure the beanstalk is there.' I take that to be a reference to the tall, German woman who testified at the trial."

It was just like Dettelbach to make such an irreverent remark. I thanked Inspector Mulligan and promised to discuss the matter with Mr. Wolff. Maybe together we could come up with a plan of action.

Curtis laughed out loud when he heard my plan, but the chance to catch Dettelbach in flagrante delicto (he had gotten into the habit of bandying lawyerly terms about like a juggler throws balls in the air) was too good to forego. Curtis wanted the chance to expose our attack dog as being in cahoots with the German Kulturbund and Ulla Scholz.

The date for the conclave of the Teutons, as I dubbed it, was still a week away. Much needed to be done to make sure my plan ran smoothly. As good fortune would have it, the German shops carrying the items I needed were within walking distance of my college. This made it convenient to sleuth out the area between classes.

However, before all this was finalized, my attention was turned to number three in the line of callers. Alexander Levary came flying in from California, and it turned out he was not only willing to talk but eager to unburden himself—better yet, justify himself.

FOUR

Alexander Levary called from the airport the moment he landed. He requested the meeting be in a place where he couldn't be seen entering and leaving or be overheard. Curtis assured him his office was absolutely soundproof, though he lacked any proof to back up this assertion. He was quickly becoming a real huckster. I wondered if they taught Prevarication 101 in law school. He set up the appointment for ten o'clock at night with the promise of total, absolute secrecy. Whether he could deliver on that was likewise uncertain. Since he had put his shingle out, newshounds often cased the neighborhood. Curtis Wolff had become a marketable item. Adding the husband of the slain diva into the mix would be a field day for the tabloids. If all these promises served the cause, though, who was I to judge?

Curtis thought it best to pick Sender up personally at a small hotel in the Village where he checked in just a few blocks from our office. I was posted outside in the street to signal when the coast was clear of members of the fourth estate.

More cloak-and-dagger activities, I thought. *Actually lots of cloak so far and no daggers, except those that flashed from Lotte Lenya's eyes into my chest.*

Levary was muffled in a dark brown fur overcoat with sable trim and a Russian ushanka fur hat with the flaps pulled down over his ears. Once he was safely inside, he threw off both coat and hat on the rack in the vestibule and kicked off a pair of Russian army boots. All of these items, he let us know, were souvenirs from his time in Siberia. If he thought this disguise would make him fade into the surroundings, he was sorely mistaken. These items would make him stand out in the streets of New York, and he had his famous limp. Maybe in Berlin he could have pulled it off but not on a clear October night in New York. Luckily my scanning of the windows in the surrounding buildings yielded no spying eyes. The newshounds had apparently turned in for the night.

While Alexander Levary divested himself of his furry hide, I put the water on for tea. I apologized for the lack of a samovar. Curtis started pouring cognac into three snifters he had acquired since Lotte Lenya's visit.

"I'm afraid we're out of vodka," he joked.

"Nothing to apologize for." Levary raised the glass to his nose, gave it an elegant swirl, and sniffed its contents. His fingernails were perfectly manicured and buffed.

"Mmm. Très, très bien!" He wrinkled his nose with the flair of the connoisseur. "I'm Hungarian. Not Russian. I know a good French drop when I smell it. This is an excellent one."

Curtis tendered the third glass to me with a nod. See, he seemed to say, I bought an extra glass for you. With the kind of days I had been having, I decided I could use a stiff drink and accepted.

I almost laughed out loud when I heard Alexander Levary say, "You understand I'm here on condition of complete confidentiality. Nothing that transpires in this meeting can be repeated in public." He anxiously searched first Curtis's face then mine.

We both crossed our hands over our hearts. It sure looked as if we were in for another long night of tales from another wanderer in the land of Nod.

The impression I had gained of him at court had to be revised again. Up close he presented an image much more in keeping with the one Viktor Erdos had drawn. He was the image of the urbane man of the world. His tailored double-breasted gray suit was a perfect fit. He was sophisticated in manner, taste, and speech and completed his look with pince-nez and Errol Flynn mustache.

Another chameleon perhaps.

To my chagrin he had become a smoker since that time in Vienna when he abhorred the habit. His cigarette brand was Melachrino Egyptians, and they perfumed the air in the room with a honeyed hookah fragrance.

Above all he was an enigma. It would take a lot more than just asking questions to draw him out. I signaled Curtis to let me have a go at it.

"Sender," I began. "May I call you Sender? It's the name by which Viktor Erdos refers to you. Somehow I too think of you as Sender."

He looked at me perplexed. "You mean to say Viktor spoke of me to you?"

"Yes. Very fondly," I partly lied. "He told us about Stella and the beginning of their friendship when she was a child in Vienna. He assured us he would never do any harm to her. As a matter of course, your name came up as well. He spoke of your long-time friendship."

"Then you also know..."

"Yes. He was very open about your relationship."

He gave me a long, probing look. "I betrayed him. I let him down. He was outraged when Stella and I got married. I had never seen him in such a state of anger. Cool, calm Viktor blew up like a volcano. I couldn't figure out what angered him so much. Was it that Stella should marry someone, or was it specifically that she married me? It was all so confusing. It was the only time I ever saw him threaten her. Then he walked out."

"Didn't Ulla Scholz testify that Stella showed him the door?"

"Whatever that woman says has to be taken with a grain of salt. Stella missed him. She often said so to me. Why she didn't call him back I never understood."

"Is it possible Ulla had something to do with it? She didn't like Jews much, did she?"

"No. I can still see her face when Stella told her she too was Jewish. She apparently had no idea. How she couldn't know is beyond me. Just goes to show how the human mind believes what it wants to believe. Total denial of the obvious. Ulla actually packed up and left when she heard it from the Nazi thugs. Two weeks later she came crawling back and was all apologetic. Why Stella took her back was always a mystery to me. One thing I'm sure of is the lesbian stuff was over, if it ever was true. For Stella everything was about her art. Our marriage was just window dressing. I never had sexual congress with Stella. I loved her but not in a husbandly way. I wish I had been able to explain this to Viktor."

"You knew where to find him, didn't you?" I said.

He looked pensively into the crystal bowl of the cognac glass in his hand. He moved his head back and forth sorrowfully. "So much lost time. So many lost years. We should have gotten together, talked it all over openly, and poured our hearts out. Instead we had all this secrecy and holding back what we felt. Out of what? Misplaced pride? And now look where we are. Stella is dead, and Viktor is in prison for her murder. It all makes no sense."

What do you mean misplace pride? What self-serving nonsense is that? What about blatant opportunism?

My patience was close to bursting over all this prevaricating and playacting.

"What about the Ulla factor? Might it have had something to do with the situation?" I chose my words carefully. I didn't want to sound suggestive or to put words in his mouth.

"The Ulla factor! Good way of putting it. It's true. She seemed to have some kind of hold over Stella that I never understood."

"Could it be she was blackmailing her?"

He sat up and gave me another long, probing look. Had I touched on something?

"Truthfully I don't know anything about her blackmailing Stella, though it would explain a lot. After all she was blackmailing me. She had some potentially embarrassing photographs of me. She was always walking around with a camera. I wouldn't have cared, but some were with Viktor. I never told him anything about it. It wasn't about money. She just wanted me to collude in whatever scheme she was hatching. I went along because of Stella and what it might do to her reputation and career if they were made public. You must understand. Everything was always about Stella. When she plotted to get rid of Viktor, I had no choice. I had to keep my peace. It was

194

the most difficult dilemma I ever faced in my life." He paused again. Tears welled up in his eyes.

Was he acting? Was this regret genuine?

"You benefitted from keeping your peace, though. Didn't you?" Curtis interjected. He had listened silently until then.

"Yes. You could say I rode to fame on Stella Berger's coattails. As her manager, though, I negotiated lucrative contracts for her. I also directed her in three highly acclaimed films. Any kind of public scandal could have ruined us both. Even in the acting world, where the practice of homoeroticism is widespread, it is not openly condoned. The moguls always have to be mindful of the sensitivities of theater- and moviegoers."

"So Viktor became the sacrificial lamb," I concluded.

"You could see it that way. In retrospect I would agree."

"Why Viktor and not you? Why not both of you if Ulla had a beef with Jews and homosexuals?"

"She definitely did not have 'a beef' with people's sexual predilections. Her Jew-hatred was an open secret. Her beef with Viktor went deeper. It was his closeness to Stella. It was the way Stella always sought his advice about any decision, even on matters concerning her craft. He was the pillar she leaned on, her father confessor, and her therapist. Nobody was closer to her. Nobody else had her complete confidence. Perhaps most galling to Ulla, however, was he had no ulterior motives. It was all about Stella. Never about him."

"You make him out to be a saint," I said. I suspected guilt was behind this glorified portrayal of his friend, but I didn't think it was my place to voice any objection. Then I heard Curtis put my thoughts into words.

"Isn't it a little late to atone for your betrayal now?" His tone had the stridency of a schoolteacher berating a pupil for a shameful act.

"I told you I am very sorry and wish I could make it up to him," he replied. He thought for a moment, and then he added, "Perhaps you should hear my story."

Only his schoolmate Chaim Erdreich called him Sender. His given name was Sándor Herz Loewy. Later he was known as Alexander

Levary to the world and Sasha to his intimates. He had his not-so-humble beginnings in a mansion in Budapest's first district in the artsy Tabán. His family had moved there from the Jewish Quarter in the seventh district before he was born. The only child of József Hertz, a business magnate and patron of the arts, and his wife, Anna Loewy, Sándor was, by his own testimony, born with a silver spoon in his mouth. His father and uncle had invested the fortune they inherited from the family's textile plants in South American copper mines. The wealth generated provided his father with the leisure to indulge his love for the arts. He became a foremost art collector and patron of the theater and opera.

Sándor's mother, his second wife and struggling, asthmatic actress, was thirty years his junior. She ran away from her Hasidic family in the eastern province of Szátmar to follow her dream of a stage career. Growing up in a home where various theater folk and artist types went in and out, Sándor caught the bug early. At age eight he played Puck in *A Midsummer Night's Dream* at the Hungarian National Theater. It won him the heart of every mother in the audience. From his stage debut to the time when he left for the gymnasium in Debrecen, he was frequently seen in small parts wherever a droll child was needed. At school he put on plays and discovered he found the greatest pleasure pulling the strings from behind the scenes.

Upon graduation from the gymnasium in Debrecen, he returned to Budapest. His plan to become a theater director was firmly established in his mind. His family connections easily got him an assistantship at the State Theater. In this version, he came to the attention of Max Reinhardt at a party his parents threw for the renowned impresario on a visit to Budapest. He invited Sándor to come to Berlin the next season.

"There might be an opening for an apprenticeship," the great man told his father. "One caveat, however. The boy will have to earn his spurs. He'll have to start at the bottom like all of us." Reinhardt shook hands with his father and slapped Sándor on the back. This was the *entretien* Sándor later described to Viktor in Vienna as a contract with Max Reinhardt whom he was on his way to join in Berlin.

Then came the war. Like everybody else the guns of August stopped him in his tracks. It blew his most grandiose plans sky-high and crash-landed all dreamers on the rough terrain of the battlefield. Viktor was drafted into the Austrian army. Sándor went home to Budapest first. If he thought he could evade the draft, he was sorely mistaken. The merciless mill of war required a limitless supply of warm bodies. He was drafted into the Hungarian infantry, and after a brief period of grueling training, he was dispatched to the wasteland of the Russian front.

Once there he decided he should make the most of it and distinguish himself through acts of bravery. He was the first to volunteer for special missions and skirmishes. To his dismay even those provided little opportunity for rising above the millions of soldiers slugging away daily against an invisible, yet lethal enemy.

Good fortune came to him, he thought, when the army command put out word for volunteers to join the newly formed aerial intelligence gathering unit. After special training back home, Sándor was flying high in a hot air balloon over enemy lines. He was surveying and mapping troop movements and positions, communication lines, and supply routes of the Czar's army. He was awarded a medal of valor, promoted to lieutenant, and shot down on his ninth mission. His captors put him in chains, worked him over, and beat him to a pulp. They finally put him on a train packed to the rafters with a similarly bleeding, bruised heap of human misery shivering in the chill of the Russian winter. It was weeks of bone-rattling stop and go to nowhere. They had next to nothing to eat, no sanitary facilities, and little protection against icy winds whistling through the cracks. They landed in a prisoner of war camp east of the Ural Mountains.

By some miracle or his own resilience, Sándor had survived the balloon crash almost unscathed. He had just minor scrapes and bruises. His body had healed fairly quickly from the torture wounds and deprivation without lasting ill effect. The limp, on the other hand, he had acquired at the camp courtesy of a drunken Cossack guard whose favorite pastime was using Jews for target practice. Fortunately the fellow was so soused up he missed Sándor's vital organs and splintered his hip instead. This wound did not heal as quickly. The overworked Russian doctor, a political prisoner who was supposedly involved in a conspiracy against the Czar, patched him up. He labored under primitive conditions and a critical shortage of medical supplies. Sándor was sent in excruciating pain to another camp with a hospital. It was hundreds of miles away, and he arrived in septic shock.

Conditions there were just a notch above primitive. An Austrian surgeon from Graz, a fellow prisoner, saved his life and limb. He prevented the gangrene from spreading by applying maggots to the infected area. He made sure the wound was properly bandaged and the dressing changed regularly. Sándor also had his first warm meal since his capture—a thick soup of indeterminate ingredients but as savory in that moment as the finest cuisine he had tasted at his mother's table. The healing process was slow and agonizing, but it kept him from being worked to death in a coal mine in godforsaken places with names such as Irkutsk or Kutznesk.

The seasons came and went, turning from scorching summers to glacial winters. Sándor lost count. One winter day he was hobbling over the icy ground between his barrack and the canteen on his crutches, which were crudely fashioned tree limbs. He noticed the guards were gone. There were no rifles or machine guns pointing down from the watchtowers. No patrols were circling the perimeter. There was no more herding the prisoners around with shouts and curses. The inmates found themselves free but without a way out.

On leaving, the Russians took most of the communications equipment and destroyed what they couldn't carry. Cut off from the outside world and without any news about the war, the inmates had no prospect for rescue or escape in the dead of winter. They had no choice but to make themselves at home in the camp and took over the guard quarters with their relatively greater comforts and better supplies.

While Sándor's bodily shell languished in limbo, his brain cells chugged away in high gear. Never, not even in his darkest moments, did he let go of his dream of becoming a stage director. He impounded every piece of writing material he could find. In the absence of a library, he reconstructed from memory modern and classical dramas mostly in German. The actors' troupe he organized from fellow prisoners put on improvised versions of plays by the likes of Chekhov, Kleist, and Oscar Wilde. He was particularly fond of Ibsen. In a production he cobbled together of *Hedda Gabler*, he took on the title role himself and found ingenious ways of making his disability enhance the drama.

Then one day the Russians came back. Sándor remembered it was spring, though he couldn't remember which spring. He had lost count of how many seasons he had played Hedda Gabler. He was taking his bow and expecting the usual tepid applause from those inmates who still came on occasion for lack of anything else to do, when he heard loud clapping and shouts of "bravo." In the back of the room stood a little man in a ragged Russian uniform. He was sporting a goatee and wire-rimmed glasses. He was boiling over with enthusiasm.

As it turned out, he was the leader of a band of peasants and work-ers. The man they addressed as "Commissar" told them Russia was now in the hands of worker and peasant Soviets who were spreading the gospel of Karl Marx. Sándor's heart leaped. Mention of that name brought back fond memories of long hours spent reading and debating those writings with his classmates at the gymnasium in Debrecen.

The commissar elaborated on the finer points of Ibsen's play and its revolutionary message in fluent Austrian German. He had acquired this through years of sitting around the coffeehouses of Vienna, read-ing newspapers in every language available, and writing revolutionary tracts in all of them. He called everybody *Genosse*, the German commu-nist moniker for "comrade." He spouted endless harangues in snarling cadences of a barking dog about world revolution, the dictatorship of the proletariat, the decadence of capitalism, and on and on. He showed a firm command of all languages represented at the camp. He charged the doomed, bedraggled band to go back to their home countries and join the revolution against the reactionary forces in the historic class struggle against the capitalist exploiters.

A dilemma arose when it wasn't altogether clear what and where these home countries were. They had been fighting the war for the empire of Kaiser Franz Josef. Now they heard for the first time that the empires had fallen. Franz Josef was dead. Kaiser Wilhelm was in exile. The Czar of all Russians and the entire Romanov family had been removed. The commissar didn't specify to where. The Central Powers had lost the war, and an army of international workers had established revolutionary governments everywhere.

Sándor took the news with a cool head. Revolution brought to his mind 1848 and the national Hungarian poets. Ever mindful of his stage career, he made a mental note to revive the dramas of Mór Jókai when he got back to civilization.

Months after the encounter with the commissar, he felt his bones had healed well enough to undertake the long, perilous, arduous journey home. An early snowfall signaled the onset of another winter. He limped along washed out highways in his Cossack boots. The heavy army overcoat, its hem dragging on the ground, bundled up his emaciated body like grown-up clothes on a child. The pulled-down flaps of his ushanka hat shielded his ears and face against frostbite. Across the Ural he went, jumping on the rare passing train. Recruits for the Red Army headed for some no-man's-land packed the cars. On he went through the vast expanse of the southern Russian steppe.

Civil war had ravaged the landscape dotted with desolate villages in which the dead outnumbered the cadaverous living due to famine and disease. Conditions were not much better when he reached the Podolian Plain, now Poland, or the snowcapped, densely forested Carpathian Mountains. He never knew exactly what country he was in. The scars of war were still open and bleeding wherever he directed his gaze. He went hungry for much of the way. He obtained food only by stealing or from the hands of kindly peasants willing to share some of their own meager scraps.

Eventually he made it back home to Budapest. What he found there bore little resemblance to the place he had left almost ten years before. His father's mansion had been turned into a camp for Gypsies and other riffraff. Traces of ransacking were visible everywhere. The costly furnishings and artwork were gone. Most of the library shelves, which had housed rare books and manuscripts collected over a century, had been stripped. They were used, he was told, for firewood. The bare walls still bore the marks of the priceless paintings that had once decorated the hallways, dining room, and parlor. His father had died of a heart attack when one of Bela Kun's thugs rammed the butt of his rifle into his stomach. A former servant told him this. Rumor had it his mother had been the victim of rape, following which she went back to Szátmar, now in Romania, to beg her father's forgiveness. The family fortune was gone.

Sándor did not mount the curved staircase to the private quarters. Whatever might have become of the items in his room, he preferred not to know. There was nothing he could do. His only hope for a future was his verbal contract with Max Reinhardt at the Deutsches Theater in Berlin. Ever the intrepid optimist, he set out with renewed determination for the German capital. He arrived in what turned out to be the month of November in the year 1923. It was a time marked by snaking food lines and the billion mark bread loaf.

The great director remembered him and the delicious meal he had enjoyed at his parents' house before the war, but he did not remember anything about a contract concerning a position for Sándor at the Deutsches.

"It wasn't anything in writing. More like a verbal promise sealed with a handshake," Sándor explained.

"That was so long ago. Ten years almost. Where have you been all this time?" Reinhardt asked perturbed.

"There was a war," Sándor stated. "I served the Kaiser on the Eastern Front when I was shot down in my surveillance balloon. The Russians took me to Siberia. We were completely isolated and didn't even know when the war was over. I was also wounded. As you can see, I still have a limp. But I always practiced my craft even under the most difficult conditions."

"Your craft?"

"Yes. Directing. I wrote down the great dramas such as Ibsen's from memory. We had no printed material, but my fellow inmates and I produced them."

"You are obviously a remarkable young man. I wish I could do something for you. But times are bad, and our budget is tight. Sorry." That ended their exchange.

Alexander Levary let out a deep sigh. He pointed toward his coat on a hook in the corner.

"I had it altered to fit me," he said. "I will never part with it. It's my talisman. So are the hat and boots. These items I took from a dead Cossack saved my life. I don't know what would have become of me without them."

Curtis nodded pensively. By now I knew him well enough to see through the workings of the wheels in his brain. Giving Levary time to regain present ground from the emotional journey into his past, Curtis struggled with how to pose his next question with enough tact to lead the subject gently down the slippery slope of the topic to which all that preceded was mere prologue. What really happened in Berlin? Why did Viktor Erdos leave Stella's company without protest?

"That is a question I never cease asking myself," Levary said with a mournful expression.

"You could have contacted him. You knew where to find him. His articles were in the papers. His travel reports from Palestine and other places in the Middle East were freely available. Didn't you read the papers?"

"Yes, of course. We were quite surprised to hear he was writing for a Zionist paper in Vienna. Stella and I thought it a bit odd he should have fallen in with those crazies who want to establish a Jewish state in Palestine."

"So did you think he had found a different circle of friends? Did you think perhaps Stella was no longer important to him?" I felt the hairs rising on the nape of my neck.

"I don't think so. Stella would always be the most important person in his life. He distanced himself because he did not want to bring any harm to her reputation and career."

"So his homosexuality wouldn't taint her reputation?"

"Exactly."

"Where does that leave you?" I interjected. "It doesn't make any sense. I've been told your sexual proclivities were well-known around town."

"In certain circles and among artists and actors such as your parents, *gnädiges Fräulein*, but not among Stella's adoring general public.

That's why she married me. To put the rumors beginning to surface in the tabloids to rest.

"Quite frankly, I was indispensable to her as her manager. I had directed her in several very successful films. I was the one who held the stirrups for her climb into the movie business and international fame. You must remember that acting was everything to Stella. Viktor was the dispensable one."

"So we've heard from other quarters." Curtis took over again. "It's still unclear why the change in the equation that had existed for eight years. What happened in 1931?"

"You could say what happened then was the Nazis, but let me go back for a moment to the time when Viktor saved my life."

FIVE

A stranger in a strange, windswept city, Sándor hit the pavement with his Cossack boots. He wandered aimlessly in drizzling rain through the gray alleys and murky side streets, and only his Russian army coat and ushanka fur hat kept him from freezing to death. At night he huddled inside the doorway of an apartment complex, the interior yard of a shopping arcade, the side nave of a church, or wherever he could find momentary shelter. He had little sleep. A shivering, noisy multitude of the dregs of humanity already crowded most of these places. He avoided public shelters for fear his coat and hat would be stolen or someone might pull off his boots while he slept.

After five days and nights, he reemerged into the light of day, as he recalled. The sheer force of an iron will pulled him up. The lousy hand he had been dealt would not continue to guide his life. As the first order of his transformation, he reassumed the name he had chosen for himself before the war: Alexander Levary. He cleaned himself up in the washroom at a railroad station and sought out the brighter areas of the city along the grand boulevards. The sun didn't shine there either. It was the same leaden sky, but Alexander marched through the Brandenburg Gate with a triumphal stride in the manner of his namesake. He strolled down Unter den Linden. He stopped by the cafés. While he consumed little, he devoured the newspapers searching for something, anything that might give him hope or a lifeline to pursue. He found it. Perusing the papers for a few days, his attention was drawn to the byline of several articles on political events and the cultural scene. It read Viktor Erdos.

My word! he thought to himself. His old chum Chaim Erdreich had come up in the world. He also noticed his glowing reviews of the performances of an actress named Stella Berger. Somehow that rang a bell. It evoked the vague memory of Viktor speaking about a young, stage-struck girl in Vienna who called herself Stella. Now she appeared on stage in Berlin. It had to be the same one.

At first he was resentful. These people had had a chance to pursue their dreams while he was cut off from the world. He had spent years in a Siberian shithole only to find his whole world destroyed on his return. But Alexander Levary wasn't one to get hung up on what was past and couldn't be changed. He wouldn't let resentment or envy pull him down. He was a man of action and determined to make his own destiny. He was sure a request for a little help from a friend would not be denied.

He found out where Viktor lived and paid him a visit. As he had expected, his longtime friend would not deny him a helping hand in getting back on his feet. That was in 1923. He folded up his Russian memorabilia and stashed them in a trunk. Reincarnated and clothed in the fashion of the day, he entered the gates to a new realm. He rediscovered his fondness for things sartorial. As he had been before the war, he became a fastidious dresser. Viktor and Sender resumed their prewar relationship, though both their lives revolved around Stella. Everything was about and for Stella. Stella was the center, the focal point, and the fulcrum from which everything devolved and to which everything gravitated. She was the Charybdis who drew in every bit of energy and breath around her.

Her career blossomed and reached its zenith by the middle of the decade. Levary's crediting of himself for pulling her out of the pool of second-tier cast members at repertory theaters to premier rank and stardom was surely exaggerated. If anybody did any pulling, it was Stella by means of her astounding talent and will. Stella and her friends moved out of the cold-water walk-ups in the depressed areas of the city. The goddess set up house in a villa in Dahlem, which was to become infamous for its opulence, lavish parties, and orgies. Supported by Viktor's journalistic activities, the two friends maintained an alternate residence away from Stella in a posh founder-period flat in the swanky neighborhood of Leipzigerstrasse near Spittelmarkt. This was how they set up a double life—a life away from Stella and a life for and with Stella.

Though naturally monogamous, Viktor went along with Sender's desire for occasional walks on the wild side. The best years of his life had been wasted away in the backwater of Siberia. Now was the time to recapture the lost years of his youth. So went Sender's reasoning for hurling himself into the campy haunt in the Kreuzberg district called "Café Vogelfrei." Located in an abandoned bridge tender's station on the Landwehrkanal, it styled itself as an intimate meeting place for discerning gentlemen rather than a cabaret. Sparse entertainment was provided in the piano bar up front, but the main attraction was the back room where the clientele indulged their diverse proclivities in discreet anonymity.

Viktor had little taste for these activities and much preferred the Taubenschlag where he could read his latest poetic output to an appreciative audience. Sender deemed it ironic and tragic, therefore, that Viktor should be the one to become entangled in a brawl at the Vogelfrei. From that fight derived a series of events that culminated in his fall from grace with the venerated Stella.

Toward the end of the decade, Nazi types increasingly swamped the Vogelfrei. They strutted about in their diarrhea-brown uniforms swathed with red armbands imprinted with swastikas. Their presence introduced a raucous tone of rowdiness and coarseness into the ambience of a gentlemen's club the management had striven to cultivate over many years. The vulgar anti-Jewish discourse was the last straw for Viktor. He urged and begged Sender to stay away from the place as long as those thugs held sway there. However, Sender refused to clear the field to the barbarian hordes. He savored the idea of a chance for a little *espièglerie*. He wanted to put one over on them and play the ruffians for fools, helped by the diffuse lighting in which the activities were conducted.

To Viktor's relief Sender had little time for such exploits, at least for a while. He was far too busy at the UFA film studio in Neubabelsberg and on location along the Baltic Sea producing and directing his first sound movie with Stella in the starring role. With her financial support, he had created their own production company, LevBerg Creations, which gave him full artistic control. Levary had directed Stella in several well-received silent films. Stella's stage obligations temporarily had curbed his desire to get in on the sound craze. Then came the tremendous success of Josef von Sternberg's *Blue Angel*. Alexander Levary was no longer content with playing second fiddle. He immediately searched for a suitable vehicle to showcase Stella's beguiling voice and elocution. He was sure audiences everywhere would rave when they heard her emote in the mellifluous, enthralling tones that had captivated Berlin theatergoers for years. He planned to take full advantage of the fact that Marlene Dietrich's emotional and vocal range was rather limited. He would unleash the full power of emotions gushing from the inner well of Stella Berger.

Levary found the perfect vehicle in *Cecile*. It was Theodor Fontane's novel about the adulterous affair of a neuralgic young woman and neglected wife. It gave Stella a chance to pull out all stops, letting her full register of emotions explode onto the screen. The director and his cameraman took full advantage of the medium. They zoomed in for facial close-ups at critical moments. Levary's hopes and expectations to make it to the top were more than fulfilled. The critics raved. Cinematic history, groundbreaking, an emotional rollercoaster, and an artistic triumph for star and director were some of the proclamations in the press. The foremost theater critic, Alfred Kerr, known as the "culture pope," who had frequently derided Stella's stage performances as maudlin sentimentality, even he expressed himself flabbergasted, bowled over, and converted. Viktor Erdos's review hedged in his kudos with a few words of criticism that were on closer reading a form of underhanded praise. Movie house audiences in town and country rose to standing ovations at the climax of the duel and suicide.

The star and producer of the film received wide press coverage. Pictures of the smiling pair on the red carpet of the first-run movie palace in Friedrichstadt and subsequent interviews appeared on the front pages of tabloids and glossy magazines.

The fountains of champagne and caviar at the Hotel Kempinski, attended by a thousand, ran dry. The lights of the private party at Stella's villa, attended by a few hundred, had gone out. The handful of select gentlemen attending an intimate, private gathering on Leipzigerstrasse had departed in the graying morning. Sasha, the life of it all, was still much too pumped up with energy to give it a rest.

"It's only four o'clock," he told the washed-out Viktor, who was in his pajamas and ready for a good night's sleep or what was left of it. "The Vogelfrei doesn't close until six."

"What about those Nazis? They'll only spoil all the fun," Viktor said to dissuade him.

"*Au contraire, mon ami.*" Sender lifted his pointer in schoolmasterly fashion. "Poking it to those loser thugs will put the crowning touch on our success."

Entering the premises, they found it packed with drunken storm-troopers singing raucously and disturbing the peace of the neighbor-hood. The Jewish owner took Sender and Viktor aside and suggested they leave right away.

"The atmosphere in our club is not what it used to be. So far they haven't attacked me personally, but I know I'll have to close down soon," he said.

Sasha insisted he wasn't about to cede the field. Acquired on the battlefield of war, this was now a favorite expression. He told the owner it would be a shame if the Vogelfrei were no longer a free and open field for anybody looking for a good time.

"Haven't you heard? Chancellor von Papen just lifted the ban against those hooligans," the owner replied. "They've been celebrating their big victory all night. They constantly brag about their bloody clashes with the communists and how many of them they killed in the streets."

Sasha refused to heed the owner's warning or Viktor's entreaties. With head held high, unflinching defiance marked his every step. He walked straight into the den of roaring, bloodthirsty rowdies. Right in the center of the back room, a flash of light stopped him dead in his tracks. He was still trying to adjust his eyes to the darkened surround-ings, a sudden flare engulfed him in a shaft of light and blinded him.

"It's the Jew from the movies!" someone shouted, and others repeated it. They obviously had a list of Jewish names in the entertainment industry, and Levary's face had been on prominent display in recent weeks.

Slogans of "Judah, bite the dust," "No more Jew smut," and "We want clean, fatherlandly, wholesome German folk movies!" resounded. There was loutish laughter, coarse obscenities, pushing, and shoving. They fell over him like a pack of cannibals. They stripped him naked and tied him to a pole, Saint Sebastian style without the loincloth. One ruffian kneeled beside him, flicked open a cigarette lighter, and brought the flame close to his exposed parts.

There were rhythmic shouts of, "Burn off his foreskin!" Then, "Oh no! He has no foreskin! Burn off his circumcised dick!"

No one paid attention to Viktor who hugged the shadows. His eyes were sharply focused on the unfolding scene. No one saw him pull out the gun. Anticipating trouble that night, he had the foresight to pack his Roth-Steyr pistol. The shot went off and shattered the hand that held the lighter. Then a second shot hit its mark and penetrated the back of the head. The target writhed and groaned on the floor.

Viktor stood unflinching with his gun held steady in his hand. A showdown seemed imminent. Then the unexpected occurred. There was no return fire. The warriors of the crooked cross fled. They turned on their heels and did what Sender had refused to do—clear the field. They took the body with them.

When the dust settled, Viktor untied his trembling friend and scooped his clothing off the floor. Viktor urged him to hurry. "We'd better get the hell out of here before the police arrives," he said while fighting off the kisses Sender tried to shower on him. Outside he kissed his Roth-Steyr good-bye and threw it into the Landwehrkanal.

"I'll have to get another one," he said. "With all the street fighting going on, we'd better be prepared to defend ourselves."

He never did. Sender still thought there was no need to panic. The communist fighters would prevail in the end. He was sure.

In the following days, they scoured the newspapers for police reports of a shooting at a bar in Kreuzberg but found nothing. Sender telephoned the Vogelfrei owner. No police ever showed up there. Obviously the thugs didn't want publicity about their secret activities. Then he bade them good-bye. He was leaving for more peaceable pastures in America.

For a few weeks, all was quiet as far as the affair was concerned. Bad publicity was not something the Nazis wanted. In other ways the street fighting between the Nazi storm troopers and the communists raged on. Brutality and savagery reached new heights on both sides.

All the while Stella was unaware of her friends' scuffle at the Café Vogelfrei. She resumed her stage career at the Deutsches. Alexander Levary cast about for fresh ideas for another movie. He needed to build on his success as quickly as possible. His motto was not to give the public time to turn its affections to other contenders. Viktor wrote his news reports and commentaries, and in quiet moments, such as they were to be had, he composed his poetry. The club owner was apparently right about the publicity-shy SA men. In the summer of 1931, however, retribution struck in an unexpected, vengeful form.

The storm troopers invaded the movie houses where *Cecile* was playing and interrupted the showing with raucous shouts of "Jewish smut!" Parading pickets outside showed photographs of the smiling Stella and Levary altered to look devilish like caricatures from the Nazi smear rag *Der Stürmer*. The picture was captioned, "Germany is in our hands." On the steps of the theater where Stella played Gretchen in a showing of Goethe's *Faust*, Nazi demonstrators were linked in solid formation to bar theatergoers from entering. Posters showed Stella as Gretchen at the spinning wheel with the caption, "What is she spinning? A net to ensnare the German Michel!"

Then the rowdies started to parade in front of the Dahlem villa shouting, "The Jews are our misfortune!" Stella had enough and took it out on Ulla. Some Germanic professor in the previous century had coined this old slogan, and Stella had heard it too many times from the mouth of her companion. She had never said anything, but now she had heard the slander against her people one time too many.

"What do you mean your people? You are not one of them. Are you?" Ulla whimpered in disbelief.

"Why should this be such a surprise to you? Of course I am one of them!"

"It never occurred to me. You're not like..."

"Like what? Come on. Explain."

Ulla was in tears. "Nobody knows." She gave it some consideration and then added, "I know what you are doing. You're trying to fool me for the sake of your Jewish gentlemen friends here." She pointed at Alexander and Viktor. Standing by with their hands in their pockets, they were taking in the scene with gloating amusement.

Stella poured out her heart. "If you didn't know, Herr Goebbels certainly is much better informed, as you can hear and see out there. I never took your hints and allusions seriously. What did they matter? They were part of many people's everyday talk. One gets used to it. But now the situation has changed. Your anti-Jewish attitude and your little digs and baits are now becoming blatant Jew-hatred. I will no longer tolerate this kind of talk in my house. Don't forget. What's at stake is nothing less than my career, and that feeds us all."

Never before had she put Ulla in her place in such a firm manner. Ulla broke down. All she was able to bring forth in response was a whimpering, "I never knew. No one knew. No one!"

Then she gathered herself up and ran out of the room. She was not seen again until the morning she appeared at the door with a suitcase. If she expected Stella to hold her back or beg her to stay, she was disappointed.

Alone with her Jewish gentlemen friends, as Ulla called them, Stella smiled. She was obviously satisfied with her performance. Only this time it wasn't a performance. She had spoken from her heart and with deep concern.

"She had it coming for a long time," she said. "But Ulla isn't the problem. It's what's happening to Germany. Anybody with eyes to see can read the writing on the wall. The barbarians are at the gate. We might all have to clear the field and seek a place of refuge."

Viktor and Sasha were astounded. She had never shown any awareness of what was going on in the world of politics or anything beyond the perimeter of matters connected with the theater. From then on she frequently involved them in discussions about the increasingly worrisome situation. She sought out Viktor's advice and opinion in particular. After all he was the one who was best informed. He was at home in the halls of power, the Reichstag and judicial courts, where he cultivated connections with prominent people in the course of gathering material for his articles. He often applied his sharpest pen to exposés about the violent excesses of the National Socialist paramilitary organizations. As such his name figured high on the list of enemies of the rising movement. The outside world was becoming a dangerous place.

Inside the villa an atmosphere of lightness made itself felt. A note of joviality entered into Stella's dealings with her gentlemen friends. Ulla's presence had previously cast a looming shadow. Now that she was gone the threesome breathed free like the three little pigs dancing on the corpse of the Big Bad Wolf. They laughed, cried, joked, exchanged anecdotes, and engaged in lighthearted or heated discussions about anything under the sun. The holiday lasted about two weeks. Ulla came crawling back. Where she had been keeping herself in all that time was never clear. It was also unclear to anyone why Stella took her back.

The two women had a private conversation from which Stella emerged seemingly reconciled. She assured her friends all was patched up. They found it hard to believe that Stella should have caved in. Ulla promised never to say anything against Jews again. She had heard that phrase, "the Jews are our misfortune," from her father and his business partners all her life. When the financial crisis in Bismarck's time ruined their businesses, it was the Jews' fault. She just repeated it without thinking. From now on she would be more guarded in what she was saying. Stella was forgiving to the dismay and incomprehension of most of her friends.

At the time of Ulla's return, the Nazi demonstrations against Stella stopped. Instead the Brownshirts directed their ire toward Viktor Erdos and Alexander Levary—two men who everybody knew were closely associated with Stella Berger. That's when Ulla lapsed in her promise. She told Stella the Jews had to go.

Words such as "faggots" and "sodomites" were heard on Leipzigerstrasse, arousing fear there might still be a police investigation into the Kreuzberg shooting. In a private conversation out of earshot of Ulla, Sasha and Viktor told Stella about the incident at the Café Vogelfrei. The relationship between her two friends had always been an open secret and of little concern to her. The way she saw the situation now, however, the sybaritic living had to end. They now had powerful enemies who would use them to destroy her.

"I absolutely cannot have any scandal or innuendo touching me about what the bourgeois mind regards as perverse activity."

The next day she appeared at the apartment on Leipzigerstrasse. To avoid being detected by the restive Brownshirts, she entered a neighboring building and cut through a connecting tunnel in the basement. She found Sasha and Viktor discussing plans for leaving Berlin together. They planned to take up residence either in Vienna or Budapest until things quieted down. Stella would not hear of it. Both of them could not leave her. Since Viktor was the shooter, and his columns put him in the crosshairs of Josef Goebbels and his minions, she thought it might be wise for him to leave Germany for a while. This suggestion was so out of the blue, it left both men speechless. Sasha was stunned. He looked at Viktor whose face was glowing red with rage. Then came the second bomb.

"I know how you feel about this." She wrestled for a moment with how to put her next proposition. She avoided looking at Viktor who stood dumbfounded as if hit in the stomach. She turned to Levary. "Sasha, you are my manager and director. You are indispensable to me. To put an end to the innuendos and hate campaign, I have decided to marry you."

Was she kidding? Who did she think would be fooled? Alexander Levary knew it was an empty gesture, but he acquiesced. His career was inexorably intertwined with Stella's. He had ridden to fame on her coattails. Without her he was nothing. He poured her a cup of black coffee and a stiff cognac for himself. They faced each other on the couch and made plans like lovebirds. It would just be a brief ceremony at the Schöneberg Rathaus. Viktor wasn't even in the room for them anymore. He seemingly ceased to exist for the pair absorbed in plotting a scheme to salvage Stella's imperiled career and reputation.

Alexander had never seen the mild-mannered Viktor in such a rage. Roaring like a wounded animal, he hurled himself at Stella, seized her by the throat with both hands, and lifted her delicate frame up to the level of his eyes. He showered her with the vilest epithets, called her whore and slut he had lifted from the gutter. The names didn't quite reflect reality, but he had lost all control. Alexander Levary feared he would choke Stella to death or break her delicate neck. It was with great exertion he managed to pry Viktor's grip off her neck. Stella collapsed on the sofa like a rag doll.

"I never want to see you again in all my life," she gasped. "And may you burn in hell!" She spit out the words like a curse.

Viktor called on her a few times in the days that followed, but she wouldn't see him. Sender moved his belongings from the apartment on Leipzigerstrasse to the villa. A few weeks later, pictures of the smiling couple, Stella Berger and Alexander Levary, exchanging rings and kisses at the registry office of Schöneberg Rathaus blazed from the front pages of every newspaper and magazine.

"We never saw Viktor again." Alexander Levary concluded his evocation of demons past with a doleful look. "All we knew was he had gone back to Vienna and was writing for a Zionist publication. I don't think Stella ever read that kind of stuff, but I followed his reports from Jerusalem and Tel Aviv and other places in the Middle East. Then I lost track." His voice broke off.

Neither Curtis nor I said anything. There was nothing to say.

Sender added, "We stayed in Berlin until March 1933. Fortunately Stella had an offer to appear on the London stage. So we all moved over there. Ulla came with us, of course."

Curtis thanked him and helped him into his Russian overcoat. At the door he turned once more. "You see why none of this could come out. Especially at the trial. It wouldn't have looked good for Viktor to be seen as someone with a history of violent outbursts. I'd like to help as much as I can but in strictest anonymity. Maybe you should take a closer look at Ulla's activities and connections. It's just a hunch, but I never believed in her change of heart."

"Just one moment," I said. "Why are you telling us this story if it cannot be used in Viktor's cause?"

"It wouldn't make him look very good, would it?" he replied. "I just wanted to set the record straight. I still don't believe he is responsible for Stella's death. The assault in Berlin took place under very different circumstances. I should have stood by him then."

Yeah. You should have, I thought.

He pushed his ushanka hat down over his ears and turned to leave.

There by the grace of God goes a hypocrite, I thought.

Things didn't look good for Viktor, even without public knowledge of the story we had just heard. It also didn't look good for Alexander Levary and his chances for making it big in Hollywood on his own now that his coattail ride was over.

SIX

The following Sunday I took the train to Ossining. Visiting hours were from two to four in the afternoon. I was nervous and unsure how he would receive me or if he wanted to see me at all. Stuck under my left arm I carried his violin. Somehow I felt the instrument might melt the ice between us.

"I see you brought my violin," he said immediately. "You shouldn't have. This is no place for music."

"I thought you might like to see your old friend is well kept."

"I had no doubt when I entrusted it to you that you would be a good caretaker."

We exchanged some pleasantries and engaged in small talk about his accommodations and the prison food.

"You should stay with your studies. Not play detective on a hopeless case," he suggested.

"Who says it's hopeless? Curtis is even now working on the appeal."

"I know he is. I appreciate what he is doing and what both of you have done for me."

I told him we had spoken with Alexander Levary. As I expected his ears and eyebrows went up.

"What could he have to say outside his testimony at the trial?" he said with suspicion.

"He had much to say about the truth of what happened in Berlin."

"What makes you think he told the truth? Sender, Sándor, Sasha, Alexander. The man has as many faces as he has names."

"He also believes you are innocent."

"Then why didn't he come out and say so in his testimony?"

"He didn't exactly say the opposite. You know certain delicate matters might have come to light..."

"Yeah, yeah. Matters embarrassing to him and Stella when she was alive."

I asked him point blank about the incident at Café Vogelfrei and his assault on Stella. He more or less confirmed Levary's account.

"What Sender might not have told you is that the SA ransacked my office more than once. I was even pistol-whipped at one point. I no longer had a gun, and even if I had, the odds were against me in a firefight. I thought it best to escape the dangers of Berlin and relocate to Vienna. For some foolish reason, I had the illusion Sender would come with me and maybe even Stella. I told him they could make movies in Austria just as well. She would no doubt be welcome at the Burgtheater. But she had other plans. Or maybe it was Ulla who had other plans."

"Do you think Stella was under Ulla's cudgel? It has been suggested she was blackmailing Stella."

"Blackmailing? What could she possibly blackmail her about?"

I dropped the subject. I feared any hint about what Stella had been doing in Zurich, the particulars of her relationship with Ulla, and the nature of certain photographs that might be smoldering in a bank vault would not only have destroyed his image of the immaculate Stella but would have been the death blow to himself.

"I always felt there was something strange and incongruous in that relationship," he pondered. "You know how it is when you have a feeling something is at odds? I could never put my finger on what it was exactly. Mostly I didn't give it much thought. And I don't believe that lesbian bit."

"Do you think Ulla's outlook on Jews was less than positive?"

"That's putting it mildly. Nobody could accuse her of love for Jews. She made no bones about it either. One gets used to this kind of talk, though, and learns to ignore it. Certain anti-Jewish figures of speech were always part of the culture and entered the language in general. The Nazis are something else. For them Jew hatred is holy gospel. She is probably at least a sympathizer. Why are we wasting our breath talking about this woman?"

"Because it has been suggested she might have had something to do with Stella's death."

He gave me a long, probing look. "Who would say that?"

"I can't tell you, but we think it's an angle worth pursuing. She is probably still in New York somewhere. Someone is helping and supporting her."

"Didn't she inherit a nice bundle? I would presume Stella had her in her will."

"If she even had a will. All that is still up in the air. Much of the estate and its assets are in England, and while the war is going on... Curtis is very interested in talking to Ulla. We just have to find her."

"You and Mr. Wolff are very kind. I am very grateful to you and appreciate what you are trying to do, but you are wasting your time. This case is sealed. The public mind is made up. For them justice has been served. The murderer sits on death row. You'll see. You'll run up against a wall."

I saw the futility of arguing with him further. There was one aspect of this whole melodrama that still bothered me, though.

"Why did you never try to contact Stella in all those years? Why did you let ten years go by? She was understandably outraged about the assault, which Sender says was not like you at all. You could have asked her forgiveness. She was a generous person. Don't you think she would have forgiven you had you shown some remorse?"

"But, my dear child, I did. My situation in Berlin had become untenable. My life was in danger. The SA thugs would not have left me alone. I had to leave. But I did write to Stella. Hundreds of times. All my letters were returned unopened and marked undeliverable. I found out where she was staying in England and wrote to her there. I looked forward to the mail delivery every day. I hoped for a response or any sign she received and read my letters. Even when I was traveling in the Middle East, I wrote to her many times. I never gave up, because holding a grudge for so long was not something the Stella I knew would do.

"Here in America it was not difficult to follow Stella's whereabouts in the papers. Then she came to New York, and you know the story from there. I left a note at the Plaza Hotel where she was staying. I suspected she never saw any of my letters and that someone was intercepting them. I had to speak with her in person. I wanted her to look me in the eye and tell me she still hated me. I tried to attract her attention with my violin outside the theater, but nothing happened. There was no sign she even noticed the mendicant fiddler. I read in the papers her theater engagement was ending. I figured she would go back to California afterward. I had no way of reaching her there. I was in a state of panic. My last chance for redemption was slipping away. I had to plead with her, throw myself at her feet, and beg her forgiveness. Maybe it was a stupid way of going about it. I am very sorry it got you in trouble. All I can say is I had reached the end of my rope."

He had looked me straight in the eye during this long speech. Now he turned that wistful gaze toward the little, barred window high up. It shed a dim light on him. I realized his tormented soul had lived suspended in purgatory all those years. I reached for his hands across the table. He did not withhold them. We sat quietly, engrossed in our own thoughts. I knew what needed to be done and hoped it wasn't too late.

"There is only one person who could and would have intercepted your letters," I said and readied to leave. "You know as well as I do who this person is. We'll find her and call her to account."

SEVEN

"You've gotta be kidding. Get this thing away from me!" Curtis put out his hands as if fending off a snake attack. "No way am I going to wear these."

"It's the latest in Bavarian fashion chic." I laughed and held up a pair of shiny, knee-high lederhosen with suspenders embroidered with edelweiss flowers. "It comes with a stylish Tyrolean hat. Come on. You'll look fetching!"

"What's that paintbrush sticking out?"

"This, my dear, I'll have you know is called a *Gamsbart*. It's a tuft of hair from a chamois, a goat antelope species common in Alpine and other mountainous regions."

"OK. That is more than I need to know. If you ask my opinion, this whole outfit is just stupid."

"I didn't ask your opinion. I don't like these rags any more than you do, but they'll serve our purpose."

"Speaking of fetching, I like your outfit much better. You *do* look fetching."

"Why, thank you." I turned around in front of him and modeled my checkered pink dirndl complete with a light blue apron. On my head was a coquettish grass-green Tyrolean hat with a white ostrich feather stuck in the corded band. "Don't ask me to yodel. I have no idea how to produce such a sound."

"All this cost me a bundle. I hope you'll reimburse me," I said. When he gave me a pained look, I pointed out he could write it off as a business expense.

When we had finished applying heavy layers of makeup and rouge to mask our features, we got a good laugh at the pair of Alpine peasants smiling back at us from the mirror.

"We really do look fetching. Both of us." He strutted back and forth in front of the mirror like a peacock.

As we were getting into our coats, I gave the hand reaching out for my waist a decisive slap. This was strictly business. He had to do a lot more penitence if he was to redeem himself. *Let him sweat in limbo.* My heart overflowed with sympathy for Viktor Erdos. Not so much for Curtis Wolff.

"Well, off to the Oktoberfest we go. I hope your dance step is up to doing the *Schuhplattler.*"

I was pleased to note that the impersonators of Alpine peasants and shepherds around us, whose ancestors probably came to America as far back as a hundred years ago, were no more adept than Curtis and I at slapping their ankles and knees to the thumping beat of the oompah band. I, at least, had spent some time in my childhood in the foothills of the Alps and had a vague remembrance of the real thing. My efforts to pass to Curtis what little knowledge I had were quite fruitless.

"You mean to say you don't have these kinds of festivities in the Midwest? Isn't Wisconsin the German diaspora site Herr Dettelbach is so proud of?"

"Could be, but it's not where I come from. My ancestors came from Westphalia in the north."

Dancing and chitchatting, however, were not the purpose of our visit to the Yorkville Oktoberfest on East Eighty-Sixth Street. As I surveyed the joint, my attention was drawn to a door in the back of the hall.

"Hold off on the beer. You need to keep a clear head," I told Curtis who gulped down a bit too much of the brew in front of him. "There's something going on in the back room. See those goons at the door? They are checking everybody entering. Looks like it's by invitation only.

Another thing. None of those people are in costume. They didn't come here to frolic."

"Maybe they know how ridiculous it would make them look."

"Be serious. Mulligan was right. Something's stewing, and it isn't sauerbraten."

We danced a few more rounds and waltzed closer to that door with each turn. Then I spotted the George Brent look-alike. He had a thin mustache and a dangling cigarette, and he wore a perfectly tailored, striped Brooks Brother's suit. He headed straight for the goon-guarded door. They stepped aside reverentially to let him pass.

I lowered my head and pulled Curtis's hand to make him do likewise. "Dettelbach just went in," I whispered. "We have to find out what is going on in there."

"And how are we going to do that?" Curtis whispered back.

"We'll have to find out if there's a window to the backyard. Maybe we can eavesdrop."

"You've been watching too many movies."

"Sometimes life copies art." I had expected more cooperation from the counsel for the defense and said so. "Don't you think this is important?"

"It could also be that the inspector is enjoying a game of poker among friends. That's what people do in back rooms. Well, among other things."

"What about the guards at the door? Does this look like an innocent get-together to you? Besides they would more likely be playing a game of Skat."

"Always finicky. It could very well be quite innocent. Since you insist, though, maybe you also have a plan for how we'll get into the backyard."

The merrymaking was in high gear. The dancing, singing, and beer swilling were taking their effect. People linked arms and reveled in good cheer and *Gemütlichkeit*. Nobody paid us any attention. We slipped out a side door unhindered and hopefully unnoticed. An acerbic smell of stale beer and sauerkraut assaulted our nostrils in the dingy yard. We stumbled over a pile of discarded crates and kegs. The next challenge was to figure out which window belonged to the room of interest.

"It must be the one with the light. It's about the right area, but it's a bit high."

"You're getting to be a real sleuth." Curtis gave me a patronizing pat on the back.

I gave him a kick in the shin and told him to hoist me up so I could get a look inside. The smudged glass pane and smoke rising from the room blurred my vision, but I would have bet my life the woman I saw was Ulla Scholz.

"Bingo!" I exclaimed and jumped down. "She's in there with a bunch of stuffed suits and our inspector."

I didn't have to explain who "she" was. Even Curtis understood the importance and magnitude of this discovery. He too seemed to catch the bug now and agreed we had to find out what was being plotted in there. We stacked up a few of the crates under the window and made sure the pile was stable enough that it wouldn't collapse under my weight. I had won the argument that I should be the one listening in. Whether the conversation was in German or English, I was the one to cover either eventuality. The bits of speech I caught through the cracks in the window were indeed mostly English with flourishes of German such as "Sieg Heil," "das Vaterland," and, most tellingly, "Der Führer." It was hard to make out the face of the man doing most of the speaking, but I had the vague sense of having seen those gestures and the overall pudgy gestalt somewhere before. Ulla Scholz sat quietly upright. Her stone-faced demeanor was impossible to read. The gist I was able to gather was they were planning to get her out of the country and back to Germany. All they had to do was wait for a signal from a U-boat close enough to either Coney Island or Sandy Hook for the boarding to occur.

This was invaluable information and just the kind of break we had been looking for. What we would do with it had to be determined later. Right then I was so filled with excitement that I began jumping up and down. This made the crates I was standing on wobble so precariously

I was thrown to the ground. As I lifted myself up, I came face-to-face with Inspector Dettelbach holding a gun.

I should have known. If somebody became aware of some movement at the window, even the slightest movement would not escape this bloodhound's notice.

"Well, aren't you two in style? I would have taken you for bona fide Bavarians if I didn't know otherwise." I looked behind me for Curtis. He was fastidiously brushing debris from the collapsing crates off his lederhosen. *What are you fussing for?* I thought. *We're up to our necks in muck.*

"Interesting to find you here so far out of your home turf. Playing detective! Did Mulligan put you up to this masquerade?"

Neither of us replied.

"OK. Let's go!" Dettelbach waved his gun in the direction of the exit.

"Are you arresting us? What for?" I asked.

"For trespassing."

"This place is open to the public. We paid the entrance fee at the door."

"Then for snooping in off-limits places. Or maybe for impersonating an ethnic group."

"You've got to be kidding. Since when is dressing up a crime?"

"In this case it is. I could have you arrested for spying. Just move." He seized my arm and pulled me toward him. "Do as I say, and you won't get hurt," he hissed between his teeth in my ear. "Let's go, Counselor, and forget about any funny stuff."

He steered us through the partying throng toward the exit. Dettelbach might have been kidding about the obviously ridiculous charges, but I had no doubt he was dead serious about using his gun.

Curtis walked next to me. Dettelbach's hot breath blew against our necks. My heart was racing, and I felt my knees softening. My eyes were darting around for some opportunity to dodge into the crowd. I knew it would be a foolish move. Dettelbach would catch us and add resisting arrest to the other trumped-up charges. Knowing him he would make it all stick somehow. Then my eyes caught something strange. It was a fleeting image that was gone before it registered completely.

A man in a dark suit, maybe one of the guys from the back room, passed close to our little group. He flashed a grin and I could have sworn flicked his thumb. Judging from the slant of his gaze, the thumb was directed at Curtis rather than Dettelbach. The incident passed so quickly I doubted it actually happened. The unlikelihood of what I was thinking bewildered me. I told myself the confusing situation was making me see things.

Outside on the sidewalk Dettelbach waved his arms about, whereupon a black limo pulled up in front of us. He shoved us into the backseat still at gunpoint. He climbed into the front seat next to the driver. His face and gun were turned toward us. Although the windows were tinted, I could see enough to notice we were turning onto Fifth Avenue at Central Park and heading south. I also noticed Curtis getting restless.

"I demand you explain what this is all about and where you are taking us. This isn't the way to the precinct." Curtis's courtroom tone didn't seem to impress Dettelbach in the least. "Let us at least get out of these outfits. I would feel much better in normal clothes."

"You made your bed." Dettelbach chuckled. He put down his gun, lit a cigarette, and blew the smoke into our cabin.

Somewhere in midtown the limo pulled over in front of a brownstone. Dettelbach motioned us to get out of the limo. From the surroundings I figured we were on the West Side in the area called Hell's Kitchen. Dettelbach shoved us up the front stoop and into what might have been at one time a concierge apartment. The vestibule still bore faint traces of the faded elegance of a bygone era through which once, most likely a century ago, must have passed a more glittering coterie of patrons than our befuddled little band trudging in now. The apartment showed equal signs of longtime neglect—flaking paint on the walls, stained wood floor, and frayed lace curtains. A tawdry lamp shed dim light on the sparse furnishings. There was a pallet with a lumpy mattress in the corner without bedding. It didn't look like anybody lived in this place. Perhaps it was another police safe house. The memory of the walk-up downtown in the Village on Bleecker Street churned my stomach. My mind flashed back to the dump where I had lost my virginity. It was the same site where I had listened over the course of a long, smoke-engulfed night to the thousand and one tales of Viktor Erdos.

There was an essential difference between these rooms, though, and it was a welcome one. This place had a couch, a chintz-covered chair with an ottoman, and a little end table with an ashtray between them. The decor was ramshackle, the fabric faded and frayed but still luxurious compared to the seating at the place in the Village.

My knees held up just long enough to carry me to the divan onto which I collapsed. Curtis had to be satisfied with the wooden chair. Dettelbach flung his large frame into the club chair. With a deep sigh of relief, satisfaction, or both, he stretched out his legs on the ottoman and fumbled for the indispensable cigarette.

"Counselor, be so kind as to put on a pot of water in the kitchen, won't you? We only have that new stuff, Nescafé, but it'll do the trick, and it's quick. You'll see. If you haven't tried it, it's not all bad."

Curtis must have smelled a rat. "Whatever game you are playing, Dettelbach, I've had enough. I'm out of here." At the other side of the door, a uniformed officer blocked his path and shuttled him back inside.

Dettelbach turned to the police officer. "Would you please oblige us and make coffee for everyone? Our counselor seems to find it beneath his dignity now that he is a famous lawyer. He wasn't so finicky before, but that's what success does to people. It spoils them. Gives them a feeling of being above ordinary mortals. Wouldn't you agree, Fräulein Safran?" For some reason, he seemed to have it in for Curtis. I was not about to humor him and fall into whatever trap he was laying.

"I wish you wouldn't smoke so much," I said.

He crushed his cigarette butt into the ashtray on the little end table next to him. "Always happy to oblige," he said.

Did he think he could pull the wool over my eyes with such bare-faced schmooze?

"You know, I am sorry we had to meet under adversarial circumstances in the past." He moved the chair in position and confronted me directly. His back was turned on Curtis. Dettelbach did nothing without calculation. I knew the configuration of the players in the room was no accident and carefully choreographed.

"How can I say this?" He reached for his cigarettes but on consideration put the pack back into his pocket. "I have always had a soft spot in my heart for you, Fräulein," he continued. "May I call you Misia? I can't help but feel like a father to you—a young girl alone in a big city. There are so many dangers and predators to fall prey to. So many wolves in sheep's clothes ready to dupe a young girl like you and lead her astray."

Beware. The bloodhound is morphing into a fox, I thought.

There seemed to be no limit to the variety of transformations this inspector was able to undergo. Once again he had me nonplussed. I avoided meeting the benevolent look with which he regarded me. What did he want from me?

My gaze wandered to Curtis. He cringed, and his face twitched as if he was in pain. Dettelbach's remark about wolves in sheep's clothes made me wonder. Then I remembered the grin on the face of the man in the dark suit and his upturned thumb. I also remembered many other things and situations. I remembered how uncomfortable Curtis Wolff was at the Friday night gatherings at Habonim and his very thin knowledge of Jewish customs. I attributed all this to his background as a member of an assimilated, wealthy, Jewish family long settled in Chicago.

Then I remembered what Viktor Erdos had said about him. He is not one of us. He does not have a *Yiddishe neshume.* What did I know about a Jewish soul? I was from Berlin. My upbringing straddled the more or less assimilated environment of the haute bourgeoisie. I observed the rational side of Jewish practices and was more versed in Kant than the Torah. My parents' bohemian lifestyle was even further removed from Jewish practices. The concept of a Jewish soul was regarded as an Eastern Jewish figment—a region some people called *yene welt* and my grandmother called "the land where the black pepper grows."

"I can't arrest our counselor here for impersonating a Bavarian, but we could come up with a reason to arrest him for impersonating a Jew." Dettelbach's voice sounded ominously low as if traveling through a long funnel.

"What are you saying?" My stomach was in an uproar as if it had received a massive blow. It was being assaulted from all sides of late. I wouldn't be surprised if I developed an ulcer.

How many more surprises am I supposed to be able to stomach?

A knock on the door postponed further revelations. The uniformed officer opened the door, and in walked Inspector Mulligan. Was this the deus ex machina? The same Thomas Mulligan who had implored me not to reveal him as an informant gave a friendly nod.

"How are we doing, Frank?" he asked Dettelbach.

"I was just about to tell Miss Safran what a fraud her friend, the counselor, is," Dettelbach replied.

Then he turned his face back to me. "We made inquiries, and I regret to inform you that Mr. Curtis Wolff is neither Jewish nor from Chicago. He is a lawyer of sorts, but his degree is not from NYU. He graduated from a second-rate school in rural Wisconsin. He hails from a farm near Fond du Lac. Being from Madison myself, I recognized the intonation. To the fine-tuned ear, that accent is definitely not from Chicago. The only thing genuine about him? He's of German descent. They chose him because he didn't even have to change his name to something more Jewish. As you know, Wolff works both ways."

"Chose him for what? Who did the choosing?" I managed to bring forth.

"He belongs to a self-styled army of militants who call themselves the Cherusker Legion after the Germanic hero who fought the Romans..."

"I am familiar with the story of Arminius. Also known as Hermann der Cherusker, he defeated the Roman legions in the Teutoburg Forest. I learned that in third grade," I snapped at him.

"Of course you wouldn't need an explanation," he held up his hands. "I should have known you learned all about this in history class." He took a sip from his now cold coffee the officer had made a half hour before.

I avoided looking at Curtis who was being talked about as if he wasn't in the room.

"Anyway," Dettelbach cleared his throat, "don't be fooled by the word 'Legion.' They are no such thing. They are a handful of backwoods thugs and card-carrying Nazi sympathizers. Their creed is absolute adoration of the Führer."

Another blow below the belt. It would have bowled me over had I not been sitting. "I don't understand anything anymore," I groaned. Tears sprang up in my eyes.

"That's why we set up this scenario. So we could break it to you gently," Mulligan said. "We knew you would follow up on this lead about a meeting at the Oktoberfest. I hope you will forgive me. The meeting of the German-American Kulturbund was real. So was the part that the fate of Frau Ulla Scholz was to be decided. Only I couldn't tell you that much and had to cast aspersions on the loyalty of my partner, for which I apologize. Frank infiltrated this group a while back when certain activities came to our attention that made us suspect not all was kosher.

"When the trial of Viktor Erdos was over, and he was convicted of the murder, we began to have grave doubts that justice had been served. Closer examination of the record of the court proceedings and testimonies opened up many questions. One question concerned the behavior of counsel for the defense. Why was he so eager to take on that job in the first place, which he bungled in the end? Was it just inexperience? It was clear we had to get to Frau Scholz. Only she was in hiding and under protection of the *Bund* or the Legion."

I shook my head in disbelief. I still understood only half of what was being said. It was too much to take in at once. What about Dettelbach?

"You took me for a Nazi, didn't you?" he said.

"You made certain remarks that could lead one to such a conclusion."

"I might have said a few unkind things about your people, Misia. My apologies. But I never subscribed to the crass racism or the Jew hatred currently being preached and practiced in Germany. This is not my Germany. I am proud of my German heritage, but I am always an American first. The *Deutschtum* of the Cheruskers, and to some extent the current Kulturbund, is abhorrent to me and most of my compatriots. Believe me. The majority of German Americans see it as an aberration of our history, culture, and everything we hold dear!"

Was this a case of protesting too much?

"I've heard enough of this crap!" Curtis jumped up. "Don't believe a word he says, Misia. He has been in on it the whole time. They planned to silence Stella Berger. I admit I was there too, but things have changed for me. I have changed. I fell in love with you, Misia. We've gone through a lot together. You can't just dismiss that."

"It was all a lie then. You have a lot of explaining to do."

"I will explain everything. Just give me a chance." He fell on his knees before me.

"Nice try, buster. Now you have us to reckon with." Dettelbach pushed him aside.

My head was spinning. I couldn't figure out who was fraud or friend. I turned to Inspector Mulligan for help. "How do the Irish stand on this subject?" I asked half-jokingly wiping the tears from my eyes.

"We like to stand aside and just watch. We have our own axes to grind." He gave me a reassuring wink.

"As I said he grew up on a farm in Wisconsin," Dettelbach continued. "They called the homestead Teutoburg. His father and uncle are the top Cheruskers. Sort of like the grand dragons of the outfit. They groomed junior here from an early age. When they sent him off into the world, he already had the name and law degree. He was even genitally credentialed as a Jew. Like many boys in America, he was circumcised in the hospital at birth. At the time his father was outraged when his mother told him what she had done. But it came in handy for duping a young, inexperienced, Jewish girl."

"I will not have you speak about private matters in that way." Curtis glowered with rage. The strong arms of the uniformed officer clamped around his chest and prevented Curtis from falling on Dettelbach.

"If you don't want me to do it, why don't you do it yourself? Go ahead. Spill your guts. The lady is waiting for an explanation. We all would like to hear what you have to say."

"I'd rather speak with her in private."

"That wish cannot be granted. Sorry."

Did anybody care to inquire about my wishes? Apparently it didn't occur to either of them to extend that courtesy to me. What I really felt like doing was run away and leave those knuckleheads to lock horns over whatever it was they were fighting about. It surely couldn't have been just about me. There was a whole lot more going on. Maybe it was some old tribal rivalry going back to the early settlement of the backwoods of Wisconsin. I didn't want to know.

Mulligan handed me a cup of hot tea. Dettelbach fixed his tie and went outside for a smoke. Curtis used his absence to plead with me to hear him out. Not wanting to make a big scene in front of the others, I put him off until some other time. I needed time to mull things over and absorb what were very disturbing revelations.

"I forswore the Cheruskers and their ideas long ago. I told my father so. Remember, I love you. It might not have started out that way, but I fell in love with you, your kindness, your concern for others, your inner strength, your persistent search for truth and justice..."

"Attributes you didn't expect to find in a Jewess. Don't lay it on too thick, Curtis, and don't bullshit me," I cut into his litany. I had learned a few things, and not falling for flattery was one of them. "I would have liked it better had you said you loved me for being the most beautiful, attractive girl in the world. But let's not belabor the point. When the time comes, we'll talk, and then we'll see."

"OK, you lovebirds, the cards are on the table, and all is clear. Let's get to work. First order of business. We have to rake Ulla Scholz over the coals, even if we have to kidnap her. I'll go back to my friends at the Kulturbund— I'm still a member in good standing—and try to find out where she is being held. No doubt they plan to get rid of her as soon as possible. She's too much of a liability. All that talk about boarding a German submarine off the coast somewhere is hogwash. They know very well this won't happen. No U-boat gets past the Coast Guard for such a transfer to take place. I have the distinct suspicion they will take her out to Sandy Hook or Fire Island. They will kill her at a given moment and sink her body into the sea.

"What we don't know is when they will act. It could be any time and any day. So we'll have to move fast. My plan is to bring her back here to this apartment where we can grill her undisturbed. We'll all meet back here when the deed is done. I'll send word when I have her in my custody."

"I have a list of questions I would like to ask her," I said.

"You'll get your chance. I promise. We'll get to the bottom of this mystery yet."

Inspector Mulligan drove me home. I refused to let Curtis accompany me. I needed time alone for solitary reflection. The first thing I did when I got to my place was throw up, and then I took a cleansing shower. It was almost early morning when I fell into an exhausted, deep sleep.

EIGHT

Dettelbach was true to his word. Three days later Inspector Mulligan came knocking on my door. The deed was done. Ulla Scholz was in their custody. He had come to take me back to the police apartment in Hell's Kitchen. For a moment I gave myself over to divining a significance of this location but gave up. I was too much in a state of anguish and trepidation to dwell on symbolic meanings. I was about to have a face-to-face meeting with Ulla Scholz. In my mind she was a formidable *éminence grise*, the power behind the throne. This woman held the key to so many unanswered questions, which possibly included the identity of Stella Berger's killer.

The woman I saw before me was anything but formidable, though. She looked haggard and wispy like a willow. She looked even thinner than I remembered. She wore that ridiculous black felt hat with netting draped over her face and tucked under her chin. This failed to conceal the creases in her face though. She constantly dabbed her long, pointed nose with a tissue. As I entered she was moving her long legs from side to side, seemingly unable to find a comfortable position on the sagging couch.

Dettelbach urged her to have a seat in a high-back chair. A recent addition to the decor, it was probably from the local Goodwill. She declined the offer.

Someone had done some fixing up of the place. The seating was arranged in a circle. All kinds of goodies were stocked in the kitchen.

There was enough food to get an army through a long siege. I was delighted to see my old friend the precinct stenographer with pencil and writing tablet at the ready. Her professional utensils were next to her on the kitchen counter while she was making coffee and stacking pieces of cake and donuts on a plate. Maybe she was the good fairy to be thanked for dusting and airing out the place. For the first time, I saw her smile with a nod of recognition when I greeted her. I had to hand it to Dettelbach. Having this hearing (or whatever it was) in a neutral place wasn't such a bad idea. For one the bottles of alcohol I spotted in the cupboard would not have been allowed at the station.

"You won't get away with this," I heard Ulla Scholz say under sniffles. "I have powerful friends."

"Lady, you might not realize it," said Dettelbach, "but I just saved your life. I snatched you from the claws of certain death. There was no U-boat out there to take you back to the fatherland. If I hadn't come along, you would be floating face-down in the ocean by now. You would be swimming with the fishes on the bottom of the Atlantic."

"What do you want from me?" She sniffled again. Mulligan tendered a big box of Kleenex.

"We want the truth," Mulligan said. Dettelbach stuffed his face with a jelly doughnut. "Nothing but the truth...about the murder of Stella Berger."

"Hasn't that been decided?" Her voice screeched like a hen chased by a rooster. "The killer has been convicted and is in prison awaiting his..."

"You are right. There is a man in prison who has been found guilty and is waiting to get jolted into eternity. We think, however, he was wrongfully convicted, and that's due in part to your testimony."

"That is outrageous!" The sofa's close proximity to the floor defeated her struggle to lift herself into an upright position.

Mulligan extended his hand, pulled her up, and gallantly led her to an armchair better suited to accommodate her stretched-out frame. She took off her hat and veil and tossed it carelessly on the floor. She crossed her legs, hugged her knees with hands folded, and expectantly looked Mulligan in the eye. When he offered something to eat or drink, she turned on that haughty gaze I remembered from the courtroom.

"Suit yourself," he shrugged. "You might get hungry later. We'll be here for a while."

"What are you going to do to me?"

"Unlike your friends from the Kulturbund, we won't lay a hand on you." Dettelbach dabbed his mouth with a napkin and got back into the ring. "You might not be aware of this, but Fire Island where they were taking you is deserted this time of the year. It's the perfect setting for doing away with a person who has outlived her usefulness. As soon as we got wind of the location, my partner and I raced out there. You are one lucky woman."

"You keep saying this. How do I know you are telling the truth?"

"You have to take my word for it. Ask yourself this. Why should we care whether you live or die? The answer is we don't. On the other hand, we didn't want you to take the truth with you to your grave, which is where you surely would be by now. A very watery one at that."

She pulled a big wad of tissues out of the Kleenex box and blew her nose with great trumpet blare.

"So let's stop the theatrics and chitchat, and let's get down to more serious stuff."

"You don't know what you are doing to my father. You just sentenced him to death," Ulla whined.

"Your father? How does he fit into this?"

"He's in Dachau. Has been there since the beginning of the war."

"Is that how they got you to do their bidding?"

"My father was a member of the Bavarian People's Party. After the war their aim was for Bavaria to secede from Germany and join Austria. The Allies wouldn't permit it. Admittedly my father never had any love for Jews. He despised them as a devout Catholic, and I might have absorbed some of his views growing up. It doesn't, however, make him a Nazi. He was actively opposed to the Nazi regime from the beginning. He warned against the evil of the movement when it gained more and more support.

"When Hitler became chancellor, he organized a Catholic resistance cell in Bavaria. The cell was small—a handful of businessmen, clergy, and farmers. There was not much they could do to prevent the Nazi government from taking control over every aspect of life in the country. At the outbreak of this war, they distributed antiwar pamphlets. This led to their arrest and most, including my father, have been in Dachau ever since."

"Good story. We are all choked up." Dettelbach sneered. "I'm sure the part about your father is all true and regrettable. But what about you? As a member of the Kulturbund, I've heard a different story. You were identified as a trusted insider."

"I had to go along or pretend. I just told you why."

"To the point of going along with plans for the murder of the woman to whom you owed everything? Your protestations won't do you any good. We know of your connection with Herr Doctor Goebbels long before your father, from whom you have been estranged, was put in a concentration camp. You admired the Nazis. You supported their political goals. You shared their hatred of Jews. You testified at the trial how appalled and shocked you were when you found out your employer and friend Stella Berger was Jewish. You left the house because you abhorred the revelation. Then you returned apparently contrite. Your friend and employer graciously took you back, but that leaves two big mysteries. Why did she take you back, and why did you come back?"

"You think you know everything. You don't know the half of it." Her eyes flared defiantly.

"Enlighten us. And don't spare us the truth. We can take it even if you can't."

One of the mysteries Dettelbach posed I was sure she would not shed any light on. She would not tell him about the contents of a certain vault in a Swiss bank. I did not see any need for him or anybody from the police to know about this aspect of the story that had been related to Curtis and me in strict confidence. Why Ulla came crawling back was a different matter. I wondered if my suspicions about where she had been keeping herself and with whom she met during those two weeks out in the cold would now be confirmed.

Dettelbach propped up his chin with a curved hand like *The Thinker*. Silence fell over the room. Dettelbach, Mulligan, and I sat in a circle. Curtis remained in the background. All eyes were on Ulla Scholz. The stenographer was ready with an assortment of sharpened pencils and writing tablets on her knees.

"Well then. Shoot!" Dettelbach finally said. With a sweeping gesture of the hand, he added, "The stage is all yours."

"All right. You shall get to know the truth. My truth."

The revelation that her adored Stella was a Jewess rattled Ulla Scholz to the core of her being. She went out into the mean streets of Berlin carrying nothing more than a small handbag. For hours she rode the U-Bahn and the S-Bahn. From the underground line, she switched to the above-ground line and back and forth again. She traversed the city she had always hated. In all the years in Berlin at Stella's side, she had never ventured out much and had always remained a stranger in this city. Its inhabitants were so alien to her. She hated the rhythm, the hectic pulse of its traffic, the hectic speech and commerce, and the intonation jarring to her southern ears. She hated the touted Berlin air and the even more famous quick-wittedness Berliners prided themselves on. She hated the climate—the arctic cold sweeping the north German plains in winter and the oppressive, hovering clouds in summer. Now she was out alone in this hostile territory with limited means.

In the haste of getting away, she hadn't thought of what she might need. Physically and mentally drained, she found a small pension in the working-class district of Moabit by nightfall. She stewed there for several days and then moved on. Her mind was made up. She had to get back into Stella's good graces. It was useless. She had devoted her life to this woman. To her mind that time had been squandered. Now she had no prospects, skills, or connections. She couldn't make it on her own. Going back to Bavaria and asking her father for help was even more abhorrent. They had had a falling out way back on account of the life she had made for herself, which went against his strict Catholic moral code.

On the way back to Dahlem, going over and over in her head what she would say and how she would say it, fate overtook her on Nollendorf Platz. As she emerged from the underground station to cross the square to another train, a cheering, jeering throng of SA Brownshirts and SS Blackshirts blocked her path. Bystanders or passers-by of every variety stood locked together in an impenetrable phalanx. It was drizzling, but no one opened an umbrella. The air was fraught with crackling anticipation. All eyes were directed toward the far end of the square where the Theater am Nollendorf Platz was located. Ulla discerned a little man on a platform mesmerizing the crowd with wild gesticulations and shrill exhortations in a high-pitched voice. Fragments of his harangue reached her ear. There were familiar allusions to November criminals, Judenrepublik, degenerate art the stock at the theater in front of which he stood, Jewish communist conspiracy, and Jewish capitalist intrigues. The phrase "die Juden sind unser Unglück" punctuated his every sentence.

With each pounding repetition Ulla's heart beat faster. She was swept up in the sensation of the moment. No. She would not return to the house of that Jewess who had pulled the wool over her eyes, betrayed her, misled her, made a fool of her. This here was her crowd, her people, and her kind. The little man had appeared as a messenger from heaven. She felt reborn and baptized in the intensifying rain. The crowd began to scatter. The messenger had charged them with the mission to go forth and spread the word. As people around her expressed awe and approval, she felt herself lifted to a higher, loftier plane.

Ulla did not want the moment to vanish. She wanted it to last. She yearned to lose herself in the warmth of like-minded bodies around her. She followed those in the uniform shirts to their haunts in nearby taverns. She listened, followed the debates, learned, and then struck up conversations. She had to find out the identity of the messenger. Didn't she know? Everybody knew Gauleiter Dr. Josef Goebbels—the right hand and mouthpiece of the Führer.

Ulla said she wanted to meet him. They laughed at her at first. Who did she think she was? The Gauleiter didn't have time for any woman who put it into her head to meet him. Many women had their eyes on him. The Nazi Party was on a spectacular rise due to his oratorical skill. These comments irked her. She was not any woman. So Ulla pulled out her trump card. Maybe the Gauleiter would have time for the confidante and personal secretary of Stella Berger. She gave them a what-do-you-say-now look.

Someone in the crowd knew someone who was close to someone in the inner party circle. An interview was arranged. The Gauleiter saw possibilities. She could be useful to the cause, he said. His interest in her lessened, however, when she assured him she was no longer in the employ of this Jewish actress. In that case she was useless to him, he told her bluntly. But she was now ready to serve the cause of the fatherland and the party.

Many were ready to jump on the bandwagon, he informed her. He thought for a while and looked her over. Then he nodded. He had a plan so she could still be turned into a valuable myrmidon. He instructed her to go back and make up some story. Show herself to be contrite. Beg on her knees if she must to be reinstated in her job. The gratitude of fatherland and party would be with her.

For the next few days, she was given the royal treatment. She was wined and dined and was put up in nice lodging. She attended lavish parties where she rubbed shoulders with the party elite. Several hours a day, she underwent an abbreviated course of intensive thought training. Before the freshly minted sleeper was sent off, she was told the Gauleiter would contact her directly when her services were required. He had full confidence she was more than up to fulfilling his expectations.

Ulla was flattered, but she was no fool. She relished the attention showered on her but was keenly aware of her utter worthlessness without Stella Berger. Even now it was all about Stella. What she didn't reveal to the Gauleiter or anybody else was how she would get Stella to forgive her and reinstate her in her former position without arousing the diva's suspicion she was now a Nazi agent. This trump card she held close to her chest. A thinly veiled reminder would be enough to make Stella dance to Ulla's tune.

To the surprise of Stella's friends and devotees, Ulla returned to the Dahlem villa. To all appearances she was back in Stella's good graces.

Outwardly it was like old times. Ulla attended to Stella's needs, ran the household, and was frequently seen with her in public. Inside the inner sanctum of the villa, and later in the private realm of exile, a different scene prevailed. If Ulla thought Stella would dance to her tune, she was greatly mistaken. Despite the hold she had over her, life with Stella turned into a hell from which there was no escape. By the time Ulla came to realize she had made a pact with the devil, it was too late. The Gauleiter would never release her from the oath she had sworn to Führer, Volk, and Fatherland. His legs might be short, but his arm was long. She was sure of it. He would find her wherever she sought refuge to collect his due. She had made her bed.

Inextricably hitched together, Stella and Ulla were forced to march in step to keep some semblance of balance. All the while the centrifugal pull of mutual hatred threatened to overturn the cart of their destiny at every turn. The Stella she returned to was not the forgiving, sweet-tempered, angelic Viennese Mädel of her public image. The Stella in Ulla's story was a vindictive and cruel shrew.

Once her Jewish origin became public knowledge, Stella became obsessed with the Nazis. She taunted the Gauleiter in public statements. She knew her worth as a precious commodity in an industry he sought to control. She ridiculed his offer to make her an honorary Aryan if she would only keep quiet. "If Herr Dr. Goebbels thinks I can be bought for thirty pieces of silver, he is sorely mistaken," she declared on more than one occasion.

If her Jewish roots had never played a role in her life, she now embraced them with a fierce cry of *davke*. She threw down the gauntlet at the Gauleiter's feet and assumed the role of standard bearer for her pilloried, oppressed people. She mounted the barricades with the fanatic resolve of a Joan of Arc. She applied herself with the same doggedness she had shown in the pursuit of her career. Her reckless battle with the Gauleiter of Berlin aroused the dismay and discomfort of her theater colleagues who feared for their security and livelihoods should the rise of the Nazis continue. The party's considerable dip in Reichstag seats in November 1932 did nothing to dampen the burnt-earth warfare in the streets of the capital city.

Ulla watched from the sidelines and prayed secretly for a Nazi victory. She hoped it would release her from her state of bondage. She egged Stella on and even applauded her nightly anti-Nazi harangues. She took care not to seem too enthusiastic lest she arouse Stella's suspicion. She knew Stella was not easily duped and did not trust her. Then Hitler was appointed chancellor, and he and his myrmidons began their seizure of power and complete control over Germany. Ulla was relieved. She heard of people in the opposition, communists and pacifists, being rounded up and put in a concentration camp near Munich that had opened just a few weeks after the *Machtergreifung*. She thought her mission was fulfilled. She would be released and could seek out other ways of serving the cause. Stella might not last much longer under the new regime she had already alienated. Even Stella's husband, Alexander Levary, cautioned her to curb her attacks lest she end up in a concentration camp herself.

Ulla's hopes seemed close to fulfillment. Her heart was beating even faster when Stella sold her villa and packed her belongings to move abroad. For some time she had had an offer to appear at the Globe Theater in London. The time had come to take up the offer. Greener pastures and world fame beckoned. Even though her German audience had abandoned her, the world was still Stella's oyster. Ulla's hopes for release, however, were dashed. Before she had a chance to let Stella know she was staying behind, word came from the office of what was now the Propaganda Ministry. It said for her to stay the course. She would still be able to serve fatherland and Führer but not in the role she had dreamed of. These were orders directly from Dr. Goebbels. She would hear from him with instructions at the appropriate moment.

Ulla stayed the course and soldiered on. She swallowed her pride and suffered Stella's rants against the fatherland in silence. Even the Brits looked askance at the expatriate's ceaseless lambasting of a regime they thought one could live with and accommodate. As a superb thespian, they showered her with adoration. As a gloom-and-doom Cassandra who regularly turned the Globe's stage and other venues where she appeared into her pulpit from which to forecast the imminence of another war, the war-weary British public found her rather irksome. At least so it was in the early years.

Aside from that, the overall reception Stella Berger received from the British public and her colleagues in the theater was warm and welcoming. Yet Ulla noticed an increasing nerviness taking hold of her nemesis. Even in the safe harbor of exile, Stella's obsession with the Nazis was turning increasingly into paranoia. She never lost her amazing ability to turn herself into the character she was portraying on stage with utter self-effacement. Offstage, she became a different person altogether. She saw Nazi agents, even assassins, lurking everywhere. She developed migraine headaches and other psychosomatic ailments. She became dependent on painkillers. Eventually she turned to drinking. One glass of wine turned to one bottle. Then she moved to harder stuff such as cognac and single-malt Scotch. She frequently lost her temper over the slightest incidents or for no reason at all. She would fly into a rage at the drop of a hat. Alexander Levary, her *soi-disant* husband, knew to duck while going on his merry way. Ulla, the long-suffering factotum, was made to bear the brunt of Stella's fury.

When Britain came under bombardment during the Blitz, Stella feared an imminent German invasion. She henceforth abandoned the country that had embraced her with open arms to its fate. She moved her show and entourage to California. Ulla was disconcerted about being so far from her homeland, but she bravely tagged along. She was staying the course even after six years of waiting in vain for word from the propaganda chief. She was glum and despondent, yet she never wavered in her belief the call would come. With the war progressing and talk of America's possible entry on the side of Germany's enemies, she had a distinct premonition her hero in Berlin would soon make his move. Something would be done to still the increasingly shrill voice of the Fury. She didn't know what form it would take, but she would have a major role to play.

In Hollywood Stella Berger became a much sought-after celebrity at émigré parties. Sasha Levary's double life as husband, manager, and man of undisguised homosexual leanings became the subject of the tabloids. As was her wont, Stella ignored this aspect of his activities. She became close friends with Hedy Lamarr, another Viennese girl and outspoken opponent of the Nazi regime. As Stella and Sasha were busily casting their bread upon various studio waters in hopes of a hefty contract, Hedy introduced Stella to Louis B. Mayer.

The MGM studio boss was more than willing to entertain the idea of showcasing a new Garbo. He scheduled a private conference with the star in her hotel suite to hash things out with the proviso they'd be alone. No manager or agent was to be present. Hearing this demand piqued Ulla's interest. Ulla overheard the conversation from the adjacent room, and the conversation between the studio boss and the star at first raised her hopes. Levary would have to go, she heard the mogul state. Then she realized her position too was in jeopardy under Mayer's conditions.

"The American public is more sensitive or, shall we say, of a more puritan bend of mind than Europeans," she heard him say. "Americans like their idols to be pure, *unbefleckt* in German. Untainted by scandal. Our stars are the idols of the marketplace. That's the reality we have to deal with. Keeping up appearances."

"So what are you implying? I am not sure I understand." Stella's voice came through the door. It sounded soft and almost cowed.

"Let me make it clear then." In contrast to Stella, he sounded gruff. It was clear he was used to wielding the cudgel of power to intimidate and get what he wanted. "I suggest you replace your manager. His lifestyle is too much of a liability."

"Mr. Levary is my manager and director, but he is also my husband." Stella had apparently regained her bearing. Her voice was more forceful now.

There was a long pause before the great man spoke again. "Then I suggest you get another husband! If you want to make it in this town and in this country, you have to play by local rules."

"And who sets these rules?" Now Stella was back to her old self. She wasn't just anybody to dance to a tyrant's tune, she let him know. Besides, from what she had seen since coming to this town, no one had the right to ride the moral high horse.

"Hollywood may not be populated by saints," he replied. "But openly being a faggot is still taboo. There are also rumors about you and the tall woman who follows you like a puppy. Personally I don't give a damn whom you fuck and who fucks you. But I have an image to protect. I have shareholders and audiences to assuage. This is a business, and we play by business rules. Without customers, we are nothing. Get rid of both of them, get a real husband, and we'll talk again."

A noise nearby blotted out Stella's response, but Ulla was sure she didn't buckle. She was far too self-assured to be bossed around.

"Think about it. I can make you the biggest thing to hit the silver screen. The brightest star in the Hollywood firmament since Garbo. You have something most of the bimbos who hang around here don't have. You are a serious actress. A professional and the best of your craft. An artist."

"Thank you. I take this as a compliment," Stella replied. "I am glad you realize I am not in the same class as the bimbos. Let me tell you this. I have an engagement on Broadway for a Shakespeare play this summer. If and when I come back to this town in autumn, I shall ring you up, and we'll talk some more."

There was a forced burst of laughter from the big man. "You know, even your Max Reinhardt eats out of my hand. Refugees can't make demands. As they say, beggars can't be choosers. Remember those glory days of Berlin are no more, gone, kaput. But my hat's off to you, lady. You've got guts and spunk, and I like that. Nevertheless, if you want in, your paramours, or whatever they are, have to go or no dice."

Ulla was in a state of fretful anxiety. She gasped for air. Her pulse raced, her heart pounded, and her stomach churned. She rushed to the nearest bathroom and spilled her guts. If Stella followed through, she would no longer have a listening post. The years of suffering abuse would have been for naught. She would no longer be able to stay the course or fulfill her mission for the fatherland and her mentor in Berlin. Something had to be done to forestall the unthinkable. She grasped at straws. One straw she decided to reach for was the person of Alexander Levary. She would tell him what she had heard. The situation warranted she set aside her profound dislike of him. They were now in the same boat together. Better to admit to eavesdropping than endure being put out to pasture at such a critical moment. As allies they might put together a plan to avert the disaster. If Stella was to give him the boot and file for divorce, his cushiony, sybaritic life would end. He had as much if not more to lose than she.

Alexander Levary laughed her in the face. Stella would never get rid of him no matter what demands the studio boss made. However, Ulla was another matter. She was dispensable. In fact he had often wondered why Stella kept her around, he said. She had no visible function to fulfill. She really served no purpose. She was as useless as an appendix. He went on deriding her and heaping scorn upon ridicule.

Stella told them both nothing was written in stone. She had more important matters to tend to. She rebuked them but remained evasive when questioned about what she planned to do. Pointing out the presence of her voice coach, she added, "Desdemona awaits." She knew the character of the ill-fated wife of the Moor of Venice inside out. She had portrayed her many times on the German stage. Now the challenge was to enact the role in Shakespearean English. Study and work to the exclusion of anything else was the regimen she set for herself. She would allow absolutely no distractions from anybody or anything. Both Ulla and Sasha knew well the menacing squint in Stella's eyes that gave emphasis to her last remark. Woe to whoever sought to sidetrack or bother her in any way with trifling personal concerns. Once immersed in her character, her lay persona ceased to exist.

Ulla took bitter note of Stella's refusal to rebuff Mr. Mayer's demand outright. The thought kept going round in her head. She took Stella's poetic remark to mean she was undecided. Everything was up in the air and put off until another time. From this Ulla deduced Stella was considering his proposal. This did not bode well. The future loomed in a gloomy light, rousing the viper in Ulla's chest. The snake ate away at her heart and soul.

Then came New York. Just as Ulla was about to give herself over to despair, the long-awaited order from Berlin came. Ulla was jubilant. She had stayed the course. Her time had come. The fruit of her endurance was within her grasp. She would not fail. Then she heard the order being given, and she blanched. Her body trembled. Her heart sank. Her spirit sagged. Murder? Murder was never part of the bargain. Stella was to be silenced nothing more.

"How did you think it was to be done?" asked the messenger who sat across from her in a dark bar downtown.

She hadn't thought that far. It had never occurred to her. She had to think it over. This was not what she expected, she told him. What did she expect? A walk in the park? She was told there was nothing to think over. These were the orders. It was up to her—the insider, the mole—to figure out how it was to be done. She should have known this was not a job for the fainthearted, he added.

Opening night came. Stella Berger's name illuminated the Great White Way. Ulla was sidelined. She had nothing much to do but observe the backstage scene. Stella was under constant siege from a bustle of producers, directors, stagehands, voice coaches, makeup artists, hair-stylists, costume designers, and tailors. Critics, journalists, writers, and fans vied for entry into her dressing room after each performance, but Stella held firm. No one was to come near her for a half hour. Absolutely no one. No colleague, attendant, producer, or manager. Not even the president of the United States or the mayor of New York. It had always been so from her early days on stage in Munich and Berlin and later in England. She required this time of complete solitude to transform herself back into Stella. Everyone respected her wish. Ulla knew it well.

Ulla also knew this time of respite was the window in which to strike. What are you thinking? Have you gone crazy? Ulla reproached herself. No. She would not...could not be involved in murder. She couldn't play a part in the murder of Stella Berger! They had a long history together. They had loved and hated each other. Fate had hitched their lives together for better or worse.

She wandered aimlessly through the streets of the huge unknown city. She was pondering a way out. From the days in Zurich when she took in the hungry, penniless girl with great ambition, she had loved and adored her. She had taken her under her wing, cosseted her, lavished care and devotion on her, and served her every whim and desire. She also served as the diva's target for her scorn and every whim. She watched her grow from a thin little duckling into a beautiful swan loved and admired by all the world. That this apple of her eye, this beautiful swan, should turn out to be a Jewess was one of those ironies life likes to play on the unsuspecting. Ulla wanted her silenced and the harangues against the fatherland stopped. But did she want to see Stella dead? No. Three times no! The horror of the thought made her skin crawl and her hair stand on end. Her entire body shook with revulsion. She felt a vise clamping her chest and squeezing the air out of her.

"We were told you were absolutely reliable," the messenger said.

She was reliable and willing to do anything for the cause, she assured him. Murder, she pleaded, was a different matter altogether, though. How could she? She was a foreigner in a foreign country.

Another turn on the vise made her gasp for air.

"We had been hoping it wouldn't come to this. Even the minister seems to have overestimated your loyalty." The messenger informed her of her father's incarceration at Dachau. He and other Catholic dissidents would be brought to trial for acts of sedition against Führer and Reich. As she might imagine, there could be only one outcome. However, Field Marshal Goering, the man in charge, might be willing to put mercy before justice in her father's case. Life imprisonment in a fortress could be entertained.

Ulla was crushed. She contemplated suicide, but what would be solved by her own death? Her father's fate would surely be sealed. She knew of his distaste for the Nazis on religious grounds. She had no doubt of his involvement in some kind of quixotic plot against the regime. They would have no difficulty rounding up witnesses and fabricating evidence against him and his friends. She and her father had their differences, and they hadn't spoken since that stormy falling out more than twenty years ago. Still she couldn't send him to his death. Not if it was in her power to save his life. It was Stella or her father.

"Quite a conundrum!" Inspector Dettelbach stated with raised eyebrows when she paused.

He poured her a shot of whiskey, and she sent it down the hatch in one fell swoop. I was still trying to figure out which side he was on. Was

246

this a tactic to keep her off guard? Was he sympathetic? He was such a master of different impersonations and theatrics. She still hadn't gotten to the actual murder yet. So he might think that arousing her ire was not a good way to draw her out. However, my ire was aroused, and I was unable to hold back.

"So you decided the life of a father you detested was worth more than the life of a woman who had given you a life of luxury and leisure and to whom you owed everything. Without her you were nothing but a slut." I knew my voice sounded shrill. Maybe I shouldn't have made that allusion to her career as a prostitute, but I went on venting my anger in mixed German and English. I had never hated anybody as much in my life as I hated this woman. "The worthless life of a worthless, subhuman Jewess, your benefactress, against an anti-Semitic, Aryan father. What an interesting conundrum, as the inspector says. I don't believe it was a conundrum for you at all, though. Was it not a foregone conclusion who the sacrificial lamb would be? Murderess! I spit on you and your Kulturbund accomplices."

"Easy, Miss Safran!" Mulligan placed a restraining hand on my arm. "We understand how you feel, but we are in America. In America a person is innocent until proven guilty."

I conceded his point with a wave of my hand and sank back in my chair. "Sorry."

"Now, if you will be so kind, Frau Scholz, enlighten us about how you planned and carried out your mission for the fatherland." Dettelbach, the fox, ever polite when it served his purpose, blatantly dripped the honey. Even Ulla had to notice she was being led around by the nose.

"I don't know what you mean." She folded her arms and sulked.

"Come on. You just told us you had to make a choice. It was either your father being tortured and hanged or Stella Berger being snuffed out."

"I didn't say I actually made the choice. I was faced with the choice. What makes you think I actually did it?"

Dettelbach leaned forward and pushed his face almost into hers. "If you think you can play us for fools, you are way out of your league!"

247

She cringed under the thundering impact of his voice and spittle sprinkling her face. "All right, I made the choice." She moved her head back. "It wasn't an easy choice. Nobody should be put in such a position. But what could I do? He is my father. I've heard rumors about what these concentration camps are like. Besides my task was only to plan for a good moment. I would not pull a trigger or actually see her die. Somebody else would do it when I gave the go-ahead. I waited for the right moment and invented reasons for putting it off. Stella's Broadway engagement was nearing its end. The pressure to act reached a boiling point. Then everything was arranged, but before it could be carried out, she was already dead."

What was she saying? I didn't trust my ears.

"Lies!" Curtis yelled. "Nothing but lies!" He had been quietly following the interrogation. Suddenly he seemed all worked up.

"Do you have any inside information to that effect, Mr. Wolff?" Dettelbach turned toward him.

"No, but she is obviously lying. Why don't you stop beating around the bush and charge her with conspiracy to commit murder?"

"Because we don't have enough evidence to charge her, Counselor. She hasn't confessed."

"Why don't you shut up, Curtis?" I felt like strangling him myself for his interference just at the moment we were getting somewhere with Ulla.

He was about to reply, but Dettelbach cut in. "We don't need any lovers' quarrels." He turned his vulpine smile again on the talebearer with an apology for the interruption. "Mrs. Scholz," he began slowly. "Why don't you take us back to the moment when you made what was no doubt a difficult choice? You can take it from there. If you will, please take us step-by-step to the moment when you made the discovery. I presume you discovered the body."

Ulla explained she had been caught in her own game. She had underestimated the propagandist in Berlin. Her back against the wall, she made her choice. Once the die was cast, she went to work on her plan. She did her research. She read up on various sensational murder cases. One thing was clear. The deed had to be done in the period of Stella's post-performance repose when nobody would be near the dressing room. She persuaded her handlers that a gunshot would be too noisy. Poison would take too long to take effect. She also wanted to spare herself from witnessing a protracted, agonizing death struggle. The violin player who sat in front of the theater every day gave her the idea of using a set of violin strings. They were not as strong as piano wire but more subtle and easier to conceal. The idea was to hide the murder weapon in the dressing room for the assassin to find.

The whole scheme threatened to fall flat when Stella took note of the violin player. She was getting out of the limousine when she suddenly halted her step and listened. "I swear that sounds just like Xaverl," she said. "That schmaltz. I'd recognize it anywhere." She sent Ulla to find out. The last thing Ulla needed at this moment was the reappearance of Viktor Erdos. She approached the violin player from the side. She got close enough to get a good look at him but distant enough he would not see her. To Stella she said she didn't think it was Viktor.

"How could it be him?" Ulla feigned. "He's not likely to be in New York. Last time we were aware of him, he was in Vienna writing for a newspaper."

"That was five years ago," Stella replied. "Have you forgotten what happened since? There was a thing called *Anschluss*. The Nazis annexed Austria into the German Reich, in case you have forgotten. I pray to God he got out in time." She added, "It's time to bring Mama over here from England. It's no longer safe for Jews there either."

That would be another complication Ulla didn't need. Having Stella's meddlesome mother around would definitely overturn her scheme. Was there no end to the trials of a sorely tried woman? She consoled herself that with war at sea hampering transatlantic crossings, the possibility of this new peril occurring anytime soon was not very likely.

A more immediate problem was Stella's growing obsession with finding out who the violinist in front of the theater was. She obviously doubted Ulla's veracity. The Kreisler melodies reaching her ear and heart convinced her that the man had to be Viktor Erdos. It happened once or twice that her attention was just deflected as she was about to approach the man. Some staffer had an urgent message or production detail to discuss, for example. How long could such luck hold out, though?

Ulla was not about to rely on coincidences being repeated indefinitely. She herself became obsessed with the fiddler whose identity was to her not in doubt. There was no question about it. He had to be eliminated from the scene before Stella wised up to who he really was. The mere thought of Viktor Erdos's return into Stella's circle robbed Ulla of sleep at night.

All these years she had managed to keep him away from Stella. She had destroyed his letters and dripped false rumors about him in her ear. She knew he was always on Stella's mind. Stella had eagerly read his articles, particularly his travelogues about Palestine and Egypt. She always asked friends from Vienna for news about him. Now fate had landed him once again on the threshold of Stella's world. They were only a few steps apart and were sure to meet in due time. She, the glittering Broadway star, and he, a homeless hobo playing the violin. Ulla knew Stella would immediately forgive him, receive him back with open arms, and even invite him to come to Hollywood. Viktor Erdos was much more discreet than Alexander Levary. No one would be the wiser about *his* sexual leanings.

Ulla tossed and turned at night. Anxiety tightened her chest. Panic over the consequences should her mission fail drenched her body in menopausal sweat. Something had to be done. Viktor Erdos had to be done away with. The question was how and who would carry out the deed.

She told the messenger an obstacle had turned up. Obstacles were bound to come up, he said. It was up to her to handle it. It was clear he was getting impatient.

"The highest cadres of the *Reichsleitung* are getting impatient," he said.

She wondered whether the field marshal and propaganda minister didn't have bigger fish to fry and more important things to worry about than an actress saying nasty things about the regime. By all reports the war on the Eastern Front was not going exactly according to the Führer's plan. She kept this thought to herself, though.

"Do something," the messenger said. "Shoot him or whatever. Just get him out of the way, and get the whole matter over with already!"

That was it. No discussion. It would be useless to point out she did not have a gun and had no idea how to get one. The messenger rose abruptly. She got up as well. Something shiny on the table where he had been sitting attracted her eye. What she saw was a silver revolver with a mother-of-pearl grip. It was no bigger than the palm of her hand. When she had its firing power assessed, she found out it was a nickel-plated ladies' derringer. The snub-nosed barrel made for a rather short range. She would have to get close up to her target. The fact that she had never fired a weapon gave her pause for a moment, but it didn't deter her. She decided this minor drawback could be overcome. She would do it and get the whole thing finally over and done with.

Once again the intended victims inadvertently played into her hands. A sealed note entrusted to her from Stella for the fiddler turned her mind toward a totally different idea for solving her problem. Before delivering the note, she had to know what was in it. Steam from a water kettle was the oldest tried-and-true trick in the book. Stella told him his violin playing enthralled her. It brought back memories of her homeland and a long-lost friend. Would he come to her dressing room on such and such a date at such and such a time? She apparently wanted to see him alone. The time indicated cut into the period she required to mutate back into herself.

All at once a light flared up in Ulla's head. A splendid opportunity opened up before her. She would get off the hook from shooting Viktor Erdos and at the same time frame him for the murder of Stella Berger. She resealed the envelope. For a few pennies a street urchin delivered it to the hands of the addressee in English: To the fiddler outside my theater, Stella had written. In German she made a slight variation: "Dem Geiger draussen vor dem Tore," to the fiddler outside the gate, an allusion to a Schubert song Viktor would understand.

NINE

As best laid plans go, this one went rather well for Ulla at first. Then she ran up against the first glitch. Stella had left it to Viktor to find a way to get into the theater and make his way around backstage. That he might not have the means for a ticket didn't seem to cross her mind. So this is where I came into the picture. This is how I became the inadvertent handmaiden in crime and was for a time suspected of complicity. Had Stella included a ticket with the note, I would never have become involved in this affair and gone on my merry way unawares. I would still have lost my job at the theater. With Stella gone I would have been out of employ anyway. I would have mourned her death but then concentrated on my studies, found other part-time work, and followed the case in the newspapers. Fate had other designs on me.

According to Ulla's account, Viktor Erdos took a seat high up in the gallery. She tried to keep her eye trained on him from her seat in a side loge. She had told Stella she would like to see the play one more time before the final curtain. This was a matinee performance, and the engagement was winding down. Seats were available in all areas. What Ulla had not been counting on was that Viktor would leave his seat before Stella finished her anti-Nazi speech. This upset the delicate balance of the timing. The assassin was already hidden behind a changing screen inside the dressing room at the ready to carry out the deed as soon as Stella entered. He would make a quick getaway and be gone before Viktor came in and found the body. In the best scenario,

Viktor would bend over her, take her pulse, break down, and leave his fingerprints all over. Ulla would then appear in the door and catch him red-handed. She would make a big hue and cry. The entire staff would stampede down the corridor to Stella's dressing room, providing enough distraction for the assassin to get out of the building.

This was the plan according to Ulla. This was not exactly how it went down, however even though, the end result was the same. Stella Berger was dead—strangled with a bundle of violin strings.

"So, tell us. How did it go down?" Inspector Dettelbach prodded. "Where did things go wrong from your standpoint?"

"I went to the dressing room door expecting the assassin, I mean the hired help, to be gone and to find Viktor Erdos with the body. Instead both men came storming out. They were screaming and dispersing in different directions. Actually they didn't come out exactly together. First I was almost run over by a man in a mask, and then Erdos bumped into me. He was tearing down the hallway as if the house was on fire. Neither one uttered a word. Both were gone in no time. Vanished."

"Go on."

"I saw Stella lying there on the floor. Lifeless. The candle extinguished. It dawned on me she was gone, and I just broke down. My legs gave way, and I was completely shook up."

"Excuse us, lady." Dettelbach's loud, sharp voice tore the air. "Excuse us if we are not all choked up over your expression of grief. She was dead because of your intrigues. You plotted her death. So cut the crap. You won't find any sympathy here. Just give us the facts. Let's start with the name of your killer."

"I don't know the man's name."

"Then what did he look like?"

"I'm not sure of that either. He wore a mask and a big hat pulled down over his face. The area where he bumped into me backstage wasn't very well lit."

"What about his overall figure. Was he tall, medium, short? Was he more like Sergeant Mulligan or like that tall, thin officer over there? You must have seen something."

She gave each of the men present a close look. Then she said, "His overall gestalt was more like that of Mr. Wolff."

Curtis had jumped up as if he had been lashed with a whip when Ulla pointed her finger at him.

"How about it, Counselor?" Dettelbach prodded him. "Why don't you fill in the missing pieces of the puzzle for us?"

"I don't know what you are talking about."

"Come on. My partner and I did a little digging. We've traced your steps and followed your tracks. You were the assassin sent by the Cheruskers all the way from Wisconsin!" Dettelbach pointed an accusing finger at him.

"I told you I no longer have any ties to that group."

"Maybe that's true now, but it wasn't back on July 19th when Stella Berger was murdered. You know your father and uncle concocted the whole murderous plot to please their Nazi masters. The Cheruskers infiltrated the German-American Kulturbund and used it as a base. By the way, I don't appreciate the disrepute you backwoods militants have brought over this once respectable, patriotic organization. But that's a matter for some other time. Right now I want you to tell us exactly what went on in that dressing room. No more evasions or I'll get you locked up for good."

"I didn't kill her. I swear."

"But you were there with the intent to kill. Attempted murder is good enough to get you thirty years."

Curtis turned toward me. His hands were extended in a helpless gesture. His eyes were running with tears. My eyes were dry. If he was looking for pity or sympathy, I was not the person to turn to.

"Tell them what you know and what you did, and leave me be!" I yelled at him at the top of my lungs.

Why hadn't I seen it? True. I had sensed something all along. All along this suspicion had gnawed on me that something didn't fit together. It was something I couldn't quite put my finger on or perhaps something I refused to face up to. When I heard about the militia group and all the lies he had been telling, I was shocked, but I just put it on the back burner for the time being. It could be dealt with later. But this? No. There was nothing more to deal with. This was the end. I felt drained of all emotion and incapable of feeling anything. I had been dunked and wrung out too many times. I couldn't even feel sorry for myself for having been duped.

"For the last time," Dettelbach scowled at him menacingly. "What happened in that dressing room? That's all we want to know. No crap like, 'Papa made me do it.'"

In the case of Curtis Wolff, it was Papa and Grandpa who made him do it. From early childhood, they had instilled in him notions of a fantasy world. The glory of the ancient Germanic tribes who brought disaster on the Roman Empire dominated these stories.

It couldn't be said he imbibed it with his mother's milk. His mother came from a hardy American stock of French, Irish, and German settlers with a sprinkling of native blood. She scorned the Wolff family's obsession with Germanic myth and their endless rehashing of Teutonic lore. When they formed a comitatus, a *Männerbund*, in the Wisconsin woods, she fled this Valhalla for parts unknown and was not seen or heard from again for years.

Curtis was five when she disappeared from his life. When she came back to reclaim her son, the teenage Curtis was irretrievably lost to her. Had she stayed with him, he might have been brought up with a kinder, less martial view of the world. Instead he was fired up at his grandfather's knee with an apocalyptic view of the twilight of gods and warriors.

While German boys back in the homeland grew up on the Western stories of Karl May, Curtis's imagination was steeped in the sagas of Germanic gods and heroes and battles against the might of Rome. His German cousins played cowboys and Indians; he and his American cousins engaged in swordplay with imaginary Romans.

They named the bund they formed "Cherusker Legion." The Germanic honor code for the warriors demanded absolute fealty and obedience to the chieftain. This included murder if it was deemed necessary to advance the cause. These American farmers' forebears came to America in 1848 fleeing poverty and political oppression in the Prussian Rhineland, and now they laid ludicrous claim to direct descent from the Germanic hero Arminius, or Hermann, who was famed for leading a massacre of three Roman legions led by the Roman general Varus, which made Emperor Augustus famously whine, "Varus, give me back my legions!"

How often did Curtis hear this story? Every September the woods around his home in rural Wisconsin exploded with fireworks marking the Varian Disaster in the Teutoburg Forest in the year nine BCE. The entire Wolff family and neighbors would get into period costume for the annual performance of Kleist's patriotic drama *Die Hermannsschlacht (Herman's Battle)*. It was hardly any wonder that when the chieftain of the National Socialists, in whom they saw the reincarnation of the glorious Hermann, seized power in the fatherland on January 30, 1933, their jubilation knew no end. The event was hailed as the fulfillment of a centuries-old dream. A torchlight procession through fields and woods and an extracurricular performance of Kleist's play marked the occasion.

Curtis did go through a short-lived period of rebellion. In his undergraduate days at university in Madison he came into contact with a different kind of German culture and ideas of the Enlightenment. His reading of Goethe, Schiller, Lessing, and Kant opened his eyes to an ideal of humanity that exulted peace and the life of the spirit rather than war and brute force. He studied English and French political thinkers as well. He even styled himself a Marxist for a brief time, discovered a gift and liking for debates, and carried a hefty volume of *Das Kapital* around campus. By the end of his sophomore year, he thoroughly derided his family's Teutonism as a primitive tribalist cult.

This phase in Curtis's life came to a quick end, however. On visits home his father made clear he would not tolerate books by the Jew Marx in his house. He would not allow his son to spread Jewish smut. One might have thought they would see in the other nation doggedly fighting Rome, namely the Jews, kindred allies. That was not the case. Even though no Jew, or person whom they could have identified as such, had ever set foot on their backwoods soil, Jew-hatred and the notions generally coupled with it were part and parcel of the Cherusker universe.

Curtis was browbeaten back into the fold by the time graduation rolled around. He was sent to law school while being groomed and trained for a mission to New York. The influx of so many Jews from Germany made the Cheruskers suspicious of what these newcomers might be up to and what anti-German plots they might be hatching. They heard of denunciations and calumnies being made against the beloved fatherland and Führer. They put out feelers to the minister of propaganda in Germany. They assured him of their readiness to oppose and counter any smear campaign against the Reich the Jews might be waging to get America into the war. A delegation of Cheruskers was sent off to New York—the whore of Jewish influence and power. Curtis was to infiltrate the Jews downtown. The rest of the gang took aim at infiltrating the German-American Kulturbund uptown.

New York hit Curtis like an epiphany. Curtis felt the irresistible pull of this strange new world. He waded into the bohemian life in the Village, bathed in the cultural offerings, and soaked up its nightlife. According to protocol he made himself out to be a Jew from Chicago. He wrote an article with information he got from the library and offered it to the German émigré paper *Aufbau*. He dated a few Jewish girls, including a young refugee named Misia Safran. He beguiled them with stories of his rich parents. He boasted about his grandparents who had come to America from Germany a century before and made a big fortune. It all followed a common American narrative. The Jews with whom he came in contact turned out to be regular guys, and the girls were pretty. All was very pleasant. Life in the big city was good. Yet every time he was overcome with a desire to strike out on his own, the tether that bound him to family and upbringing reined him back in. No hacksaw could sever this chain.

Then the order filtered down through the command chain to the New York Cheruskers. The pesky German actress appearing on Broadway with her harangues against the Reich, a thorn in the side of the propaganda minister, had to be eliminated. They drew lots. Curtis was the lucky one or the unlucky one, depending on one's point of view. It fell to him to carry out the deed. He did not shirk his duty.

On the appointed day and time, he appeared at the theater in disguise and following Ulla's plan, she took him to the dressing room while all eyes were fixed on the action on stage. He lay in wait behind the dressing screen expecting Stella to come in alone. Ulla had assured the messenger with whom she hashed out the details of the plot, Stella never deviated from her habit. As it happened on this day, she did deviate. She was not alone. She entered the room engaged in animated conversation with a man. Presumably he was the man to be framed, but somehow he had gotten there too early.

Curtis understood only a little of what they were saying. They were speaking Austrian German. The German he heard growing up, but never learned to speak fluently, was a bastardized version of the dialect his great grandfather had brought over from the lower Rhine area a century before. From the chattering banter in her voice, Curtis discerned she was happy to see this man. Then there was mention of letters written but never answered or received. The details escaped him. Next Curtis picked up more familiar words such as California, Hollywood, and studio. He heard the name Sasha Levary. As everybody who followed the entertainment news knew, he was Stella Berger's husband. The conversation became very heated and accusatory on the man's part.

Then it happened all very suddenly. From behind the screen, Curtis saw the man's face glowing red. It looked ready to bursting. Next thing he seized her by the throat, and before Curtis could let out his breath, he heard the woman make a gagging sound followed by a thump. He came out from behind the screen as the man was heading for the door. On the floor lay the lifeless body of Stella Berger. He wasted no time and bolted. Relieved to have been spared the unpleasant task with which he had been entrusted, he nevertheless planned to keep a low profile and leave town as soon as possible.

To his initial horror, the police called him down to the precinct the day after the murder. It was not, however, as a murder suspect but as the boyfriend of a woman who was suspected of being an accomplice of the murderer. They hoped she would lead them to the violin player they suspected of being the killer and he was to keep her under surveillance.

TEN

The train to Ossining chugged along the Hudson River Valley at an excruciatingly slow pace. What would I tell him? Strangely I felt no anger in my heart. I had no desire to accuse him of deceit or lying. Everybody in this drama lied for personal reasons. I just wanted to know the truth of what happened. He had nothing more to lose now. I wanted him to trust me with the truth. I felt I had a right to know. What drove him over the edge? She must have said something. Did it have to do with Levary and Hollywood? Was it her ambition?

We sat for a long time without speaking. As I looked through the glass window separating us, I tried to penetrate the wistful gaze that had struck me the first time I saw him sitting on a crate on the sidewalk opposite the theater playing the violin. I had learned so much about him and his life since then, and yet he was still a mystery to me. He opened up a book he had on his lap. It was the collected works of William Shakespeare. Slowly and haltingly, he began to read in English. "I pray you in your letter, when you shall these unlucky deeds relate, speak of me as I am; nothing extenuate, nor set down aught in malice. Then must you speak of one that loved not wisely, but too well...one whose hand threw a pearl away richer than all his tribe."

Tears flooded my eyes. I promised to look for a German translation of Shakespeare's works, which was understandably not available at the prison library. The lines from a poem by Oscar Wilde came to my mind.

"He looked upon the garish day with such a wistful eye; the man had killed the thing he loved and so he had to die."

His love for the little girl from the tenements in Vienna and the woman who rose to world fame had no strings attached. He loved her not for personal gain, for what she could do for him, or how her fame reflected on him. He didn't even love her to possess her. He loved her unconditionally for who she was—the eight-year-old girl who won his heart with a poise and spunk beyond her age. He loved the girl who dreamed of being on stage not for fame and fortune but for fulfilling a calling she felt inside.

The note the boy in the street handed to him had come from her. He recognized the curves of her handwriting. He also noticed the envelope had been opened and resealed. He knew Ulla had read Stella's note asking him to come to her dressing room right after the matinee performance the following Wednesday. He was well aware this was her time for complete rest. This was a sign she meant their rendezvous to be a tête-à-tête, a sign she wanted be alone with him.

He watched the last act of the drama from the darkened perch in the gallery. The magic of seeing her onstage once more after all those years was overwhelming. The strange words flowing from her mouth were incomprehensible to him, but that wasn't important. The timbre of her voice and the emotion bursting forth from her diminutive person, even in sotto voce, resounded within the walls of the intimate theater like an echo call in a mountain gorge. Viktor realized how empty his life had been, how shallow his pursuits, and how trifling his qualms. Without her he was but a forager for meaning. Without her he was a wanderer adrift in the land of Nod.

Then came the last scene and Desdemona's death at the hands of Othello. Seeing the smothered, lifeless body slumped on the bed raised Viktor's heartbeat to near bursting. He was in desperate need of a cigarette. He descended from the gallery before Stella took her bows and missed her subsequent plea to the audience to pray with her for the defeat of the Nazi tyranny.

Consequently they arrived at her dressing room door almost simultaneously. She took both his hands into hers and pulled him inside.

"I am so happy to see you!" She covered his face with kisses and pressed him so close to her as if she never wanted to let him go. Then she held him at arms' length and looked him over with a critical eye. "You don't look well. You're not ill, are you? Are you getting enough to eat?"

He assured her he was well though a bit weathered. "Emigrant life isn't easy. But my violin helps me get by."

"You should have come to me earlier. Whatever you need, just ask."

"No, no. I'm all right. All I want is to speak with you."

"One more reason you should have come to me right away."

"It's not easy. All kinds of people watch over you. They surround their precious commodity. A homeless street musician would be chased away."

"Precious commodity! That's my Xaverl! Hitting the nail right on the head!"

"Besides I didn't know if you would want to see me after all those years."

"And why not?" Her face took on a serious expression. "Why did I never hear from you after our little altercation in Berlin? Did you think I was holding a grudge all this time?"

"I was wondering. It wasn't like you. Not like the girl I knew. But you never answered my letters, and that made me think fame had changed you."

"What letters?"

"All the letters I sent you from Vienna, Madrid, Rome. Even Cairo and Jerusalem. Wherever my assignments took me."

"I was reading your reports from those places in the papers, but I never received a letter."

"When I heard you had gone to England, I found out where you were staying and wrote you there. I begged your forgiveness. I never gave up hope you would change your mind about having sent me away."

"We were both being had," she said with a pensive expression. "You know there is only one person responsible. I promise she will pay for this."

"I'm surprised she is still with you. I never understood."

261

"She has been a millstone around my neck for many years. One day I'll tell you about it. It's a complicated matter."

This intimation perplexed him. She had always confided in him and told him about everything that was going on in her life. Had she deceived him even back in the days when they were on intimate terms? Did she keep secrets from him? He didn't want a sour note to mar their reunion. He pushed back the anger brewing in his innards and did not insist on an explanation.

"How is Sender? Or Sasha as you call him. I read in the papers he's in Hollywood negotiating with the studios. The columnists predict a lucrative contract will come out of it for you."

"You shouldn't believe everything you read in the papers." She puckered her lips and raised her eyebrows. Her face suddenly took on a harsh, haughty expression. "We released this story to the press to avoid questions about his whereabouts. He is in Hollywood all right, but he is not negotiating anything on my behalf."

"Isn't he your agent and your manager?"

"Yes, but that will soon change. I'm also filing for divorce."

"Has he outlived his usefulness then?"

"You could put it that way. I'm in contact with MGM on my own. With the help and advice of some savvy American lawyers, of course. Louis B. Mayer has plans for a new Garbo."

Viktor looked at her in shock. There suddenly was a side of her he had never seen before. The face he saw was that of a cold, calculating business woman. There was a hardness around her mouth and eyes. Maybe it was a sign of aging. In Hollywood actresses her age were washed up. True. Everything had always been about Stella. The marriage with Alexander Levary was a blatant move for her advancement. He had made her a movie star in return. Shouldn't he expect a measure of loyalty if not gratitude now she saw a future for herself in Hollywood?

"A new Garbo? Is that what you want to be?"

"It's just a publicity ploy. I'll still be Stella Berger and better than Garbo."

"What about Levary? He can still be useful. He has savoir faire. He's always been a great wheeler-dealer if that's what you need."

"Very high-minded of you to stand up for the man who scorned you. He had no qualms about leaving you in the lurch."

"You are tossing him out like so much trash?"

"That's a good description. Trash. His behavior in Hollywood has raised quite a few eyebrows. Hollywood is not Berlin. Louis B. Mayer himself advised me that he is a liability and a hindrance for my career rather than an asset. Americans are a puritanical people. Much more so than Europeans. The American public likes its stars untainted by scandal. The way he flaunts his perverse sexual appetites casts a bad light on me."

Viktor felt his stomach churning. The anger he had been holding back burst forth like a river breaking through a dam.

"Why...you never before...you're turning into a whore for Hollywood fame?"

"Yes. You always thought of me as being so pure so snow-white. Well, I have news for you. The little girl you worshipped ceased to exist a long time ago. From the very beginning in Zurich I've always been a whore. That's why I couldn't get rid of Ulla. She held the evidence over my head every time I threatened to put her out to pasture. How do you think I became such a big star? My talent alone? Yes, I have the talent, but talent counts for only so much among the sharks. Maybe the moguls will exact their piece of flesh as well, but it will be done discreetly and without scandal. One thing is clear. I won't let that faggot stand in my way."

Viktor Erdos fell silent. He lit a cigarette and took a few hasty puffs. Then with a sudden move he crushed the burning end into the open palms of his hands.

"What on earth are you doing?" I screamed.

He held up his hands to show me the burn marks with a triumphant, crazed smile. I understood. He was stigmatizing the hands that had snuffed out the thing he loved more than anything on this earth.

My body was still shaking as I mounted the train back to New York. The horror of the sight of Viktor Erdos holding up the burn marks would not let go of me. Gradually I was able to collect my thoughts. He

263

held up his hands to indicate he had choked her with his hands—the way he had done in Berlin. Only Alexander Levary had stopped him then.

It became clear to me Viktor never used a violin string. That was Ulla's ruse. The assassin was to use a violin string to implicate the violin player who had been playing outside the theater. Something was awry here. The autopsy report stated Stella Berger had been found with violin strings tied around her neck. The same story was repeated over and over in the press. Both Ulla Scholz and Curtis Wolff told Dettelbach during the interrogation that Viktor had used the violin strings lying on a table. Someone put the strings around Stella's neck after the fact. A horrible doubt crept into my mind. What if Stella was only unconscious but not dead when Ulla entered the room?

CODA I

Northampton, Massachusetts, Summer 1945
Shortly after the war ended, I left the city. I looked around for a quiet place removed from the turmoil of the time and the bustle of the city but not too far from civilization. I needed a place where I could collect my thoughts and memories and write down the peculiar love story of Stella Berger and Viktor Erdos. Since I had only one brief encounter with her, and her tragic death made it impossible to interview her in person, I can only relate what has been related to me by those who knew her and were closest to her. Unfortunately the people I am dealing with are all unreliable narrators. Each witness had a personal agenda, and each brought a skewed perspective to the story. Each had a multitude of sins and motives to sweep under the carpet woven of lies and distortions. I have attempted to give an account of what I heard without adding to the confusion. I avoided piling on my own speculations and conclusions about what happened to the thicket of lies, deception, and evasions.

Viktor Erdos remained on death row. No more appeals were filed following the dramatic revelations Ulla Scholz and Curtis Wolff gave of what happened in Stella Berger's dressing room at the time of her murder. Their versions of the events, though unsubstantiated, had everybody convinced once again that the actual murderer had been brought to justice.

A few days after the interrogation, Ulla Scholz went missing. Her decomposed body washed up on a Staten Island beach the following spring. A note was found among her effects. Without Stella Berger her life had lost its raison d'être. No mention was made of the content in a Swiss bank vault. Whatever it was and whether it ever existed will never be known.

Lotte Lenya had a brilliant run on Broadway for several years in a musical composed by her husband Kurt Weill. After his premature death in 1945, she went on to a successful stage and film career on her own.

Curtis Wolff waylaid me on several occasions. When I refused to hear him out, he resorted to writing. At first he sent little notes begging forgiveness. Then he sent more and more long-winded epistles about his childhood, upbringing, and family and the Cherusker Legion. He didn't expect me to understand, but he wanted me to know where he came from and why he acted the way he did. Mostly he wanted me to know he had totally abjured the way of thinking his grandfather and father had instilled in him in the course of his childhood. His last missive to me, a short note, was dated December 12, 1941, a few days after Pearl Harbor. He had signed up with the Marine Corps. He hoped to redeem himself through service to his country. He assured me he would not shy away from a hero's death. Still that romantic warrior talk. Had he learned anything? A German expression came to my mind. It is impossible to escape one's own skin. Though I left his letters unanswered, I kept them for the record.

The cabaret duo Paul Safran and Tillie Werther moved back to New York. With the money they made in films, they set up a club in Chelsea called The Dovecote. It was in memoriam of the magic, lost world of Weimar Berlin that they still hankered after. Though they never achieved their dream of becoming famed like Weill and Lenya, they gathered a loyal following of regulars at their club. Many were from the old homeland and like them bemoaned the passing of that dream world called Weimar. Also more and more Americans came to appreciate their cabaret style of musical performance.

News about the war in Europe and the fate of the Jews of Europe preoccupied much of our time and exacted its toll on our nerves and emotions. Stella Berger's warnings, which many had branded the product of the vivid, even hysterical imagination of a modern-day Cassandra, turned out more than timely and prescient. Not even she foresaw the horrifying reality gradually unraveling before our eyes with each report about the fate of the Jews. Every day the news exceeded the direst predictions.

The last letter from my Aunt Trudi was dated February 19, 1943. It reached me in late August 1943, long after Berlin had been made *judenrein*. She wrote in code, but we were able to read between the lines. She was still doing slave labor in a munitions factory in Berlin, but the situation was tenuous with Jews being rounded up daily and transported to unknown destinations in the East. We were greatly disturbed to hear my Omi had already been placed on a transport for elderly people several months before on Rosh Hashanah of 1942 to some place in the East. My aunt knew nothing of her fate from then on. Neither did we ever find out what had befallen her after her letters stopped coming.

As of this writing, Viktor Erdos is still on death row in Sing-Sing Correctional Facility. When the war ended, Alexander Levary engaged a high-powered team of lawyers to work the case. So far all appeals for a retrial or clemency have been turned down. Sender is the one who actually made it big. He became a Hollywood mogul and head of his own studio, albeit in the burgeoning porno film industry.

Until I moved out of the city, I was a regular on the train to Ossining. The stationmaster thought I was the wife or companion of a convict. The actual wives I met regularly on the train adopted me and treated me as one of their own. I stopped the visits when I just couldn't take that resigned, wistful look anymore. We had nothing more to discuss after I handed him a copy of a German translation of Shakespeare's works. He was writing poetry, he told me, but he never showed me any of his work. He had made his peace and was waiting to die. With Stella gone he seemed to think there was no point in going on. I assured him Sender wouldn't give up.

Frank Dettelbach and Thomas Mulligan have become good, steadfast friends. I suspect this is mostly because of my coffee made with the newfangled Melitta filter. Whenever I am in the city, they stop by my place for a cup of what they call the tastiest coffee in all of the New World.

As for me I never went to medical school. After graduating college I became a seeker. I studied the texts of a great many academic fields. Not even the thoughts of the greatest practitioners of their disciplines (not philosophers, psychologists, historians, anthropologist, sociologists, or pedagogues) were able to still my hunger for answers to questions about what bestirs the human heart. I found more of a kindred spirit and understanding of the human soul in the works of fiction writers. The novels and plays by Thomas Mann Tolstoy, Pushkin, Balzac, Flaubert, Victor Hugo, Thomas Hardy, and Herman Melville were among those who became my constant companions. The conclusion I finally reached was, if I wanted to get a grasp, however tenuous, on the mysteries of the human mind and soul, in order to peer inside the human heart and find the motivation behind the human drama, I had to become a writer.

CODA II

Northampton, Massachusetts, September 25, 1945

A glimmer of hope appeared at my doorstep this afternoon. I was exercising my fingers on my newly acquired typewriter. They were not yet very nimble, but consistent practice would give me good use of this tool of my chosen vocation. Suddenly into the clattering of the keys intruded the rattling of a motorcar huffing up the dirt road to where I was staying in a small, wood house on the edge of town. As it came closer, the fumes billowing from the exhaust aroused my considerable displeasure. I had come to this place to sort things out in the clean, bracing New England autumn air. The location afforded me mind-clearing walks in the nearby fields and woods, a short hop into town for concerts and lectures at the college, and access to its libraries.

I did not expect any visitors and was surprised to see the face of a stranger in the yellow New York City taxicab that pulled up in front of my door. The driver opened the passenger door and reached inside to help the man disembark. He then handed him a pair of crutches. The man who saluted me with a friendly smile was an amputee, and since he was in a US Marine uniform, I presumed he had acquired his disability in the war.

"I am looking for the fiancée of US Marine Lieutenant Curtis Wolff," he said with a southern drawl.

This was not the way I would describe myself, but my curiosity was aroused. I nodded.

"Am I then speaking with Miss Misia Safran?"

I assured him of the truth of his assumption. I invited him in, and he instructed the driver to wait.

"You came all the way from New York?" I asked to say something. "And you are going back today?

"Yes. I have a plane to catch to Texas early tomorrow morning."

"Can I at least get you some tea?"

"That would be swell."

He looked haggard and washed out. I presumed he had been on the road for a long time. Had he come all the way from Texas to see me?

We sat silently for a while on the termite-infested porch. We quaffed tea and nibbled a few biscuits I scrounged up in the cupboard. Suddenly he tried to jump up but immediately fell back.

"I beg your pardon, ma'am. I'm forgetting my manners. Gunnery Sergeant William Williamson, US Marine Corps." He rummaged around in his coat pocket and pulled out a battered envelope. "I've come to deliver this letter to Miss Misia Safran from Lieutenant Curtis Wolff who, as you probably know, died for his country in the battle of the Solomon Islands on November 2, 1942."

I did not know. I looked at the crumpled, stained envelope he had handed me. There it stated: To the hands of Miss Misia Safran, New York City from Lt. Curtis Wolff, US Marine Corps.

"Did you know Lieutenant Wolff?"

"No, ma'am. Not personally. But I was told to let you know he died a hero's death."

"This letter looks as if it's been in war." It was a measly attempt at a joke, but he took it in good stead.

"You could say that, ma'am." He laughed. "It's been handed down through maybe six or seven hands. I'm the last one alive," he added with a look back to a place from which I was barred from following.

"The lieutenant served in a special advance unit of the brightest and bravest. The Second Marine Raiders Battalion. On the night they were to hit that beachhead, he instructed his comrades, in case he should be killed, to take the letter he carried on him and make sure it reached his fiancée. It was a matter of life and death. He said it with such urgency they made a sacred promise the letter would get to you no matter what. I didn't know most of the guys who passed the letter along to the next guy who then passed it along again. It reached me in the spring of 1944." He paused.

"You must excuse the delay. I was wounded in battle and captured by the enemy. Didn't get stateside until the war was over. They didn't do too good of a job patching me up. So now I have to get back to my home in Texas, and hopefully the care for veterans is better there."

I was speechless. I was barely able to bring forth a thank you. Anything I could say seemed too meek an expression of the gratitude I felt for him. I appreciated not so much the letter but the incredible loyalty to a comrade's dying wish. I wanted to embrace and kiss him, but I didn't know if I should. He was so formal and proper. I shook his hand and asked him if he had family. Yes. He had a wife and three children who grew up without him. He was eager to be with them now.

"And you made this huge detour to deliver a four-year-old letter from someone you didn't even know?"

"Semper fi," he said with a grin over his shoulder as he struggled back into the cab.

The letter was lying in front of me on the table. My eyes were pinned on it. I didn't dare touch it. What could it possibly contain? Another apology? Another plea for forgiveness? Another justification for what he did? Four years had gone by. He had been dead for three already, and he was still reaching out to me from the great beyond. No matter what was in this letter, it would change nothing. It would not change how I felt about him. What he did to Stella was unforgiveable, even if he didn't actually kill her. He was the assassin sent to kill her, and all the while, he curried favor with Viktor to gain his trust. A wolf in sheepskin. Then again, I wondered whether Viktor was really deceived as I was. I suspected he saw behind the mask and accepted him as his attorney for reasons of his own.

A gust of wind almost lifted up the letter together with the fallen leaves gathered on the porch. I clutched it and felt its thickness. What had the sergeant said? He was told it was a matter of life and death. Without knowing what the letter contained, he had tracked me down on good faith to this remote place. I was certainly remote from the battlefield where he had been severely wounded thousands of miles from his home. Whoever had passed it to him had impressed him with the urgency of its content. A matter of life and death. Whose life? Whose death? Maybe it wasn't about me at all. Maybe my private battle with the dead letter writer had nothing to do with any of this. The suspicion rose in my mind it might have something to do with Viktor Erdos. It was his life hanging in the balance. It was he who dwelled in limbo at death's door. So I picked it up and started to read.

My dear Misia,

I have long lost hope you will ever find it in your heart to forgive me. So I will no longer beseech you with apologies and assurances of my love for you. Neither of them matter to you, and so it must be. I have to live and die with profound regrets about the wrongs I committed and the pain I caused you.

You said once you might be able to forgive me for what I did to you, but never for what I did to Viktor Erdos and Stella Berger. I no longer seek to justify any of this. I don't seek absolution. I must make my peace with myself, however, and do what's right for Viktor. Since the beginning of this war, death has been staring me in the face every day. I won't bore you with the horrors of war. Just know I have witnessed the kind of human suffering unimaginable in my grandfather's stories of glory and valor. How much bunk all that was! But this is not the purpose of my writing either.

Faced with my own mortality, I, Lieutenant Curtis Wolff, US Marine Corps, Second Raider Battalion, swear by all that is dear to me and in the name of God Almighty, to the truthfulness of the testimony I am about to give in the matter of the unlawful death of Stella Berger. I hope it will somehow aid the case of Viktor Erdos and maybe gain him clemency or a retrial.

Let me take you back to the moment in the dressing room at the Schubert Theater in New York City on July 19, 1941. On that day I became witness to an argument between Stella Berger and Viktor Erdos. I want to state with absolute clarity that the purpose of my presence was to murder the actress, a deed for which I had drawn the lot. As I told the police at the time, since they were speaking Austrian German, I was unable to understand in detail what they were arguing about. All I can say is it was a heated exchange that ended when the male (I did not yet know Viktor Erdos) left in a hurry. Thereupon I came out of hiding and found the actress Stella Berger lying on the floor. Her face was all blue. I bent down to search for her pulse. It was faint, but she was alive. At that moment Ulla Scholz, the woman who had been my contact at the theater, came dashing in. I told her what happened. A man had assaulted the victim, but she was still hanging on. If we could get a doctor or an ambulance, she might be revived.

"Are you out of your mind?" the woman yelled. "This is a most fortunate turn of events. All you have to do is finish the job you came here to do."

The half-dead woman on the floor started to stir. I lost my nerve and refused.

"Just give me those strings then." Ulla Scholz tore the violin strings I still held in my hand from me, and before I knew what was happening, she completed the deed. She strangled her friend with the strings as had been the plan. It was a perfect frame of the violin player who had somehow made his way into the theater and the dressing room to take revenge for a wrong done to him years before.

"It's done. Now get out of here before I alarm the staff and call the police. Some kind of assassin you are!" Ulla turned a triumphant smile on her handiwork, the dead woman on the floor. I never forgot that crazed, evil look. To this day I blame myself for not having had the courage to stop her. But how could I have explained my presence at the scene without incriminating myself? I should add I was disguised and she did not see my face.

What happened thereafter is well known to you, my dear Misia. I am not proud of my actions and role in the course of these proceedings. I hope I can somehow redeem myself in the eyes of God if not in your eyes. I, therefore, welcome the opportunity to offer up my life for my country.

Be well, and have a wonderful life. You are a strong, spirited woman, and you will no doubt make your mark.

Your most devoted servant, Curtis Wolff

I reread the letter countless times. Thinking about the long, winding trail it took to get into my hands, I felt a sense of gratitude to the carriers and Curtis who had inspired so much admiration for his valor among his comrades.

I took the early morning train back to New York City. The long train ride afforded me plenty of time to ponder its implication and how to use this information. Would it even help Viktor's case? He would still be accused of assault with intent to kill. He might get a reversal of the verdict and get life with or without parole. He was not likely to agree to this. He was ready to die. A long prison term would be worse than death for him.

I contacted Dettelbach and Mulligan. They looked over the document while savoring a cup of my Melitta filter coffee with doughnuts at the place I still kept in the Village.

"Very impressive," said Dettelbach. "We should be able to get the judge to grant a retrial."

"'We'? No offense, but you guys are off the case. As far as we are concerned, it is closed. Remember, you saw to it. Levary's lawyers will know what to do. I just wanted to share the letter with you for old times' sake and in the spirit of our friendship. I trust there won't be any leaks to the press?"

"Of course not," said Mulligan. "We appreciate you showing it to us."

"Dettelbach?" I poked him in the side with my elbow. "Can I rely on you?"

"What makes you think you couldn't? It's a shame it's out of our hands now." He licked his chops like a hungry fox.

"In case of a retrial, you'll probably have to testify." I tried to console him. "I'm sure you'll get your day in court and in the limelight."

I typed up several copies of the letter and put them in a bank vault. The original I passed on to Alexander Levary who had his lawyers run with it. It took me a while to track him down. He was a very busy man. I finally got him on the telephone. He must have dropped everything he was doing and jumped on the next plane out of Los Angeles, for he appeared at my door less than twenty-four hours later. He was salivating with excitement and immediately roused one of his top lawyers.

He made me go with him to the office, even though it was ten o'clock at night.

"This is good stuff!" The lawyer waved the letter at me and ground his teeth as if chewing a delectable piece of meat. It obviously never occurred to him that to the recipient of this letter "good stuff" was not exactly an apt description. He had a few questions I would be able to answer much better in the morning when I was more alert. As it was, I was pleased with Levary's quick response. It told me a lot about the man.

The following Sunday I was once again back on the train to Ossining. Viktor ignored my joyous announcement that I was the bearer of good news. Instead he pushed a piece of paper through the slot in the glass that separated us. It was a poem. I was touched. For the first time he allowed me to read one of his poems. This one had the title "Götzendienst" ("Idol Worship").

With the hands of the potter I formed you in clay
With the hands of the sculptor I chiseled you in marble
With the hands of the gilder I fashioned you in gold
With the hands of the shaman I carved you in wood
With the hands of the artist I colored you in paints of oil
With the hands of the builder I erected a pedestal towering like a cathedral.

With the mind of the fool, I mistook you for a figure of clay
With the mind of the fool, I mistook you for a statue of stone
With the mind of the fool, I mistook you for an amulet of gold
With the mind of the fool, I mistook you for an image splashed on a canvas
With the mind of the fool I enthroned you on a pedestal made for gods.

My fool's mind made you an object of clay
My fool's mind made you an object of stone
My fool's mind made you an object of gold
My fool's mind made you an object of wood
My fool's mind made you an idol, lifeless and cold
A thing, inanimate without a soul.

The hands of this fool extinguished the flame,
A woman's life flesh and blood had made,
A woman who defied marble, clay, and gold,
A woman who defied frame and throne,
A woman who defied the crown of thorn
For love without lust and desire she had forsworn.

"You needn't say anything," he said. "It's for you to keep."

"I am sorry you had to bear so much anguish and pain as a result of this affair," he said when I told him about the letter. "You should never have become involved."

I was deeply touched. It was the first time he had addressed me in the familiar "Du." I felt a bond with this strange man as with no one else in the world.

"I'm not sorry," I said. "I think it helped me become a better, more mature person."

"Next time you come...you will come again, won't you?" His eyes rested questioningly on mine. I nodded emphatically and held his wistful gaze. "Bring me the violin then, if you please."

The retrial was granted after much legal maneuvering. It got underway in the summer of 1946. Viktor Erdos had spent almost five years on death row. The defending counsel made much of Othello's line of loving not wisely but too much. He sketched out a melodrama worthy of an Italian opera—a drama of love and passion unrequited. He enjoined the all-male jury to put themselves in the defendant's shoes—walking for years in the shadow of his beloved, always rejected and dejected, his hopes of fulfillment dashed again and again. Tweaking the truth of the friendship between victim and defendant was considered a wise strategy. Mention of homosexuality would surely prejudice the jury against him and give the story of the defense the lie.

Figuring largely in the defense's argument was Curtis Wolff's letter to me, written on the front line of some faraway Pacific island; the defense called it a "deathbed confession." I was put in the uncomfortable position of being cross-examined by both prosecution and defense about my relationship with the confessed assassin. My mother sat weeping in the gallery. Next to her were Hedy Lamarr, in all her beauty, and Lotte Lenya. I nodded in their direction, imperceptibly I hoped. Yes. I submitted to the grueling questions in the name of justice so the true murderers would become known, even though they could no longer be held accountable. The top instigator had evaded justice by poisoning himself and his wife and children in a bunker in Berlin. The world should add this one to all his other crimes. I held out under the strain. I did it for Stella but mostly for Viktor.

The melodramatic staging in the courtroom came off brilliantly. The lawyers worked their magic on the minds of the jury. Viktor Erdos was found guilty of assault and battery and subsequently sentenced to five years imprisonment including time served. He walked out a free man. As for Alexander Levary, he was not in the courtroom. He remained in California. This was probably one of the more thoughtful things he did in his life.

On nice days I can hear the Kreisler and Sarasate melodies floating in through the open window of my studio on Waverly Place. Their lilting sounds mingle with the clatter of my typewriter. In the afternoons I like to walk around Washington Square Park where Viktor stands near the fountain playing his violin with that wistful gaze lifted toward the open sky.

On late Saturday nights, one can catch him reading his poetry at the Dovecot to a gathering of exiles from the lost paradise of Weimar Berlin. On such nights the dim, cramped establishment, complete with sawdust-strewn floors, offers ample opportunity to rub elbows with the likes of Lotte Lenya and Hedy Lamarr. Marlene appears now and then. So does Peter Lorre when he's in town. Ernst Lubitsch, before his untimely death, would show up with Pola Negri on his arm. The exiles, however, looked upon her somewhat askance. She wasn't fully accepted into the club as an equal. A bevy of writers and actors still wedded to a language now in disrepute found a homely, congenial atmosphere there. The owners, Paul Safran and Tillie Werther, are doing their best in this city of refuge to recreate the hallowed milieu of Der Taubenschlag, their cabaret once located in a dark factory yard off Friedrichstrasse. With greater maturity, I have even come to appreciate my mother's silky, suggestive voice warbling my father's compositions. My grandmother would unjustly call them *Gassenhauer*—gutter songs—to most other people they were the expression of a dream called Weimar, a time and place that was the best and also the worst.

The war was over and the Nazi scourge defeated. Stella's watchword, expatriates, might be a better term to describe this talented lot of émigrés. I like to think of them as wanderers in the land of Nod, wanderers on the face of the earth. They had found a new haven after yet another expulsion in the course of centuries. For how long? Who can tell what the future holds?

CPSIA information can be obtained at www.ICGtesting.com
Printed in the USA
LVOW07s0703140216

475021LV00001B/34/P